PLOTS and PANS

KELLY EILEEN HAKE

PLOTS and PANS

SHILOH RUN PRESS

Print ISBN 978-1-62029-958-6

eBook Editions:
Adobe Digital Edition (.epub) 978-1-63058-027-8
Kindle and MobiPocket Edition (.prc) 978-1-63058-028-5

All scripture quotations are taken from the King James Version of the Bible.

Cover Design: Kirk DouPonce, DogEared Design

Published by Shiloh Run Press, an imprint of Barbour Publishing, Inc.,
P.O. Box 719, Uhrichsville, OH 44683, www.shilohrunpress.com

*Our mission is to publish and distribute inspirational products offering exceptional
value and biblical encouragement to the masses.*

 Member of the
Evangelical Christian
Publishers Association

Printed in the United States of America.

DEDICATION

For God, first and foremost, and my husband—you inspire and
humble me with your love and encouragement!
I cannot thank you enough. . . .

PROLOGUE

Bar None Ranch, Texas
1872

Don't let go, Jessie!" Her brother's shouts somehow made it past the sound of her pounding pulse.

I won't! With no breath to spare for screeching, she gritted her teeth too tight for words anyhow. *I can't,* she reminded herself, swallowing a sob. *Papa wants to send me away. . . .*

Jessalyn half rose out of the saddle as the horse's hooves hit the ground with bone-rattling force. Seconds spooled past, as if time itself couldn't keep up with her battle against the bronco. He reared, hooves flailing in the air as though beating back defeat. Jessalyn felt like she was doing the same thing, fighting a force she couldn't see but that would change her life if she lost.

If she could just break this bronco—the meanest, wiliest mustang ever brought to the Bar None Ranch—she'd prove she belonged here. The horse moved into a series of hops. Faster than thought, Jess turned her toes inward and clamped her thighs tight against the saddle, hanging on as the horse twisted. His vicious determination to unseat her was matched by her will to master him.

But strength of will, Jessalyn was coming to realize, just might not be strength enough. The horse showed no signs of tiring, but Jess gripped the reins so tight her fingers started prickling—an unwelcome warning they were going numb.

No! Gasping, she tried to tighten her fists, but it was too late. The bronco reared, went into a twist, and bucked again before Jess could compensate. She sailed over his head, crashing into a fence post. In the moment before pain cracked through her arm and ribs, Jess saw her father jump into the corral and head toward her. The spark in his eyes spoke her sentence loud and clear, even though she couldn't make out the words he was yelling.

I lost. Jess struggled for air, unsure whether it was her bruised ribs or her determination not to cry that made breathing so hard. *He'll send me away for sure.*

CHAPTER 1

Bar None Ranch, Texas
April 1879

Come quick, Boss! Doc says Culpepper's fixin' to rope a rainbow, saddle a cloud, and ride to the Great Beyond."

Tucker Carmichael spurred his mount to a gallop before the cowhand finished talking. He raced back to the ranch house, slid from his horse while it was still slowing, and hit the ground running. He barreled up the stairs, snatched the hat off his head, and didn't stop moving until he reached his mentor's bedside.

"You made it." Simon Culpepper gave a hacking cough, those three simple words enough to tax his strength. He nodded at Tucker but looked to where his son already hovered beside the bed. He squeezed Ed's hand as though drawing strength for the journey ahead.

From where Tucker was standing, it didn't look like Edward Culpepper had much strength to spare. His best friend had aged a good ten years in the two days since his dad's latest relapse.

"Yep." Tucker said nothing more—no words could fix the problem.

Seven years ago Simon Culpepper lost his head, running past a bronco that had just thrown his twelve-year-old daughter. She'd gotten a broken arm and a trip to a British boarding school out of the deal, but her dad suffered a kick to the ribs and a collapsed lung.

It healed, but Culpepper ignored medical advice and kept riding the range, smoking cigars, breaking broncos, and generally living

9

hard enough to wear out a much healthier man. During the past half-dozen years, the damaged lung collapsed twice more. This time Tucker didn't need to be a physician to see that Simon wouldn't pull through.

"Tell. . ."—Culpepper drew a painful, rattling breath—"him."

"Pa's changed his will." Ed's throat worked visibly as he stifled his grief. Still, he met Tucker's gaze and held up his free hand to forestall any protest. "Now twenty percent of the Bar None goes to you. We'll continue to manage things as we've always done, but now you'll own a solid stake in the business. As you should."

"I can't accept." Tucker slid his Stetson brim between his hands to keep from crushing it. Guilt made his fingers tense.

"We're not asking. Whether you want to acknowledge it or not, the property will be in your name from here on out." The ghost of a smile passed over Ed's face. "Besides, you've earned it. The Bar None wouldn't be what she is today if it weren't for you. Pa's right to do this."

"I don't deserve it." He squeezed the protest through a windpipe that suddenly seemed two sizes too small. Didn't they remember this was his fault? That he'd been the greenhorn foolish enough to let Culpepper's daughter saddle the bronco in the first place? Without his mistake—and Jessalyn's arrogance—that wild ride wouldn't have cost the Culpepper family so dearly.

"Take it." Culpepper slapped his palm against the bedcovers, his agitation stronger than his ability to express it. Even his voice sounded fretful and weak as he fought to speak. "Just. . ."

"Let him pass in peace," Ed growled at him over his father's coughs.

When Simon rested a bit easier, Tucker managed a short nod.

Culpepper sucked in a scraggly breath. "One thing. . ."

"Yes?" Ed and Tucker leaned close to catch his last whisper.

"Take care. . ." The old man's eyes gleamed with a familiar determination. His soul might be moving on, but his stubborn streak stayed long enough to see his sentence finished. ". . .my Jessie."

"We will," they promised immediately. Ed reached out at the same moment Tucker did, joining the three men in a three-point circle—a wordless enforcement of a pledge that couldn't be broken.

Tucker managed a gruff prayer as Culpepper breathed his last. Without his outsize personality, the figure on the bed seemed small and infinitely sad. The room started to stifle Tucker, but he and Ed stood for several moments before Ed broke the silence.

"Thank you for accepting his last wish." His friend couldn't meet his eyes, but Tucker caught the glassy glint of tears Ed wouldn't let fall just yet. "For letting him pass in peace."

"I'll sign it back over to you as soon as I can," he promised.

"No." Ed swung around and glared at him. "I won't dishonor my father's wishes. So put down whatever blame you've been packing since Jess left and help me get on with making the Bar None into something befitting Papa's memory."

Emotions already rubbed raw from Simon's loss, his friend's reproach pained him worse than it would have on any other day. Tucker stiffened. "I've been doing that for half a dozen years!"

"Working the Bar None? Yes." Ed's acknowledgment sapped away some of the sting, only to lash him again with fresh accusation. "Trying to order everything and everyone on the ranch to atone for the past? Yes. Letting go of the guilt? Not even close. You still blame yourself."

"Our mistakes make us who we are." *And show who we should be.*

"We're more than our mistakes." Ed clapped him on the shoulder. "They're just part of what we grow from. God gives us grace, and even Pa gave you another chance. So why refuse to forgive yourself?"

Tucker shrugged away from his friend's hand and the orders that went with it. "Quit preaching at me. It's done and over with."

"It's not over until you face it." Ed moved to block the doorway. "It's not just about you anymore. You have to forgive yourself, and you have to prepare for the fact Jess is coming home and sure as the sun shines you won't be able to control her."

"I don't need to control her. Just help take care of her."

"And how do you plan to take care of a woman who won't follow orders?"

"Easy. I order the men to keep their eyes open and their hands off—that's my part done." Tucker shoved his hat back on his head. "When it comes to anything more personal, you can take care of your sister!"

England
April 1879

"I can take care of myself," Jessalyn assured her new roommate—her sixth roommate to date at Miss Pennyworth's Penitentiary.

More generally—if less honestly—known as Miss Pennyworth's Academy, the institution locked up everything from the sugar bowls to the stables in an effort to "mould young women into fine ladies whose appearance and behavior are a credit to society." This meant that everything about Jess, from her sweet tooth to her "unseemly inclination toward independence" was unwelcome within these walls. Unfortunately, her father's money had thus far convinced Miss Pennyworth to overlook Jessalyn's faults for far longer than the four academies she'd attended previously. Miss Pennyworth's staunch determination was almost enough to win Jess's admiration.

Almost. Because teatime inevitably rolled around, serving dry soda biscuits instead of cake with a measly half a sugar cube allotted each student. Then Jess's rebellious spirit flared to life, and an entire pot of tepid tea couldn't quench the blaze. Miss Pennyworth cited society's admiration for "trim waists, tightly laced"—but Jess preferred buttered crumpets and breathing.

"But Miss Pennyworth sent us to our rooms because it's time for our afternoon rest," Cecily Something-or-Other squeaked, following Jess onto the balcony she could no longer call her own.

Right now all the girls were draping themselves artistically across a myriad of lounges, poufs, and settees provided for just such a purpose by the academy. Supposedly every young lady of quality should be attractively exhausted after a morning filled with such taxing pursuits as letter writing and—Jess suppressed a shudder at the memory—embroidery.

"You're right," she soothed, wondering whether it was her imagination or if her roommates were becoming mousier. Jess strongly suspected Miss Pennyworth assigned them based on their lack of spine and willingness to turn rat if she did anything unconventional.

For instance, when she shimmied over the wrought-iron railing of the balcony to the library terrace, then snuck down the servants' stairs to swipe a treat from the kitchen on her way to the stables. She'd repeated and perfected this maneuver until she probably could have done it in her sleep. Which might come in handy if she was finally forced to follow the rules and nap along with everyone else.

"Oh, good!" Cecily gladly turned tail and followed Jess back into the room. She gracefully sank onto the chaise lounge by the door and arranged her skirts to hide her ankles. Ladies, Miss Pennyworth lectured, hid their ankles at all times. Apparently a mere glimpse could make men mad with lustful, animal urges.

Jess snorted and plunked herself down atop her bed, hoping that Cecily proved to be a champion napper. Sound-sleeping roommates who dozed off quickly were valuable commodities.

"Aren't you going to remove your boots?" Cecily wiggled pink little stockinged toes as though relishing a forbidden freedom. "It's ever so much more comfortable on a warm day."

"It's not warm to me." Jess clicked the heels of her boots together and rolled her ankles, glad to have a truthful response besides "I'm going to sneak out and steal some fresh air."

"Oh!" Cecily propped herself up on an elbow, now looking interested and disappointingly alert. "Is it much warmer in the Americas then?"

Quite so. Jess clamped her lips shut against the tickle of such an oh-so-proper response. This sort of incident—times when she began to think like a British miss instead of the Texas cowgirl half born in the saddle—had been sneaking up on her with increasing frequency during the past couple of years. Without fail, each of these moments made her wonder how many times she *hadn't* caught herself and whether anyone would recognize her when she finally got home.

If I ever do get back. The dangerous doubt pricked her. *It's been seven years now. . . .*

Cecily's worried glance broke through that dismaying line of thought, letting her know she'd taken too long to answer the girl's insipid question about Texas weather.

Jess kept her answer short and hoped Cecily stopped talking. "Yep."

"Yes."

"Yes, what?" Jess reached for her pillow and punched it into something comfy.

"Yes," Cecily clarified. "Ladies don't say things like 'yep.' Miss Pennyworth asked me to take notice of your American habits and help you work to correct them."

"Please don't trouble yourself." *Or myself,* Jess added silently, surprisingly unsurprised that Miss Pennyworth had already recruited Cecily to help monitor her "mistakes."

Cecily's sweet smile swiftly gave way to a delicate yawn. "It's no trouble at all, Jessalyn. I'm always happy to help a friend." Then she kindly fell asleep, which was all the help Jess needed to creep back out to the balcony and be on her way.

The grandfather clock in the hall warned Jess how much of her free time Cecily's chatter nibbled away, so she hastened to the kitchen. Usually she made a point of shooting the breeze with the cook and other servants. Largely unappreciated by the students they served, the staff became valuable allies whenever Jess needed to stretch her legs or—after an academy-approved breakfast of stewed tomatoes and kippers—her stomach.

"We heard you had a new roommate." The cook waggled her ladle at a small, linen-wrapped bundle neatly tucked atop the baking table. "Carrots for your mare and fresh-baked shortbread for you."

Jess grinned her thanks and slid the bundle into the pocket of her skirts. "No danger of me getting those mixed up. Carrots are wonderful, of course, but Morning Glory is welcome to them when there's shortbread nearby." She waved good-bye and didn't mention that she'd be sharing the shortbread with the stable boy next door.

Little Ben's sweet tooth rivaled her own—she'd once caught him sucking on the tea cubes of sugar she'd brought for Morning Glory. Since then, she'd made a point of passing along a treat whenever she snuck into the stables. In return, Ben had Morning Glory saddled and ready for her every afternoon, kept her split riding skirts well hidden in the tack room, and acted as lookout for the other grooms while she changed. The gap-toothed smile of her nine-year-old friend made one more thing to love about visiting the stables. No one really smiled in an academy. Manners nixed vulgar things like grinning or laughing louder than a bell-like tinkle.

She'd heard many of the girls complaining about riding lessons, deploring the filth of the stable yards and the smell of the horses. But Jess didn't mind getting her boots and hands dirty, and to her way of thinking, horses, hay, and grit smelled like home. England's gloomy weather hid the sun, but something about hay reminded her of sunshine, open air, and things growing wild. Jess drew in a deep breath as she left school grounds and made her way to the stables.

"There you is." Ben put down a grooming brush and came out to greet her. "Mornin' Glory an' I was wondering if you would make it."

"Got held up," Jess admitted, drawing the bundle from her

pocket. "I might be a little later tomorrow, too. Miss Pennyworth gave me a new roommate, so it's harder to get away."

"Wot say I 'as Morning Glory ready at same time, but if you isn't over by 'alf past, I put her back?" Ben suggested, happily cramming half the shortbread into his mouth in one blissful bite.

"Good idea," Jess called from the tack room as she slid out of her day skirt and shimmied into her split riding skirts. Luckily the legs were wide enough to pull on over her boots, so she moved quickly. At first Jess couldn't decide what part of her afternoon escapes Miss Pennyworth would find most troubling—her climbing over the balcony rail and swinging onto the library terrace, or the split skirts themselves. Then Miss Pennyworth found her first pair hanging in the wardrobe—she searched student rooms at will—and confiscated them as scandalous. Since she started changing in the stables, Jess figured the skirts won as "most likely to give the headmistress apoplexy" when she finally found out about the whole procedure.

Because Miss Pennyworth *would* catch her sooner or later. Jess didn't fool herself about that—after all, she'd been caught at three of the four schools she'd previously attended. She hadn't been caught at the first school she'd gone to for one reason: Jess hadn't broken the rules. She'd been convinced that if she behaved, applied herself to her lessons, and became a perfect little lady, Papa would want her back. She'd been a model student right up until the day the doddering headmistress died and her father arrived to pick her up—and took her to another school before boarding a steamship and returning home without her.

After that Jess saw no point in pretending Lady Lessons didn't bore her senseless. She warred with headmistress after headmistress until they gave her the boot, always hoping that this would be the time Papa realized she belonged back home at the ranch. But it didn't work. Year after year, school after school, he always found another headmistress-turned-warden to keep Jess corralled an ocean away.

Exiled from the Bar None. The irony never wore off, but years of use certainly wore it thin.

"She's chomped up them carrots," Ben informed her when she hustled back to the stalls, his collar coated in buttery crumbs.

"How's my girl?" She stroked Morning Glory's velvety nose.

The mare whickered softly, shifting to the side and pulling her nose from Jess's hand to gently nudge her shoulder. Horses had an uncanny sense of time, and Jess could tell Morning Glory had grown anxious, waiting for her to show up. They both wanted to get out in the open for a while. Jess didn't waste any more time and swung up into the saddle. That was one of the many nice things about riding astride—she didn't need a mounting block or a man's assistance.

Why ladies—who were supposed to be so very delicate and sheltered—were required to perch so precariously atop their mounts made no sense to Jess. Sidesaddles were downright dangerous. Papa had plunked her on a pony at age four, and even *she* felt off balance and unsteady on the silly things. The way a woman had to hook her knee around a pommel and tangle her limbs in heavy skirts effectively hobbled her as a rider. She couldn't center herself well, nor adjust her seat to match the horse's gait, or even tighten her knees for stability. She certainly couldn't jump off if the need arose.

Compromised control with no ability to escape. . .sidesaddles were the riding equivalent of all the other fussy, foolish rules Jess rode to get away from. She kept Morning Glory reined in at a trot past the corral, waiting until they reached the overgrown fields. Then she gave the mare her head, settling into the fluid rhythm of an all-out gallop. Together they ran from all the people, procedures, and never-ending sets of expectations that confined them. Just her, Morning Glory, and the wind cooling their faces.

During these precious, stolen moments, Jess could breathe. It seemed like she never got enough air in the stifled halls of the academy. Only outside, one with the grass and trees and the horse helping her fly away, could she clear her lungs and her thoughts. When she rode, she could remember Mama's voice, feel the safety of Papa's bear hugs, and see the home she'd lost.

But time ran faster than she could, and today she turned Morning Glory back to the stables long before the halfway mark of their usual circuit. Jess swung off the mare's back, giving her one last pat before entrusting Morning Glory back to Ben. She trusted the stable boy to water and brush Morning Glory down after their afternoon jaunts, grateful her little friend didn't mind the extra work. If she had to tend the mare after each run, they'd hardly have any time to ride.

Jess was thankful for Ben—and even more thankful that she didn't have to worry about her escapades getting him in trouble. Miss Pennyworth didn't have the acreage or, Jess suspected, the funds to operate a stable for her students on school grounds, so she'd made arrangements for the students' horses to be stabled at the establishment next door. That way the students still learned the valuable social skill of sedate, sidesaddle riding, but the stables weren't part of the academy.

She hurriedly changed back into her day skirts and ran back to the school, sneaking in the back and taking the servants' stairs two at a time. Once upstairs, she slowly tiptoed along the edge of the hallway—the center creaked—eased open her door, and prayed Cecily stayed asleep.

No such luck. Cecily's chaise lay empty, and Jess couldn't quell the first stirrings of panic as she turned toward the beds. There sat Cecily, wringing her hands. And across from Cecily, holding herself so stiffly that she hadn't so much as wrinkled the counterpane, sat Miss Pennyworth.

The jig was up.

CHAPTER 2

Bar None Ranch, Texas
May 1879

She's in it up to her eyeballs, that's for shore." Ralph Runkle, long-time cowboy for the Bar None, gestured southward. "Tried to pull her out, but it's gonna take more than me and Samson here"—he patted the powerful neck of his oversized mount—"to get the job done. Anyone in particular you want to have ride the line with me and rescue her, or can I grab whoever crosses my path?"

"No need." Tucker stuffed his bandanna in his back pocket. "I'll go—it's been too long since I rode the south pasture anyhow." He headed for the stables housing his favorite stallion.

"Hold up there, Boss." Ralph swung out of the saddle and ambled after him, his long stride catching him up quick. "I heard tell you was up all night helping birth those twin foals."

"Yep." He didn't elaborate. Tucker could see where Ralph was heading, and the ranch hand needed to take the hint that the boss spent his time wherever and however he pleased.

"Boss." Ralph took a half step into Tucker's path, forcing him to stop. "I know it ain't my place and all, but you didn't get any shut-eye the night before that neither. It's almost sundown. Why don't you let Virgil help me get the cow while you grab some grub and catch a few winks?"

Tucker thumbed back the brim of his hat and pinned Ralph with a steely glare. Staring down a man when you had to tilt your head back to look at him made for a tall order, but Tucker could fill it. Ralph's size made him an asset on the ranch, so long as his mouth didn't get too big.

"Sorry, Boss." The ranch hand fell back a step, raising ham-like hands apologetically. "But ain't no secrets in the bunkhouse. You're taking Culpepper's passing mighty hard."

"I wouldn't have guessed that a man who snores as loud as you do manages to keep track of who's awake." Tucker started walking, making Ralph back-step and get out of his way. The last thing he wanted to do was talk about Culpepper's death—or his troublesome final bequest.

Ralph guffawed, white teeth flashing in his dark face, massive shoulders shaking with mirth. "All of us are rafter-rattlers. It's best to fall asleep first, else you couldn't pick out a single snorer from the bunch if you tried." He made a good point—Tucker knew because he'd tried two nights ago, the first time in seven years when he hadn't fallen asleep as soon as his head hit the pillow.

Not that he planned to tell Ralph, who kept hovering as he grabbed his saddle and headed to Happy Jack's stall. Not appreciating Ralph's interference but understanding what drove him, Tucker unbent a bit to say, "Hard work makes for deep sleep. I aim to out-snore everyone tonight."

Ralph raised his brows but kept his mouth shut, retreating from the stables and getting back to his own horse. He'd mounted up again by the time Tucker rode up on Happy Jack. Even better, he didn't say anything more as the two of them headed out in search of the distressed cow.

With the sun sliding down to meet the horizon, a breeze cooling the back of his neck, and a welcome exhaustion pulling at him, Tucker figured that tonight he'd beat the restlessness keeping him from a good night's sleep. Since Culpepper's passing, Tucker's brain worked harder than his body—that was the problem. Lucky for him, spring meant the busy season, and after today he'd have worked hard enough to earn some peace—even if quiet wasn't an option in the bunkhouse.

Tucker grinned at the thought and settled into the sway of Happy Jack's walk. Not everyone would agree, but riding the range relaxed him. Something about the almost endless expanse of land, green grass shooting up to tickle a stormy sky, put him at peace. No buildings in sight, no train tracks taming the wilderness. . .just open earth and the quiet companionship of a fellow cowhand. Thunder banks rolled toward them from a distance, but they'd probably outpace the rain back home.

"Just up ahead now." Ralph shifted in his saddle, veering toward the rain-swollen stream running to the left. Spring streaked the skies with lightning, deluging them with downpours in a haphazard and unsuccessful attempt to make up for the dry winter. This wasn't the first cow to get stuck in a bog this spring, and it certainly wouldn't be the last before the mud holes started to dry out.

Another couple of miles and Tucker spotted the lone calf, sloshing in mud up to its knees and edging around the deeper pit trapping its mother. At first he couldn't make out the cow—mud caked her ears and muzzle. He knew Ralph wasn't given to exaggeration, so Tucker wasn't surprised to find she was in up to her eyes, having to tilt her head back to get some air and let loose piteous moans.

"She's in a bad way, but calf's well padded," Tucker noted.

If the calf were nothing but bones, they'd know she'd been stuck for days, starving. Weakened, her bones wouldn't be strong enough to withstand the mud's suction without breaking, and the kindest thing would be to shoot her. Lucky for the cow, she hadn't been in long before Ralph found her. Good news for the beeve—bad news for his afternoon. Rain or no rain, he'd be getting wet.

"I'll go in." Tucker dismounted and started stripping off layers. Hat, bandanna, coat, chaps, work shirt, boots, socks, and finally Levi's hit the nearest patch of grass. Now down to his drawers, Tucker changed his estimation of the weather. Thunderheads had moved several miles in the past half hour, the wind had picked up, and its new bite warned they didn't have long to get the job done.

Ralph was always first to volunteer, but for once the burly ranch hand didn't protest about letting someone else, even the boss, do the dirty work. This time they both knew his mass made him a poor choice—he'd displace enough mud to drown the almost-buried beeve. With the calf's pathetic lowing growing louder and more anxious, Tucker headed into the mud a ways away from the cow.

He cautiously worked his way deeper through the mud sucking at his toes, legs, and finally his arms until he reached the trapped animal. Her wide eyes rolled in panic, her neck straining against Tucker's hand in a futile attempt to pull free. He crooned to the cow, running a palm down her shoulder and her side until forced to lay his own head in the muck. Only then could he find the indentation where her leg met her belly. Pulling his free arm from the mud with a sickening slurp, he caught the rope Ralph tossed over.

Rope in one hand, he plunged it into the mud, passed it behind the cow's leg, and grabbed it with the other hand, performing a sort of sideways crab-walk so he stood in front of the animal. Moving fast so she wouldn't butt him with her jaw, he passed the rope behind the other leg and up her other side. Then he knotted the lasso and repeated the entire maneuver with her back end.

Finally, he fought his way out of the sludge, mud sucking at his heels. Ralph tossed him a coarse blanket Tucker used for a rough towel-dry before swinging up into Happy Jack's saddle. He wrapped the end of one lasso around the pommel as Ralph had done with the other, and together they backed the horses up. Slowly, squelchily, the cow emerged from the pit. Since they didn't know how tired the cow might be, they kept backing up until the mud rose halfway above her knees. Then Ralph hustled over to undo the knots before she could free herself enough to kick him. If she hadn't been rocking and pulling on her own, he would've looped a line around her neck to pull again. But this cow was on the move and finished sludging loose without further help.

In no time, she'd reached a clump of grass and lowered her head for a welcome meal. The calf raced to its mother, all gangly legs, knobby knees, and flying slobber. It slid in a slick patch and crashed into the cow's side before righting itself and latching on for supper.

Ralph slicked mud from the ropes while Tucker unbuckled the blanket from his own saddle, cleaned up a bit more, and pulled on his gear. By now temps had dropped and the rain clouds lurked almost overhead, so they gave the horses their heads and ran for it until the outlying buildings of the ranch house came into view. Then they reined in to a more sedate pace. Any horseman worth his salt knew better than to give the horse his head back to the stables or they'd run wild.

By the time they'd put up the horses, the dinner bell sounded. Stomach rumbling, Tucker headed for the bunkhouse instead of the mess hall, determined to grab a few moments of privacy. Working fast with a bar of oatmeal-lye soap, he scrubbed away the remnants of the mud hole. All cattlemen expected to carry a certain amount of dirt and dust around with them, but dried mud itched something awful. Once Tucker could stand himself again, he went in search of supper.

By the dim light flickering from a handful of lanterns hung over the long tables, Tucker could see that he'd come too late. Charlie, the old-timer cattleman-turned-cook, stood in front of the fireplace dominating the far wall, dumping water into the already-empty stewpot. Cutlery and tin bowls smeared with gravy overflowed from the half barrel by the door. Biscuit crumbs spotted tables where the men, made peaceable by full bellies, lingered over coffee, cards, and checkers.

He should've known. Spring brought a trail of grub-line riders, workers riding from ranch to ranch for a few days' or weeks' worth of work in return for a bunk and three square meals a day. In addition to the Bar None crew, he saw two grubbers he'd given the go-ahead and three he didn't recognize. Most likely they'd gone to the big house while he'd been out helping Ralph, and Ed approved them to settle in for the night and report to Tucker the next morning.

Most likely, but not necessarily. Sometimes grub-line riders made it a point of arriving just before supper or just before a storm, banking on ranch-land hospitality for a meal and a bunk. Then after breakfast or the storm passed—whichever lasted longest—they headed out before putting in a day's work. Larger ranches, like the Bar None, left more room for these rascals to work their scam.

Just in case, Tucker needed to check with Ed. Stomach now rumbling loud enough to be mistaken for thunder, he left the mess hall and hit the big house at the same time as the downpour. Shutting the door behind him, Tucker scuffed his boots on the doormat and called out a greeting.

His "hello!" got a distant "Tucker?" in reply, which he followed down the hall to the dining room. There he found Ed, a lone figure dwarfed by the immense table. He couldn't help but notice Ed's overflowing plate and tried to ignore the way his mouth started watering as he drew close.

"Tucker!" Ed half rose out of his seat and made an expansive gesture. "Join me, will you?"

Neither of them could count the number of times Tucker turned down invitations to join Ed and his father for a meal at the big house. As foreman, he felt he belonged in the mess hall, rubbing shoulders with his men and keeping an eye on things. When the bosses got too comfortable or seemed too distant, things began to deteriorate in the bunkhouse. The men got restless or complacent, work slipped, and unless someone in charge caught it immediately, the ranch suffered.

But tonight Tucker didn't have it in him to turn down a hot meal with the friend whose father had just died. Grief made something new to share with Ed, who'd always treated him like a brother and insisted on accepting him as a new business partner. Besides, Tucker's stomach wouldn't let him pass up anything edible at this point. He nodded and grabbed the nearest chair.

"Hang on and let me get Desta." Ed shoved back from the table.

"Last night she said she wasn't hungry, but she needs to join us tonight. She always did when Dad was alive, and. . ."

"If me being here puts her off, I can come back." Tucker ignored his belly's protest. If the Culpeppers' black housekeeper usually ate with the family, he wasn't going to mess with protocol.

He didn't know the woman, but he'd delivered a fair number of warnings to the ranch hands about steering clear of the pretty, light-skinned housekeeper. Her status as the only woman on the ranch, and a servant, mistakenly made some men think of her as fair game. Tucker found himself wondering every once in a while whether Jessalyn Culpepper would've caused those sorts of problems, but decided her position as the big boss's daughter would cut back on that. From what little he'd known of Jessalyn, she would've managed to find other sorts of trouble instead.

Then again, she'd been a pretty little mite—all sun-kissed curls and freckles. Tucker couldn't be sure how many times he'd done it before, but he winged up another little prayer of gratitude that Simon Culpepper had the sense to send his daughter somewhere safe. Safe for her, and safe for everyone at the Bar None. He and Ed agreed they couldn't bring her back until after this season—and Tucker was more than happy to push back that problem until after the cattle drive this summer.

"She'll be out in a minute." Ed pulled his chair back up to the table, looked down at his plate, and heaved a deep sigh. Passing his palm over his face as though wiping away worry, he sprawled back against the ornately carved support of his seat. "Something I should tell you."

"Shoot." Tucker wondered whether Ed was having trouble dredging up the words to ask for his share of the ranch back. He'd happily sign it back over, but considering how Ed jumped all over him the last time he offered, Tucker wasn't in any hurry to bring up the subject first.

"It's Desta." His friend leaned forward so fast his chair creaked.

His voice dropped to a whisper. "Just found out when the lawyer went over Pa's will. She's not just the housekeeper, which makes sense. You'll find out when you try to eat supper—made me wonder whether Pa..." He cleared his throat. "Well, that is to say, we never discussed... But since she got here, she always ate at the table with us. And she can't cook a lick, so I figured there was some connection..."

"If she's your secret stepmother, I won't say a word against it." Tucker took a wild guess to save them both from Ed's hemming and hawing through a botched explanation. Though it didn't sound like Simon Culpepper. The man he'd seen as a second father didn't hide behind secrets.

"Naw." Ed shook his head, still looking poleaxed. "She's my aunt."

Tucker felt his brows shoot up, but couldn't find any right way to ask the obvious.

Luckily, Ed saved him from the struggle. "Half aunt, I should say. I guess the farm Grandpa lost in the war was bigger than Pa let on—more of a..."—he paused—"plantation?"

It didn't take much to read between the lines on this one. Apparently Grandpa Culpepper owned slaves and made one of them his mistress. The fact that the scenario had been more or less typical for the times made it no less abhorrent, and Tucker's tongue glued itself to the roof of his mouth. It wasn't like he could congratulate his friend on finding a long-lost relative; she'd been living in his house for half a dozen years now. The real questions—whether it was her choice or her brother's that they kept it quiet, and whether Ed would do the same—weren't Tucker's to ask.

If quiet could creep through a room to knock a person sideways, Desta figured she wouldn't still be standing. Wiping damp palms against her apron, she pressed her ear tight against the doorjamb.

Nothin'.

She didn't know what was worse—the two men sitting in there, not finding a single thing to say, or her bone-deep conviction that anything they might've said would've weighed on her mind even worse. With time running out, Desta dug deep and decided to be grateful that her nephew and the foreman weren't the sort to flap their gums and whip up a tornado of troubles.

Desta shifted, resting her forehead against the wood, and sent up a small prayer. *Lord, You know I've got doubts, but You haven't brought me this far to forsake me now. Please give me patience, wisdom, and skin thick enough to weather the difficulties waiting ahead. Amen.*

There was nothing for it but to grab an extra bowl for their guest and brave her way into the dining room. She slid it in front of the foreman how Mammy taught her, from the left, before lifting the lid off the large tureen and ladling him a healthy portion of stew. Then she sidled around the table to spoon out a much smaller portion for herself. No point in wasting food, and she didn't see how she'd manage to swallow so much as a bite.

Which was a cryin' shame, considering how even she couldn't mess up stew too badly.

Desta busied herself with placing the napkin in her lap, nudged her water glass a smidge farther from her plate, and tried to talk herself out of being so nervous. True, she and the foreman had gone six years without wasting more than a hundred words on each other. But as a woman with eyes to see and ears to hear, Desta knew enough about the man to like and respect him.

So she hitched a smile on her face and looked up to find Mr. Carmichael giving her a grin in return. Not a penetrating stare, as though he were trying to see her brother in her features, or determine how much white or black blood she might have, or questioning why she and Simon had decided to keep their relationship a secret—just a regular old friendly smile. Desta started to relax.

"Thank you, Miss Desta." He scooped a spoonful of stew to his mouth and started to chew. And chew...and chew...then he chewed some more before giving a mighty swallow.

Oh no. Desta looked down at her own unassuming bowl. *What went wrong* this *time?*

She'd gone a clear four months since the last time she'd made a busted batch of stew. That's what made it her best dish. Sticking everything in a pot of boiling water and leaving it alone made for practically foolproof cooking. Best part was if you changed what vegetables and meat you added in, you came out with something different every time. Last night she'd used fish and carrots, and it hadn't been half-bad. Yes, the fish flaked and carrots made the whole thing sweeter than she'd reckoned, but a healthy sprinkling of salt sorted it out well enough.

So what could've gone wrong tonight? She'd aimed for something hearty and chosen rabbit with beans. The pot had been on the fire since this morning, long enough that the meat should've been melting in the man's mouth. *So why all the chewing?*

She looked at Ed, who looked from his own bowl back to her. He picked up his spoon, flourished it in her direction in a wordless "you try it first!" sort of gesture, and put it back down.

Desta gave a small huff at this ingratitude, shrugged her shoulders, and tried a tiny bite. The gamey flavor of the rabbit didn't bother her, the meat was soft, the stew heartily thick. All things considered, it ranked as one of her better efforts! She swallowed easily and shot Ed a there's-nothing-wrong-with-this-here-stew look before spooning up a larger bite to prove it.

Again, the meat and thick broth satisfied. But the first taste hadn't held any beans. . . .

"I forgot to soak the beans last night," she croaked out after she finally choked them down. Guilt and humiliation burned her cheeks, and Desta just knew her face was turning darker.

"Grief makes a powerful distraction," Mr. Carmichael observed, his voice kind.

Desta nodded but didn't trust herself to speak. Luckily, she didn't need to. He kept on.

"Loss and change are two of the hardest things life throws at us. It's easy to let something small slip when your hands are full. Why don't we just eat around the beans for tonight?"

"For tonight?" Disbelief echoed in Ed's words, and she shot him a glare so he'd hush up.

"Thank you, Mr. Carmichael." Desta pushed her chair back and grabbed the handles of the tureen. "I'll just take this into the kitchen and bring out plates of rabbit. Won't take but a minute."

She cleared the table in two blinks and retreated to the quiet of the kitchen. Putting down the tureen, she started picking hunks of rabbit out and placing them on a platter. Desta tried to keep her mind on the task, but she knew trouble when she found herself in it. She was a housekeeper who couldn't cook, for a half brother who'd gone on to his reward. For tonight, putting rabbit on a platter would do. But without Simon to look after, what she was going to do every other night?

CHAPTER 3

Things hadn't looked any better in the cool light of morning—possibly because her new cell of a room didn't have any windows. Miss Pennyworth made sure of that. No light came in, and no students could shimmy their way out. For good measure, she locked the door at night and during naptime.

Naturally an early riser, Jessalyn awoke just after dawn every day. BC—Before Capture—she used the extra time to slip out to the stables. Morning Glory matched her name, and they both adored the precious hours before the rest of the world awoke and the demands of the day set in.

But for the past two weeks, since Cecily snitched on her, there'd been no illicit visits to the stables. Perhaps fearing Jess would try and make a run for it, Miss Pennyworth barred her from even the standard, scheduled riding instruction. She didn't so much as glimpse Morning Glory, though the headmistress had grudgingly promised not to send the horse away. Then again, she probably would have tried if Jess's father didn't pay the stables directly for Morning Glory's boarding.

Jess could do nothing but wait until Miss Pennyworth's report of her many misdeeds reached her father and he handed down a decision. Her stomach churned in an uneasy mix of hope and dread. Despite seven years away from home, she couldn't help hoping that he'd come for her and take her back to Texas. Because of those same seven years, she dreaded what might come next. She turned nineteen in a couple of days—at this point she'd outgrown boarding academies.

She was the right age for marriage, and weren't these sorts of schools nothing more or less than training grounds for well-behaved wives? Her grandparents were well placed to introduce her to society and pawn her off on an unsuspecting groom. Panic threatened at the possibility.

Steps tapped down the hallway, and Jess watched the sudden depression of the door handle. The door flung wide so fast it knocked into the wall.

Miss Pennyworth burst into the room, large nostrils quivering as though scenting misbehavior. Given nearly twice the normal amount of nose—the better to stick it into other people's business—but rather sparse eyebrows, she perpetually looked somewhat shocked by whatever she discovered. Today she seemed surprised to find Jess sitting up in the straight-backed chair. She probably hoped to startle Jess awake, leaving her groggy and at a disadvantage.

The woman evidently hadn't learned from her past mistakes, so Jess turned the tables.

"Miss Pennyworth, such a surprise to see you! Shouldn't the entire school be resting for another. . ."—Jess picked up the clock on her desk and eyed it in disbelief—"twenty minutes?"

"My schedule is not that of the students I teach." She sniffed in derision and fixed Jess with a beady gaze. "I'm a very busy woman and don't have the luxury of such leisure time as you enjoy."

Somehow Jess managed not to question what luxuries she enjoyed while locked in a windowless room. Antagonizing the head-mistress could wait until after Jess knew where she was going, for how long, and whether or not Miss Pennyworth would join her.

"Very good, Miss Culpepper," the headmistress praised. "You're learning to hold your tongue. It's good to see that your time with us has not been entirely wasted after all."

Abandoning all pretense of pleasantness, Jess gave a surprised echo. "You're sure?"

"No, Miss Culpepper, it has not," Miss Pennyworth snapped back. "In spite of your deplorable habits, there are certain aspects of your behavior which we've managed to refine."

"You misunderstand. I did not question the worthiness of my time here." *I wouldn't waste my breath.* "I questioned your implication that our time together has reached its end."

The headmistress clicked bony fingers, and a maid edged into the room, carrying a familiar, half-packed valise. "We will discuss your departure in the salon while your bags are packed." She sailed from the room, obviously assuming Jess would trail at her heels like some eager pup.

She didn't. Jess resisted, determined to prove herself more powerful than the pull of her own curiosity, hopes, and fears. Miss Pennyworth might dictate her future for a little while longer, but Jess remained in control of herself. Instead of chasing after the head-mistress for answers, she calmly helped the maid finish packing her belongings. Then she took a few more moments—both to compose herself and further enrage a waiting Miss Pennyworth—to rinse her face and hands.

In a way she felt like she was washing away any remnants of this place. It relaxed her, giving her something tangible to do as preparation for moving on. Only then, when she felt good and ready, did she make her way down the stairs to the parlor. By now other students were stir-ring. She even spotted Cecily down the hall and drew encouragement from her smile. In the end, it didn't matter where Miss Pennyworth chose to send her—eventually she'd make her way home.

"Close the door behind you," the headmistress directed when she stepped into the salon. Once Jess obeyed, she gestured to the uncomfortable horse-hair stuffed settee across from her. "Go ahead and sit down. You should probably pour yourself a bracing cup of tea before we begin."

She might have responded that there was no such thing as a "bracing" cup of tea—particularly when served lukewarm—but something in Miss Pennyworth's expression stopped her.

Suspicion, frustration, judgment, and even resignation were reg-ularly served up with the headmistress's everlasting disapproval, but here was something different. Softer somehow.

Then she spotted the platter of cakes and tartlets beside the tea-pot. Miss Pennyworth never served sweets, and she never looked at Jess kindly. The changes completely flummoxed Jess, bringing back the anxious panic. She couldn't even consider a tartlet, her thoughts too full of what horrors could move the headmistress to pity.

"No thank you." Jess kept her spine straight and her chin up. She'd meet this head-on.

"Stubborn." Miss Pennyworth shook an admonishing forefinger, and Jess took heart.

"I've no illusions that you're sorry to see me go." She tried to sound businesslike. "But I'd rather not spend my last moments being chided. Tell me where you're sending me, and I'll be off."

"You're going to your grandparents' in Wiltshire." The older woman rose to her feet and pinned her with a stare. "It is my fond hope that there you will cease secluding yourself and find that people hand out rules and advice not only to instruct, but to protect the people they care for."

Already smarting from this latest proof that Papa still didn't want her to come home, Jess bristled at Miss Pennyworth's censure. "I doubt I'll be secluded, considering I don't go about locking *myself* in rooms. There's a vast difference between protection and imprisonment."

"And there are ways to isolate yourself without ever shutting a door." The headmistress pursed her lips as though trying to hold something back. Then she sighed and held out a letter.

That's not Papa's writing. Jess's pulse picked up as she took the envelope. It pressed heavily against her hand, as though burdened by the weight of its words. Her brother's spiky scrawl sent streaks of fear shooting up her spine. Ed didn't write to her very often, and even then he enclosed his notes with Papa's longer letters. *It's been too long since I heard from Papa. . . .*

Jess jerked her gaze away from the envelope, glaring at Miss

Pennyworth's sympathetic expression. "You've been holding my letters as part of my punishment." At least, she assumed so. Papa usually wrote every week, and she hadn't received a letter since she switched rooms. She pushed back the panic clawing up her throat to demand, "Where are the others?"

"There are no others." The headmistress's hands fluttered, empty and helpless.

Turning away to give herself some privacy, Jess forced a few deep breaths. She slid her finger beneath the flap of the envelope, ripping it open in a single, rough motion. She delved inside and pulled out the letter. Either her brother's penmanship had actually gotten worse, or he'd struggled to put down the words.

> *Dear Jess,*
>   *This is my third try to get this out, but every time it keeps coming out wrong. Maybe it's because there isn't a right way to tell someone bad news. Well, maybe in person, but I'd probably botch that as bad as this letter. It's hard to believe and harder to tell you that Pa's passed on—*

A tiny mewling sound escaped Jess, far too small to unload the sudden weight of grief. Her gaze locked on that line, blurring the script until it made no sense. She staggered backward, groping for the arm of a nearby chair and collapsing into it. Darkness edged her vision.

"Breathe, Miss Culpepper." Miss Pennyworth's voice sounded muted, as though coming from a long distance, even though Jess felt her hand bracing her back. "Breathe deeply now."

The vile smell of ammonia burned its way through Jess's stupor, making her gasp for air and splutter back to her senses. She waved the headmistress and her smelling salts away, heart racing.

Miss Pennyworth took away the vial and stepped back. "You were coming over faint."

"Culpeppers don't faint." Aghast at such weakness, stricken by loss, Jess swallowed a sob.

"You didn't," the headmistress assured her. "But you must admit you're better now."

Better? Jess looked up blankly. Nothing could make this better. *My breathing won't bring him back—but my stubbornness made his lung collapse in the first place. It's my fault he's gone.*

She looked back at the letter, needing to be sure. After all, people died of fevers and falls every day. Maybe something else took Papa. Maybe it had nothing to do with that terrible day seven years ago when the bronco threw her, then kicked her father when he tried to reach her.

> *Yes, it was his lung, and NO, you can't go around feeling like it's your fault he died. Don't shake your head at that, Jess.*

She gave a strangled cough. Her brother hadn't seen her in years, but he'd known she'd blame herself. Then again, they both knew she had good reason to feel responsible. Guilt intensified her grief as she scanned the next few lines.

> *Pa didn't blame you—his last words were how much he loved you and how he wanted to be sure you'd be looked after. He always talked about bringing you home, but didn't think he could keep you safe out here and raise you into the sort of woman Ma would have wanted. He didn't send you away because he was mad about you riding the bronco or him getting injured.*
>
> *After all, he knew better than to jump in a corral and try to skirt around that bronco—you remember what he taught us? "Never approach a bull from the front, a horse from the rear, or a fool from any direction."*

Jess mouthed the words as she read them, remembering happy

days filled with sunlight and sage advice when their father taught them everything he knew about ranching. For a moment the memory eased her pain. Then it rushed back, heavier and harder than before.

Jess bowed her head. *She'd* been the fool who'd tried to bust a bronco she had no business riding. If Papa hadn't been so worried about her, he wouldn't have jumped into the pen, run past the wild horse, and gotten kicked in the chest. Without that injury, he wouldn't have struggled through having his lung collapse the other times, and he almost certainly would still be alive.

Miss Pennyworth cleared her throat, breaking into Jess's self-remonstrance. Abruptly she recalled that a carriage waited for her at the door to take her to her grandparents' home. She needed to finish reading Ed's letter and wrestle her emotions under control until she reached the privacy of the carriage. Once alone, she could sit in stunned silence or let her tears fall. But not now. Not here.

> *Most likely you'll want to be close to family now and will choose to stay with Ma's parents. But just in case I'm wrong and you want to stay at the academy, I sent Miss Pennyworth the next semester's tuition with a good bit extra for mourning dresses and whatever else you might need.*

Here she paused then scanned back up to reread the passage. The words scattered through her thoughts like buckshot, hitting every possible emotion. Disbelief and hurt that he'd leave her here—abandoned—warred with outrage at his high-handedness. For a moment rage overshadowed the more difficult realms of grief and remorse. Anger lent her strength to keep reading.

> *I'll try to write more often, though I don't know how regular my letters will go out once we hit the Chisholm Trail. You know I can't come fetch you now—the county roundup's scheduled for early June, and we'll take the trail directly after—but*

Carmichael and I decided the Bar None will forgo an autumn drive this year so I can be there as early as September.

Write back and tell me where you plan to camp out until then.

All my love,
Ed

P.S. You'll still be in mourning by the time I make it out to England, so it shouldn't be a problem, but I don't want to leave this to chance. If some smart fellow asks for your hand between now and then—or already has—you be sure and wait until I can meet him and make sure he's good enough for my baby sister. Promise me that in your next letter so I can rest easy.

Jess couldn't hold back a snort that her brother's final worry was whether some man would snatch her away. Obviously he hadn't been in contact with any of the headmistresses whose schools she'd attended and failed. Otherwise they would have put paid to the notion that any English gentleman would see her as a desirable bride. She'd grown into a woman, but not even seven years of cloistered lessons could turn Jessalyn Culpepper into their idea of a lady.

True ladies didn't shimmy over terraces, ride astride. . .or use tuition money to book passage back to Texas. Which was why she wasn't going to write back and let her brother rest easy.

Jessalyn might not be a lady. . .but she wasn't a liar, either.

CHAPTER 4

W e don't tolerate that sort of thing at the Bar None." Tucker
fisted his hand around the placket of a grub-liner's shirt and yanked
him down off his horse. When he released his grip, the man stumbled.

"What're ya talkin" bout?" the stranger sneered. "I wasn't tryin' ter
steal the thing."

Tucker hooked his thumb over his belt, drawing attention to
the holster against his hip. As foreman, he took the responsibility of
wearing his firearm seriously. The other ranch hands weren't allowed
the privilege. "It's not about stealing, though we don't tolerate that
either."

"We tried ta tell him, Boss," Cookie hollered from the door of
the mess hall, where he kept vigil. His shout brought a round of sol-
emn nods from the cowboys clustered outside the bunkhouse.

"What're you jawin' on 'bout?" the culprit protested. "Didn't try
ter tell me nuthin'."

"Dig her loose—and don't be rough about it." Tucker waited
while the cowhand considered.

The man looked from him to the chicken at his feet and
scratched his head. "Fer serious?"

A raised brow served for his answer. No sense wasting words
on a fool, and Tucker didn't doubt this man ranked as a fool. In
the regular run of things, he probably wasn't a vicious man. Plenty
of cowboys didn't think Chicken Pickin' was anything more than
an amusing pastime. They figured chickens were for eating, so the
manner of killing didn't much matter. But it had mattered to Simon
Culpepper, and the senseless practice stuck in Tucker's craw, too.

The confused cowhand squatted down and started scooping dirt away from the bird. "Aw right. I didn't know this'un were some kinda pet. I kin grab another'un jest as easy anyways."

"Ya might as well try scratchin' yer ear with yer elbow, mister." Old Virgil tongued his tobacco to the other cheek and spat into the dirt. "It ain't the bird ya picked that's yer problem."

Burt added, "It's the game itself what chaps the bosses' hides. Think it's cruel."

"Cruel? How is it any crueler'n branding a calf?" With a loud squawk, the hapless hen escaped from the loosened earth around her, flapping her wings in the face of the startled cowhand.

"You want us to bury you up to your neck and line up to gallop by, trying to pull you out?" Tucker waited for the man's vehement protests to end then added, "You know we brand because we have to identify who the cattle belongs to. It's not done for sport, and it doesn't kill them."

"They all get butchered and chickens go from the coop to the kettle, so what's the fuss?" He didn't sound belligerent, just baffled, so Tucker gave him the benefit of the doubt.

"You work with animals. Horses, cattle. . .you know they have a strong instinct for survival and show fear when they're cornered. Am I right?" He waited until the man—and several of the others—nodded their understanding. "Chickens are no different that way. So when you start burying the chicken, it's helpless and scared. When a great big horse thunders by, almost trampling it, it's even more frightened. And if someone manages to grab hold and pull it loose without strangling the poor thing or breaking its neck, that little bird has been put through the wringer."

"That's a terrible truth, Boss." The man looked humbled. "Never thought of it like that."

"Good." Tucker shrugged. "It's just mean-spirited to treat any living thing that way."

"I get what yer sayin'!" The grub-line rider snapped his fingers. "Kill the bird first!"

At that Tucker stopped talking and simply walked away. He wasn't going to keep arguing with a man who boasted less brains than the bird. Besides, he'd promised Ed he'd swing by the ranch house after dinner to discuss a few things.

"C'mon in!" Ed invited in response to Tucker's halfhearted holler from the front porch.

Tucker let himself through the front door and headed for the study, only to find Ed in the dining room. Again. Sending up a thankful prayer that he'd already eaten in the mess hall, Tucker wandered in. He waved howdy when Desta bustled through the kitchen door and relaxed when he realized she was clearing the table. No chance for him to hurt her feelings by refusing food.

"Grab a chair." Ed gestured toward his left. "You can join me for some dessert."

Tucker paused in the act of pulling out a seat. He muttered so Desta wouldn't hear. "I filled up at the mess hall. You know good and well that I told you I'd swing by *after* supper ended." Ed invited him for supper, but he couldn't fool Tucker into that situation twice. Miss Desta might be a paragon of womanly virtues in every other area, but she couldn't cook a square meal if someone laid it out at right angles for her in advance.

A mischievous grin lit his friend's face. "Stop giving me the hairy eyeball. According to Desta, cooking and baking are as different as mules and mares. One's too stubborn and ornery for her to get a handle on, the other settles in sweet and works out every time. You're in for a treat."

"I've known some women who could cook but not bake, but never the other way around." Tucker sank down into his seat, reluctantly intrigued. Come to think of it, Desta's disastrous stew came with unblemished biscuits last time.

Ed gave a great, loud sniff as Desta backed into the room, a pie in each hand. "Those pies sure do smell wonderful. Are they sweet potato?"

"One's sweet potato, and the other's pecan. I planned to serve the pecan tomorrow, but since Mr. Carmichael joined us in time, I figured you might like a choice. Or even a slice of each."

"Please call me Tucker," he reminded. "Otherwise I can't go on calling you Miss Desta." While she thought it over and finally gave him a nod of agreement, he took the opportunity to eye the pies. They looked tempting, but Ed played the trickster often enough to make a wise man pause.

"Pecan, please." Tucker decided to try one before committing to a slice of both. There'd be no harm asking for a second slice, but trying to swallow a set might prove an impossible task.

"Both for me!" Ed slanted him a sideways look that said he knew Tucker doubted him. "Sometimes two are better than one!"

Soon the only sounds at the table were the scraping of forks and the gobbling of two truly superior pies. Sweet and satisfying, baked goods lulled a man into a contented stupor. A reliable reaction Miss Desta must have planned to use to her advantage. As soon as they'd eaten their fill and let their forks fall, she dabbed her lips with a napkin and let fly what was on her mind.

"Speaking of two being better than one," she began as though there hadn't been a twenty-minute, dessert-devouring interlude since Ed's comment, "I'm hoping you'll agree with me, Mr. Tucker, that my nephew needs to send for Jessalyn as soon as possible. That girl's been away from home for far too long, and it's only natural to keep family near after a loss. The pair of them will do better together than apart."

Tucker registered that she'd used his name, but the rest of her speech left him tongue-tied. He turned to Ed, unable to tell the well-meaning housekeeper that he thought her niece should stay as far away from the ranch as possible, for as long as possible, until things settled down. There surely weren't any appropriate words to say that. Given what he remembered of little Jessalyn Culpepper, she'd bring along more trouble than the Bar None was equipped to handle just yet. Women—especially women who didn't know what they were doing—made a powerful liability.

But he couldn't say that to another woman—especially one who'd proven she didn't know what she was doing when it came to cooking up a main meal. Or, to look at it another way, a woman who was the disastrous young lady's loving aunt. Tucker knew he'd bring a heap of trouble down on his own head, so instead he kept his mouth shut and waited for the majority owner of the ranch—not to mention brother of the problem in question—to handle Miss Desta's demand.

Ed finally sighed and bellied up to his responsibility. "Now, Aunt Desta, I already explained to you why it's just not possible to bring Jess back until the fall. There was no cause for you to ambush poor Tucker like that. When it's all said and done, the decision belongs to me."

"Well, the decision might belong to you, but I figured you'd be open to some good advice before you went and settled on the wrong one." She started to sound huffy, and Tucker wondered how long it would be before she started shaking an admonishing finger at her errant nephew.

It'd probably be entertaining, so long as she didn't try and drag him into it again.

"You're thinking with your heart; I'm thinking about what's practical for the ranch. You know what's practical for the ranch is what's best for all of us, Jess included," Ed defended.

"Calving season, roundups, cattle drives, and so on." Desta waved away their lives' work as though it were less than air. "It's all taken precedence over yore sister for seven years. Why doesn't yore own flesh and blood matter more to you than a bunch of cows you replace every year?"

"Unfair!" Ed half rose out of his seat. "You know we care more about Jess than we do about the cows. Even Tucker, and she's not related to him. Dad thought England kept her safe and helped her grow into the sort of woman Mama would want her to be, so she could marry well and have children and live a long, happy life. Who are we to say Pa raised his daughter the wrong way?"

"You know I won't speak ill of yore papa." Desta raised a fluttering hand and laid it over her heart. "But that man got intimidated by the idea of trying to raise a daughter on his own after yore mama passed on. Maybe he had good reason—a daughter needs a mother figure—but she's been gone more than long enough to become lady-like. I suspect he got so used to having her gone, he just didn't know what he'd do with her when he brought her home."

"And you think *we'll* know what to do with her when she comes back?" Tucker's astonishment had him talking before he made the decision to join the conversation.

"You don't have to know what to do with her," Desta promised. "I'll settle her in."

"My sister doesn't settle into anything she does." Ed reached for his coffee mug, realized it was empty, and thumped it back on the table. "You never met her, Aunt Desta, but Jess grew up half wild and more than a little willful. She's shuffled from school to school in merry ol' England because she doesn't take orders. Five academies for fine ladies, and I got an expulsion notice from the last one two days ago—crossed in the mail with my letter sending the next semester's tuition."

"Well, there you are!" She positively beamed at her nephew while Tucker looked at him aghast. "If the school's turning her out, it's the perfect time to bring her back home to Texas."

"No." Ed shook his head. "I already wrote the headmistress to send Jess to her grandparents. For all we know, it would be worse to move her from the country where she's lived for so long. She doesn't need any more shocks. When I bring her home, she'll turn the Bar None on its head—first trying to get involved in everything and then when fellows start coming to court her. From the day she arrives to the day she marries, everything around here will change."

While Ed talked, Tucker felt the pie he'd just eaten settle heavier and heavier in his stomach. The two of them had decided to leave Jessalyn in England until autumn because the ranch took every bit of their attention. Other ranchers tried to range their cattle around the plentiful water holes of Bar None land, and rustlers, hearing that the Big Boss died, grew bolder in stealing unbranded calves. Until they made it through the roundup and drive and established to the entire county that the Bar None remained strong, they didn't have time to fetch a schoolgirl and help her settle in.

They both knew all of this, so they hadn't needed to discuss it in detail. Now, hearing Ed reminisce about his sister made Tucker anxious. His friend painted an awful grim picture. Even as Desta gave up pestering them, he couldn't stop the churning in his gut over the troubles Jess would bring home. Come fall, he and Ed would talk again. Maybe, just maybe, there'd be good reason to keep Jessalyn Culpepper away from the Bar None for a little bit longer.

Not much longer. Jess arched her back, trying to ease the aches from hours in the saddle. Her muscles protested the shift and then tensed when the motion tilted her hat brim, dousing the back of her neck with a fresh run of rainwater. It didn't make her much wetter or colder, but it didn't help either. She stretched and settled back in the saddle, trying in vain to get comfortable.

It didn't work. If she were being honest, she hadn't been comfortable since the hour she'd left Miss Pennyworth's Penitentiary two weeks ago. The strictures of the place chafed, but for the most part they provided soft, clean beds and chairs. After seventeen days of travel, Jess was in a mood to deeply appreciate a soft, clean bed. Or a hot bath. She let out a moan at the very thought.

From the small quarters she'd shared with the steamship captain's very pregnant—and very seasick—daughter, to the sooty train cars and the few disreputable hotels Jess stopped in, each leg of the journey proved cramped, uncomfortable, and downright stinky. Though, to be fair, at this point Jess doubted she smelled much better than any of the other travelers she'd met on the way.

The company crammed eight passengers into the stagecoach she'd chartered for the final leg of her journey. For her own sake, as well as whatever small measure of extra space her fellow customers might enjoy, Jess had taken to riding Morning Glory rather than wedge into the jarring coach. Her afternoon escapes from the academy might not have prepared her for such long hours in the saddle, but living in England had bolstered her ability to tough out a little rain squall.

Not that she liked riding all day in a downpour, but it made a marginally better option than bouncing along on a narrow wooden bench, jammed between two men who hadn't bathed in months. Especially when they insisted on shutting the window coverings against the rain, making the scant air even more stagnant. Stares from the other women—every bit as icy as the water now trickling down her back—encouraged her to stay outside until they went their separate ways.

Every day, every mile brought her closer to home. From gloomy England, across the wave-tossed Atlantic, through bustling cities along the railroad, she'd refused to slacken her pace. The only concession she'd made had been a morning's worth of shopping once she hit American soil. About the only useful things she'd brought with her were her trusty horse and her pistol.

The pistol proved the single concession Papa granted her after she moved to England. He'd taught her to shoot when she turned ten, and she guilted him into letting her keep it. Headmistresses didn't approve, but Papa kept his promise and wrangled permission at each and every school. He never came out and said so, but Jess got the impression he found it comforting that she could protect herself. She knew it helped her feel safe in unfamiliar surroundings—or on the long journey home.

So she landed in America armed with her pistol and her pony, but no way to ride. While students were encouraged to keep their own mounts, they'd been forced to use tack provided by the stables. This time Jess gladly bypassed sidesaddles, sniffing out a Denver-style rig with a three-quarter cinch, something sturdy enough for roping. She transferred the meager contents of her valise into a set of saddlebags and turned her attention toward finding hard-wearing, comfortable clothing.

Replacing the set of split skirts Miss Pennyworth had burned back at the academy presented the greatest challenge, but Jess found a seamstress willing to make alterations overnight. After that, she'd rustled up the rest of her gear without too much trouble. The ban-dannas, Stetson, and boots she'd worn ever since. By looking at her now, no one would guess they were practically new.

Her backside protested the many miles spent in her saddle, and Jess didn't care to count the blisters breaking in her boots, but it was worth it. She'd finally arrived in Texas and, after a dismal dinner stop at a knock-together café, parted ways with the stage. The Bar None sat a mere sixteen miles down the road. After so many years, she couldn't believe she'd be home for supper.

Home. Her stomach fluttered with nervous hope. No matter how often she told herself things would be different after so many years and that Papa wasn't going to be waiting in the doorway to sweep her into a hug, treasured memories kept welling to the fore. She expected to find the Bar None changed after so many years, but this was home. Nothing could change that.

The jitters got worse as she drew within two miles and saw the vague outline of the main fence. No one knew she was coming. Ed refused to come get her and he'd sure as shooting be surprised when she showed up, but would he be glad to see his sister after so long? The part of her heart that had withered without her family desperately needed someone to welcome her back, and her brother was the only relation she had left. Jess pushed down a growing fear that he'd be angry, see her as an inconvenience, and want to send her away again. Heaven help them both if he tried.

I'm back, I'm a grown woman, and this time no one can force me to leave.

The wind kicked up as she reached the gate, driving the rain at an angle. Jess raised her bandanna over her nose, trying to guard against the stinging chill. The last thing she needed was to ride up coughing like a weakling and give everyone the idea she couldn't handle harsh conditions. It didn't hurt that the fabric would help conceal her identity until she could get to Ed. He might not recognize her at the start, but a woman on a ranch always attracted a fair share of attention.

At the thought, Jess reached up and stuffed her braid into her hat. Stetson designed his hats with Western weather in mind, creating a high crown to allow an extra insulating layer of air between the hat and head. He probably never planned on that space being used to hide a woman's hair, but it worked surprisingly well. With her gloves, the bandanna, and Jess's long duster coat, the split skirts might escape notice. She'd ordered them black in honor of her father, so at a glance the extra girth might be mistaken for chaps—particularly in the midst of a passing storm.

Hiding her identity helped Jess squash her worries. She wouldn't go undetected for long, nor did she want to, but at least now she held a decent chance of making it to the house first. Ed would probably be more receptive to her sudden appearance if she could wrangle a private reunion. She dropped from the saddle to open the gate, fingers tracing the dripping Bar None brand, feeling the truth of her homecoming. Driving rain stung her eyes, making her blink as she led Morning Glory through. The wind blew the fence shut behind them, but she made sure the latch caught.

Then Jess stood for a minute, stretching her legs and her heartstrings. Stiff, aching, and cold, neither one had been used properly for far too many miles. But the pain felt good. Like a loosening of muscles and memories clenched too tight for too long. She squinted ahead, making out the house and the stables with the accompanying bunkhouse and cook shack. The buildings looked both bigger and smaller than she remembered. Smaller because she'd grown bigger and the rain blurred everything down, but bigger because they'd added on to everything over the years.

She blinked a few more times before grabbing the pommel and willing her nerves to steady. Jess swung back up into the saddle and rode the last few hundred feet home. As she drew near the stables, a figure rode out to meet her.

Even on horseback, the man gave the impression of height and power. He rode smoothly, making the ride look easy even when the horse shied from a particularly stinging lash of wind. Jess reined in and waited for him to reach her, wondering if she was about to meet her brother face-to-face. She remembered Ed as stockier than this man.

"Hey!" When he reached her, Jess battled conflicting surges of relief and disappointment. He wasn't her brother. But he looked over Morning Glory with a discerning eye, noting that her sides steamed in the cold, and got right down to business. "Been riding all day?"

"Yep." Jess deepened her voice and kept her chin tilted downward, avoiding his gaze.

"Take her to the stables—they'll see to her. Grab some coffee and stow your bags in the bunkhouse then grab a rag bag and a fresh mount." He shouted too loud for the wind to snatch his words. "Ride the northern line. Flag any weak wire, but don't work it or you'll slice yourself to ribbons in this weather. Won't be too long until you hear the supper bell anyway."

Jess nodded her agreement, not trusting the wind to disguise her voice and not willing to challenge a man who wore authority so easily. Bossy and brusque, he spoke knowledgeably and issued orders like a foreman. But beneath the orders ran a kind streak Jess found comforting and curious—he'd noticed Morning Glory's state and directed her to the stables. That alone would've endeared the man to her, but he'd also told a cold grub-line rider to take the time for a hot cup of coffee before riding the fences and specified a job that wouldn't be made dangerous by the rain.

Intrigued, she tilted her head and tried to make out his features beneath the brim of his dripping hat. Thick brows slammed together over a strong nose whose bump tattled of a break. He squinted, so she couldn't make out the color or shape of his eyes. Jess just got the impression of a fierce intelligence that would've seen through her garb in an instant if it weren't for the storm.

"Name?" he barked, a stubborn jut to his jaw as he peered at her through the elements.

"J." Deepening her voice for the single syllable, Jess figured she rode a fine line between truth and lies. Before he sent her away, Papa used to call her his "little J Bird" because she peppered him with questions from sunup to sundown. Her throat tightened at the remembrance, but Jess figured it would help her croak like a man if the cowboy in front of her asked anything else.

He didn't. Just gave a short nod and a pull on the reins before riding south, toward the windmills. As a good foreman should, he probably went to check that the raging wind didn't damage the water pumps. Nevertheless, Jess caught herself watching him ride away and hoping he planned a cursory look rather than an in-depth inspection. She didn't know his name, but she liked his style of leadership. The Bar None needed workers she and Ed could trust, and it'd be a shame to lose this one because he went scrambling up the side of a windmill in this weather.

Once he disappeared from view, Jess turned in Morning Glory at the stables. Avoiding conversation with the stable master, she kept her head down and grabbed her saddlebags. It cost her a twinge to leave Morning Glory behind when she'd been such a stalwart and constant companion, but she squared her shoulders and moved away from the warmth of the stables.

I made it. She kept her eyes on the house as she headed for the door. *Now we'll see what they make of me.*

CHAPTER 5

Desta didn't know what to make of the young man dripping all over the front porch. Cowhands and pass-through workers knew better than to come to the ranch house without explicit instruction from Ed or Tucker. Even then, they usually made their way around back to the kitchen out of respect.

So when she heard the knock at the front door without Tucker's accompanying greeting, she didn't know what to expect. Folks from town stopped coming by with their condolences weeks ago, and other than that Ed didn't invite many people over or encourage random visitors. Yet here stood a cowpoke—a very young cowpoke, judging by his small size and smooth cheeks—gawking at her and peering around her into the entryway without so much as a word of explanation.

"Did Tucker send you?" Desta knew better, but figured it would prompt a response.

The figure on the porch jerked back, muttering *"Tucker?"* as though recognizing the name and finding it surprising. But he recovered quickly, giving a short shake before answering in a respectful murmur. "No, ma'am. I'm looking for Ed—Edward Culpepper. Can I talk to him?"

"He's not here." She couldn't have put it into words, since the youngster didn't strike her as dangerous or intimidating, but she wasn't sorry to send him on his way. Desta sensed something was off here, even if she couldn't distinguish the cause. "You'll have to talk to Tucker Carmichael. Ask for him at the stables or even in the mess hall. He's in charge while Mr. Culpepper's away."

"Away?" The voice sharpened in distress, losing any pretense of a low rumble and exposing the speaker as even younger than Desta imagined. "For how long? When will he be back?"

"Talk to Tucker, child." She stepped back to close the door. Desta knew Tucker wouldn't take on the youngster, but he'd give him a dry spot to sleep tonight and a meal or two to fill him up before sending him down the line.

"I can't." The voice sounded so small, so lost, it made her pause. "It has to be Edward."

"Why?" In spite of herself, Desta opened the door wider. She gasped as the stranger reached up and jerked the Stetson away, letting a long, thick golden braid fall over her shoulder.

"Because. . ." Lonesome brown eyes blinked back tears as she confessed, "He's my brother."

"Jessalyn?" The black woman breathed her name so softly that at first Jess wasn't sure she'd heard right. Then the woman let out a whoop, flung herself through the door, and just about smothered her in a joyous hug. "Praise the good Lord, if it ain't little Miss Jessalyn, come home at last!"

Taken completely off guard, Jess stood stock-still, unable to return the embrace or end it. Everything about this was *wrong*. Papa dead, Ed gone away, and her only welcome after seven years came from a complete stranger. The bone-deep chill she'd warded away with hopes of home seeped toward her soul, streaked with disappointment and jealousy. Just who was this woman who guarded *her* father's house, knew her name, and greeted her like a long-lost loved one?

"Yes." She drew away from the suddenly suffocating clasp. "And you are?"

"Oh, but you wouldn't know about me." The woman took a step back, far more subdued as her eyes flickered over Jess's face without meeting her gaze. "I was yore daddy's housekeeper."

"Right." She'd committed all of Papa's letters to memory, and now Jess remembered. The very fact that he'd told her helped Jess feel less cut off from the Bar None and more comfortable accepting the woman's welcome. She dredged up a small smile. "Desta. I do know about you."

"You do?" Startled, her eyes went so wide Jess could see white all the way around.

"Papa wrote me when you came to the ranch," she elaborated somewhat defensively. The housekeeper's surprise made her feel her role of outsider, as did the humiliating recollection that she'd written Papa back, telling him he didn't need a housekeeper if he just brought her home. She'd promised to take good care of him and the rest of the Bar None, but he'd firmly maintained she was too young. Six years later, she stood on the stoop, trying to explain herself to the woman who'd served as her replacement without revealing how heart-sore the whole thing made her.

"I'm sorry I didn't recognize you from his description so long ago. It's a bit of a shock. . . ."

Understanding dawned on her face, and she broke in, "He didn't tell you I was black?"

Nettled that the housekeeper thought that would matter so much, Jess shook her head. "It's not the sort of thing he'd bother mentioning. I'm thrown off by Ed's absence. Somehow I didn't imagine I'd get all the way out here and not see him right away. It's been a long journey."

"And a long overdue one." The woman shook her head as though in remorse then snapped to attention as though just realizing Jess still stood out in the rain. She reached out and all but dragged Jess through the door, clucking like a distressed hen. "Come in! As if you ain't been through enough, my brains joggle at the sight of you and I leave you in the cold. You must be terrible tired and horrible hungry, but I'll get you fed up and settled in before you know it!"

"Thank you." Jess allowed herself to be led through the door but halted in the hallway.

Home. Dark wainscoting paneled the lower half of the walls, familiar but faded damask wall hangings stretched to the ceiling. Jess breathed in the scent of beeswax tinged with lemon oil, laid over the earthier fragrances of ranch living and rain. For one mad moment she fought the urge to race along the hardwood floors and take the turn into Papa's office so fast her feet slipped.

No matter how fast she ran or how hard she wished, she wouldn't find him. Never again.

Her chest constricted painfully until Jess drew a jagged breath. The tight ache eased enough to allow a few steps, taking her past the round occasional table gracing the entry. She fought the urge to reach out and finger the fresh wildflowers filling her mama's blue willow-patterned vase. If she stopped, she feared she might do something unutterably foolish—like snatch the vase to her chest, sink to the floor, and weep until she ran dry.

Instead she continued to the right, down the hall, and opened the door to Papa's study. Bookcases cushioned the walls, bracing the massive claw-foot desk she remembered so well. But the desk sat empty. No cheery fire cast flickering light around the room. The stale smell of cigars long since smoked teased her memories and sparked sudden outrage. Her grip tightened on the door handle, unwilling to let go as she turned to face the woman her father chose to take care of him.

The woman who'd let him continue smoking cigars, even after the doctor cautioned against them. Papa's lung might have been weakened by the bronco's kick seven years ago—old guilt grabbed her at the thought—but was it any wonder it kept collapsing if he kept doing the work of younger men and refused to give up something as insignificant as cigars? Was this why he died?

"You let him smoke?" Accusation bit through the words, questioning more than mere cigars.

"I didn't *let* Simon do anything, or *make* him do anything." The housekeeper sounded sympathetic. "No one did. He laid down his own laws.

"Simon?" Jess caught hold of the familiarity, partly out of curiosity but mostly because she didn't want to admit the woman made a valid point. She knew better than anyone that when Papa set out on a path, no amount of reasoned arguments or emotional pleas could make him change course.

"Simon," Desta repeated softly, not defensive or apologetic. If anything, the woman looked thoughtful. "I wondered if you were just surprised by my coloring, but you don't know the other."

The blatant reference to things she didn't know made Jess's teeth clench. "Other?"

"You've suffered a long day capped with disappointment. What say we get you upstairs and I'll bring up water for a hot bath? Once you're rested, you can ask all the questions you like." If she'd sounded superior and issued orders, Jess would've demanded answers straightaway. But even after she'd snapped questions about her place in the household and implied the woman hadn't cared properly for Papa, the housekeeper remained calm and kind, trying to ease Jess's homecoming.

Something about this woman spoke of strength and called for the same in others. For the first time since she hit the porch and the door opened, Jess spared a thought for someone else.

What must it be like for this woman, who'd looked after the Bar None for a half-dozen years, to find Jess on her doorstep? Did she chafe at her subservient position to an unexpected visitor? What deep-seated decency made her welcome the daughter of the man she'd worked for, fielding insolent questions with quiet understanding? Shame cooled Jess's rioting emotions.

"Whatever my disappointments, you're not one of them." Jess frowned. "I've been rude."

"Tired, more like." An encouraging smile lit her face. "Traveling takes a toll on the body, grief grabs the soul, and it's only natural to have questions after you've been gone so long."

"It's one thing to have questions and another to demand answers." A rueful smile crossed her lips. "But maybe you'll appease some of my curiosity while we work on filling that bath?"

The housekeeper looked her over and let loose a sigh. "I say you could us a good night's sleep before unpacking all yore questions, but I see you won't rest easy until after the askin'."

"Would you, ma'am?" Jess followed her into the kitchen, forbearing to look in the rooms they passed for fear of getting distracted—or worse, overwhelmed.

"Don't 'ma'am' me. Even if I didn't work here, we aren't that formal or fussy."

"Thank goodness. I've had enough pomp and pretension to last a lifetime." Jess reached for a bucket and waited while the other woman pumped water into the first. "So what do I call you?"

"I'm hoping..."—for the first time the woman looked nervous—"you won't mind calling me 'Aunt.'"

"Mind?" Her niece barely breathed the word as the bucket slipped from her hands. Jessalyn didn't so much as blink at the metallic clang of it hitting the floor, her eyes too busy staring at Desta.

Childhood lessons of fearful subservience, painstakingly set aside over the past two decades, surged to the fore with frightening power. It took every ounce of courage not to fix her eyes upon the ground and wait, trembling, for rebuke and retribution. Pale skin no longer gave anyone the right to hurt her, but Desta feared the pain of rejection. Since her mama died and her husband left her childless, her heart's longing was for another woman to call family... to call friend.

"You're my *aunt*?" Disbelief dripped from every syllable, but gave way to wonder. Warmth sparkled behind tears as her niece reached out and pulled her close, ignoring the way Desta's own full bucket sloshed water all over the pair of them. Jessalyn just stared. "I have an aunt."

"You have me." Desta set down the bucket and skirted around it. "If you want."

"If I—" She broke off and started again. "Ed's my brother, and I'm sorry he's not here, but now I find that my family welcomed me home anyway. You've *doubled* my family!"

Then they both were awash. They hugged for a long time, not saying anything more that couldn't be said by holding each other: *I'm here. You're not alone. I'm grateful you're in my life.*

Desta drank it in and poured it back out in prayer, her heart full of fervent, silent thanks.

Eventually, after the tears ran their course, little realities began to intrude on the moment. Her niece's slight frame was warm at heart, but cold to the touch and soaked clean through. Jessalyn didn't offer any protest when Desta sat her down at the kitchen table and took charge.

"We need to warm you up on the inside while we're filling the tub. Tea leaves are in the cupboard to the left, and I keep the honey right alongside of it." She moved to the washroom near the pantry, where she kept the big tub whenever it wasn't being hauled upstairs for Simon. As Desta crossed the kitchen, Jessalyn dutifully moved over to the cabinet and grimaced at the tea tin.

"Aunt Desta?" She tentatively tried the title out, smiling as she said it before wrinkling her nose at the tea leaves once again. "Is there any chance I might have some coffee instead?"

"Of course." She pulled down the grinder. "I thought tea might make you feel at home."

"Tea is for England, where the women make tepid conversation about weak weather. But in Texas, where the rain makes a racket and the people more than match it?" Jess found the beans and all but buried her head in the bag, breathing deep before declaring, "*Coffee* says home!"

❧

The promise of hot coffee had Tucker swinging by the mess hall. He planned to fall into his bunk—most likely with his boots still on—and sleep himself into a better mood, but the lure of coffee kept him sociable. By sociable, he meant not shouting at every man who got between him and the pot.

Thankfully, no one proved fool enough to try and engage him in cards or conversation. Either the rest of the men worked themselves into the ground same as Tucker, or they scratched together enough sense not to let him know otherwise. In any case, no one blocked his path to the stove where Cookie always kept a vat of coffee hot and strong enough to steam the hide off a hog.

Tucker grabbed a mug from the nearby pile, reached for the handle, and all but upended the pot before acknowledging the unpleasant and unprecedented truth. It was empty.

"Which man," he roared, plunking the useless pot back atop the burner and whipping around to face his workers, "which abysmally inconsiderate *fool*, poured the last cup and put the pot back?"

Astonished silence met his demand, cowhands casting furtive glances from their own steaming mugs to the empty one Tucker waved in accusation. No one fessed up, and no one pointed fingers. This last was to be expected; his men knew better than to butt in or carry on. That didn't bother Tucker. He didn't have the patience to waste catching the culprit and coming up with a memorable, amusing punishment. Venting his spleen made him a little less grumpy, warned everyone to keep their distance, and most importantly warned them not to let the pot go dry again.

Though if he'd had to guess—and he didn't have to do a single blessed thing but accept the full mug Cookie rushed out to him— Tucker figured one of the grub-line riders as the guilty man. He recalled that the previous influx headed out this morning, so Bar None only played host to one transient tonight. But the youngster who'd ridden up in the rainstorm couldn't be blamed for the empty coffeepot. Tucker recognized each and every cowboy who'd avoided eye contact, so he'd probably find the newcomer in the bunkhouse, snoring off a long, cold day in the saddle.

Tucker could respect that, considering he planned to do the same. He drained the rest of his coffee in a scalding glug, plunked down the mug with the rest of the dirty dishware, and left the mess hall without another word. A well-timed break in the rain saw him to the bunkhouse without a further dousing. Between that small mercy and a stomach of hot coffee, things looked up. After a solid night's sleep, Tucker figured he'd feel almost human again come morning.

But when he sank down onto his bunk, biting back a groan of relief, he noticed something. Actually, he noticed there wasn't anything or anyone to notice—he had the bunkhouse all to himself. Typically this would be a welcome rarity. Tonight it ranked as an unpleasant surprise because Tucker knew, without a shadow of a doubt, the stranger remained at the Bar None.

When he'd turned in Happy Jack at the stables, Tucker took a moment and looked in on the grubber's mount. He'd harbored some concern since she'd been ridden hard in poor weather. If she'd looked underfed, sickly, or otherwise abused, Tucker would've found a way to buy her. He'd done it before with a few mounts who deserved better treatment from a no-good grubber and had no qualms about sending a man away on foot with a few dollars in his pocket and a bug in his ear. But that hadn't been the case. The sturdy little pony looked well fed and beautifully maintained.

With the horse accounted for, Tucker needed to track down her rider. If any of the Bar None mounts were still out this late and in this weather, the stable master would've warned him. He hadn't said a word, so that meant the mysterious "J" hadn't gotten caught out on the range. Tucker should've spotted the man around the stables, mess hall, or bunks. There wasn't anywhere else any of the hands—especially a stranger—belonged. Abruptly, Tucker realized he hadn't checked on Desta since midday. With Ed gone on business, she was alone.

The chill traipsing down the back of his neck owed nothing to the inclement weather. Tucker surged to his feet, unholstered his pistol, and all but mowed down a cowhand when he hit the door. Not stopping to apologize or explain, he hot-footed it up to the ranch house. He almost reached the porch before making a quick decision to veer around the house to the kitchen. Tucker forced himself to move slowly and quietly, refusing to give any warning of his approach.

If something were wrong, he'd get a jump on the situation. If nothing were wrong, he didn't want to alarm Miss Desta. After all, no lone woman wanted to be reminded of her vulnerability, and the last thing Tucker wanted to do was worry her out of sleeping until Ed got back.

Flickering light from oil lamps illuminated the kitchen window, throwing a sizeable gap between the curtains into sharp relief. Tucker slid closer, ears perked for any sign of distress. Nothing struck him as out of the ordinary, but an uneasy prickle across the back of his neck whispered a warning. That disruption, that sense of something awry without any concrete confirmation, saved his life more than once. Cattle stampeded, horses bolted, flash floods burst through barriers, and often that tingly, indefinable sense of disturbance gave the only warning.

After countless close calls, Tucker trusted that tingle—and tonight it told of trouble.

He crept onto the back porch. Unable to avoid the runoff from the overhanging eaves, Tucker ignored the chilly rainwater sluicing over his shoulders and pressed his back against the wall. Slow sideways steps brought him to the window, where a sudden burst of sound startled him.

Laughter. He stiffened in surprise, then suspicion, as he made out more than one voice.

No longer concerned for Miss Desta's safety, he turned to face the window, peering through the gap he'd noted in the curtains. At first all he could make out were the things he expected to see, like the stove. Its merrily burning wood fire made a fool of him for lurking in the cold rain, but Tucker resisted the urge to abandon his post and head inside. First he needed to know what he'd be dealing with. The laughter sounded feminine, but Desta was the only woman at the Bar None.

He pressed tighter against the wall and angled his line of vision toward the other half of the room. *There.* Tucker sucked in a sharp breath as he caught sight of the woman sitting with Desta.

She sat facing away from him, toward Desta, so he couldn't see her face. At first he didn't need to. A riot of honey-colored curls tumbled past her hips, picking up glints of red in the flickering firelight. Her dress, a spritely pale green, dipped in to reveal a trim waist. It might've been the way she perched on the stool, but the skirts seemed short on her. Tucker made out finely turned ankles above rosy toes. While he watched, the vision tilted her head back in another laugh.

Her glorious mane cascaded to the side, giving him a glimpse of her profile. Full lips parted in mirth, her smile generous and her amusement honest. A pert nose and strong chin told of a woman with character, though long lashes several degrees darker than her hair shaded her eyes.

The coffee he'd craved mere moments before soured in Tucker's stomach. Here sat the disturbance he'd sensed, and now he knew his instincts were right on the money. Women—especially women who turned up where they didn't belong—were unpredictable and problematic.

This one might be pretty as all get-out, but to Tucker, she just looked like trouble.

CHAPTER 6

Good thing he made it his policy to meet trouble head-on.

Tucker pushed away from the wall but slid sideways past the window before straightening up. After going to such lengths to be sure Desta wasn't frightened by any unwelcome visitors, it would be a fine thing if he fulfilled the role himself by looming at her window. The thought made him pause before knocking—he'd raced up here to make sure the young grub-line rider hadn't broken in or caused mischief. Instead he'd found a beautiful woman visiting with Desta.

A few things didn't sit straight, and the possibilities didn't explain them away.

Had the youngster followed the lady to the Bar None? If so, why? And where was he?

How had a lady sashayed onto the property—even in the midst of a storm—and not caused an almighty ruckus among the men? Why hadn't Desta sent him word and let him know who'd arrived? Come to think of it, there weren't any other new horses in the stables and Tucker knew no carriages or coaches rolled up to the ranch with visitors. How had the woman gotten here at all?

Water rolled from the brim of his hat to drip on his nose. Tucker shook his head, hoping to dispel the annoyance and redirect the course of his thoughts. No such luck. He couldn't reject the one explanation to account for this scenario, no matter how deeply it pricked his pride.

It'd been dark and raining this afternoon. The young cowpoke sheltered behind hat, bandanna, and jacket. Tucker didn't make much of it when a man didn't waste his words—he valued peace and quiet and thought more of folks who didn't speak unless they had something to say. But now looking back, he realized that the youth uttered no more than two words, a single syllable each. For pity's sake, one of them might not even be a word—just a letter! "J."

I've been duped. Tucker gritted his teeth and drew in a cold, rain-scented breath. If word got out that a gorgeous woman rode up to the Bar None and fooled him into seeing a tired cowhand, he'd never live it down. A small, honest part of him thought he probably didn't deserve to.

Any boss who required instant, unswerving obedience from his men had to earn their respect. Every hand on the Bar None needed to trust Tucker's judgment because a moment might be the difference between life and death. They followed him now because he made solid decisions and his instincts provided reliable warning in dangerous situations, much as they had tonight.

So what happened this afternoon? He scowled. The only thing he could figure was that his senses didn't see mistaking a woman for a ranch hand as a dangerous situation. Stood to reason. History showed that if there was one thing to throw off a man's primal instincts and interfere with his God-given good sense, it was a woman. For the first time, Tucker felt sympathy for Adam.

Privately, he'd always thought the first man fell embarrassingly short of the mark. Adam knew better than to eat the fruit. He'd walked into sin with his eyes wide open, so in Tucker's book, the man should've owned up to his share of the blame. Instead he pointed at Eve as the instigator. Now Tucker reconsidered. Maybe his forbear wasn't just pointing at Eve. Maybe the world's first hapless male had been trying to explain that his good sense misfired when confronted with a female. Adam made the first mistake, and men had been falling for women ever since.

Too bad that didn't make the impact any less painful. Or any less embarrassing. *He'd* fallen for the little lady's trick. Tucker raised his hand and rapped on the door. But now *she'd* be the one standing her ground and offering an explanation.

When Desta opened the door, he brushed past her into the welcome warmth of the kitchen. He ambled toward the interloper, never letting his gaze leave her face. Not that it wanted to—up close the woman made an even prettier picture than he'd expected; all big brown eyes and rosy lips softly parted in surprise. She'd risen to her feet before he'd crossed the threshold, and Tucker noted she stood unusually tall for a woman. Also that he'd been right before—her skirts hung short.

She didn't move as he walked toward her, and Tucker found he appreciated her courage. As any cowboy would, he removed his hat before confronting a misbehaving lady. " 'J,' I presume?"

The knock on the door startled Jess to her feet. She reached for her holster before remembering she'd left it with the rest of her clothes. For years she'd kept it as close as possible—a reminder of who she was and that Papa wanted her to be safe even if he wasn't close enough to do the protecting. Once she'd found her way back home, it didn't seem as necessary anymore.

Then, too, it somehow seemed wrong to strap her pistol over one of Mama's fine dresses. Desta insisted she wear it since her traveling clothes could practically stand on their own and everything in her saddlebags got soaked by the rain. She hadn't imagined that an irritated man would burst through the kitchen doors and cut her off from the washroom, where her pistol lay.

Close enough for comfort, but not close enough to count, Jess berated herself.

Desta looked more amused than alarmed, and Jess took her cue from that. As her tension eased and the man drew closer, Jess identified him as the foreman from that afternoon. Almost immediately she confirmed her impression that he was irritated—the man practically simmered. She wouldn't have been surprised to see some of the rainwater coating his clothing rise up in steam.

But he leveled all that heated intensity on Jess as he stalked across the room. A lesser woman would've taken a step back or shifted so she didn't meet his gaze. But Jess refused to step back and find herself penned against the table. On a visceral level, she recognized in this man the innate tendency to dominate. If she lowered her eyes, he'd see it as a sign of submission.

Refusing to let an employee get the upper hand on her first night back, Jess wouldn't even blink. He crossed the room in a matter of seconds, but the man made a powerful impression.

Earlier that afternoon, even through the storm and while on horseback, he projected an air of authority, a sense of stubbornness, and gave an impression of physical height and strength. Up close and out of the rain, Jess saw that she wouldn't be revising any of those opinions anytime soon.

He stood a full head taller than she, which made him unusually tall. She saw eye to eye or close enough with most men, but Jess got the feeling she wouldn't be seeing eye to eye with this one on any level. A square jaw, dusted with several days' growth of whiskers, jutted toward her like a hound dog after a hare. Sweeping the hat from his head, he flung water across the kitchen floor.

" 'J,' I presume?" He bit off the words, making a mockery of his fine manners.

Intelligent. Jess added to his list of attributes. *And angry as all get-out that I fooled him.*

"Tucker Carmichael, you stop frowning so fierce or I'm going to take offense." Desta bustled up to provide a buffer. "No man should walk into a kitchen looking so put out."

Tucker. Jess kept herself from gasping, but it took some effort. Suddenly she remembered standing on the porch, hearing Desta tell her to talk to Tucker. She'd had the same reaction then, but forgotten it in the revelations that followed. Now her surprise came rushing back.

The memory unspooled of a rangy—even gangly—young

greenhorn, taken on for the spring and eager to prove himself. The boy stood tall, waiting for manhood to fill out his shoulders and a few seasons at the Bar None to round out his skills. He evinced the wiry strength not uncommon in young cowhands, with a quick mind and an eye for horses. His way with animals convinced Papa to hire him in spite of his inexperience—and his inexperience made it easy for a twelve-year-old Jess, in desperation, to convince young Tucker Carmichael to saddle an unbroken bronco for her.

Now, seven years later, Jess couldn't say what surprised her more—that Tucker Carmichael hadn't left the Bar None years ago or that he'd grown into a man strong enough and skilled enough to oversee the entire operation. Whether or not the intervening years had been kind, he wore the changes well—and Jess was woman enough to be intrigued by the differences time wrought.

Though she couldn't be sure, she thought he'd grown taller. Certainly, his shoulders broadened and he'd gained muscle through the chest and arms. He moved with equal parts deliberation and easy confidence. Beneath the whiskers, his jawline sharpened since she'd last seen him, his brows seemed thicker and more thoughtful. She'd never thought about how expressive eyebrows could be, but Tucker Carmichael's transmitted his mood loud and clear.

Especially drawn together like that, scowling at her. It made Jess wonder whether she'd earned his ire this afternoon or if he harbored a deeper grudge from seven years before. She couldn't tell whether Tucker recognized her as more than "J," but suspected he hadn't fit that piece to the puzzle yet. Perhaps her position as a member of the Culpepper family would elicit respect.

Or maybe he'll start seeing the wayward girl I was instead of the woman who's standing in front of him. She bit back a sigh. *Nothing like a conversation guaranteed to feed a man's temper.*

For a second his attention shifted to Desta. "I'm not put out. I'm fed up, that's all."

"That sounds more appropriate to a kitchen," Jess pointed out agreeably, unable to resist.

"I've been busy tracking down a stranger wandering on Bar None grounds," he snapped back. "So you'll have to forgive me if I'm less concerned with what's appropriate in a kitchen."

Stranger? Jess wondered if he referred to "J," the mysterious grub-line rider, or if he still included her now. It sounded like Tucker Carmichael pegged her as the rider from this afternoon, but didn't recognize her as Jessalyn Culpepper. And why should he? She hadn't recognized him either.

"And I turned out to be even stranger than you expected," Jess hazarded, unwilling to apologize but feeling it was only fair to acknowledge the upset she'd caused. It didn't take much to see that he'd rushed over to the big house to keep her aunt protected from the missing "stranger."

"That's not the—" her aunt broke in, obviously intending to protest Jess's characterization.

"Well," Jess headed her off. "It's pretty clear Mr. Carmichael didn't expect to find me."

"Oh, now, wait a minute, ma'am." His quaint manners caught her for a moment, and Jess fought a smile at the novelty of being addressed as ma'am. As he continued, her amusement faded.

"Granted, I was on the lookout for the grub-line rider, but I still ran you to ground. Whether you're wearing a waterlogged duster or some fussy party dress doesn't make a lick of difference."

His disdain made it all too clear how much he would've preferred finding a fellow cowboy to discovering her as a woman. Some small corner of Jess's feminine heart sputtered with indignation.

First he thinks I'm a man. She'd wanted him to make that mistake at the time, but now it seemed a smidge more insulting. *And now he acts as though I can't wear a dress properly either!*

Jess knew an evening gown when she saw one, and she knew she'd do better to find something more serviceable. But tonight she hadn't been able to resist the fanciful notion that wearing

Mama's favorite dress would be like wearing a hug. She'd craved that closeness.

Besides, it buttoned. None of the others fit across Jess's chest. And even though the man standing in front of her didn't know any of that, she couldn't help but stew over his remarks.

"If it makes no difference, then there's no need to insult me," she gritted out, suddenly reminded that the past weeks had worn her patience even harder than the traveling clothes abandoned on the washroom floor. Both were to the point of fraying under duress. "Or *my mama's* dress."

He surveyed her in silence for a moment, perusing her up and down in a way that wasn't lascivious, but still took her measure. Then he announced, "Skirts are too short for you. Don't get me wrong, it's nice—looks a lot better than that awful getup you were sporting when you rode in."

Fighting the urge to tug her skirts, knowing he'd notice even the most surreptitious attempt to lengthen them, Jess was forced to confront a great and terrible truth. *Miss Pennyworth was right.*

How many times had Jess laughed at a headmistress's earnest exhortations that men couldn't behave when faced with bare ankles? The man earned a special sort of eternal enmity for proving the prudes of the world right. Jess took refuge in outrage. Making no attempt to conceal herself, Jess straightened to her full height. She eyed Tucker as he'd eyed her.

"That 'awful getup' matched yours almost exactly!" she crowed, triumphantly dismissive.

Instead of being properly put in his place, the man had the effrontery to smirk. "Exactly."

Heaven help him, she got even prettier when riled. Those big brown eyes of hers threw off sparks to shame a lightning storm. He even liked the way she talked when she got mad. She became so tightly controlled that her sentences sounded clipped and crisp, each word a sharp dagger. After all the trouble she'd given him—and all the trouble she'd surely make tomorrow—Tucker figured he deserved to siphon some of his frustration back to its cause.

Besides, it worked. The more she bristled, the more he enjoyed the conversation. Since he didn't say anything hurtful, just the honest truths that her dress was short and her other gear was made for men, Tucker didn't even feel guilty for giving the girl a hard time. She'd duped him, so now she faced his judgment. It wasn't *his* fault that her ruse centered around how she looked.

And if she thought he'd been insulting about her mama's dress, well, that was probably safer than if he'd offered an honest compliment. Tucker didn't know much about women and understood even less, but he suspected the woman would've been more offended if he'd shared his first thought, which frolicked along the lines of, *If her mama filled out that dress half so well as her daughter, then her family produces the most happily proportioned females I've ever seen.*

His second thought—about the dress being an improvement on the cowboy gear, though too short—he'd shared. Sure, it came out a little raw and obviously rubbed her the wrong way, but it served a purpose. It kept the most inappropriate nuggets rattling around in his head instead of clattering through his teeth and earning him a slap across the face. Because hard on the heels of notions one and two came observation number three—that hussies wore short skirts to show off their legs, which was part of why women of loose morals were called lightskirts.

The Bar None would certainly bar someone if Tucker thought Desta's friend would try to cause trouble among the men. He didn't see any possible way she could avoid distracting every man within a half mile, but he could keep the hands reined for a couple of days until she left. Maybe she didn't have any dresses that weren't passed down or maybe everything else got drenched in her travels. In any case, her defense of her attire relieved his mind almost as much as it amused him.

What sort of woman thinks she'll win an argument by admitting she wore men's clothes?

She looked so pleased, proclaiming her outfit matched his, that Tucker did the polite thing.

He agreed. "Exactly."

"Exactly?" she echoed, eyes narrowing in suspicion of his sudden affability.

"Yep." Tucker didn't blame her. In fact, her distrust of an easy capitulation did her credit. It made him savor the sparring, so he paused a beat before plunging ahead. "If you didn't look like a cowboy, I never would have offered you a place in the bunkhouse or a job to finish." He raised a brow and added pointedly. "Work I'll need to reassign tomorrow."

"I'll take care of it." She'd pursed her lips so tight he marveled that any sound emerged.

Yeah. He managed not to roll his eyes. *She'll probably "take care of it" by batting her lashes at the first ranch hand she runs across—as though I won't already have given them work.*

"Don't trouble yourself." Tucker waved away her offer. "While everyone around here pulls his or her own weight, we don't press guests into service. We try to be hospitable."

Her brows winged toward her hairline. "Well, I'm glad to hear you make an effort. I can't imagine what sort of welcome would await a new arrival when you *weren't* being hospitable."

Tucker appreciated her restrained way of taking him to task. He tried to think of a diplomatic way of asking his next question, but either he'd gotten too tired or there just wasn't one. So he let fly. "I know your visit came as a surprise to Miss Desta, or she would've let me know to expect you. So I hope you won't mind filling me in. How long do you plan on staying?"

A satisfied smile brightened her face as she uttered the last words Tucker wanted to hear. "A good long while, I think."

"Don't be acting coy now, child." Desta crossed her arms.

"I can't be more exact." The smile faltered in a flash of swiftly suppressed fear, then grew hopeful. "You know I have to talk to Ed when he gets home. It all depends on him."

"Ed?" A wayward surge of jealousy kicked in his gut. Then came a deeper horror as Tucker realized the ramifications.

If she came for Ed, I'll never get her off the Bar None. Because only a fool would send a woman like that away, and my partner is no fool. The idea fair boggled the mind, but he couldn't dispute the truth. *We'll be stuck with her forever.*

"You know I'm not just talking about timetables, young lady." Desta's hands traveled to fist on her hips. "Tucker's ranch foreman. He looks after everything and everyone, making sure things work as they should and stay where they belong."

Tucker stifled a smile. *I knew I liked Miss Desta.*

"You know I belong here!" the girl cried, somehow staking a claim and pleading for acceptance in the same breath.

Her fervency struck Tucker as peculiar. A beautiful woman could make a place for herself anywhere she chose to go. *So why is she here? What makes the Bar None so special?*

"Yes, you belong." The housekeeper's words seemed to calm her a little. "But like it or not, you're going to throw things off around here. You'll need Tucker to rebuild the balance."

She spoke almost as if he weren't present, and the intensity of the women's interaction suddenly sent shivers down Tucker's spine. An appalling idea snaked through his thoughts, and he reacted the way he would if facing an angry rattler.

He froze. Breath hitched in his chest, vision narrowing onto the threat as he searched for further signs of danger.

And he found them. *Golden curls and brown eyes. She speaks with an* accent, *not anger. Her determination to stay. She asks for Ed.* Now that the scales slid from his eyes, Tucker spotted so many warnings he winced at his own obtuseness.

Of course it's her mama's dress. He eyed her trim figure, now knowing he'd been right. Simon Culpepper built this fine house for the fancy, foreign wife who'd wrapped him around her little finger. And her daughter turned out just as pretty and probably as manipulative. *Call her "J." How blind could I be?*

"A man doesn't like to be wrong, but I'm hoping tonight is one of those rare times I'm holding nothing but a handful of horse feathers. Please tell me she isn't. . ." He looked to Desta, hope sinking fast as she shook her head.

Dumbstruck, he turned his attention back to the woman who'd ridden onto his ranch to turn it inside out. *"Jessalyn?"*

CHAPTER 7

Desta knew her niece's arrival would turn the ranch on its ear, but she hadn't foreseen Tucker's reaction. From the moment the man stalked into the kitchen, all fired up over mistaking Jess for a man, the two threw sparks. Unfortunately, they seemed intent on heating up arguments, not warming up to each other.

"Yes, Tucker." Her niece raised her chin. "I've come home."

Oh, please don't say the wrong thing. Desta closed her eyes. If only Tucker pulled himself together enough to welcome Jess, things would smooth over. *Then they could stop looking for insults and start noticing the ways they match each other.*

"You're supposed to be in England!" Tucker's protest smashed that dream.

If the man has a bad taste in his mouth, it's not from Jess's arrival. Desta frowned. *Hopefully he recognizes the tang of leather quick enough to pull his boot from outta his mouth.*

"That's *your* opinion." Her niece sniffed, sounding uppity enough to set up any cowboy's back. "I'd say I should've been here long ago. I'm *supposed* to be home, with my family."

"And we're glad to have you here, safe and sound." Desta shot Tucker an agree-with-me-before-you-lose-the-chance glare.

Too bad the man didn't prove fluent in meaningful glances.

"If you traveled," Tucker pressed, "where's the other one?"

"The other one of what?" Jess voiced Desta's question.

"Well, everybody knows women are like oxen—" He broke off beneath the weight of the women's splutters, looking bemused.

"Oxen!" Desta burst out, unable to contain her horror.

Her niece protested, too. "Women are *nothing* like oxen!"

"Don't get your dander up, ladies!" He put up his hands in a conciliatory gesture, then tried again. "You all are like ox—"

"Think careful before you continue." Desta stopped him again, shaking with the strength of her own emotion. "No human being should be equated with a beast of burden. Never. You know what it leads to, so don't go comparing women to livestock."

Dimly, she noticed that Jess skirted around Tucker and slipped an arm around her shoulders. Her niece's silent support both bolstered and destroyed her ability to say another word. Desta reached up and patted Jess's hand, drawing and returning comfort. Logically, she knew Tucker didn't mean any harm—the man worked a ranch and just about every waking thought in his head had to do with cattle. But some things crossed beyond logic.

"I'm so sorry." Tucker swallowed, looking appropriately horrified by what he'd said and humbled at her reaction. "You know I didn't mean women should be treated like animals. Please forgive me for it coming out that way, Miss Desta."

Jess made a soothing murmur, not accepting the apology on her behalf, but trying to soften the impact for everyone. The girl showed a deep-running compassion in her handling of the situation, accepting Desta's distress and understanding Tucker hadn't meant to cause it. It gave Desta something more to be thankful for; otherwise she might have worried that her reaction would make things even more difficult between them. But she could rest easy. Jess wouldn't hold Tucker's mistake against him—or over his head—as they got to know each other.

Desta pulled herself together enough to nod so things could move on. Enough of her life had gone in service of other men's mistakes—she didn't pay the tithe of regret any longer and didn't want these people to get caught in that trap either.

"It was just a fool way of trying to say ladies usually go in pairs."

Tucker looked abashed, but doggedly returned the conversation back to his main concern. "Women travel together, and I couldn't figure out what happened to Jess's companion."

Now that he mentioned it, Desta could see his concern. The poor man worried for Jess and worried for the woman who'd supposedly made the journey with her. Too bad it wouldn't settle his mind any when he found out that no such woman existed.

"After I parted ways with the stage in town, I rode up the last few miles unaccompanied." Jess pointed out the obvious, considering how Tucker saw her arrive. But she didn't mention anything about the thousands of miles she covered before. Her niece's evasion confirmed Desta's suspicions; Jess returned to the Bar None the same way she'd lived for so long—on her own.

"But before the stage got to town. . . ," Tucker prodded.

"Before then she traveled a long way, and I doubt it'd make for a short story." Desta decided the time had come for her to act like an aunt and take care of things. "She's near enough dead on her feet, and I aim to put her in bed. Come back in the morning for breakfast, when you've both rested up a bit."

"In just a minute, Miss Desta. This is important." Tucker showed no signs of leaving and every indication that he shared Desta's suspicions. Trouble was, if Jess confirmed them, not a one of them would see a pillow that night. He'd take offense and most likely berate Jess for lack of propriety and good sense.

Desta couldn't disagree with the sentiment—she'd praise God for the miracle of her niece's safe arrival for years to come—but it wasn't Tucker's place to take her to task. He wasn't her kin and had no say in what she did. Both of them were too tired to see straight and too stubborn to stop the inevitable fight.

"A closed mouth gathers no boots." Desta shrugged away from Jess's embrace. As she spoke, she swung open the door. "Since we're all tired and liable to step on each other's toes, we'll see you at the breakfast table."

For the first time in weeks, Jess didn't jackknife awake, groping for her gun and searching her surroundings. Still, her heart pounded as she peered into the darkness, hunting any threats that managed to slip past her locked and barricaded door. Once satisfied that her precautions hadn't been breached, she breathed easier, recognizing her surroundings.

My first morning home. She sighed and snuggled back into the soft warmth of a clean bed. Jess breathed in the scent of soap and spice, pushing back the lurking knowledge that Papa hadn't left the scent when he came in to check on her, as in years long past. She'd sprinkled his aftershave across the pillows last night, wanting to surround her senses with the reassurance that she'd come home.

Jess kept her eyes closed, holding tight to the memory of her father and the proof of her homecoming for a few extra heartbeats, postponing the moment she'd have to face the truth: her loving family hadn't brought her home. Loss allowed her to sneak back before her brother could prevent it.

Now she'd have to face whatever challenges arose from her unconventional decision.

The vague thought of challenges brought to mind a handsome face, strong jaw clenched with disapproval. The image seemed so real, Jess's eyes flew open. The empty room almost surprised her— she'd half expected to see Tucker Carmichael, shaking his head.

Vexed that the churlish foreman troubled her thoughts before she'd gotten out of bed, Jess stopped stalling. She pushed back the pillows and cautiously raised her arms overhead. Wincing, she tried not to catalogue the protests from what seemed like every muscle in her shoulders, back, and even stomach. Last night's rain promised the sort of damp morning that wouldn't make things any easier, so it would be slow going until movement worked away the worst of the stiffness. It made Jess seriously consider snuggling back under the covers. Besides, it seemed early even by Jess's rise-at-daybreak standards. No hint of morning light glimmered around the curtain edges.

No one here would blame me for sneaking some extra sleep, she mused. *For all they know, I typically languish in bed until after nine o'clock, like any other milksop miss trained in academies.*

Heaven knew she could use a chance to rest up and regroup before facing Tucker—and his questions about her improper journey home.

Agitated by the prospect of another interrogation, Jess swung her legs over the side of the bed and got to her feet. Moving gingerly in deference to a body-wide chorus of *ouch-ow-ouch-ooh*, she reached the fireplace. She carefully selected a few of the smaller pieces of wood piled on the hearth and stoked the blaze until heat reached across the stones. Jess sank into the wingback chair someone—Aunt Desta, most likely—had pushed away from its old corner by the bed and angled near the fire. She wiggled her toes, relishing the spreading warmth as she pondered what to do next.

I'm home, but how much of it will be the home I remember? How much more will have changed? She'd known Papa wouldn't be waiting, but a part of her still expected to hear his booming laugh. Tucker Carmichael took her by surprise, but she'd hoped to see a few familiar faces from the bunkhouse. Aunt Desta defied expectation. Never did Jess imagine she'd discover a new relation, much less a woman who brought her so much comfort alongside such controversy.

I've missed so much. Jess's heart squeezed. *There's so much to learn, so many questions to ask, so many pitfalls to avoid. . . .*

Abruptly, she realized she might as well have laid back down if she planned to sit there, stung into stillness by her own musings. Shaking her head, Jess went back to considering how to spend her morning. Aside from doing as she always did and slipping out to visit Morning Glory, the only thing that occurred to her was picking up Papa's Bible. It lay on a small table beside her, well loved.

Papa always said the Word soothed the soul and offered answers for a worried heart. She brushed her fingertips across leather worn smooth against her father's calluses, imagining him sitting where she sat, thumbing through the treasured text. A sudden swell of loss made her breath catch. *What answers can this book offer me now?*

None. She pushed the tome to the far end of the table, salt stinging eyes still sore from last night's tears. *The wisdom of the ages never convinced Papa to bring me home. It won't tell me what Ed will say when he finds me here, or help me handle Tucker until then.*

Jess wrapped her arms around her chest and rocked forward, dwarfed by a dawning truth. *I'm home, but I'm still on my own.*

She rocked a few moments, letting her aching muscles distract her from the ache in her heart. The pain galvanized her, a reminder of her underlying strength. Her bruises might burrow to the bone and span clear to her soul, but she wasn't broken. Jess moved her hands to the arms of the chair and levered herself upward. *I make my own way and stand on my own two feet, just as I always have.*

So she'd do as she'd always done and go visit Morning Glory. Jess found her soreness eased by the time she'd dressed in the blouse and skirt Desta hung up for her last night. They'd dried by the fire, residue from the rainwater leaving them somewhat stiff. No matter— Jess figured they'd loosen up along with the rest of her. By the time she'd shoved her feet into her boots and buttoned her coat against the morning chill, Jess looked almost the same as when she rode into the ranch the day before.

Only difference was her skirts—she couldn't stomach sliding into her split skirts until they'd gone through a good washing, and she didn't have a spare set to wear until then. From the hips down— after the holster, anyway—she looked like a lady. Otherwise, she could probably pass for any other ranch hand. The thought made her smile and put some speed into her step. She wanted to visit Morning Glory and get back before the real ranch hands were up and about.

I'm not going to hide in the house until Ed gets home, she assured herself as she crept down the stairs and slipped through the kitchen door. If Jess ran into someone in the stables it wouldn't be the end of the world, but she knew better than to flaunt her arrival. Things on a ranch ran to a rhythm, and disrupting things wouldn't endear her to the workers. She and Tucker needed to iron out an understanding before she stepped fully onto the scene.

Jess drew deep breaths, soaking in the earthy fragrance left by fresh rainfall. English rain didn't smell the same—it lacked that special, spicy-sweet pungent aroma of chaparral and mesquite. She'd forgotten how invigorating and comforting the scent could be, twining half-forgotten memories with fresh hopes for the day ahead.

Violet tinged the darkness, making it look more like twilight than morning. But a more varied, cheerful twittering slowly usurped the song of blackbirds. The first thin washes of morning light would paint the landscape soon, so Jess lengthened her stride and hurried.

That swift stroll to the stables did her a world of good. By the time she slipped inside she'd swapped the worst of her aches for a nose tingling from the morning's dew-rich air. Smells of horses and hay mingled with leather and saddle oil. Deep breaths of slumbering animals and the rustle of bedstraw accompanied Jess's steps toward the end of the row, where Morning Glory stretched her neck over the rope and nickered a soft welcome.

Jess patted the mare's neck, wishing she'd put on the split skirts after all. Now that she was up and moving, it seemed that a ride would help dispel some of the lingering aches. Besides, Morning Glory expected the exercise. Even now, the horse butted her head against the partition and stamped one hoof in delicate demand.

"I can't," Jess whispered apologetically. "By the time we get back, everyone will be up and I won't escape notice." Particularly if she rode astride in skirts. Granted, her boots covered halfway up her shins, but even cowboys expected a certain propriety. She wouldn't win their respect or welcome if they saw her knees.

But to ride the ranch, seeing the sunrise and breathing in more of that special, rain-fresh air. . . Jess gave a wistful sigh, her resolve weakening when Morning Glory echoed in a windier version. She bit the inside of her lip, considering. If she traveled north, she could circle back behind the house and hitch Morning Glory there. That way she'd avoid the stables, mess hall, and bunkhouse.

"All right." Jess laid her forehead against her mare's for a second then hastened to get her equipment. Morning Glory stood still and patient as Jess saddled her, ears perked to whispered promises of carrots, apples, or oats to be filched from Desta's pantry until she returned to the stables for a proper breakfast.

As she led the horse down the row, Jess faltered. If Tucker caught her out before breakfast, he'd be angry—and he'd even have some right to be disgruntled. What could she say if he railed that she had no business setting off on her own without telling anyone where she was going? Stopping before the stable door, she caught sight of the perfect excuse to ride the northern line.

Grinning, she grabbed one of the bags, stuffed it into her pocket, and led Morning Glory out the door. *Problem solved.*

CHAPTER 8

W e've got a problem, Boss." Hank, who'd run the Bar None stables since long before Tucker arrived, frowned grooves into his forehead.

"You're telling me." Tucker gulped down his first mug of scalding coffee then went ahead and poured himself another cup. When it came to coffee, one-mug mornings were mighty rare, and Tucker didn't need Hank to tell him today wasn't one of them.

Obviously Hank hadn't searched him out to talk about the real trouble that had descended upon them. But it wasn't as though Tucker managed to think of anything but Jessalyn Culpepper since he'd caught sight of her through that gap in the kitchen curtains. She'd plagued his thoughts and invaded his sleep, leaving snatches of half-remembered dreams to serve as a warning when he woke up.

"I shoulda known ya sent the young'un away already." Hank's forehead unfurrowed, and he turned away. "Forgit I bothered ya."

"Hold up." Tucker tried to figure out a way to ask why Hank thought he'd sent away "the young'un" without revealing he hadn't. Since no new grub rider stayed over in the bunkhouse or appeared for a slug of coffee, he'd be hard-pressed to explain the absence without getting into the whole story. And until he had the whole story from the women, Tucker knew better than to try. "No bother. You know I'd rather you come to me than sit on a suspicion."

"A' right." Hank lifted the coffeepot and grabbed a mug. "I know you don't hold with sending folks or critters away empty-bellied. Caught me off guard to find the mare already gone, is all."

Tucker blinked, trying to connect this information with any type of plausible explanation and coming up empty-handed. "Gone?"

Gone. A few moments after he'd stormed out of the mess hall. Tucker looked at the tracks leading from the barn toward the north pasture in disbelief. Hank assured him all the other horses were accounted for, and the ranch regulars had more sense than to ride a stranger's mount. Besides, Tucker knew for a fact none of the men had headed out: old Cookie just started serving breakfast.

Within minutes, Tucker saddled his favorite mount and followed the trail. Happy Jack, known for his cheerful disposition, seemed about as pleased as his master to be pulled away from breakfast and sent on a wild-goose chase. Or a *silly*-goose chase, as things stood.

What can that fool woman be thinking? Tucker kept a sharp eye out and urged Happy Jack to pick up the pace. For the life of him, he couldn't figure out what drove her. *How harebrained does she have to be to sneak into the stables and ride off on her own?*

He knew without so much as stopping by the house that Jessalyn hadn't mentioned her plans to Miss Desta. Her aunt would've either put a stop to such madness, or if her niece proved too headstrong to listen to sense, Miss Desta would've gotten word to him. A lone woman would be easy prey if an unscrupulous man happened to be wandering by at the wrong moment and take an interest in her.

Ironically, given his irritation from the previous day, Tucker took some comfort from the knowledge any such man might have difficulty pegging Jessalyn Culpepper as a woman. Given the sort of getup she wore, few would guess her gender from any distance. But even that didn't ease his mind. *She shouldn't be out here alone.*

Whether following direct orders from Tucker or acting on their own judgment, none of the ranch hands rode out before making sure others knew where they headed, what they planned to do, and accordingly, a rough idea of when they should return. Basic common sense demanded some accountability—there were a hundred ways to get hurt or worse out here. From barbed-wire fences to ornery longhorns and even poorly placed snake holes, danger lurked around every bend.

Most riders knew the risks of the range, but the once-familiar terrain would have become foreign to Jessalyn after her years away. The thought made him wonder if maybe that was why she'd gone for a ride. Early morning offered the calmest time on a ranch, and maybe she'd wanted a quiet moment to reacquaint herself with the land.

I wouldn't want company either, Tucker admitted to himself. He could almost understand that she'd want to rediscover her home before the demands of the day distracted her. *But she should've let someone know in case she strayed too far or stayed out too long.*

Tucker offered a prayer of thanks that yesterday's storm softened the earth. Her horse's impressions proved easy to track, even if the same couldn't be said for her mistress's thoughts. *What weighs so heavy on her mind that she can't sleep through the night?*

Truly, no one had any business getting up so early unless they were working a roundup or on a cattle drive. For the life of him, Tucker couldn't imagine why a member of the weaker gender—particularly one who'd endured a grueling journey through a downpour and should've been downright exhausted—would leave a soft, warm bed. The only thing he knew was that Jessalyn Culpepper was proving him right on one of the rare occasions he'd much rather be proven wrong.

Whether the woman intended to be a pain in the backside or not didn't make much difference. Either way, this morning she continued what she'd begun when she stepped foot on the ranch—*causing me trouble when I've already got more than enough to take care of.*

As he reached the pasture, he pushed past surprise that he couldn't see her yet. This particular area followed a curve in the typically straight landscape, dipping down to a river marking the far boundary. They'd gone through a fairly dry winter, so the low water level would make a bigger difference in the terrain than usual. If she'd made it that far, Tucker hadn't missed her by a matter of mere minutes—she'd beat him by the better part of an hour.

A sudden movement caught his peripheral vision, making him turn. For a moment he saw only what he expected to see—a long line of fence picking its way through morning shadows across lush grass. Then the breeze shifted, and he spotted what caught his eye before— a thin strip of rag fluttered from the fence. Tucker pulled up short, eyes narrowed as he recalled a snippet of last night's conversation.

"If you didn't look like a cowboy, I never would have offered you a place in the bunkhouse or a job to finish," he'd chastised. *"Work I'll need to reassign tomorrow."*

"I'll take care of it."

The promise Tucker so easily dismissed the night before came back with vindictive clarity, and he groaned.

She wouldn't. He tried to reassure himself, but the damaged fence lay before him, temporarily patched and flagged for fixing. The evidence waved in the wind, forcing him to reconsider. *Would she?*

I did it! Jess slid the fencing pliers back into their canvas bag, enjoying the soft clink as they rubbed against a few stray staples. In all fairness, there hadn't been a surfeit of neglected stretches along the fence line. She'd discovered just two broken lines in need of attention and made only temporary repairs before marking them.

It would take at least two men the better part of two days to address the problem. They'd need to pull the posts clean out of the ground and stretch new lengths of wire high and tight between them. To Jess's mind, there wasn't really any such thing as "fixing" a barbed-wire fence. Once patched, it would have to be replaced.

As things stood, it took her longer than it should have to tend those two patches. Well, longer than it would've taken any of the ranch hands. But considering she hadn't so much as glimpsed a length of barbed wire in seven years, and only helped her father a handful of times before that, Jess decided to give herself credit.

I remembered. She pulled off the heavy leather gloves she'd snagged from the stables. The things were so large, she didn't actually need to pull—they slid right off when she straightened her fingers. Jess crammed them into her saddlebag along with the fencing kit. Then she walked back and squatted down to inspect her handiwork. It hadn't been easy, but after struggling to figure out how to handle the first one, she'd managed this one much quicker.

I'll manage even better once I get gloves that fit. Trying to grasp barbed wire proved tricky under the best of circumstances, so Jess hadn't expected to walk away without a fair number of cuts. That didn't matter. If anything, she saw the stripes as badges of honor. Flushed with success, proud to contribute even in a small way, she knotted the second strip of rag next to her workmanship.

It waved in the wind like a flag of victory. Jess smiled at the sight before the sound of an approaching horse caught her attention. Someone was coming up fast. Jess had a fair idea who that someone was, but moved her hand to her holster just in case she was wrong.

She wasn't. In no time at all, Tucker Carmichael pulled to a stop, glaring down at her from a massive black-spotted paint. The man didn't even bother to dismount before he started in on her.

"Just what," he gritted, "do you think you're doing out here?"

Jess refused to let the irritable man ruin her good mood. For all she knew—and certainly from what she'd seen firsthand—the man was a perpetual grump. So she reached deep and dredged up a smile.

"Probably just what *you* think I'm doing. And I'm sure we can both take satisfaction in being proved right. So. . ."—she gestured toward her fine, fine workmanship and asked—"what do you think?"

Think? Tucker blinked, caught off guard by her bright smile. It transformed her fine features, the laughing warmth making mere beauty something irresistible. That smile tugged at him, unraveling his iron control and filling his mind with unspeakable responses.

I don't know how I ever mistook you for a man. Sounded random.

I think if I undid your braid, those lush waves I saw last night would feel soft as corn silk. If anything, even worse.

Tucker could feel time running out as she stared up at him, waiting for him to cobble together some sort of coherent answer. Her smile started to slip, and he fought a sudden need to bring it back. It struck him that he could do a better job of thinking straight if she stopped looking at him with those big, expectant brown eyes.

So he looked down, tracing the gesture she'd made toward the fence. But his gaze didn't make it to the fence—he snagged on the sight of her hands. Red lines, some thin, some jagged and still bleeding, lashed around her wrists to creep across the backs of her hands. If he knew anything about barbed wire, her palms looked even worse.

Tucker stared until red spread across his vision. *She's hurt.*

His own hands clenched into fists, fighting to keep from reaching out and grabbing her so he could see the worst of her injuries. Suddenly his thoughts narrowed to a single focus. *I promised her father I'd take care of her. I have to keep her safe, make her understand that she can't put herself in dangerous situations.*

"I think you have a habit of doing things you have no business trying and showing up in places you know you don't belong."

"I belong here." The spark in her eyes went cold. "I've *always* belonged here. Who do you think you are to say otherwise?"

"The foreman of the Bar None, same as I have been for half a decade." Tucker found her far easier to handle when she went flinty. Smiles could addle a man's thinking, but scowls kept him on track.

"Strange." She wrinkled her nose as though rejecting something rancid. "I don't remember 'passing judgment on family members' as part of the foreman's responsibilities—or one of his privileges."

"Good judgment is part of doing anything responsibly. I use mine just fine—you're the one who's 'passing' it by," he shot back.

"You're tangling my meaning, and you know it!" Her voice rose a notch. "It's not your job to decide how or where I spend my time."

No. It's my job to keep you safe. Problem is, that means monitoring where you are, who you're with, and what you're doing for just about every minute until your brother gets back to take over.

Tucker kept the thought to himself. It made no sense to stick a burr beneath the saddle of a bucking filly in need of breaking.

"I'm responsible for the safety of everyone on the ranch." He shifted, making her tilt her head back farther to keep glaring at him. Only then did Tucker give up the literal high ground in favor of besting her in conversation. He didn't have time to waste arguing the woman dizzy—and he needed to see the worst of her wounds.

Tucker swung from the saddle, landing close enough to snag her elbow and turn her hands palm up. As he'd expected, the vicious wire left marks here, slicing into the soft pads of her palm and fingers.

"What are you doing?" She tried to tug her arm from his grasp, words falling fast and furious. "Ensuring the safety of your men surely doesn't include playing nursemaid over a few scratches!"

"Easy now." He murmured to her the same way he did with any other skittish creature. "I need to see how bad you hurt yourself."

He kept one hand wrapped around her elbow—tight enough to hold her but not cause harm. Tucker raised his other hand to his mouth, biting the tips of his glove and pulling it off. He unclenched his teeth and let the glove fall to the ground as his bare hand reached hers, tenderly tracing around what looked to be the deepest cut.

She hissed at him like an angry cat, so he knew the slash stung. But her sun-warmed skin gave softly beneath the questing pressure of his fingertips without revealing any deep gashes. He checked both hands from palms to wrists before deciding he didn't need to worry about stitching her up. He'd expected a lot worse.

What he hadn't expected was the silent testimony of her skin. Milky white and fine-boned though her hands may be, they didn't tell tales of a privileged lady. Beneath the scratches from today's foolishness he'd traced scars and calluses. Jessalyn Culpepper's hands spoke of skills earned with hard work—*and a hard head.*

"Enough!" She yanked free, though by now Tucker's grip slackened so she could slip loose at any time. "You don't need to concern yourself with every little mishap. Especially mine."

Not every little mishap, he silently conceded. *But especially yours. I'll count us blessed if your scrapes stay so small.*

"I feared I'd find worse." It cost him nothing to admit that much and might bring her around to a more manageable mood. "But you're right—Desta can clean those scrapes up and bandage them."

"There you go again!" Apparently unable to stand still, she stooped to pick up his glove and slap it against his chest. "Stop acting as though it's up to you to make decisions on my behalf!"

Tucker tugged his glove from her grasp and tried again. "It's not just on your behalf. The foreman gives orders for everyone."

"Not everyone," she fumed, eyeing his glove as though wishing she could smack him with it again. "That isn't your responsibility."

"You seem awful preoccupied with telling me just what does and doesn't make up my job." He frowned and shoved the glove in place. "Particularly for someone who hasn't stepped foot on a ranch in years. Things might go smoother if you took a look around first."

"Oh, I plan to." Her crossed arms transformed her agreement into a threat. "But you seem awful preoccupied with trying to convince me that it's your job to order around everybody else."

"How many times do I have to say it?" Tucker felt the muscle in his jaw start twitching. "It *is* my job to decide what needs to be done around here and then assign the right man for the work."

She smirked. "Then you've no cause to complain, Mr. Carmichael. Yesterday afternoon you gave me the task of flagging this fence."

Stung by the injustice of this argument—and the scrap of truth behind it, Tucker roared, "You aren't the man I thought you were!"

For a moment he thought she wasn't going to respond. The obstinate woman turned her back on him and walked over to her mount and unknotted the reins. She left him hanging just long enough to let him start feeling foolish and consider offering an apology.

"No, I'm not the man you thought I was." She spoke in the soft tones of disappointment. "I guess that makes us just about even."

CHAPTER 9

*Y*ou're not the man I thought you were either. Jess didn't bother to speak the final indictment aloud. Disappointing though he might be, Tucker Carmichael proved intelligent enough to understand an insult. *Especially such a clever one.*

She knew better than to pat herself on the back for snarky comments, but a well-spoken reprimand required a certain sort of panache. The man most likely needed a boot to the backside, but until Ed got home and Jess got the lay of the land, she'd have to settle for serving up a masterful set down.

"Haven't you dealt with enough barbs for one morning?" the man rebounded swiftly, his quick wit making Jess struggle not to smile.

I shouldn't be enjoying this. He's clever, but teaching him that he can't order me around isn't going to be easy for either of us. The stern reminder did little good. She'd always enjoyed a good round of repartee, and Tucker Carmichael gave as good as he got. Besides, even though she wasn't going to admit it, Jess wanted to get back to the house. Her hands stung, her stomach rumbled, and deep down she knew the two of them needed to reach a truce.

"I suppose." She glanced back at the fence, her spirits rising at the sight of the waving rag. "Since I haven't been on a ranch for a good long while, I'm willing to defer to the foreman. What do you say? Are we finished riding this line and ready to move on?"

"Yep." Without so much as pretending to look over her hard work, he stuck his boot in a stirrup and got back in the saddle.

As she followed suit, Jess debated whether or not she should insist that he inspect the fence. The first place she'd patched looked haphazard, but she didn't think anyone would be able to tell this second site had been handled by a novice. She'd done a good job bending the broken barbed line into two loops then passing baling wire through them and binding the whole thing tightly.

"We don't want Desta to find you missing and start worrying, if she isn't already." Tucker's call made the decision an easy one.

Jess could live without the foreman's approval of her fencing skills, but guilt gnawed at the idea she'd make Desta worry. She hadn't planned on working in the pasture when she left that morning or she would've left a note in the kitchen. Since Tucker mentioned it, it seemed almost certain her aunt would be missing her by now.

Oops. Jess urged Morning Glory into a canter, easily catching up to Tucker before adjusting her pace to the gait of his taller paint. Although sorely tempted to see whether Tucker would condescend to race back, Jess didn't spur her mare into a gallop. Morning Glory would go where Jess bid, but the barn was home to Tucker's mount. If he gave the horse his head, the paint would run for breakfast.

More importantly, Jess didn't want to draw further censure. If she kept to his side and he didn't stare, he might not notice that she was wearing skirts while riding astride. So in the interest of preserving their newfound peace, Jess kept her gaze fixed ahead, her mouth closed, and her pace steady. Unfortunately, her companion didn't seem inclined to offer the same courtesy. She heard an odd, disgruntled sort of snort before Tucker maneuvered his mount to an angled stop—right in front of Morning Glory so she had to halt, too.

Determined not to show her rising irritation, Jess took a deep breath and forced away a frown before addressing the man. "Yes?"

"You're wearing *skirts*," came his terse accusation. "*Astride.*"

"Yes." *I should've known he'd catch me out before we got back.* Really, the surprising thing was that it took him this long to notice. Apparently he'd been too worked up over telling her off and checking her hands to think about her type of saddle any sooner.

"Unacceptable." He gave the pronouncement with such conviction and authority Jess wondered whether he expected immediate change.

"Once in a while necessity trumps convention, Mr. Carmichael."

"Don't try hornswoggling me, Miss Culpepper. Necessity had nothing to do with your decision to go riding fences this morning."

Hornswoggle? Jess bit her lip, sure that her laughter wouldn't soothe Tucker's offended notions of propriety. Luckily, her delight at hearing the phrase restored some of her own good humor. *How could a woman fail to appreciate a man who keeps a straight face at all times—even when accusing her of attempting to "hornswoggle" him?*

" 'Necessity' referred to the manner of riding, not my purpose or my destination. What choice was there but to ride astride when I didn't find any sidesaddles in the barn?" *Not that I looked very hard.*

"Which is why you should've forgone riding." He wagged an admonishing finger at her. "Necessity didn't make this choice for you, as you claim. No looming calamity forced you to abandon propriety in an urgent attempt to make the best of a bad situation."

"I've been making the best out of bad situations for years without the benefit of your exalted opinion," Jess pointed out.

He raised a mocking brow. "From what I can see of the way you make decisions, you could've used with a few doses of wisdom."

And what does he know about it? Jess steadied Morning Glory as the horse started moving sideways, shying away from Tucker's mount. *I've made my own way in a foreign country for a third of my life, then managed to make my way back home without anyone's help.*

The idea that she might need to justify her decisions to a mere stranger rankled, but maybe Tucker thought she was flighty. *It's not as though I run off without considering my options—maybe he doesn't realize I thought things through before setting off this morning.*

"I'm wise enough to ride around back and hitch her behind the house, then walk her back to the stables," she grudgingly revealed.

"That's something." Tucker's concession sapped some of her ire. "Not much, but we'll go ahead with that plan and ride around back. It's good to know you haven't completely abandoned propriety."

If the man had been gracious enough to accept her plan without casting further aspersions, Jess would've happily headed for the house when Tucker spurred his mount forward. But if he thought he could lob an insult at her and have her trail behind him like a whipped pup, the man needed a lesson. She waited for him to realize she hadn't moved.

"What's wrong?" Irritation stiffened the line of his shoulders as he swung back.

"Plenty. We'll start with your misplaced love of propriety."

He snorted. "Misplaced? I think not. Propriety serves an important purpose in helping protect women who abide by the rules."

Jess took a moment to consider his response, appreciating that his core concern was for others but rejecting his logic. She looked down to make sure her skirts still covered her knees before answering. "So your first and foremost concern is for my safety?"

"Safety in general." He shrugged. "But since I've never met another woman who rode astride, this situation is unique to you."

"Fair enough. Then while we ride back, I have a question for you to think over." She tugged the reins, edging Morning Glory around him. "Exactly how much danger would I be in, riding on my own ranch, even if someone did happen to catch a glimpse of my knee?"

With that, she rescinded her earlier decision, urging Morning Glory to run back to the house. Let him lag behind—the sooner he stopped expecting her to follow his lead, the sooner they could stop butting heads and start working together. Besides, he probably needed a little extra time to figure out an answer to her question!

As she neared the hub of the ranch, Jess took care to carve a wide path, veering away from the outbuildings to come in behind the big house. In spite of the fact she'd only known the stables for a single night, Morning Glory required some forceful steering to keep her on track. Whether instinct or just a keen sense of smell guided her toward breakfast didn't much matter, but she strained toward the stables when Jess slid from the saddle.

For a moment she wondered whether Tucker raced his mount back to the stables, signaling her mare to follow. But to her great surprise, he pulled up right beside her—mere seconds after she stopped. Not only did he cut a fine figure, but he showed significant skill in handling horses. In spite of herself, Jess was impressed.

At least until the troublesome man opened his mouth again.

"How much danger would you be in?" He repeated the challenge she'd thrown as he dismounted. "If the wrong man spotted you, you could be hurt in ways I won't even discuss. And since you didn't tell anyone where you were going, you could have been kidnapped or killed before we got out there to start looking for you."

"Compare the chances of that to the odds of breaking a leg in a sidesaddle," she challenged. "Not that there was one available, but in terms of safety, that ridiculous contraption presents a much larger threat than any hypothetical villain lurking around here."

"You act as though sidesaddles are dangerous," he snorted.

"They are. Not only does a woman have to crook her knee and offset her hips in a precarious perch, but she's trapped by her own twisted skirts." Jess had no trouble expounding on this old complaint. "If her mount shies, jumps, or even stumbles in a snake hole, a woman in a sidesaddle is at great risk. It's senseless to put a woman in danger for the sake of her own protection. Propriety isn't sensible or safe in this instance."

"Even if you're right about the saddle—and I won't agree or disagree since I've never sat in one and never intend to"—he started sounding downright reasonable, but didn't stop there—"it's not just that a lone female looks like easy pickings, it's that you present a picture that would encourage an unscrupulous man to entertain lustful thoughts. You need to guard against that, no matter where you are, how you're dressed, or what you're doing."

"If my skirts happened to shift at the precise moment some villain rode by, he'd have to catch me to wreak any havoc. Assuming he managed that—which is a mighty big assumption—he'd have to deal with my pistol at point-blank range before dragging me from the saddle."

"It's not the danger of a single moment." Tucker crossed his arms over his chest, an immovable mountain of mulish man. "Attract unwanted attention, and it's not just for one morning; you've changed the way men look at you forever."

The way he looked at her now, his gaze full of intensity and a heat that might not be entirely due to anger, held her transfixed.

"And if you only listen to one thing I say, make sure it's this." He paused, making sure he'd snared her attention. Tucker leaned in and lowered his voice, his final words taking on a deeper husk: "Once a man decides you're fair game, he won't take kindly to hearing that he's wrong."

CHAPTER 10

Desta heard hooves pounding the ground and burned yet another flapjack. Jess hadn't been in her bed this morning, nor anywhere else in the house. That had been enough to weigh on Desta's mind, but now that weight dropped down to press the breath from her lungs. No one raced up to the house like that except for an emergency.

Somethin's gone wrong. And like as not her niece had gotten caught up in it. She hurried to the window, shoving the curtains aside and pressing her face right up against the glass for the best view. When she caught sight of Jess, her breath hitched then eased. Mischief, not panic, lit her niece's face as Tucker came thundering up behind her. Now that Desta knew no emergency awaited, she quietly retreated from the window—no one liked to feel spied on.

Besides, she reasoned with a mischievous smile of her own, *I don't need to watch them when I can hear every blessed word they say.*

For the first time in her life, she didn't regret burning something. She'd been so distracted, worrying over where Jess had wandered off to and whether it would cause problems with Tucker, that she'd burned more than a few flapjacks. She'd opened the window long before the pair of them came riding up. So she left it up.

Once she caught the gist of their argument, Desta almost snuck a peek to make sure she'd heard aright. Instead she hurried to the washroom. A glance told her all she needed to know—Jess's traveling clothes lay where they'd fallen the night before. She'd heard right.

Jess went out riding in regular skirts, and Tucker caught her. Desta rushed back to the kitchen, ears open to catch the rest of the conversation. Even though she couldn't help but side with Tucker, it did her heart good to hear Jess standing up for herself. *And doing a mighty good job of arguing her way around the problem, too.*

Which just went to show how much Jess took after her father. She gave a wistful smile, remembering how her brother managed to do the same thing. Every time someone backed him into a corner and he couldn't outright win an argument, Simon stopped trying. He shifted the focus of the conversation to something more advantageous.

Now that she knew her niece inherited those debating abilities, it felt like getting back a small part of Simon. Grief grabbed at her, trying to tarnish the joy of getting to know Jessalyn.

Lord, You know I only got to know Simon after he fetched me here. That's a mighty short time for someone to leave behind such a big hole. I see Yore hand in bringing Jess to help fill the lonely places, but easing the ache ain't the same as removing it. Help me pour Yore love on my niece. Don't let her be so quick to butt heads that she misses a chance to make her heart whole.

She felt more at peace by the time she finished praying, but that calm didn't carry outside. From the sound of things, Tucker refused to be swayed. He set her straight with clear, carrying statements of fact—and then, all of a sudden, his voice lowered. Even with her ear pressed against the wall, Desta couldn't make out what they were saying anymore. She listened for a moment longer, sensing the conversation turned, but not knowing which way it went.

Either they'd lapsed into frosty silence or reached an accord.

But for the life of her, Desta couldn't figure out which. If they'd come to an agreement, she figured they would've moved on into the kitchen. If things devolved to a staring contest, it would take a force greater than their combined tempers to shake them loose.

Galvanized by the thought, Desta squared her shoulders and flung open the door. "I don't know where you two have been or what you've been up to, but I figured the pair of you could scrape up enough manners to get in here before the day's half done."

Jess and Tucker both startled at the interruption, and Desta noted that she'd been partly right. They'd left off arguing to stand there in silence, staring at each other. *Staring—but not angry.*

Desta filed that away and worked mighty hard to hide her satisfaction. There'd be a time for smiling at some point, but she foresaw plenty of fighting before those two joined forces. She bit back a sigh, impatient at the knowledge Tucker and Jess would be locking horns again. *Prob'ly won't even make it through breakfast.*

Tucker tried to look away after delivering his final warning, but found himself caught fast by the sudden vulnerability in her expression. Her eyes searched his face as though in question. Tucker wasn't sure he wanted to know what question—most likely she wouldn't care for his answer, and they'd be right back to arguing.

Desta shoving open the kitchen door and hollering at them brought him to his senses. He hoped the housekeeper never knew how big a debt of gratitude he owed her for such excellent timing. Even better, she didn't try to join them and nose into their business. Tucker didn't relish the idea of reliving half a morning's worth of arguments. Particularly since he suspected that breakfast would bring fresh contentions.

It hadn't escaped his attention that Jessalyn hadn't answered his questions about how she arranged the long journey from England to Texas. Nor had he failed to notice the way Desta helped her niece avoid the issue. When two women actively tried not to talk about something, it didn't take a bloodhound to scent trouble on the air.

"We'd better go." Jessalyn brushed past him to the back-porch step. "I owe Aunt Desta an apology and Morning Glory a treat."

Tucker noticed she didn't mention owing him an apology, but decided she wouldn't appreciate any teasing. Besides, he'd spoken harshly and raised his voice a time or two today, so she'd be within her rights to claim that he owed her an apology in return.

He made a point of always paying his debts, but "sorrys" cost more than he cared to spend if he could work his way around it.

He stuck his head through the door but stayed outside. A strong smell of burned. . .something. . .hit him hard. An uneasy feeling that owed little to his hunger settled in his stomach. Tucker craned his neck, trying to figure out whether or not he'd be expected to consume charcoal for breakfast or if Desta scraped together something else to serve. He couldn't see past the women to be sure.

He cleared his throat, ignoring the sting of smoke as the women looked up. They hadn't gotten into the swing of their conversation yet, so Tucker forged ahead with his plan.

"While you and Miss Desta get your hands cleaned up and tended to, I'm going to take Happy Jack and Morning Glory back to the stables. They deserve full feed bags as much as we do, and it'll help avoid awkward questions until we can arrange when and how you want to meet the ranch hands. Won't take more than a minute." He pulled back from the doorway without waiting for agreement, but heard a feminine call of "thank you!" float across the porch behind him.

She's making an effort to be agreeable. The thought made him move a little faster—not because he appreciated the courtesy, but because he found her sudden sweetness suspicious. All of a sudden, leaving her alone with her aunt to plot out the morning's conversation seemed like a downright foolish decision.

Tucker picked up the pace until he moved more at a trot than the horses did, determined to be back in that burned-smelling kitchen before the women could concoct anything too damaging. He all but threw the reins to Hank, holding up a hand and shaking his head to forestall the inevitable questions about the mysterious missing rider.

It was a testament to the training of his workers—and the seriousness of his expression—that no one tried to stop him. Everyone could see he wouldn't be handing out work orders the way he did most mornings—and everyone had brains enough to get busy anyway. With no one to stand in his way, his step only faltered once.

Should I stop for the seltzer? A grumble from his gut urged him to make time for a dash-and-grab. Tucker blazed through the mess hall, sweeping a handful of the tablets into his pockets and hitting the doors again before they so much as had a chance to swing shut behind him.

He hot-footed it back, whipping the hat from his head and all but leaping over the porch and into the kitchen. His boots hit the mat with a thud audible enough to turn the women's heads toward the door.

Jessalyn's glance took his measure, the corners of her mouth tilted as though keeping back a smile. "Hungry, Mr. Carmichael?"

"Must be." Miss Desta's grin flashed white and welcoming as she twisted the lid back down on a jar of unguent, finished tending her niece's barbed-wire cuts and scrapes. "He rushed back awful fast."

"I am hungry. How could I not be when something smells so. . . ready."

For the compost heap or the hog slops bucket anyway. Tucker bit his tongue and mentally gave himself a boot to the behind. He should've buttoned his lip after agreeing he was hungry.

Desta didn't seem to take offense, though her niece wrinkled her nose in disbelief. "Whether the food's ready or not, it's a fact: men only move that fast when they're heading for the table."

"Or away from it." Jessalyn's smile escaped her for a second, unleashing the incandescent warmth that drove out any other thought.

Tucker caught himself staring. That he looked away as quickly as possible was small comfort. *At least I caught myself before Desta managed to—though that's twice she might have noticed. . . .*

Luckily, the housekeeper focused on her niece's sassy remark to the exclusion of anything else. She planted her hands on her hips. "What are you talking about, men running away from my table?"

He didn't know whether to wince or chuckle at Jessalyn's mistake. Miss Desta had more reason than most to get touchy over the topic of men racing from her cooking because the scenario wasn't entirely outside the realm of possibility.

"Not *your* table," Jessalyn assured her aunt, making Tucker wonder whether something counted as a lie if the person speaking it didn't know any better. "On the ship over I saw some folks rushing out of the dining room with their hands clapped over their mouths. I could blame the swaying motion of the sea for their troubles, but in truth the food might've garnered the same reaction on dry land."

"If that's the worst part of your travels, I'll be thankful." Tucker wasted no time pouncing on the opening. "Waiting all night to hear the details of your journey just whetted my appetite."

"Looks like Aunt Desta's whipped up more than enough food to satisfy the strongest stomach pangs." Her ingenious attempt to change the subject didn't fool him for a second.

In spite of the looming threat of a charcoal breakfast, Tucker led the way with a light step. Tables made great places to corner someone, and their surprise visitor wouldn't slip past his questions for much longer.

Then he caught sight of the meal. He blinked, wondering if he'd gotten hungry enough to imagine food where none existed. These heaps of flapjacks, golden and glistening with butter, made his mouth water. He breathed deep, amused and reassured to still catch the acrid tinge of the ruined batch left behind in the kitchen.

"This looks amazing, Aunt Desta!" Jessalyn reached for the platter nearest her, which Tucker happily saw was filled with sausage.

"Hold on now." Desta's look made everyone freeze. "Let's thank the Lord for the food before us and a shaky start to the morning behind. Tucker, why don't you go on ahead and do the honors?"

He spotted Jessalyn giving the platters a longing glance before she ducked her head and laid her hands one over the other. It made him smile, though he knew her tendency toward impatient and impulsive decisions threatened his peace of mind. But when chaos loomed, a man couldn't do better than to bow his head and pray.

"Lord, we thank You that Miss Jessalyn arrived here safely yesterday. We ask for Your hand on Ed while he's away and offer sincere thanks for the breakfast before us. Please bless the food and the day, and let us enjoy both to the fullest. Amen."

By the time he lifted his head, Jessalyn had her platter and started spearing sausage to her plate. "Fullest was a good word."

Not wanting to miss out, Tucker loaded his own dish with four flapjacks. He added two fried eggs before Desta passed him the sausage. Though butter glistened atop the flapjacks, he piled on a healthy-sized pat before reaching for the maple syrup.

"You warmed it!" Delighted, he poured out a generous measure. The thick, luscious stream melted and melded with the butter. By the time he reached for his cutlery, a lake of creamy sweetness spread over his entire plate, dipping against the eggs and sausage. He tried not to drool while he cut the flapjacks into smaller slices.

"Careful." Miss Desta's warning pulled his attention from the plate—but just barely. "You know it does a woman's heart a lot of good to see a man tuck into her cooking with so much enthusiasm—especially after all that talk in the kitchen about running away. All the same, ain't neither one of us gonna be happy if you drip syrup and butter onto my nice, clean tablecloth. You do a lot around here, so don't make me add washing linen to the list."

Women sure do fuss. But Tucker wasn't inclined to grump at anyone who offered an edible meal, much less a delectable one. So he glanced at the pristine tablecloth and agreed. "Yes, Miss Desta."

Except that was easier said than done. Now that he got a gander at the snowy linen beneath his dish, it seemed maybe Miss Desta wasn't just fussing. The syrup-and-butter combination sluiced around everything on his plate, pushing up against the raised edge and threatening to spill over. Not only would that be a sin in the eyes of the housekeeper, it'd be a shameful waste.

"If you'd cut your hotcakes before making free with the syrup, you'd be in better shape." Jessalyn's amusement came through loud and clear, but she didn't stop there. No, she waved her fork over her own overflowing plate with a smaller stack of flapjacks.

Only difference was hers sat perfectly sliced. Even squares marched across her plate, tapering into rounded edges soaking up the sweetness with no risk to Miss Desta's tablecloth. While he watched, unsure whether to be envious or irked, she speared a bite.

Then it didn't matter. A bead of syrup clung to the fullness of her lower lip, making Tucker swallow at the same time she did.

Delicious. Mouth somehow dry and watering at the same time, he reached for his coffee mug. A restoring gulp of the bitter brew would help clear his head, but he found the mug empty and the pot across the table. Right where it couldn't help him—by Jessalyn.

Reduced to washing down his own foolishness with nothing but water, Tucker decided he didn't care if he wound up washing every piece of linen on the entire ranch. *Flapjacks aren't getting the best of me.*

"I understand my brother will be back in the next week or so with about six hundred head of cattle from Victoria. Did Ed take some of the men with him from here, or did he hire on the way?" Jessalyn began the conversation, but it wasn't the talk Tucker planned on.

Better nip this in the bud. He didn't doubt that once she started asking questions about the ranch, she'd hit her stride and refuse to turn back. Tucker never let a filly get the bit between her teeth to run as she pleased, and he didn't plan on making Jessalyn Culpepper the exception. *She's flouted enough rules.*

CHAPTER 11

Jess felt no compunctions about taking advantage of Tucker's distraction. If the man let breakfast catch his attention too thoroughly to launch an interrogation, so much the better. Besides, it was fun to join Aunt Desta in teasing him.

When it looked like he'd recovered enough to start asking questions, she launched a few of her own about Ed's whereabouts. With a little luck—or through sheer determination, if that worked better—she could talk about the ranch and sidestep anything else.

"I understand my brother will be back in the next week or so with about six hundred head of cattle from Victoria. Did Ed take some of the men with him from here, or did he hire on the way?"

"Both," he answered but kept talking before she could follow up. "But before we get to talking about Bar None business, back up the story a mite. I'm itching to know how you got here from England."

Drat. He rode around her maneuver in no time flat, and Jess suspected he knew exactly what game they played. The man looked far too self-satisfied for a man whose cheeks bulged with breakfast. Well, maybe he just appreciated the food. Jess knew she did.

"And I'm itching to do justice to this breakfast, so you'll have to wait a bit longer if you want a detailed description of my entire trip." She took another delicious bite and took her sweet time chewing. Filling her stomach and annoying Tucker were two enjoyable pastimes, and she delayed talking for as long as possible. Only when her stomach began to protest did she slow down enough for conversation to resume.

By then Tucker had put away an impressive amount of food. Most folks would be moving slow and looking dull-witted, having eaten themselves into a stupor, but he proved he wasn't like most folks. Instead he raised his fork and pointed it at her, skewering her with his question. "Now that you've slowed down, tell me. How did you get here all the way from England without anyone expecting you?"

"The usual way. The academy coach took me to the docks." She started out with the most respectable-sounding slant possible. Why mention that Miss Pennyworth instructed the coachman to take her to her grandparents, and she'd bribed the man into changing course?

"From there, I boarded a steamship for the journey overseas. The train brought me westward for most of the rest of the way, and I rode with a stage for the last part." She summoned up a rueful, though not repentant, grin and admitted the one thing Tucker already knew.

"I rode inside for part of the first day, but couldn't abide being cooped up and cramped for any longer than that. After the close confines of the steamship and train, I hungered for a space to call my own."

"And you made it here." Aunt Desta reached across the table to clasp her hand, but looked down and settled for a light, loving pat. "Home is the space you can always call yore own, and I have been thanking the Lord all morning, so glad to have you here again."

"Not nearly as glad as I am to be here." Her eyelids twitched, signaling yet another spate of tears. Jess blinked them back, but didn't suppress the well of gratitude toward her aunt. Ignoring her scrapes, she folded her aunt's hand in hers and held tight.

"And, maybe even more important, I'm glad you were waiting here. I never expected to find a female relation unless Ed married someone I could rub along with. Coming here and finding my brother gone left me at a loss. You made it feel like home again."

"I can't take credit for that. Ain't a soul in the world hadn't had to deal with feeling out of place and out of sorts at some point in life's unfolding. But not here and now." Her aunt pulled away to dab at the corners of her eyes with a napkin. "Finding you on the doorstep changes things for both of us. It'll change things for that brother of yores, too."

"I'm counting down the days until he gets back." She wanted to smile, but her throat got tight and her lips followed suit. The Ed she remembered, the hero of an older brother who taught her how to rope and a hundred other things, might have grown into a man she wouldn't recognize. A man who might not recognize—or even like—the woman she'd become. *We haven't seen each other in so many years.*

Tucker cleared his throat, and Jess suddenly realized he'd been staying quiet while she and Desta became emotional. *The poor man.*

I wonder if our girlishness made him uncomfortable. She almost grinned again at the thought of how he would've reacted if she and Aunt Desta stopped trying to be strong and burst into tears. *I bet then we'd get to see a man running from the table!*

But now he jumped back into the conversation by agreeing with her. "I'm sure we're *all* counting down the days until Ed gets back." Somehow he sounded less like he waited for Ed with a friend's anticipation, and more as if he couldn't wait to get through something unpleasant. The thought made her stomach churn because she couldn't ask if he dreaded Ed's reaction to finding her home, or if he looked forward to handing her off like an unwanted chore.

He assumes too much. Jess frowned. *Not just about me, but in general. One man can't run a ranch alone. Maybe he works in tandem with Ed and things will be better later, but if not, Tucker Carmichael's going to have to learn to ease up on the reins.*

"Yes, well, until that day arrives"—she heard the stiffness in her own voice and made an effort to stop clipping her syllables—"I don't plan to hide in the house, but I don't want my presence to cause upheaval with the men. They're bound to ask questions eventually, so I think it's best if we answer them outright."

Tucker shook his head at this reasonable suggestion. Apparently he didn't have any interest in being reasonable—or at least his presumption outweighed it. "I've got a few questions of my own I'd like to hear answered before we plan how to handle the men."

Jess summoned one of the few useful things she'd learned from all those years of refined schooling—an air of regal disdain. *Spine straight, shoulders back, lips pursed*, she recited to herself. *Brow raised, eyes icy, and words sharp to convey contempt.*

She followed the established protocol and finished the performance off by waving a dismissive hand. "Such as?"

Tucker blinked, looked her up and down, and blinked again. Then he found his words, and with them his bad temper. "Don't go putting on uppity airs around here."

Uppity airs, indeed. Another woman might feel a bit deflated after he poked a hole in her efforts. But Jessalyn couldn't take offense that he'd called her out on the carpet. She could, however, be put out for other reasons. His sheer arrogance stiffened Jess's resolve. *If the man can identify the tactic, at the very least he should accept the hint and stop trying to force the discussion!*

She wouldn't soften her stance one bit to suit Tucker Carmichael. If anyone changed their approach, it would be him. "I won't get uppity with you if stop acting so briggity with me."

"Briggity?" Something that could have passed for amusement flashed across his face before he marshaled his expression. "You've got the wrong end of the steer there. I'm no greenhorn who's gotten too big for his britches and needs to be taken down a peg. Nor am I a braggart who puts on airs and struts around above his station."

"That's a matter of opinion—and based on what I've seen, my opinion is that you might not put on airs, but you give orders even when you lack the authority." She paused, faltering over whether or not to speak the last part. The Miss Pennyworth part of her brain whispered that a woman never spoke of a man strutting, but the Culpepper part of her pointed out that he'd brought the matter up.

While she wavered, he broke in. "No. I don't lack authority."

"You can claim no authority over me, but you've already made numerous attempts." Irked beyond vacillating over decorum, she added, "And you *definitely* strut around here like you own the place."

Desta's fork clattered to the table, striking the rim of her plate. Her aunt reached for her water and took an overlarge gulp, coming up sputtering.

"Are you all right?" Tucker scooted back his chair at the same time Jess did, ready if her aunt needed a solid thump on the back.

"Fine," Desta gasped, waving her away. "Don't you worry none."

"Nothing's wrong?" Jess started to relax as Desta drank more.

"Naw, not a thing to start fussing over, Jess." She summoned a smile, but it looked like hard work. "Don't let me interrupt. A li'l bitty piece of egg tried sliding down the wrong pipe, is all."

Jess dubiously took in her aunt's flushed face, but didn't contradict.

Tucker, on the other hand, didn't seem inclined to do the same. His attention remained fixed on Desta even after she'd recovered, but he looked less sympathetic than... Jess couldn't put her finger on it, but the main thing was that he didn't look sympathetic anymore.

"Looked to me like something stuck in your craw." Tucker could've been commiserating about the egg, but something still seemed off. "Are you sure it wasn't something your niece said that struck you the wrong way? I'm sure she'd want to hear it from you."

"No, Mr. Carmichael. She's fine." When Desta didn't call him Tucker, Jess knew she'd been right about sensing an undercurrent. "And for now you don't want my opinion iff'n yore actin' briggity."

"I think you just gave it." Jess beamed at her aunt. An ally made for a nice, if unexpected, change.

Tucker blew out his breath in an impatient huff, fixing Desta with a beady stare. "You know that's not what I'm getting at."

Wait. A chill of foreboding had Jess reaching for some coffee to help heat her insides. *Something's going on here....*

"Yore attitude *is* what Jess was talking 'bout," Desta maintained, her finely carved features turning stony. For the first time, Jess realized they shared a family trait: stubbornness.

"Yep." He leaned back in the chair, avoiding Jess's avid stare and keeping Desta on the spot. "What exactly did she say about it?"

"That you give too many orders and strut around like. . ." Jess faltered. This time it wasn't the word *strut* that caught her tongue. It was a sudden conviction that she understood the byplay between her aunt and the foreman.

Her mouth dry, she forced herself to ask. "You own the place?"

CHAPTER 12

But I don't strut." Tucker couldn't say why he felt the need to press this point. The reasons seemed hodgepodge at best. For one thing, he honestly didn't strut and never could abide the full-of-himself sort of fellows who did. Then, too, he didn't like the notion that she saw him that way and wanted to change that. But mostly, it gave him a way to answer her without having to claim ownership.

He hadn't yet accepted the shares, though Ed kept him from rejecting the bequest outright. Since his initial reaction, he'd started to reconsider the benefits of taking his place as part owner. Now, eying the mutinous expression on Jessalyn's face, those benefits became more pronounced. As foreman, he ran the ranch but ultimately had to knuckle under to the family. As joint owner, he earned equal status with the spitfire. He'd be a fool to give up any advantage before Ed got back and they could assess the situation.

I might be a fool to give up the advantage even after Ed gets back. Tucker considered for another minute, suddenly uncertain Ed would prove the same ally he'd been before. For all he knew, Ed's guilt over not fetching Jessalyn in person, or even simple gratitude to have his sister back, might make him side with the women.

The uncertainty made his stomach clench, upsetting the huge breakfast he'd gobbled down mere moments before. From the look on Jessalyn's face, she fought the same sick sort of feeling. Tucker worried for Desta's pride...and tablecloth...for the second time that morning.

"When?" she whispered, so pale that her smattering of freckles stood out in sharp relief. "How?"

"Your father's will." He didn't try to comfort her—for one thing, it would probably make her even less comfortable. For another, she had an aunt sitting not three feet away who'd do a much better job than any platitudes he could scrape together.

"Ed's letter didn't mention anything about the will." She drew her napkin from her lap and laid it beside her plate, fingering its folds as though hoping to discover an explanation hidden there.

"It ain't the sort of thing anyone wants to detail in a letter." Desta stretched over to smooth a hand down her niece's shoulder and upper arm. "He wrestled with every word he wrote you. It's particularly hard to write 'bout things you ain't come to terms with yoreself. Yore brother's struggled since yore pa's passing."

"I can understand that." Spine stiff, she leaned awkwardly into her aunt's caress. "I assumed Papa left the Bar None to me and Ed."

In a flash, Tucker realized that Jessalyn took the news as such a blow because she misunderstood it. At least in part. He rushed to correct her. "He didn't disinherit you, Miss Jessalyn. I didn't mean for you to think he split it between Ed and me."

As stiff as she'd sat the moment before, she suddenly seemed boneless. It was a wonder she didn't sag straight out of her chair, and Tucker figured Desta's hand helped keep Jessalyn upright.

"Heavens, no. Simon left it to Ed first, then you second, then Tucker third." The housekeeper slipped out of her chair to stand behind her niece—and help steady her. Her next words came out so softly Tucker wouldn't have been able to make it out if he hadn't already been familiar with the terms of the will. "Then some to me."

"You're family." It seemed as though her aunt's vulnerability summoned Jess's strength when her own sadness would have sapped her. "Don't you dare sound so small when you deserved Papa's honor."

And I didn't? Tucker bit his tongue to keep from demanding she acknowledge the worth of his own contributions. Beneath the resentment of her rejection, his logical streak told him the girl had no way of knowing what he'd done for the Bar None during the past half-dozen years. Then, too, she had every reason to assume her aunt deserved to inherit part of the family estate—particularly given the details of Desta's inclusion in their family. A percentage of the ranch in no way made up for the circumstances of Desta's birth, nor the way she'd lived the first half of her life.

Jessalyn's swift support brought tears to Desta's eyes and shamed Tucker for his self-absorbed thoughts. For now, emotion guided her opinions. Simon and Ed were the ones who'd worked alongside him and judged him worthy of joining their ranks. Their acceptance and approval should be enough for him. *More* than enough.

"Yore right." Desta lifted her chin then slanted a sideways look from her niece to him then back again. "But you should know Tucker's earned his stake in the Bar None. He might not be born family, but he's proven himself time and again with the work of his hands and strength of his character. The good Lord tells us the laborer is worthy of his hire, and Tucker's poured enough sweat into this here ranch to earn a piece. Yore brother knows it and agrees with it."

The unexpected defense brought heat to Tucker's cheeks. No matter that he'd been thinking along the same lines and wishing Jessalyn understood the reasoning behind Simon's decision—hearing such praise spoken aloud made him want to change the subject.

For one thing, all this talking and thinking wore away at his belief that Simon made a mistake in portioning out the Bar None this way. With so much uncertainty swimming around the place, Tucker didn't need to start doubting his decisions. *Especially when Miss Jessalyn's traveled thousands of miles to doubt them for me.*

"I'm sure you've worked very hard on behalf of the Bar None. I never meant to imply otherwise." Jessalyn struggled to speak around her emotion—he could tell by the careful, clipped way she shaped her words. "My surprise isn't a reflection on you personally."

"Understood." He couldn't give her a hard time when she already fought back so many feelings. Tucker gave her an encouraging grin. "I'll give you a couple weeks around here to see how we operate firsthand before I start taking your remarks personally."

Her nod lacked the spirit he'd already come to expect from her, but she gave a game little grin. That smile acknowledged his offer—and gave him a warning. No doubt Miss Jessalyn expected to find plenty of things to stick her nose in after she got settled.

Tucker almost looked forward to it. Given the choice between a wound-up spitfire and this silent, stricken version of Jessalyn, he'd take the former any day. Fires could be doused, but sorrowing women flooded a man's life and carried away his peace of mind. Since she looked like the next statement could push her over the edge or make her rally, Tucker decided to bedevil the blue mood out of her.

"It won't take long for you to see I'm not briggity and I don't strut." He saw her shoulders square and couldn't resist throwing one last jab. "I'll be happy to accept your apology when the day comes."

"Happier than I'll be to give it, I'm sure." She got some starch back in her spine. "Of course, I wonder whether you'll be able to admit it if I prove you wrong?"

"I can admit when I'm wrong," he protested. "I just get rusty since that doesn't happen very often."

Her indelicate snort would have been off-putting from another female. "Well, I'm sure I can help you polish up the skill, Mr. Carmichael."

"So long as you're willing to let me return the favor, Miss Jess." He shortened her name on purpose, wanting to test it on his tongue and see whether or not she'd let him get away with it.

"Miss Jessalyn will do." Shorter than he was and from across the table, she managed to look down her nose at him like a disapproving schoolmarm. "Someone reminded me this morning that once boundaries are crossed, it's difficult to reestablish them."

"Good to know you're willing and able to listen and learn." He sat a little taller to match her, taking a particular pleasure in the fact that, for all her arguing, she'd chosen to take his warning to heart.

"You'll discover that I'm willing and able to do many things."

She gave her aunt a grateful smile as Desta returned to her own seat. "Though I've no doubt you'll disapprove of some of my choices."

"Most likely." He folded his hands over his full stomach, his breakfast and his mind much more settled now that they'd gone over the hardest parts of the conversation. Truth be told, he figured he'd disapprove of almost all of her choices. Based on what he'd seen. . .

Tucker snapped back to attention, palms flat against the table. He'd been lulled into complacency far too easily and almost let her sidle by without giving a full accounting for her travels!

"Speaking of choices you've made, let's get back to that trip of yours. I asked last night what happened to your traveling companion. Somehow that part got left out again this morning."

"Why does it matter?" she countered. "I'm here now, safe and sound."

"It matters because I suspect you acted on impulse and set off on your own, without letting anyone know your plans." He stopped circling the issue and plunked it on the table.

"Even if you're right, it's in the past. What does it have to do with how we proceed now that I'm at the Bar None?"

"Because you did the same thing when you rode off this morning." He fought to keep his voice level as he ticked off the pertinent points. "You abandoned basic propriety, didn't inform anyone of your plans, and generally exposed yourself to danger while you relegated everyone else to worrying. A single incident is bad enough, but you're establishing a pattern of impetuous decisions."

"Careful, Mr. Carmichael." Her voice went dangerously soft. "You're starting to sound briggity again."

Desta swooped in before Tucker could work his outrage into a coherent comeback. Usually he didn't appreciate it when a woman's mouth moved faster than a man's mind, but he couldn't complain this time. She rounded on her niece. "You can't go throwing that word in the man's face every time he opposes you, Jess. It's not arrogant for him to hold a mirror to yore actions when you done wrong.

It's arrogant of you to try and turn it back on him."

"Wait!" Jessalyn recoiled from her aunt's chiding, but refused to back down. "I'm not saying it's arrogant of him to point out where I've gone wrong. But he's got no right to act as though I owed him any sort of prior notice before I made a decision or even an explanation afterward. I don't even know the man!"

You will. He tried not to enjoy the flash in her brown eyes, but couldn't help admiring her spunk. Same way he couldn't help but deplore her headstrong streak. Maybe she'd settle down now that she'd gotten home. . .then again, maybe she'd be a handful until her brother got back. *What are you thinking? Remember seven years ago? She was more than a handful at twelve, and she's going to keep on that way until she's put in the grave or she puts you there first.*

"We're all getting to know each other. And now that you're getting to know the way we run things around here, it's more than reasonable for us to expect you to—" *fall in line.* Tucker caught himself before he spoke the words aloud. A comment like that, even well meaning, would be tantamount to waving something red in a bull's face. Today none of them had the patience for that sort of bull. He groped for a substitution and finished, "compromise."

Jessalyn traced the rim of her water glass before taking a sip. She set down the glass before responding. "What sort of compromise?"

"I'd guess we won't know all of 'em until after the fact." Miss Desta tapped her chin absentmindedly. "You'll wind up breaking rules that haven't been used or don't even exist yet, on account of the fact there hasn't been another woman on the ranch in so many years."

"Ignorance doesn't dismiss anyone on this ranch from using horse sense." He broke in before he could get backed into a corner. If he didn't head her off, Jessalyn was wily enough to claim amnesty from any rules she broke on the grounds no one told her different. "I think things'll go smoother if we establish some ground rules."

"Agreed. Guidelines to govern our interactions will reduce misunderstandings. I think the first, most basic issue revolves around respect." Jessalyn got the upper hand by listing the first rule, and her smirk told him that she knew it. "When speaking with me, it is not acceptable to address me like one of your ranch hands. Handing down orders won't work, but I'll happily consider requests."

He gritted his teeth to keep from correcting her. "If something puts you or anyone else in danger, or an emergency crops up, I'm not going to take the time to frame a request."

"Emergency situations are separate," she agreed. "But otherwise, after we lay these ground rules, any other concerns should be broached as politely and as patiently as possible."

"I don't hem and haw around things or have time to waste." Tucker didn't plan on being wrong-footed in conversation just because she didn't like the way he said what needed to be said. "The meaning of my words holds more weight than the way they come out. Don't overlook a valid warning for no better reason than disliking how I said it."

"That would be childish. As I am not a child"—she threw him a peeved glance—"and you will not be trying to treat me like one, that won't become an issue."

"Good. Respect and good manners unless an emergency crops up. And while we're at it, no one around here takes off without letting someone else know." He gestured toward the wall opposite him because Jess knew it was the direction of the stable yard. "Tell me, Miss Desta, or even the stable master when you go saddle up. It lets us know when you're safe—and if you might be in trouble."

"That shouldn't be a problem." When she drew breath, he hurried to start talking before she could say something less agreeable.

"Next ground rule—a ranch is no place for frills and fussiness, but you'll stick to essential proprieties. Wear the split skirts when you ride. Don't loiter near the mess hall or bunkhouse, and don't get chatty with the ranch hands. I don't want you distracting them, and I don't want anyone to get the idea you're overly familiar."

"Don't worry." Her sweet smile gave him an eerie chill. "I plan to keep myself far too busy to 'loiter' anywhere."

CHAPTER 13

Jessalyn enjoyed watching the corners of Tucker's mouth tighten as he gave a nervous swallow. As she'd noted before, the man was intelligent. He recognized the threat wrapped up in her promise, just as she'd seen the put-down hidden in his rules.

"Busy?" he repeated. "That's probably a good thing to discuss. How do you plan to fill your days?"

"Today's washing clothes and, if the space between my ears is still good for anything, I figure we'll be breaking out the needles," Aunt Desta answered for her, giving that sense of being part of a team again. "Jessalyn's going to want some more split skirts, since she'll be doing a lot of riding to get familiar with the place again."

"Thank you, Aunt Desta." Since Tucker looked about ready to chew his own tongue, Jess figured she should cut him some slack before he hung himself. "It's a good idea to keep close to the house until Tucker can arrange introductions with the ranch hands."

"Right." He looked taken aback by her thoughtfulness—or maybe just the proof that she possessed and even exercised some measure of what he called "horse sense." "Speaking of which, I figure tonight after supper should be a good time."

"Is this one of those rare instances I'll be allowed in the mess hall?" She tried to keep her words light instead of sounding bitter. Even though she knew Tucker was right about keeping her distance from the men, it rankled to have places around the ranch closed to her.

Walking through the mess hall would be part of coming home for her. Tucker had no way of knowing how many meals she'd eaten

and memories she'd made in that old place, but little girls traipsing along behind their father could do things grown ladies couldn't.
She'd accept that as one of the compromises.

"Yes. It'd be best if Miss Desta came along with you." He hesitated, no longer looking her way, but at her aunt. "I know you haven't
decided to say anything to the community at large, but if she's going
to be calling you 'aunt,' tonight might be time to enlighten the men."

"They don't know?" Jess saw the way Desta's cheeks paled and
understood that she hadn't been the only one who didn't know she
had an aunt. She and Papa kept it a secret from everybody—maybe
even Ed.

For a brief moment, relief selfishly overshadowed her concern.
She didn't want things to be more difficult for Desta, but knowing
that even Ed, whom Papa kept all these years and trained to take
over the ranch, had been kept in the dark made her feel less alone.
Now it was time to make sure Aunt Desta didn't feel like an outsider.

"Simon and I kept it hushed when he brought me back because
things were still so unsettled. You've been away, and even before that
you probably didn't have much of anything to do with slavery, so you
can't know about the upheaval and hard feelings of Reconstruction.
Even eight years after the end of the War between the States, lots
of Texas still felt plumb torn apart. It's better now. The last six years
marked a lot of progress."

What can I say to ease her hurt? A familiar aching caught at Jess's
chest as she realized how much she didn't know and how much she'd
never share with the people she loved. She could offer no words
of understanding or even encouragement that wouldn't come out
sounding hollow and half thought out. She settled for scooting back
her chair and going to catch her aunt in a tight hug.

"It's not my decision to make, what you tell other people and
what you hold private." That'd be the first thing Jess would want to
hear if their situations were reversed. Sometimes the best gift was
a simple acknowledgment that a woman was more than capable of

making her own choices. "And I can't pretend I know firsthand why you and Papa made the choices you did, and I'm not going to say they were the wrong ones. But what I can say is I'm proud to claim you as my family whenever and wherever you'll let me."

Desta rocked a bit in her embrace, the cries she tried to hold back turning into a set of hiccups the likes of which Jess had never heard. Wrenching and loud, it sounded as though her stomach were creaking and calling to be tightened.

Without meaning to, Desta's hiccups broke the heaviness of the conversation, and Jess giggled. Thankfully, Tucker chuckled at about the same time, and even Desta started laughing around the spasms. Between the emotion, the strength of her hiccups, and the breath-lessness of her laughter, tears still shone in her eyes. But the sadness slipped away by the time she spoke again.

"I'm the one who's proud to hear you say that, Jess." She blotted her face with her napkin then twisted it between her hands. "What with you goin' abroad to be trained as a fine lady, I worried a fair bit that I'd shock yore delicate sensibilities."

"You dress up a person or a truth to look like something else, but it doesn't change what they are." Jess straightened up but kept a hand on her aunt's shoulder. "Deep down I'm still a cowgirl—I'm just out of practice, is all."

"Cowgirl?" He didn't sound scornful or amused, just considering. All the same it struck a nerve.

"Cowgirl. Born and raised on a ranch for a dozen years," she defended. "I'm rusty, but all things considered I've got half a decade more than you do."

"First of all, I just hadn't really heard the term before." He held up his hands, palms out as though to forestall any further attacks. "But if there's such a thing as a cowboy, it's only fair. And since you mention it, I'm going to say I don't think those first five years of yours count for too much."

"Then that puts you about equal." Her aunt broke in before Jess could point out that Papa put her on a horse and taught her to ride before she learned to walk.

She swallowed the argument. It seemed like they'd done an awful lot of arguing when they could be doing good instead. Her aunt spoke of people being equal—she could use that.

"You talk of people being equal." She spoke slowly, giving Desta time to hear where she was going and head her off if she chose. "But you don't count yourself among us. That strikes me as wrong, Aunt Desta. I don't want you to hesitate to claim the family we've got living or the bequest Papa left you."

"Folks won't like it," she fretted. "Once people look at you a certain way, it's hard to change the way they think about you."

"Tucker told me the same thing, in just about the same words, this morning. I'm supposed to guard my reputation, but for you, coming forward would be a step up." She gentled her voice. "What are you trying to protect yourself against?"

Her aunt blew out the breath she'd been holding in a long gust, rubbing her hands along her arms as though cold. She looked like she was walking through a time half-forgotten, so Jess waited.

"Circumstances and times have changed around here, like you said." Tucker pulled her attention back to the here and now, and Jess gave him a grateful nod. "Jessalyn stands beside you. Maybe it's time to change the way you let folks see you?"

Desta tilted her head to the side, looking up at Jess for an encouraging smile before she confessed her deepest fear. "Maybe folks will accept it, and maybe not. I guess I have my own troubles with it. Change is hard when you don't know where it's gonna lead."

Tucker led Happy Jack out of the stables with the sun rising toward noon. The day would be busy. He couldn't remember the last time he'd let so much of a morning slide by without getting more under his belt than a hearty breakfast.

Then again, if he didn't look at it like a normal morning, he'd tackled enough to send a stronger, smarter man straight to bed. But Tucker Carmichael didn't get to this point in his life by being the strongest or the smartest. Stubbornness could take a man a lot further than most people suspected. Stubbornness kept you in the saddle long past the point when strength gave way to exhaustion and intellect told him to knock off for the day.

Persistence. . .patience. . .perseverance. . .the Bible named it lots of ways. But for Tucker, when a job needed to get done and he didn't trust someone else to do it right—or there was no one else to try— it came down to determination. If a man asked hard enough, God granted him the ability to grit his teeth and get on with whatever needed doing.

Something always needs doing on a ranch—enough hard work for a man to lose himself in from dawn till dusk. It kind of figured that just when things started getting routine around the Bar None, God shook the place up.

First, You took Simon home. Then, almost like You wanted to be sure I stayed on my toes, You brought his daughter home to the Bar None. It won't come as a surprise to hear me say that my itch for activity would've waited until the roundup.

Tucker hoisted himself into the saddle and opened up his running conversation with the Almighty. Some people maintained that prayer required knees on the ground and eyes screwed tight against distraction. But the way he saw it, God made man for company, and he could talk while riding. If anything, working in tandem with another of God's creatures struck him as appropriate. The humble wonders of this world, from his trusty horse to a fresh breeze, strengthened his connection with the Creator.

I know You challenge us, and I know Jessalyn belongs here. But from where I'm sitting, it would've made things a lot simpler if she'd waited to come back. My guess is You'll hear me asking for patience even more than usual during the days—and maybe weeks and months—ahead. Please help me handle the complication with a measure of Your grace. I'd also be obliged if You'd help her hurry up with settling in so things can settle back down, Lord. Thank You for getting her here safely in spite of herself. Amen.

Tucker pointed his mount toward the north pasture and sped up. Earlier, he'd refused to let himself so much as glance at the fence. It wouldn't help things any to antagonize Jessalyn by looking over her work and finding it wasn't up to par. Nor did he want to encourage her by telling her she'd done a good job. Either way, he would've come out behind.

I'm still behind. He rubbed the back of his neck as he spotted the first flag. For all the ground he'd gained with their new arrival—though he fought back a niggling suspicion Jessalyn didn't see things that way—he'd done nothing else. The only to-do he could cross off his long list, if this inspection satisfied his standards, wasn't anything he'd gotten done. Jessalyn did the work.

And, once he'd gotten past the dried blood crusting up the wire around the first patch job, he didn't mind admitting she'd done the work well enough to pass muster. The temporary fixes would hold until he assigned a team to come out, dig up the posts, and string fresh wire. By the time he hit the saddle again, Tucker caught a smile before it could spread.

He couldn't let her continue trying her hand at new things—or even old skills only half remembered—if it meant she'd hurt that hand. Or any part of her.

Except maybe her feelings. For all the talk about soft skin, a woman's feelings seemed easiest to bruise. He grimaced. At some point after breakfast he'd been tempted to count the number of times the womenfolk cried or barely kept from crying—only to let loose a few moments later. Between Miss Desta and Jessalyn, they'd wasted more water than a leaky washbasin.

He knew clear down to his bones that calm and quiet wouldn't be nearly as common as they had been just last week. Tucker would tell her something she didn't like, or she'd do something foolish, and they'd be bickering long before Ed showed up. It didn't take a particularly tall man to see that far ahead.

Tucker shook his head and tried to stuff thoughts of Jessalyn to the back burner. Now wasn't the time to try and anticipate the next argument—no man could predict what would ruffle a woman's feathers under the best of circumstances. For now, he needed to go check on the farthest windmill and try to find where it was creaking.

Then he'd need to make sure the flat area he'd marked for the last day of roundup hadn't flooded from yesterday's storm. And if he found a spare minute, he'd assign someone to check the eastern stretch and make sure no cows got stuck in that prickly patch.

Yessir. There was plenty to do on a ranch, and Tucker Carmichael planned to keep so busy that Jessalyn Culpepper didn't cross his mind until they crossed paths—and maybe words—again.

CHAPTER 14

"Not again!" Jessalyn pulled out the needle and stuck her finger in her mouth. Good thing they'd picked a dark skirt. Black wool might not be particularly pretty, but it didn't show stains and made an appropriate choice for mourning.

"Didn't they teach you how ta sew at them fancy schools?" Desta clucked her tongue and kept drawing her own needle in even, rhythmic stitches.

Jess shrugged. "They taught me to sew, but I've never mastered the fine art of sitting still. The sun's been shining all day in an invitation I couldn't accept. Now it's packing in and setting for the night, and I missed it. My first beautiful day on the ranch, and I stayed cooped up like a chuckleheaded chicken."

Desta let loose a chuckle of her own. "You do have a way with words, but I understand yore disappointed. Tomorrow you can go for another ride in any one of yore three clean sets of split skirts." She lifted the finished item and gave it a good shake, loosening any wrinkles before carefully folding.

Chastened, Jess followed her aunt into the kitchen where the scent of three custard pies baking in the oven made her mouth water.

"I've waited so many years to be back, it's silly to think I could soak it all in the first day anyway." Jess grabbed a dishcloth.

"Mmmmhmmm." Padding her palm with a cloth of her own, Desta tugged open the oven door, peeked inside, and opened it wide. Together they pulled the pies from the oven and set them to cool. Her aunt didn't seem eager to leave the warmth and aroma of the kitchen, so they sat down at the butcher-block baking table.

"I know 'zactly what yore talking about, wanting to take every-thin' in at once." Desta ran a palm over the thick wooden tabletop, smoothing the scars left by knives and hot pans. "There come a day I waited for my whole life. I remember it well. When freedom came, my eyes didn't seem big enough to see the world in a whole new way."

Nothing could have convinced Jess to interrupt. Here was her aunt's heart, laid bare and needing to be loved. She hoped Tucker held off for a while longer to pick them up, until Desta was ready to take that next step away from the chains of the past.

"I goggled anyway, trying to take it all in." A bittersweet smile sketched across her lips. "Even the most common thing takes on a new light when you've waited on it."

"That's how I feel," Jess agreed then sucked in a breath. *Is it all right to agree? Seven years made me long for the silliest little details, but that's nothing compared to being born with no freedom.* How many years did Aunt Desta wait before the Emancipation Proclamation? Then another two years to end the War between the States. How long did she have to accept that other people ordered her life and she couldn't be her own woman?

"Don't poker up on me, child." Desta slanted on her stool to nudge Jess with her shoulder. "I wasn't tryin' to take away yore feel-ings or yore rights to them. Thought it might do you good to know somebody understands and even shares some."

"It does more good than you know." She hesitated then plunged ahead. "Didn't mean to poker up on you, but for all the years I thought of schools as penitentiaries and called them cages, I was wrong. Even on the worst of days, I wouldn't have thought to compare it to the way you grew up. When you were talking, I didn't want to interrupt because there's so much I don't know about you, so many questions that seem rude to ask."

Desta rubbed a rough spot on the lip of the table. "I don't mind you asking, and if'n sometimes I mind answering just then, you can let me think on it awhile longer until I'm ready. We'll do fine thataway."

"I can do that, so long as you're not offended." Once she started talking, the words poured out fast and furious. "I didn't want to belittle your struggle by comparing our lives. It feels fine if you want to, but presumptuous for me to even think that way."

"You wanna know the worst part of bein' a slave?" Desta stopped running her fingers across the table, pinning Jess with the force of her full attention. "It's prob'ly not what you'd expect, though I won't play and make you guess."

"Being separated from your family." The answer popped out before Jess even considered it. Only when she heard herself say it did she realize she was talking about her own struggle as much as guessing about her aunt's.

"Many of my people lived that out, but it wasn't my cross to bear." They sat in silence for a moment, paying respect to those who'd suffered so, seeing their families torn apart.

"Suddenly strikes me that plenty of former slaves might choose a different answer, and they'd all be ev'ry bit as right as me. I shoulda said the worst part for me."

"No need to split hairs. Speaking from the heart means it's personal. It doesn't rope in anyone else's opinion. If you want to say what crossed your mind, I'm still listening."

"All right. You were talking about how you didn't want to compare our lives. And I know you meant it out of respect, but to me that's a terrible thing. Most of my life, people wouldn't think to compare my life with theirs. Because they were different. Because I was different." Her jaw worked and eyes shone, but she kept on. "And the more differences they heaped between us, the more comfortable they felt keeping me at a distance. You see. . .when you stop looking for what you have in common with other people, it's the first step to not seeing them as people a'tal."

Jess couldn't speak. There were no words good enough to give.

Aunt Desta wiped her eyes with the corner of her apron, hiding her face until she was ready to finish. "Slavery took the freedom of thousands. But the real power behind it all—the real horror—was how it stole away our very humanity. You think it's presumption to think we share things in common—I think it's a gift to want to understand each other."

"You're the gift." She wrapped her arms around her aunt and held her tight. "That's the easiest thing to understand, and also the best. We can take our time figuring out the rest."

"That's what I started out trying to tell you." Desta drew back and raised a hand to cup Jess's cheek. "After you been dreamin' on something for so long, it's only natural to want to take it all in at once. But if you try, you'll miss some of the smaller, more special parts."

"The best parts," Jess agreed.

"Right. So take yore time letting life unfold. You'll enjoy it more."

"We could enjoy these right now and go visit the mess hall tomorrow night," Tucker suggested. He didn't think for half a second the women would revise their plans so he could eat more pie, but the luscious look of those custard treats, baked golden brown, beckoned. No man worth the name wouldn't at least try to claim an extra share.

Or two. Or maybe an entire pie all to himself.

"Best not start sounding greedy, or you'll miss out." Desta shook a finger at him. "'Specially seein' as how you filled up on my flapjacks this morning, and the other men got nothing more than breakfast as usual."

She looked serious, so Tucker settled on flattery. "Fine flapjacks, too. Instead of getting riled that I'm slavering for another taste of your baking, you should see it as a compliment."

He made sure to say "baking" because while he had no problems offering a sincere compliment if the conversation called for it, he wouldn't stoop to outright falsehood. Not even for pie.

"Wouldja listen to Mr. Tucker trying to sweet-talk his way into dessert!" Desta teased. "I never thought he hid a silver tongue."

"He keeps it hidden." Jessalyn smoothed the front of her apron and joined in. "It's hard to see any silver under so much slobber!"

"Slobber?" Revolted, Tucker stopped eyeing the pies. "We don't use that word for people much. Calves get the slobbers—and let me tell you, it's not a pretty picture."

"I know!" She hooted, and Desta joined in. Since their laughter made a big improvement from the morning's weeping, he played along.

"Are you done insulting me?" he grumbled. "I can't have you calling me greedy or saying I've got the slobbers around the other men. No undermining the foreman's dignity."

They were all funning around, but it seemed a good idea to work in the warning. Jessalyn in particular might well need a reminder before he let her within earshot of the others.

"It's not your dignity we'll be undermining if you try and sneak off with that pie." She slid one of the tins into his hands and picked up another, leaving Desta to carry the third. "It's your sweet tooth."

"Children have sweet teeth. Men have appetites." As soon as he said it, the words chased themselves around, clanging against his ears with a bad note. It was too much to hope the women wouldn't notice. Their eyes sparkled and mouths opened at the same time, savoring his misspoken phrase.

He glowered at them. "Don't say it. If you want this pie to make it out of this kitchen in one piece, let it slide." His warning fell on deaf ears. Neither woman could hear him through the sound of their cackles.

"Sweet teeth?!" they chorused, delighted and disbelieving.

"I've heard something can be lip-smacking, finger-licking good," Jess gasped, "but teeth-tasting is a new one. Sweet teeth. . ."

"You know 'tooths' isn't a word," he defended himself, if somewhat sheepishly. "It didn't sound right either way, so I chose good grammar."

"Reading rules don't much apply to sayin's," Desta told him. "Part of the reason I like 'em so much."

Tucker muttered one of his favorites. "The old one saying not to go around 'brayin' like a jackass eatin' cactus' comes to mind."

"Such language!" Jessalyn's eyes sparkled with mirth, but she sounded genuinely surprised. Looked like the lady lessons finally kicked in.

"It's another term for donkey," he elaborated. "But it's not funny to say it that way. That's all."

"I knew what you meant. But you say you don't slobber, and I say ladies don't bray."

"Leastwise, we don't," Desta agreed. "Though I've met a few women who put me in mind of mules more'n once in my life. Course, mule-headed men outnumber those without even trying!"

Mule-headed. Tucker compared it to his earlier thoughts on the nature of stubbornness and couldn't help but grin. Little wonder the Good Book stuck to all those *p* words. Perseverance sounded much more virtuous.

"Well, if you want introductions to the men on the ranch so you can decide whether or not they fit that description, we'd better get a move on. Every minute spent dillydallying around is another chance for me to find a fork."

Finally the women decided they were ready. As they ambled over to the mess hall, where he'd told the men to grab a seat for supper and stay put after they'd finished, Tucker breathed in the scent of custard. It was enough to make a man forgive the extra time waiting on the women. He looked at the pie, glanced over at Jessalyn, and nodded to himself.

Yep. *Some things are just worth waiting for.*

CHAPTER 15

W ait one second." Desta's request brought everyone up short about four paces from the front of the mess hall.

Jess fidgeted. It felt like she'd been doing nothing but waiting—and some sewing, which didn't improve the time or speed things up any—all day. Until she met the ranch hands, she wouldn't be able to roam freely around the Bar None. If it weren't for the way her aunt confided in her earlier and how nervous Desta looked now, Jess would've protested this delay.

"Something wrong?" Tucker tilted his head the same way an animal perked its ears, straining to hear telltale signs of trouble.

"No, but I want to be sure we do this right. I meant to bring it up back in the kitchen, but got the giggles and forgot all about it." She shifted the pie she held to free up one of her hands then used it to snag Jess's elbow. "Before we get started changing things around the ranch, we should ask God's blessing on how we handle it."

"Now?" Despite her best intentions, she couldn't keep her astonishment to herself. After hanging around all day, the need for prayer became so urgent they needed to juggle pies?

"Now." To her surprise, Tucker nestled his pie in the crook of his arm and scooted close enough to touch their arms, joining the circle. His eyes met hers. "Any time is a good time to pray, but this is particularly appropriate. It would make your dad's heart happy to know you started off asking the direction of the Almighty."

"Go ahead, honey." A squeeze to her elbow accompanied the order as her aunt and Tucker both bowed their heads in expectation.

"Erhm." Jessalyn cleared her throat. "You do the honors, Aunt

Desta. It's your idea, and I'm not quite caught up enough to act as the leader in anything important. I'm sure Tucker'll agree with me."

Actually, she wasn't so sure. He'd raised his head a fraction and was giving her a quizzical look. "Go on ahead."

Thankfully, Desta hadn't opened her eyes and took his encouragement in Jess's stead. The sudden weight on her shoulders eased a bit as her aunt started praying.

"Lord, we thank You for all the good You've given us and for bringing Jessalyn home to us. We pray for Ed and the others that You keep them safe while they're gone. You know our hearts. Please help us find the words to speak and the ears to listen as we go in there and meet the men. Amen."

Jess breathed easier once the prayer ended, but couldn't tell why. A lot of people claimed they felt the loving peace of the Lord settle their hearts. But in her case, it was probably relief because she'd wriggled her way out of praying aloud in front of people she wanted to have respect her. She didn't like being put on the spot, and she didn't want to mislead them into thinking she'd be more than happy to pray over them on a regular basis.

It wasn't that she minded when other people chose to pray. Jess didn't—she'd happily join in. But something inside her shied away when someone chose for her to pray. Sure, she usually balked at being told what to do—but if it were that simple, she probably would've gone along just for the chance to make people listen to what she had to say.

"Better now?" This time Tucker looked at Aunt Desta, but Jess chose to answer. It only seemed fair since they'd swapped before.

"Better." If anything, she kind of hoped answering this question made him wonder less about why she hadn't responded to his other invitation. Jessalyn got the impression he—and Aunt Desta—took their prayer the same way Papa had. Serious.

And if they found out she didn't feel the same, they might not be willing to shrug it off. *I've already got too much to learn about, adjust to, and brush up on without getting my mind examined. They should let me concentrate on wrestling all of that under control. Helping will give them plenty to do, and trying to keep them from doing more than helping will keep me hopping.*

"Lemme go in and make 'em simmer down." He handed off his pie with obvious reluctance. "I wouldn't let this go, but I'm afraid they'll mob me for it if they think there's only one. Then there's no chance of this going well."

"Why don't we all go in together, at the same time?" Jessalyn pressed, anxious to move on. "Side by side, bearing equal amounts of pie—a united front!"

"Because it ain't just us that'll want to make a good impression." Desta scooted the pies to get a better grip. "Tucker's right to give the men a chance to sit up straight—or at least sit still—before we waltz in and surprise 'em."

"Okay." Jess stared at the door as the foreman went in to marshal his troops. She shuffled her feet, sick and tired of being left behind.

The door opened and a hand poked through, waving them in. For a second she and her aunt looked at each other without moving, silently waiting for the other one to take the lead. Jess hesitated out of respect for her elder and because the men would already be familiar with Desta, even if they didn't speak much.

"Go on." Her aunt waved a pie toward the door, and Jess realized her aunt didn't hesitate out of nerves. Tucker left the door cracked open, probably so they could take their time and walk in when they were ready, but this caused a problem.

With both hands full, Desta would have to shoulder her way through and walk in backward. No woman wanted to introduce herself to a room full of men backside first!

"Oh!" Jess hurried to take one of the pies so they could do the thing in the right order. As soon as she had a firm hold, she followed Desta through the door, stepping to the side so she could stand next to her aunt.

Squinting at the change from soft violet twilight to a room

filled with dark corners and furniture thrown in shadow, she tried to get her bearings. The door blew shut behind her with a loud slam. Jumping at the sound, she came within a hairbreadth of letting one of the pies topple to the floor.

"Lemme give yer a hand!" The nearest man leapt to his feet and snatched the confection before she could thank him. He turned to go back to his seat, but found his way blocked.

His friends murmured about being happy to help as they relieved her and Desta of the remaining pies, bearing them back to their respective tables with the air of marauding Vikings displaying their plunder. The ridiculousness of the whole scene made Jess want to giggle. Then she snuck a look at Tucker.

The woebegone expression on his face as his eyes darted from table to table, trying to keep track of the vanishing pies, did her in. The giggle grew to a loud laugh she couldn't keep in. At the sound, everyone's attention snapped her way, but she didn't mind. The men grinned right along with her, and she figured they were off to a fine start before she so much as said hello.

"Nice of so many of you to lend a hand," Tucker's voice broke through. "But if you want to keep those hands attached, don't be touching those pies until after the ladies have their say."

"He's worried we won't save him a slice," someone stage-whispered loud enough to make everyone chuckle again.

Tucker snorted loud enough to rival an occupant from the stables. "Why would I worry about a fool thing like that? Every one of you boys knows that if my share goes missing, you oughta be the ones worried."

Groans and jeers mingled before he gestured for everyone to hush up. Everyone seemed to be directing his attention to her and Desta, but at the same time trying not to look too interested. Jess counted only a half dozen men and counted again. There should've been a good deal more men. Even accounting for some going with Ed, the numbers were low.

Even so, there'd seemed to be far more when they were jockeying for pies. These men took up more than their fair share of space with physical strength and outsized personalities to match. But despite evidence of those personalities as they joked with Tucker, none of them spoke up to ask about the pie bakers. *Then it's not just me—he makes a habit of keeping everyone waiting.*

"You boys are the lucky ones, since you're here tonight. No, I'm not just talking about the pie." He pointed at one of the men, who sat rubbing his stomach comically. "The men who hit the road with Ed and the ones riding roundup duty will have to hear the news secondhand when they get back."

"Or the ladies could come back with more treats," one of the two older men shouted. "We promise to keep our pieholes shut real respectful and listen like we ain't heard none of it afore!"

"Hush up there, Virgil! You'll talk us out of the first batch if'n you flap yore gums hoping for a second."

"I dunno what any of you rascals is hollerin' fer." A third older gentleman stepped onto the main floor from where he'd stood half behind the stove, hidden in the shadows. Half-stooped with wisps of white hair waving, he brandished a ladle with majestic outrage. "Actin' as though you ain't seen a pie in years. Didn't I make you shoofly pie last week? Sweet tater pie afore that 'un?"

"Mighty good it were, Cookie," the man called Virgil humbly assured the cook to a chorus of agreement.

"Dern tootin' it were good. Ain't a one of you ungrateful cusses who's been starved for dessert, but here you sit like plumb fools in front of these ladies. Yore makin' it seem as though I don't do my job, and I"—he drew himself up and pointed the dented ladle at each man in turn—"take umbrage with every one of yers!"

"Umbrage?" Someone slapped his knee. "If that ain't a five-cent word."

Jessalyn thought about interrupting them so they could get on with the introductions, but couldn't stop smiling long enough to be stern. The men might be a handful, but they were a hoot and a half. Until they knew who she was, she'd leave it to Tucker to give orders.

"Calm down, Cookie." Silence fell the instant Tucker spoke, and Jess couldn't help but be impressed. "You've been gut-griping more than usual since the roundup crew left, and I've let it slide since you suffered a disappointment. But that's enough. Everybody needs to sit down, shut their gobs, and open their ears."

"Yessir." He laid down the ladle in a disconsolate sort of way and shuffled over to join the other old-timer.

Rheumatism, Jessalyn guessed, trying not to wince in sympathy. It wouldn't make him hurt any less, and she didn't need to be one of his objects of umbrage!

"Good. By now you've all done a fine job of ruining your chance to make a good first impression on these ladies. Even though you all know Miss Desta, Simon, Ed, and I didn't see any need for formal introductions because there was no need to say more than howdy."

He stopped for a second. Even though Jess didn't turn her head to check, by the way the men straightened up and nodded, Tucker was glaring each of them into agreement. She hadn't bothered to wonder why Desta needed an introduction beyond coming clean about her family connections. Now, looking at the boisterous crew and imagining it tripled, Jess suddenly understood. They didn't know her because Tucker didn't allow them to talk to Desta.

A housekeeper could be vulnerable if a man's attentions proved unwanted. She often had the house to herself, and a former slave would be in more danger than most. Jessalyn didn't agree with it, but she knew it was true. *Tucker's been protecting my aunt from the same things he worked so hard to warn me about!*

Her chest squeezed, caught up in too many layers of emotion. Gratitude that Tucker looked after her aunt came easy. Something stronger, having to do with the realization that his lectures hadn't just been because he looked down on her as a wayward child, pinched more. *Tucker sees me as a woman, and one worth his protection.*

CHAPTER 16

*K*eeping *an eye on this woman is going to drive me insane.* Two evenings after he'd introduced her to the men and allowed her to start taking her place on the ranch, Tucker gritted his teeth and thought he heard a crack.

Not even five days since she rode up dressed like a man and only two days since he'd taken her to the mess hall, and Jessalyn Culpepper just about managed to fray his final nerve.

The men flat-out adored her and happily accepted Miss Desta because, as they pointed out, none of the other outfits could boast two ladies of the ranch. And even if they did, theirs weren't "half so purty or baked near as nice." Cookie made a point of ambling by and doing a dance step whenever Tucker looked his way, swearing by Jessalyn's poultice for helping ease his knee and "put the spring back in m' step."

Traitors. Down to a man, they raced to do anything "Miss Jess" asked. If it meant leaving something else half-done, they shrugged and promised to finish it later. If it meant showing her where to find something or how to use it, they volunteered to demonstrate. And the worst part about it was she took such care to precisely follow their agreement that he didn't have a leg to stand on when he needed to boot her out of ranch business.

She rode and flagged fences every morning. By day three Tucker anticipated her trick and made sure he got to the stables early enough to accompany her. He couldn't forbid it because she let someone know where she planned to ride, wore the split skirts to cover her creamy skin, and proved capable—if not adept—at getting the work done.

135

But that didn't mean he had to like it. Trying to get her to stop riding around her own property without an escort made for a losing battle. Even if Jessalyn weren't the sort to dig in her heels, he would've had a job arguing against it. So tomorrow morning would find him lurking in the stables, waiting to shadow her ride to whichever stretch of fence or pretty pastureland she wanted to visit.

His mornings spoken for, he tried to cram everything else into the rest of the day with limited success. Somehow the schedule got more and more scattered every time he ran into Jessalyn, and he ran into her at every turn.

In the corral where Virgil should've been working with an almost-broken filly, no horse bucked. The post lay empty—at least, it lay empty right up until the moment Jessalyn lassoed it. Thanks to Virgil, she'd already started to fine-tune her rusty roping skills.

Virgil beamed at her progress and seemed blithely unconcerned when she mentioned practicing hard so she could help in next year's roundup. But then, Virgil probably thought she was joking. Tucker knew better, but couldn't say much against it until Ed got here to back him up. So Tucker held his tongue.

In the stables, where Hank should've known better, Tucker had spotted Jessalyn cozying up to a stallion. What with all the changes around the ranch since Simon fell ill that last time, Tucker hadn't managed to more than start breaking the powerful horse. Yet here stood a slip of a girl, palming sugar cubes and spinning stories of moonlight rides she planned to take.

Tucker told her in no uncertain terms that she wouldn't be riding another unbroken horse as long as he remained at the Bar None. She'd sweet-talked her way into disaster once, and he wouldn't let it happen again. He gave Hank an earful, waving away the stable master's protests that "of course she ain't planning ta ride 'im. She just likes petting the horses. Thinks they get wistful when she treats Morning Glory special."

Thankfully, Tucker gained a reprieve. Miss Desta told him she

and Jessalyn would be working in the garden today. He half suspected the housekeeper-turned-aunt intentionally arranged to keep
her niece out of his hair for a day. As soon as he could figure out a
way, he'd thank her for it—then ask her to do it on a regular basis.

With the troublemaker neatly tucked away, he went to check on
Burt's progress with the lollygagging windmill. The horse grazing
nearby bore the distinctive markings of Jess's beloved Appaloosa, but
it didn't worry him. With the exception of unbroken mounts, the
men were allowed to use any horse in the stables. So Tucker's first
thought centered around changing that policy. The men needed to
be warned that Morning Glory served as Jess's personal mount so
they didn't take out an inexperienced pony.

He never made it beyond that first thought. The sight of her
split-skirted derriere ascending the windmill ladder had his heart
stuttering too fast and too loud to let him breathe properly, much less
think straight. Besides, why should he think straight when everyone
else on the Bar None abandoned the practice?

"Stop!" Tucker hollered the second he worked enough air into
his lungs. "Do not look down. Do not turn. Do not keep climbing or
try descending. Don't move a muscle."

She heard him because she paused for a beat with her hand mid-
air before reaching for the next rung. Tucker figured he'd have to
allow that because he wanted her to be as stable as possible, and that
meant gripping the ladder in as many ways as she could. It didn't
count as disobedience, he decided as he jumped from the saddle and
ran the last few steps.

But that *does*. In the time it took Burt to scramble out of Tucker's
way, Jessalyn moved up the ladder. Tucker knew because he heard
the soft clang of her heel against the metal and felt the accompanying vibration right down to his gritted-down teeth.

He grabbed the ladder and roared, "I told you not to climb any
more!"

"You also said not to look down," she called, looking down at him. "Or to descend. Since you left no other options than to cling to this ladder until Kingdom Come, I disregarded the order."

"You don't get to disregard an order because you think it doesn't leave you enough options," he seethed, slowly ascending. He went slowly because he didn't want his shifting weight to vibrate through the metal and disorient her. "And I don't want you getting dizzy. Stop looking down."

"Burt?" She kept looking down. "Would you mind taking the poultice from Morning Glory's saddlebag and running it over to Cookie? I planned to get back earlier, and I don't want him to be uncomfortable."

"Er. . .Boss?" Burt's uncertainty brought to mind a man scratching his head, but Tucker kept his attention fixed forward.

"And we don't want dinner to suffer either." Jessalyn's final prompting had the man scrambling to do as bid. Hooves thundered away from the scene by the time Tucker could touch the bottom of her boots.

He stopped, not sure what to do now that he'd gotten there. It wasn't as though carrying her down would be any safer than letting her do it under her own steam. Suddenly he was glad she'd sent Burt away. Tucker didn't need a witness to his foolishness.

"Well?" Jessalyn peered down at him.

"Well?" He looked up at her.

"I believe we've reached an impasse," she ventured, scraping one boot across the rung and lifting it to the next.

"That doesn't mean you keep going up!" He kept himself from grabbing her ankle, fearing he'd startle her.

"You've made it so I can't go down." Jessalyn tensed for the next step. "If you're afraid of heights, I won't tell anyone. Burt can't hear us. You can just work your way back down, and I'll be fine."

"Afraid of heights?" he echoed in disbelief. "No, I'm not afraid of heights. That's foolishness. I scale these things most every week."

"Then why all the carrying-on?" She made an *I'm disgusted*

sound in the back of her throat.

"Plenty of men start climbing, thinking it's fine. Then they look down and get dizzy. Their hands turn clammy. They freeze up or start to shake, and sometimes they fall." Tucker pushed back memories of digging a grave the one and only time he'd seen this happen. Since then he'd instituted a blanket policy at the Bar None.

He rode out with every hire then put him through the paces. He'd have the man climb halfway, practice checking for wasps, then come back down. If the man had no problems, he could go all the way up, grease the mill, and come back down. He found out real quick if the man went wobbly-kneed, forgot to check for wasps, or was otherwise unfit for duty.

"Not me. Stop worrying." With that, Jessalyn resumed climbing.

Fear, cold and unreasoning, pierced him. "I do this all the time," he burst out, following her upward. "You don't. And those skirts of yours could easily get tangled or throw off your balance. It's not safe."

She pshawed and kept going. He shadowed her, keeping a few rungs between them so he didn't crowd her, until they reached the top. Jessalyn ducked beneath the wheel blades then edged to the end of the platform to make room for him.

He sent up snatches of prayer—gratitude for the iron railing he'd insisted be installed around the platform. Thanks that the rod holding the wheel still against the wind looked unlikely to give way. Hope that he'd get Jessalyn back down the infernal ladder in one piece.

But until then, he'd give her a piece of his mind. He glared at her, but she didn't even notice. Hands braced against the railing—which was a foolish thing to do, considering she didn't know he had the thing regularly inspected—she looked out across the land.

A smile played about her lips; her shoulders rose and slowly lowered as she drew a deep breath. What might have been a gentle breeze on the ground moved faster up here, with enough force to lift the tip of her braid. Jessalyn just drank it all in.

I'll wait until she turns around, he decided, loathe to interrupt her delight. *A few more moments won't make any difference now that we're up here, so might as well let her enjoy the view.*

For the first time in many months, he found himself enjoying it. Part of that was the basic appreciation for a beautiful woman, no matter how infuriating he found her. But more than that, her love of the land made him recall his own. If nothing else came of this episode—aside from wrangling her promise not to scurry up any more windmills—she'd reminded him to look around with the eyes to see and appreciate God's handiwork.

When she finally spoke, the wind snatched the words from her lips and carried them to his ears. "You know, it used to drive Mama half mad when Papa took me along to the windmills. He started before I could even walk, you know."

Now that his heart beat at a normal rate again, Tucker's tension eased. Memories were a part of grieving someone. Sometimes they hurt, sometimes they healed, but they all helped loved ones hold on. How could he yell at her when she was talking about her papa? *Especially when I had a hand in creating the condition that killed him. . .* Guilt clutched him, keeping his words short.

"No, I didn't know that."

"He did the same thing with Ed. Mama didn't feel well a lot of the time, so Papa took us with him more often than you'd think. He said no child of his needed a wooden rocking horse when the rocking motion of a real one calmed babies better than anything. Papa lashed together a sort of holder, cobbled together out of bits of old harnesses. He slung it over his shoulders, plunked us down to sit against his chest, and would go riding. Lucky thing Papa was tall with long arms." She flashed him a sideways glance and grin.

Tucker grinned back, charmed in spite of himself at the picture her words painted. He still thought women and children shouldn't be toted up high ladders, but a bigger part ached at the silvery tracks glistening on her cheeks.

He tried to help her hold on to the good part of the feelings. "Yeah. Simon always said people learned by doing, and he made sure everyone on the ranch lived that out."

"Papa used to joke that if Mama wanted me to settle down for the night or a nap, she should dip the corner of a bandanna in leather polish and tuck it in the crib." She gave a tremulous smile, wiping the evidence of her sorrow with the back of her hand. "He teased, but one of the things Mama told me during her last days was that she took his advice. Except she used his shaving lotion instead."

As Jessalyn spoke, she rubbed her fingers along the side of the railing. Tucker imagined her wishing the motion could press her recollections into something she could hold on to. Whether she saw the past when she looked out at the horizon or the Bar None as it stood today, he didn't know.

Reliving the past took you half out of the present. If she'd been alone up here, that would be dangerous. But he could reach out and grab her in less than an instant if something went wrong. *She can fall into her memories. I'm here to catch her.*

CHAPTER 17

Looking out over the vista spread before her, Jessalyn fell in love with the Bar None all over again. How many canvasses had she sacrificed to abysmal watercolors that never captured the feeling of home? How many nights had she dreamt of this place, reliving cherished memories of a time when Papa went out of his way to keep her close?

Standing on the platform of the fancy new windmill, she realized she'd been more afraid to climb up here than she'd admitted to Tucker. Heights didn't frighten her—her own doubts had. *I was afraid the reality of this place wouldn't meet my memories.*

"I don't remember the last time I stood here and drank in the view." Tucker's voice rumbled next to her, deep and reassuring.

"That's a shame," Jessalyn acknowledged, but didn't follow up by saying anything more. Remembering so much left her feeling like half of her stayed stuck in the past. She wouldn't be able to keep up with much in the way of a current conversation.

But even though she didn't want to talk anymore and she'd wanted to swat at him like a fly when he followed her up here, bellowing orders, Jess didn't mind sharing the view with Tucker. His ridiculous worries helped keep her from growing too maudlin. More surprisingly, his company seasoned and softened her memories. Sweet things only half remembered gained strength when she shared them, enough to ease the bitterness of loss.

"I didn't used to think so, but you might be right." He pivoted slightly, his shoulders turning from hers then turning back as he took in the entire panorama. "When it comes down to it, the view

I remember looking at when I first got here is the same one you're navigating by."

The stubborn part of her still holding on to the past lifted its head. "Much remains unchanged. The pasture fences, the snaking path of the stream, the horizon line all stay the same."

"What God paints, man isn't big enough to alter. The landscape spraddles out the same as the first day I saw it, and probably the first day your pa saw it." His agreement eased her defensiveness. "The only exceptions would be where we diverted some of the streams and dammed them up to make watering holes."

She unbent enough to give him an accolade. For whatever reason, she always found it easier to offer a compliment once it wasn't expected any longer. Contrary though it might be, at least people knew she meant what she said. "I see you've expanded the western drink. That must've taken a good bit of work since the soil gets rocky out that way."

"We took it on in stages over two years since timing proved tricky. Too early in spring, the water load in the mud made it hard to haul and impossible to shore up in any kind of shape. Too late in the summer and it baked through." He looked that direction, approval softening the grooves bracketing his mouth.

"Two years," Jess echoed, hoping that would suffice. *Two years*, echoed her thoughts. He looked out over her land—part his, now, because Papa knew he earned it—and saw the results of a project years in the making. *What time or talent have I invested in the Bar None? What do I have to show for those same years? Nothing. Not a single blasted thing of any worth out here.*

Oblivious to the way her hands fisted on the railing, Tucker kept pointing things out. "The real differences are mostly from construction. The addition to the stables. The summer kitchen around the side of the mess hall. Even the windmill we're standing on are all new."

"Yes. I noticed the windmills." She tapped the railing. "White woodwork, ironwork painted green, blade and vane tips bright red.

Turns counterclockwise instead of normally. Very fancy rig."

"Fancy?" He pointed at the blades. "Curved blades, not straight slats, reduce wind damage. It's more efficient. They're stronger, sturdier, and much safer. I can't imagine even you would attempt climbing the old ones. Split skirts make a good choice for riding, but there's still too much fabric to go climbing ladders."

"Have you noticed," she began conversationally, "that no matter what I happen to be wearing, you object? My mama's dress was too short. Normal skirts were indecent for riding. Split skirts made you think I was a man and aren't safe enough for ladders. Why do I think it wouldn't make you any happier if I'd donned a pair of britches?"

His brows drew together so fast Jess almost expected to hear them crash. "Don't be ridiculous. We agreed you'd observe proprieties."

"When I do, you complain. I've followed each and every one of your guidelines, but every time I turn around you're glaring at me. Stop hovering. You act as though I put myself in mortal danger."

"You do!" Tucker burst out. "One second up here of not paying close attention can cost you your life. Grown men with full range of motion die every year from falling off a windmill. Vertigo, clumsiness, surprised by wasps after they build under the platform. It's risky at best to climb so high."

"You sound like my mother, worrying about what she couldn't control."

"Avoiding dangerous situations is the best way to control them, if you ask me." Tucker huffed. "I know you used to be close to your pa, but did you ever stop to think maybe your ma was right?"

Used to be close. . . The words hit hard. *We were close, until he sent me so far away, saying it was to keep me safe. Maybe Mama was right.*

"Mama always swore it'd be the death of her, the way we all ran wild on the ranch. She was almost right." Jess wrapped both hands around the rail, grappling with those memories. "Instead, it was Papa who died. I have no one to blame but myself for the fact I'm looking over his grave instead of talking to him now."

"I shouldn't have let you try to bust the bronco." In spite of their differences, Tucker wouldn't let her shoulder all the blame. "And Simon knew better than to jump the fence and rush up behind a bucking horse."

"He was worried for me, so he wasn't thinking. Just like I was worried about being sent away, so I tried to prove I belonged."

"You don't have to prove you belong. You never did."

His words slammed into Jessalyn's heart, and if she'd had any room, she would've staggered back. She couldn't. Nor could she walk away. No way to avoid the painful truth behind his observation. She braced herself as she would against a strong wind, hunching over and hoping the worst of its force would blow by. *I will not fall apart. Not up here. Not in front of him.*

The longed-for landscape, which had so deeply delighted her moments before, blurred. She thought she'd held herself together better than to start crying. Again.

Jess blinked, furious. Then she stopped. Her eyes felt. . .dry and gritty. She blinked again and felt better. *I stared down my own tears,* she thought with grim satisfaction.

"That didn't come out right," he apologized. Even after knowing him for such a short amount of time, it startled her to hear him sound so awkward. If his characteristic confidence deserted him for any other reason, it might have been endearing.

"Oh, I think it came out exactly right," she said dismissively, proud of the way her voice didn't catch. "I never did belong here—otherwise Papa wouldn't have sent me away."

"I meant you never needed to prove yourself!"

"Of course I did, but I failed, and so did my father." Jess swallowed her sorrow and pivoted to meet Tucker's gaze. "That day fear ruled me and my father, and we paid a terrible price for our poor decisions. Now that I'm finally home, I won't let fears stand in my way again. Not mine, and certainly not yours. So step back, stop shadowing me, and start treating me like you really believe I belong!"

❦

You don't have to prove you belong. . . . You never did. This ridiculous loop spun through Tucker's thoughts like a dropped dime. His off-hand remark did more than strike a vein—it hit an artery. Only when she'd curled in on herself, going pale, did he realize he'd dealt such a brutal blow.

Still, she withstood it. Tucker couldn't shake the memory of Jessalyn, stricken but strong, as she faced him atop the windmill. She refused to allow someone else's decisions to define or defeat her. Jessalyn accepted neither her father's perceived rejection nor Tucker's attempts at protection.

His unthinking comment knocked her back, but couldn't make her knuckle under. To the contrary. Past pain pushed her forward, driving her determination and inspiring her to issue edicts of her own. *Step back. . . . Stop shadowing me. . . .*

After his foolhardy rush up the ladder, Tucker didn't think he had legitimate grounds to refuse her. She'd adhered to his guidelines, but today he'd failed to follow her single rule—speak to her with respect. And he couldn't deny that he'd trailed hard on her heels since her first morning on the ranch.

Of course she noticed—and so had every other man on the place. He planned it that way. Tucker made sure everyone knew Jessalyn was under his protection. By now the men got the message. They understood and accepted that he'd be keeping a close eye on her. It played out so well he hadn't seen the flaw until after the fact.

What works on the men will never work the same with women. Jessalyn did not recognize the need for him to keep a close watch over her—and her unconventional pursuits—and would no longer tolerate it. *I have to find a new way to watch her. Sneakier this time.*

He couldn't argue with the timing—Tucker already postponed things more than he should have to keep an eye on Jessalyn. Now that she'd settled in as much as a woman like her could be settled, he had no time to lose. With Ed coming back with that supplemental herd, Tucker needed to get a de-horning corral and run built by the end of the week. The seller warned they'd be getting a temperamental lot—otherwise he wouldn't be selling so cheap. He wanted them off his hands and no one local wanted to buy.

The fact no one in the Victoria area would purchase the beef at such a low price and put it on the trail made Tucker leery. When Simon died, some of the standard crew packed up and moved on. No surprise there, but it left them shorthanded right at the start of the busy season. This year's trail drive would be hard slogging as things stood, and they didn't need cattle so cantankerous nobody else would take them on.

Ed disagreed enough to pull rank—something he'd never done before. This was the latest in a string of differences his partner displayed, and by now Tucker was downright worried about Ed's behavior. After folks stopped dropping by with condolences and cooked meals—which Tucker knew Ed never refused, as it gave Desta a break from the kitchen—he isolated himself.

Aside from church and any town trips Desta initiated, Ed didn't leave the Bar None at all anymore. He accepted no invitations to visit other spreads and gave none out. Worse, he'd increasingly withdrawn from ranch activities. He hadn't joined the men after church in so many weeks he'd finally forfeited his five-month run as checkers champion.

So when Ed dug in his heels and insisted on buying the bargain herd hundreds of miles away, Tucker tried to persuade him otherwise. But when Ed threw out that he'd go personally to supervise the transfer and transport, Tucker got on board. He'd take on a hard-to-handle herd if they pulled his partner back into the saddle. Besides, the dry winter pushed back the county roundup to early June. They'd be taking a late start since the cattle needed feeding up before they turned travel-ready.

The three-sentence letter Ed sent right before leaving Victoria sounded downright gregarious compared to his conversation before the trip. Ed reported that he found the animals as advertised—stringy, stubborn, and surprisingly aggressive for such a slow-moving set. He warned Tucker they'd need to clip their horns before trying to integrate the newcomers with the standing herd.

It only took a couple of ornery longhorns to throw off an entire herd. A couple of aggressive bulls made the others territorial and adversarial until the beeves got anxious. They didn't feed as well, they didn't travel well, and they caused all sorts of rumpus during round-ups. Basically, cattle were like people—bad habits spread quickest and were hardest to get rid of.

And with the county roundup already making its way to the Bar None, Tucker needed to move fast. Since the cattle proved so slow moving, Ed was behind schedule and didn't think he could make up much time over the last stretch. According to his telegram at the halfway point, he'd make it before roundup reached the ranch—but barely. They'd scramble to get the new additions ready, settled, and out of the way.

So even if Jessalyn hadn't flat-out ordered him to stop hovering, Tucker wouldn't have been able to stick close anymore. It bothered him. He no longer questioned whether or not Jess would find trouble if not watched closely. But he still questioned whether or not she'd be able to handle whatever mess she made.

I can't watch after her. Tucker hitched Happy Jack and headed for the mess hall, late for the midday meal but not feeling much hunger. He'd been planning on enlisting Miss Desta to keep an eye on her niece, figuring that once Jess settled in he wouldn't need to worry so much. *But now that I've seen her notion of "settled," I know better. Worse, now I know Desta can't keep track of her—or Jess wouldn't have made it out to the windmill today.*

Tucker decided to ask for guidance. *Lord, I know You watch over us from above, but down here Jess gets pretty hard to handle. I'd appreciate it if You saw fit to send help a little closer to home.*

CHAPTER 18

Y ore sportin' more wrinkles 'n a hard-boiled shirt, Boss." Ralph's comment caught Tucker before he walked right past the mess hall. "Means somethin's been wearin' on you. Why all the frownin'?"

"Trying to work out a plan, Ralph." Tucker backtracked a bit to where his friend propped up a wall. For most people that was just an expression for someone leaning around doing nothing, but Ralph Runkle stood taller and wider than anyone Tucker ever saw before. It seemed anyone's guess whether the man or the wall was the one doing the leaning.

"Chewing over a problem can get easier if'n you siddown and chew on somethin' else for a while. Fill yore stomach, clear yore mind, and when yore done, you might see things in a new light."

Tucker eased his hat up off his forehead, the better to look at his friend. "Seems to me most of your advice centers around eating, but I reckon that makes sense. You're so big it takes up half your time just to keep fueled. But for the rest of us, there's plenty of problems food can't fix."

"The right food from big enough platters could near 'nough fix the world, Boss." Ralph drew in a deep breath, as though smelling a far-off feast. Or maybe the smell of beef stew wafting from the mess hall. Either way, it underlined his statement with a sense of conviction.

"I doubt it. A good meal can't fix every problem." Though hearing Ralph talk about it so much prodded Tucker's appetite enough to have him walking into the mess hall.

"Think on it." His friend followed him in. "It's hard to find kindness in a man with his stomach lickin' his backbone. Hunger makes even the best of folks plain ornery."

"True enough." Tucker scraped the sides of the stewpot, rustling up enough to fill a tin. He found a pan of biscuits left warming in the oven and pulled out the whole thing. He carried the lot over to the nearest table, plunked it down, and looked up to see Ralph holding out a cup of water and a mug of coffee. "Thanks."

"So take away hunger, and already the world smiles more and squabbles less." Ralph hunkered down on the bench opposite Tucker. "Then you add in something sweet—like those custard pies from the other night—and a special sort of happiness perks up the place."

"Don't let Cookie hear you talk about those pies," Tucker warned after he swallowed half his stew. By focusing on the cook, he put off thinking about the women for a little longer. "He's riled over not going out on roundup and knowing he'll sit out the cattle drive. Rubs him wrong to see the men whose guts he keeps from grumbling go wild over someone else's grub."

"Nah. He might act persnickety, but Cookie knows there's a world of difference atween hearty chuck and a tasty tidbit," Ralph explained. "The meal sticks to a man's ribs, but somethin' with a li'l sugar sticks in his memory. Beans and sowbelly keep a man going through fair weather and foul with no bones 'bout it—but he'll go a whole lot farther on a whole lot less for that hint of sweetness."

"Why do you think that is?" Jessalyn's smile flashed through Tucker's thoughts. "Something might be sweet enough to stick in a man's mind, but it's gone and done with almost before he gets to enjoy it. How is something so fleeting powerful enough to make such a strong impression?"

"'Cuz it *is* strong. Sweetness lingers long past the last swallow, so when you think back on it, you can almost taste it again. Kind of like the best sort of dreams, the ones that leave you warm and hopeful even after you wake up and can't remember most of it." Ralph looked at the wall without seeing it then shook his head, looking sheepish. "Fanciful, but there you go. Sounds silly when you say it out loud."

"Nah, I know what the problem is." Tucker snorted with laughter at a sudden memory. "Sweet teeth. Some folks have a powerful sweet tooth, but you sound like you've got a whole set."

Ralph's deep, booming laugh joined his. "I like that," his friend decided after their mirth had run its course. "And not just because I have an excuse to hog the next pie. You stopped frowning."

"Thanks for that." Though now that he mentioned it, Tucker had a hard time keeping from doing it. "Though I haven't solved the problem yet. It's the kind I think I might never be able to solve."

"Well, how 'bout you tell me what set yore brain itchin' in the first place?" Ralph stretched and looked at him expectantly. "Maybe a spare pair of eyeballs can spot a solution."

"Funny you should say that." Tucker couldn't help but grin at the irony of Ralph's choice of words. "Because a spare pair of eyeballs is just what I need."

"Here I sit with two in fine working condition." Ralph widened his eyes and blinked for emphasis. "I can probably help you out."

That's it! The answer hit him so hard and so fast Tucker figured he should've seen it coming from a mile away. *Thank You, Lord. Ralph's my best worker and I'll have to come down heavy on everyone else to make up the difference, but I'd trust no one else to watch the women anyway. Now I just have to get him to agree.*

"Ralph, I think you can help me." Tucker planted his forearms on the table and leaned closer. "I need someone with a sharp set of eyes to take on. . .a special project for a little while. Up at the house, so I can't trust it to just anyone while I'm out all day."

"The house? To be working near the women while you're gone?" Ralph's eyes narrowed in determination, his chest puffed up in pride at being chosen. "You can trust me to look after 'em, all right."

"Yep." Tucker thought fast. "It's late to be starting, but Miss Desta's wanted a second garden for ages, and with all the upset this year we didn't do more than earmark a patch of ground. But it needs to be cleared, leveled, plowed under, fertilized, and fenced."

"I started in the fields early in life so land likes me just fine." Ralph raised a brow. "But I know it weren't no garden giving you frowning fits and making you need extra eyes. It's the part that goes alongside. Yore bothered 'bout not staying near enough to watch the women."

"Exactly so." Tucker paused, realizing he might be putting Ralph in a difficult position. His first in command didn't know Simon Culpepper left Tucker as part owner, and even so, Jess wouldn't take kindly to being babysat. "Now, Miss Jessalyn's been gone a long while, but she's come back raring to take her place at the Bar None. Her brother's not here to rein her in and show her the ropes, and she doesn't take kindly to being thwarted."

Ralph crossed his arms over his massive chest, looking like a warrior of old blocking an invading army. He said nothing, not letting on whether he was amused or disgusted at the thought of playing nursemaid to a grown woman who could fire him at will.

Tucker decided to spell out the worst of it before asking Ralph if he'd take the job. "Keeping an eye on her is more than making sure no one comes up to the house bringing problems—the biggest part is making sure she doesn't get loose to make her own."

"Mmmhmmm," Ralph rumbled, obviously lost in thought. He kept Tucker waiting for a minute before asking, "You want me followin' her if she leaves? 'Cuz I'll tell you, she'll know in a hot second. I'm a hard man to hide in a forest, much less on the open range."

"Do your best to keep her busy—we'll have Miss Desta helping with that. Maybe set them on some baking whenever you need them out of the garden." Tucker saw Ralph's shoulders straighten and his eyes gleam with what he now considered the Light of Pies Past.

"Yessir, that's a fine plan. Not one I woulda thought up, but I'm all for keeping them busy in the kitchen. If it'll help, I won't go to the mess hall for meals." Ralph's enthusiasm suddenly made Tucker wince. The man obviously never tasted Miss Desta's cooking.

"I'll leave that up to you. Head to the mess hall if you need a minute. If you've spent your days with women before, it's been long enough now that you might not remember longing for peace and quiet." Tucker figured that was fair enough. He'd given Ralph a way to avoid Desta's dishes without warning him away from the plan.

"Maybe they could chatter like magpies. Miss Jessalyn's new around here, and there's lots I don't know about Miss Desta on account of how it wouldn't be proper to mingle. I never knew she could whip up desserts like that or it might've been harder to stay so standoffish." The man's mouth practically started watering, and Tucker knew he had Ralph Runkle over a barrel. "I reckon a man can forgive an awful lot of yammering if'n the women follow it up with a li'l bit of baking."

"Then we'll tell her one of the perks I promised is something sweet every day until the garden gets done or Mr. Culpepper gets back. What do you say?"

Ralph clapped his hat back on his head, eager to get going. "Not much beyond the obvious—you ain't gonna hafta ask twice!"

Lord, what am I lookin' at? Desta paused, half hidden by the door she'd started to pull open before she caught sight of what was coming her way. She'd backed up and almost slammed the door before stopping herself. Last thing she wanted was for the men to think of her as the door-slamming sort.

Desta peeked around the edge, just to check and make sure she saw two men still heading toward her. She slipped back and softly pressed the door shut, yanking on her apron strings, grabbing a fresh one from its peg, and switching the two while she ran from the kitchen to the front hall. She prayed the whole way.

I know I bin prayin' for what seems like ages, tellin' myself You answer in Yore own good time and even then I might not hear what I'm hopin' for. Even with Simon here, my heart hurt with havin' so much room to spare, but nothin' ever got passed down from on high to change it until

You brought Jess home. Just a coupla days and that girl's done me a world of good already. I thank You for it.

She slid to a stop in front of the big mirror near the window, the one that got all the good light. If she'd wanted to keep close to the kitchen, Desta knew she could just as easily have stepped into the washroom. But it had no window in there, and taking time to light the lamps would've been all she could spare.

Desta peered at her reflection, swiftly straightening her collar and tugging a few curls free to soften her forehead and nestle beside her ears. A lick and a prayer smoothed her brows and the frizzles along her crown.

Tensing to start back, she halted and had to put a hand to the wall to keep from falling over. She twisted back to bare her teeth at her reflection, glad to see nothing stuck along the in-betweens. Satisfied but stifling a pang over her vanity, Desta bustled back to the kitchen, finishing her prayer along the way.

And I'm not one to question Yore gifts when You plunk 'em down on my doorstep, but I can't help but wonder why Yore seein' fit to set so much in motion all at once? It's got me downright frazzled. The Bible says we should try and be less like ourselves and more like You, so I'm gonna go ahead and ask right now for a measure of Yore peace to replace my own foolishness! And if'n Tucker's bringing that man here has nothin' to do with me, I pray You help me keep from feelin' disappointed. I try not to have hope unless I think Yore leading me that way, but sometimes I get a false start.

Desta gave a real start when a knock on the door shattered the stillness, even though she'd been expecting it. Putting a hand to her heart in a futile attempt to slow its frantic beating, she measured her pace to the door and took a deep breath before turning the handle. As she pulled it toward her, the opening widened to reveal two figures waiting—much like she'd waited and wondered over one of them for years before finally meeting him a few nights ago.

She sent up one more quick thought, unable to keep from asking. *Lord, please let him be worth all that wasted time!*

CHAPTER 19

Isn't it a bit late to be digging a garden?" Jess plunked down the bucket of milk she'd fetched from the springhouse and addressed her question to the room at large.

A room much fuller than it had been when she'd left it a few minutes ago. Something struck her as strange, a sort of untraceable tension that told her someone was up to something. She eyed the three people shooting looks at each other and revised her assessment. *They're* all *up to something. But what can it be?*

Whatever their plan, she deduced that it centered around the hulking black man with the blinding smile—Ralph, she remembered from meeting the men with Desta. That night, seeing him sitting down in a dimly lit room, his girth seemed immutably large—and largely immovable. Kind of like a big boulder that'd rolled farther than expected, adding interest to the landscape where it settled.

Now, seeing him standing so close, his sheer size struck her anew. Ralph held his arms tight against his sides and kept his chin tucked low as though trying to fold himself into a normal-sized person— a feat at which he failed extravagantly. The top of his head came within inches of the ceiling, shoulders stretching wide enough to make it seem as though the kitchen were shrinking, the encroaching walls compressing him. But the way he dwarfed Desta meant the kitchen hadn't diminished. It had been invaded by a giant.

Fee-fi-fo-fum! Jess recalled the lines from an old nursery tale as she stared at the massive man who wouldn't meet her gaze. She suppressed a smile as she changed the next line of the tale to suit her thoughts: *Are you an angry giant, or a friendly one?*

She noted again the way he tried to squeeze himself into a smaller amount of space than God intended, hunching so the others could speak with him more easily. Jess especially liked the way he smiled and tucked his chin against his chest when he looked at Desta, as though the special effort it took to meet her gaze was worth every uncomfortable second.

Of course, he wouldn't meet *her* gaze. Nor, come to think of it, did Tucker—though the set of his shoulders didn't look even remotely sheepish. If anything, Jess noticed a smug curve raising the side of his mouth, as though in satisfaction. Altogether, it looked as though she'd missed an awful lot during the short minutes she'd spent visiting the springhouse. Tucker had brought Ralph up to the house and talked her aunt into some sort of plot.

Jess could tell because Desta looked so nervous. Her aunt didn't exhibit any single mannerism to indicate anxiety—she fluttered through an entire supply. Jess pursed her lips and took stock of the way her usually calm aunt fidgeted. Toying with the tendrils near her ears, glancing up at Ralph and then away again, as though not wanting to get caught conspiring. Edging her feet closer to the men and farther from Jess in a clear sign of misplaced allegiance. Smoothing the front of her apron—

Wait. Jess blinked, but the snowy-white linen knotted around her aunt's waist didn't change. When Jess left, she had on the stained, worn-in one. They'd just spilled water on the table and she used the bottom of her apron to mop it up, so it looked crinkled and damp. Desta had laughed and told her it didn't matter because no one who came into her kitchen would give her a hard time about it except maybe Tucker, and that didn't cause her any concern.

As Jess stood there, trying to figure out when and why she'd made the change, Desta swayed a little. Jess spied the apron strings—not hastily looped in a quick pull-out design for easy removal, but tied in a perfect, jaunty bow. Her aunt half turned so her torso angled toward Ralph, her smile flickering bright before she sent Jess a guilty glance.

And while she looked over at Jess, the smile Ralph sent down to Desta burst into a beaming grin. Suddenly her aunt's nervous tics made sense. Desta wasn't just nervous about whatever the trio planned to spring on her niece. *She's preening.* Jess marveled. *They like each other, but don't know if the other one is interested!*

The whole scene suddenly seemed downright adorable, and Jess had no difficulty plastering a smile on her own face. Whatever plan the three of them had thrown together, it couldn't be very sound. Not when two of the conspirators were hatching plans of their own. When it came right down to it, she wouldn't need to worry much about the circling couple—it all came back down to her and Tucker.

"If I'd known I'd find you two here when I got back, I'd have brought more milk." She nonchalantly crossed the room, passing directly in front of them to put the cheese on the shelf. "Though I expect you'd be just as happy with coffee. Perhaps even more so."

"Probably, ma'am." The deep bass of Ralph's voice rumbled through the room, making Jess wonder if the forks in the drawer were set into motion, vibrating in concert to his low pitch. "Thank you."

"Let me!" Desta spun on her heels, setting her skirts and snowy apron swirling in a pretty display as she hurried to the stove and started preparing mugs for their unexpected visitors.

"Though no one answered me when I asked about the garden?" She repeated the question, absolutely certain that a vegetable patch was the least of what these three were planning to put in place. "It's the end of May. Especially after such a dry winter and unpredictable spring, we've missed the spring planting. Wouldn't we do better to try for the second season in July so we reap a late harvest and can manage winter plantings?"

"Oh, believe you me, Miss Jessalyn." Tucker's smirk grew. "I wouldn't let myself lose Ralph's help for the next couple days without making sure I'll reap something worthwhile."

"A couple days?" she repeated, mind snagging on that phrase and Tucker's assurance that he'd be getting something out of the deal.

"I can move a lotta land when I puts my mind to it and my back into it," Ralph promised with that easy grin of his. "Grew up working in fields. Started out so early on account of my size, cultivating earth feels almost like catching up with an old friend."

"Shorely we can offer you better comp'ny than that." Desta summoned enough bravery to make the offer, but her courage got caught up after that. She kept her eyes fixed on her too-clean apron and missed Ralph's expression of surprised delight.

"You wouldn't have to stretch yourself either," Ralph agreed with touching eagerness. "Whoever invented the description 'dull as dirt' must've spent time plowing. Mammy always said, 'Corn grows ears and taters sprout eyes, but ain't a crop yet that can chitchat.'"

Desta's laughter brought her chin back up. "Maybe we'll make my garden the first to cultivate corn. . .with conversation on the side!"

All those years of academy classes on clever discourse and genteel flirtation—wasted. Jess marveled at her aunt's version of witty repartee. *Some things can never be taught in a classroom.*

"Sounds like you'll be serving up something special." Tension eased from Ralph's shoulders, his loosened stance edging his bulk a bit closer. "Tucker here can tell you, I never turn down a meal."

Desta fairly glowed up at Ralph, while Tucker started to look uneasy for the first time in the conversation. He shifted his weight as though trying to find more room. Given his proximity to Ralph, who took up even more space now that he'd relaxed his rigid posture, that seemed a reasonable assumption. But something Jess pegged as concern crossed Tucker's face, making her think he wanted to distance himself from the discussion, too.

Maybe it's taken him this long to realize they're talking about more than crops. Jess corralled a smirk of her own, not wanting the other occupants of the room to misread her expression. *And now that there's some kind of emotion attached, it unsettles him.*

She saw a chance to capitalize on his discomfort, cashing in on his awkwardness to earn some answers. Jess wasn't about to let her suspicions lie fallow like that untouched patch of ground out-side. Tucker swore it'd be worth the sacrifice, but what they planted would almost certainly wither in the heat. Obviously he stood to gain something else. *But what?*

"I believe you don't turn down meals, Ralph." Jess kept her voice even and unthreatening. "What I'm hoping you can help me under-stand is why Tucker's willing to sacrifice your assistance for the sake of a too-late garden."

"I can't rightly say, Miz Jess. Maybe just the satisfaction of knowin' he's got things squared away like yore father would've wanted." Ralph paused respectfully at the mention of her father, and Jess was grateful he hadn't plowed ahead. That extra moment meant she wouldn't miss the rest of his words because the mention of her father still brought with it a cold shock of grief.

"Lotsa things got pushed back this year, but Tucker is a better-late-than-never sort of man. Even if he has to put somethin' off, he still makes sure it gits done as soon as can be."

"It's our final chance, even if it does fail." Tucker looked both abashed and determined. "We won't have a second to spare once Ed gets home."

Yes. Other things will change once Ed gets home, she tried to reassure herself, doubt hollowing her stomach as it did every time she men-tioned her brother's return. It made the tiny, vicious voice from the back of her brain start wondering whether or not Ed would welcome her at all. It'd be the shock of his life to find her already ensconced at the Bar None when he thought she'd stayed in England—and the brother she remembered didn't like surprises.

Jess swallowed and tried to recall the peace she'd felt up on the windmill, calming as she thought about the change she'd set in motion. *Even if Tucker were inclined to keep nipping at my heels, I laid down the law. And it looks like he actually listened, since he's turning his focus back to getting the ranch caught up again.*

At that heartening thought, she wondered how he'd react if she excused herself from the kitchen and headed for the stables right then and there. Surely he wouldn't dare tag along? *Maybe I'll tell Aunt Desta not to bother with supper yet. I'll grab a fishing pole and head for the old stunted oak to catch a fresh supper instead.*

She eyed the trio standing with unnatural stillness near the shelves and tried to figure out how many fish she'd need to catch since Desta all but invited the men to dinner. Ralph alone would eat heaven-only-knew how many. Tucker couldn't match his friend's appetite and wouldn't set the pace, but he'd do his best to keep up. The man couldn't stand to be left behind or left out.

Which was why she wanted to test him by taking off. *Even if he's inclined to buck my orders and ride along, he won't have the time. By planting Ralph here to sow the garden, Tucker won't have a moment to spare, much less hours to waste playing my new shadow.*

Her eyes fell on Ralph while she mused. The man took up most of the kitchen, so he naturally drew the eye—and suddenly Jess saw things clearly. She looked from Tucker to Ralph and back again, fuming. *I forbade Tucker from shadowing me, but he hasn't abandoned the job. Instead he's trying to outmaneuver me by delegating it!*

Even worse, he thought he'd gotten away with it. Jess's fingers curled with frustration as the entire plan took shape in her thoughts. No one planted a garden when it was nearly June, and she'd been absolutely right about Tucker not having manpower to lose right now. But for him the timing was perfect. In a couple of days, Ed would be home and could ostensibly take her in hand without Tucker dirtying his anymore.

But until then, he'd concocted a scheme to free up his time and still keep an eye on her. Ralph might make a garden, but his true work was making sure Jess didn't fly free in Tucker's absence. She opened her mouth to denounce their plot and tell them they couldn't keep her cooped up like a willy-nilly peahen.

But Desta spoke first. "Well, I reckon we all know there's gonna be plenty of changes 'round here, so why don't we start with a good'un? Jess and I'd be honored if you two would share our supper."

Ralph's enthusiastic acceptance overrode whatever Tucker muttered about how he might not make it back to the main grounds before supper. It also overrode Jess's need to let them know they hadn't fooled her. Watching Ralph and Desta fan their tail feathers and dance around made her realize there were worse things than letting someone think they got the best of her.

Like stealing away what's best for someone I love. Jess's jaw unclenched, and her fingers uncurled as she looked at her aunt's eyes, shining emerald bright. Exposing Tucker's plot would make him cancel the whole thing, which meant Jess needed to consider her options.

Cut someone's schemes short, or cut everyone a little slack. Jess caught herself bristling at that one, since the whole group denied her any leeway while they reined her in. But a choice went deeper than the decision, so she looked at the reasons beneath:

Be selfish to appease my temper and call Tucker on the carpet—or be patient for Desta and give Ralph the chance to come calling. Jess smiled. When you got to the heart of the matter, the only thing that mattered was the hearts involved. *I'll table my temper and keep quiet long enough for Aunt Desta to cultivate that conversation.*

CHAPTER 20

*S*ay something! Desta couldn't figure whether the voice in her head and the voice in her heart joined forces to yell at her or if one of them was trying to holler at Ralph. Either way, her nerves jangled.

She and Ralph left Tucker and Jess in the kitchen to talk over whatever crossed their minds, which meant they'd be crossing a lot of other things before they got through. Swords if they could've reached such a pair of weapons, words since those could cut just as deep, and—though Desta hadn't seen it firsthand as of yet, she felt sure the day would come—even crossed eyes when the whole hullabaloo got to be too much.

But however they chose to say it, at least those two were talking to each other instead of themselves. Desta couldn't think of a single thing that didn't sound false, forward, or flat-out silly, and Ralph showed no signs of opening a discussion. She started to sigh, caught herself, and glanced sideways to see if Ralph took notice of the odd, hiccuping sort of noise that came out instead.

"Thinkin' on how you want to get on with things?" He gestured in the general direction of her garden and the barren plot beyond.

You got no idea. Desta tightened her lips against the laugh, refusing to let loose another strange sound. It got harder the more she thought about it. *For all that back-and-forth about cultivating conversation, I sure don't have much to get to work with!*

"Always thinkin' out how to get on with something or other, but as for the garden, Simon and I mapped it out ages ago. I'll dig it out of his study for us to follow—wouldn't set right to change anything now that he can't have his say anymore." She drew a shallow breath, unable to avoid the pricks of grief imbedded in the memory.

Funny thing about painful memories—once you got prepared for the pain in them, you stopped thinking of those times as often. Maybe that was how it worked; time wore away the sharp edges until even the worst memories slid alongside less hurtful ones. But grief for Simon was still fresh enough to catch her off guard—and often.

"Some folks like flowers, but Mr. Culpepper had a practical bent. I'm thinking he'd appreciate yore choice to honor his memory this way. Keeps a bit of him alive and growing alongside you."

She sniffed again, comforted by his understanding. "I hadn't thought of it like a tribute, but now I will. A place to think on him surrounded by life and plenty. . .we have to make sure it thrives."

"Lotsa ways to go 'bout building something up," he told her, "with only one way to tear it down. We'll build this garden yore brother's way, but lay the groundwork with extra-special care."

"I don't think I could stand it if'n I saw Simon's memory garden full of withered, dying things," she admitted. "So tear away anything that's kept it from bearing fruit so we can start fresh."

"Could say the same thing 'bout most folks I know needing a fresh start so they can make their days fruitful. Soil ain't got soul, but the promise of either one can be buried beneath rough spots, thorny patches, and rocks until nothing good takes root."

"You got a special way with explainin' things. If'n you ever get tired chasin' cows and don't want to plow more fields, you might could consider preachin'." Desta slanted a sideways glance at him and smiled.

"Readin' catches me up most times," he admitted. "Though if I sit with a pencil I can usually make sense of the words before me."

"Making sense of scripture sometimes takes a lot more sense than regular reading folk can boast." Desta paused, considering whether or not she should tell him she couldn't read a lick. In the end, she decided to keep the focus on what she wanted to know about Ralph Runkle instead of what she didn't like telling about herself.

"That don't qualify me to preach. God's got to call a man to that."

His voice, so deep it never seemed truly quiet, deepened another notch. "So I'll be sticking around awhile longer."

"Then we can settle this here garden!" She tried to leave it light and playful, but something prodded her toward honesty. "And I'm glad. Selfish though it may be, I'd hate to think I drove you off the very first time we talked."

"You think atwixt the both of us, one or the other would've figured out a way to strike up an acquaintance long ago." His message hit her heart-deep, and she breathed it in like air itself. "But I wouldn't do it. Not when Tucker and Mr. Culpepper worked so hard to make sure the men wouldn't dare to pester you. Me trailing around after you would give others the wrong idea and undo too much of yore protection. I couldn't risk it. I wouldn't risk you."

"I can make up my own mind 'bout taking risks, Ralph Runkle." She had to chide him, but the words lacked heat. *I held back, too.*

"Now things 'round here is changing, yore more protected with the men knowing yore connection to the family, and having Miz Jess in the house helps keep things proper if'n I'm around. I thought that straight off when you two came to the mess hall—that now I might find a chance to get to know you better." He grinned, and she did the same. "So now that we're standing here, tell me about yoreself. Even after that announcement, yore still made up of mysteries."

Not so much mysteries as secrets. The light, joyous feeling he brought her began to evaporate as she tried to figure out what to tell him and how much she could venture before the old ghosts raised by the conversation haunted her once more. *Start slow and easy.*

"My mamma was mulatto." Desta started with the obvious. "So with my father bein' white, I'm what they call a quadroon." Black enough to be a slave, too light to be accepted by the others. Quadroon seemed a good description, since it spoke to having her life parceled out in pieces that cut her off from everyone else.

"God decided what went into making you, and that's all I need to know 'bout that. Pretty as you are, it ain't yore hide that makes you who you are. That's just the covering." For the first time that day, Ralph's smile disappeared. He suddenly seemed even bigger than before, staring down at her so fierce. "Don't tell me about *what* you think you are, Desta. Tell me *who* you've grown into on the inside."

Dumbstruck, Desta stared at him. Her heart softened and stretched toward the man standing in front of her, the sensation both a wonder and a warning. She fought to find the right words. "All my life, people seen my skin and thought they knew everything they needed or cared to know. Going deeper's going to take some getting used to." She hesitated. "It's going to take some time."

Ralph's smile returned. "It takes time to grow anything worth keeping. I don't mind the time spent cultivating our conversations, if it means we grow together. I'll put in however long it takes."

"Ten minutes!" Tucker bellowed loud enough to rattle the house windows as he pulled up the buckboard. "Or I leave without you!"

He snorted at that, knowing full well he wouldn't dare head to church and leave the ladies behind. Not on any Sunday morning, but especially not on Jess's first churchgoing. If she didn't strip his hide over a move like that, Miss Desta would gladly do the honors.

For all he knew, even Ralph would side with the women. He'd spent so much time over at the house these past couple of days, Tucker wouldn't put it past him to change camps. He handed out orders; the women served up those sweets Ralph hankered after. Maybe Ralph caught on to something. Since getting his daily ration of dessert, he'd been in such a good mood it got downright irritating at times.

For Tucker's part, he'd gotten the branding chute built and pretty much everything ready for whenever Ed showed up. He figured it would probably be another two days, and thanks to Ralph, Tucker felt pretty good about that. They'd kept Jess safe this long; they could handle another two days. Especially with one of them a church day.

Not even Jess can get herself into trouble at church.

It was one of those rare one-mug mornings, when a man had things well in hand without needing a few extra cups of coffee to shore him up. And given all the upset at the Bar None over the past few months—and past few days in particular—Tucker planned to relish the short-lived satisfaction of having everything under control.

Then Jessalyn stepped onto the porch to grind his sense of peace beneath the heel of her dainty dress shoes. "I'm ready!"

I'm not. She gave a little twirl so he could take in the whole picture. She might as well have come out and punched him in the gut. From the look of her, he didn't think the town would be ready either. It wasn't as though he'd expected her to trot out the door in those split skirts, riding boots, hat, and braid he'd come to think of as her ranch uniform, but no one would have expected this. *Weren't they supposed to teach her the finer points of etiquette at those fancy academies she'd stayed at for so long?*

But time was running out. It looked like he'd have to point out the problem himself without damaging her delicate feelings.

"What's that you're wearing?" There. He'd started out with something vague and not insulting. Maybe he'd get lucky and Jess would realize she needed to change without him having to say anything specific.

"My Sunday best." She reached back to tug her bustle into a better position. "I didn't bring much from England, but this was my favorite dress. Lucky thing that I brought it along, really."

Lucky? His pulse picked up to pound at his temples. It would be bad enough that she looked like some sort of picture from a magazine come to life. The dress might be high necked, long sleeved, and hung far enough to cover everything but the tips of her toes, but that didn't make it prim or proper. The design showcased her figure to the point Tucker wouldn't want her wearing it in any color combination, much less today's attention-grabbing getup.

A row of buttons dotted the bodice from the collar to her hips, drawing a man's eye from her nipped-in waist up to the curves encased by her corset beneath. The bustle emphasized the line of her hips, meaning men would be staring at her whether she was coming up to them or leaving them behind. The fabric didn't cling or pull, but it followed her lines in a loving manner that made a man's hands itch to do the same.

"Lucky or not, you can't wear that!" he burst out, unable to stay quiet at the thought of every man in town getting an eyeful of her in this getup. He worried when she ran around the ranch in those split skirts, but now he saw the true horrors ahead. After today she wouldn't be running around under her own steam—she'd be going full-tilt trying to escape the horde of men who'd come chasing after her!

That'd be a sight to make a strong man break out in a cold sweat.

"Why not?" She planted her hands on her hips, making his eyes follow the line laid out by those blasted buttons all over again. "I can't believe you're criticizing my clothing yet again. It's the gospel truth that you'd object if you found me wearing sackcloth and ashes!"

CHAPTER 21

Let's find out. Go try that on and come back." He knew she'd been half-joking, but Tucker wasn't. Truth of the matter was, sackcloth and ashes would come across more appropriate than this getup.

"There's not a thing wrong with this dress, Tucker Carmichael. It's not so fancy that it can't be worn into a church." She sounded outraged and sad all at once, and Tucker felt the pinch of remorse that he'd hurt her feelings. Then she took a deep enough breath to make those buttons dance.

He just about choked on his own tongue, his remorse going the way of the buffalo. When Tucker regained enough control to speak, he tried to be kind. "It's not because it's too fancy, Jess. It's because you should be in mourning for your father. This is the first time the townsfolk will see you since your childhood. You don't want to leave them thinking you came back from England with your nose so high in the air you can't be bothered to honor him. I know it's not true, but that's how folks'll see it."

"He's right, and I told you the same thing." Miss Desta finally chose to make an appearance, and Tucker didn't know whether to glare at her for taking so long or hug her for taking his side. "So don't open and close yore mouth like a bullfrog hopin' for flies. Tucker might not have the prettiest manners, but his heart's in the right place and he wants you to get the best welcome possible once we get to town."

He gave a fervent nod but kept his mouth closed tight. When things were going his way, a man shouldn't toss around too many words. More often than not, they tripped him up.

Jessalyn nibbled on her lower lip, lost in thought. Then she rallied. "I thought you agreed with me, Aunt Desta, that people would understand I left England as soon as I got word and haven't had time to get mourning clothes made up. Surely it speaks well of me that I used all haste to return home?"

"O' course it does. I'm just sayin' Tucker didn't think about that, and it does no good to get spittin' mad when, in his own awkward way, he tried to do you a kindness. Not every man would speak up." She raised a finger in warning. "You know as well as I do that even under these circumstances yore gonna have a job explainin' away that color."

"It's the only church dress I brought along." Jess smoothed a hand down the side of her skirts in evident enjoyment, and Tucker's fingers tingled to follow suit. "It's my favorite color." Her voice softened, so he strained to hear it. "On the rainy days in England, it always reminded me of home."

The comment caught at something inside him and held fast. Suddenly it didn't matter what anybody else in the whole county thought about Jess's dress. *It's a fine choice. I'll defend it to anyone who dares say otherwise.*

"I can see that." His voice sounded like he'd been stuck in a sandstorm. "It's cheerful." The very words had her brightening back up.

"Like sunshine," Jess agreed. "And summer straw, and shortcake… some of my favorite things in the world."

Warm, sweet-smelling, welcoming things, Tucker noticed. Each one a way to connect a different sense to what she'd missed. Sight, smell, taste. . . Jessalyn's favorite things revealed how hard she'd fought against feeling homesick. It made him appreciate anew how much she loved this place.

"There's the shoes and parasol to help sober it up," she added, looking down at herself. "And at least the buttons are black."

"I noticed." He croaked the words and cleared his throat, wishing for some water. "I did notice the buttons." Tucker ignored the look Desta threw him.

"Black and yellow like a li'l honeybee. And pretty enough to bring all the menfolk buzzing around." Desta confirmed his worst fears. "Be careful."

"She's in mourning,"Tucker snapped. "If the men have any sense of respect, they'll keep their distance until she's had time to grieve and settle in."

"She's mourning, all right, but in that dress she don't look it." Desta raised a brow. "Men have always followed what they see first and what someone tells 'em second. You mark my words—they'll start to swarm until she swats enough of 'em away. Even then. . ." Her comment trailed off, and Tucker's thoughts followed.

Even then, she's too pretty for them not to pester. How did I ever think Jessalyn wouldn't find trouble in a church? He could've kicked himself. *That's where they hold weddings!*

But Desta's comments hadn't just given him pause. Jessalyn stepped back onto the porch, closed her parasol, and fingered the ruffled edge. "This would all be so much easier if my brother were here. And if I had some time to get to the dressmaker. Maybe it would be better to wait."

Overcome with relief at her sensible suggestion and trying not to beam from ear to ear, Tucker didn't notice how wide her eyes got until Desta elbowed him. While he took note of Jess's sudden stiffness, she whispered one word.

"Ed?"

At first Jess had been so wrapped up in defending her dress that she didn't see Tucker's objection as anything other than his perversely persistent need to insult whatever she wore.

Once she realized his concern, her indignation lessened. Whatever else she could say about Tucker Carmichael—and Jess could come up with an awful lot even after so short a time—he truly respected her father and went out of his way to honor his memory.

Then when Aunt Desta couldn't resist making another comment about the color of her dress, Jess finally saw her inappropriate clothing as the golden opportunity she'd hoped for. Here was a valid, inarguable—since both Tucker and Desta had already made the arguments for her!—reason to wriggle out of going to church.

Under normal circumstances Jess disliked wasting a morning sitting on a hard bench, listening to another lecture. She figured she got enough of that on a daily basis, thanks to whatever academy she was stuck in. Because no matter what anyone said, that was what sermons really were—lectures. Chock full of "thou shalt nots," which invariably sounded a lot more interesting than the much shorter group of "thou shalts." Why was it no one in the whole wide world ever instructed in terms of "thou could if thou didst wish"?

Now that she'd gotten home, going to church was a gauntlet she didn't want to face. All the people she'd known seven years ago, whom she might or might not recognize, trying to see whether or not they recognized her... She hadn't considered that any of the local men might be interested in pursuing her until Tucker mentioned it. Since men outnumbered women by such a wide margin, it added to an already long list of challenges sure to be lurking in the church.

The biddies would stick up their noses at her dress, how she spoke, the fact she was proud to claim Desta as her aunt. The gossips would ask overly solicitous, stabbing questions about her long years away, searching for scandal. Worse, they'd find it. Jess and Desta decided they weren't going to hide their relationship for even half a second. Partly because Desta already got the ball rolling back in the mess hall and didn't want to lose momentum, but mostly because Jess knew she'd slip up and say "aunt."

Making that announcement while Ed was away would add fuel to the flames, making people speculate that he didn't approve. It didn't feel as though that would be fair to her brother, but Jess couldn't see a way around it. It also didn't seem fair that Ed would literally be the last in town to know she'd come home, but again, she couldn't switch the days of the week to better accommodate his arrival.

Swapping days of the week wasn't an option, but thanks to her dress, swapping the week itself was something she *could* arrange. It went to show there were more benefits to packing light than she'd ever suspected. The more she thought about it, the more relieved and excited she became. By staying behind when Tucker and everyone else went to church, she'd have the Bar None all to herself. It seemed like the perfect reward for holding her peace over what she liked to call the Great Garden Plot.

I can go anywhere I want with no one to stop me.

When she started to say that she'd rather wait for her brother, she spotted a lone rider making his way up the drive. The figure headed toward the stables, but suddenly veered to the left and made his way toward the house. Jess figured he'd seen the buckboard.

"Ed." She whispered his name, unsure why she felt so certain, but nevertheless knowing it all the way through her bones. *My brother's come home.*

Jess watched him ride up as if frozen, unable to move a muscle or even repeat his name. Dimly, she realized Desta noticed her reaction first, then Tucker. By the time they figured out she wasn't the one they should be looking at, Ed had all but reached them.

"Ed!" Tucker boomed out.

When she finally convinced one of her feet to move, Jess considered slipping into the house while the men greeted each other. But it was too late. The bright dress that should have been her saving grace became a beacon. She saw her brother gesture toward her, saw the awkwardness of Tucker's stance, the pause before he shook his head.

He didn't tell Ed who I am. The realization would've robbed her of breath if her lungs had been working. Gratitude that Tucker would let her greet her brother on her own terms and get to see his reaction firsthand swirled against a cowardly regret.

It would've been so much simpler to watch from a distance. In fact, after spending so many years on opposite shores of an ocean, a reunion from opposite sides of a wagon seemed almost like a logical progression. It made sense to close the gap in stages, leaving a little space to act as a buffer.

I might need that buffer. Ed's anger would be easier to bear if she had time to compose herself before facing it. A little distance now couldn't guarantee they'd be close later.

Tucker came back around the buckboard. He looked up at her and touched the brim of his hat in a gesture of respect and reassurance. Then, without a word, he led the horses and the wagon back to the stables. Once he'd gone, Jess suddenly realized Desta had disappeared, too.

Because she wanted to give us privacy, or because she didn't want to get caught in the middle? As soon as Jess thought it, shame assailed her. The aunt she'd never expected had been more supportive than she could've hoped. If she thought Jess might need help holding her own against Ed, she would've stayed.

And so would Tucker. She didn't know why the thought crossed her mind, but Jess realized its truth in the same way she'd recognized her brother from afar. Some things went beyond what the eyes could see.

"Hello." Ed approached the porch cautiously, as though uncertain of his own welcome. Dusty, disheveled, and sporting the unkempt beard of a man who'd spent weeks driving cattle, he looked nothing like she remembered. Jess knew he didn't recognize her yet, and that brought on a bittersweet rush of emotion. *If I hadn't been waiting for him to get back, would I have marked him as my brother?*

She hated to admit it, but she probably would've walked right past him on the street. He cleared his throat, and belatedly she realized she hadn't returned his greeting. For all he knew, a stranger stood on his porch, blocking his door and refusing to talk to him.

"Hello, Edward." Jess thought her voice sounded thin, as though the words were squeezed through a tea strainer.

"You have me at a disadvantage, ma'am." Ed dragged the hat from his head as though only just remembering he should do so when talking with a woman. "I'm afraid I can't place you."

"It's been a long time." Jess wanted to smile, but her face felt frozen.

He peered up at her, and now that half his face wasn't hidden beneath his hat, Jess could see the green of his eyes. *Papa's eyes.*

Desta shared the color, but not the same shape. Jess's throat tightened when she spied the crinkly lines gathered around the corners of Ed's eyes—even that was just like Papa's. Suddenly, getting to know her brother all over again didn't seem like something scary at all. Same eyes, same person, only older.

"How long?" Ed wanted to know. He tilted his head, looking at her face as though trying to read the answer for himself. Maybe he could, if she waited long enough.

But I've already waited too long. It's past time to close the distance between us. With that decision, Jess discovered she could move again. She gave a tentative smile and stepped forward—a step of faith in the older brother she'd adored.

"So long that the last time I saw you, your voice cracked whenever something got you excited." She bit her lip to keep from chuckling at the sudden surge of memories. Jess saw Ed's eyes narrow in thought then widen with recognition.

"Jessie?" Ed rushed toward her. He stopped one step below where she stood. Close enough to hug, but hesitating until she confirmed his guess.

With the stair staggering their heights, they could look each other straight in the eye. It seemed a fitting thing for their first face-to-face meeting in half a decade.

"Good to see you, Eddie." Jess surprised herself by not holding still until he hugged her, but instead reaching for him at the same time he took the final step up the stairs to close his arms around her.

For a while they stood that way, as though a hug could reach back through the years. Maybe, if they held on tight enough, the embrace would link them back to the life they'd once shared—and help connect them to each other again.

Jess leaned in close, resting her cheek against his shoulder and reveling in the unconditional acceptance from the last member of the family she'd missed so long. *Mama's gone. Papa went to join her while I was too far away to say good-bye. . .but Ed's still here. Even better, he wants me here.*

His hand rubbed circles on her back, much the same way Mama used to soothe them when they were sick. Ed rested his chin on the top of her head, so the embrace completely enfolded her. She closed her eyes and breathed deep, wanting to both draw out the moment and draw in the sense of closeness. Her eyes flew open as reality, unpleasant and unapologetic, horned in on her reunion.

Her brother might be happy to see her and give some of the best hugs in the world, but Ed was fresh off a cattle drive. . .and fresh would be the last word Jess could use to describe him. Once she got past all the worry making her hold her breath, resting her cheek against his slicker didn't seem like such a good idea anymore. He stank.

When she lifted her head, he drew back—but only to arm's length. He cupped his hands atop her shoulders as though he needed to be able to pull her close again. Ed stared at her as though to memorize her features—or maybe he searched for the girl he'd known within the woman who'd come home.

"I can't believe you're home. It's so good to have you back, Jessie." Happiness made his volume rise with each syllable. "Last I heard from your headmistress, she'd refunded your tuition and sent you packing back to Ma's parents. How is it you're already here?"

"Oh, I made alternate arrangements." Jess decided now wasn't the time to discuss the details of those arrangements. She'd avoided going into the particulars with Tucker, and the practice in evading probing questions would serve her in good stead now. "The important thing is I'm home safe and sound and ready to help you run the Bar None."

His brows almost hit his hairline, but Ed didn't disagree. With one swift motion, he turned them both, keeping one arm slung about her shoulders as he guided her inside. "We've got a lot to talk about."

CHAPTER 22

Y ou should've told me." Ed didn't mince words when he came to check on Tucker's progress with the herd later that morning. Freshly bathed, shaved, and dressed in the first clean set of clothes he'd seen in weeks, Ed looked too pleased with himself to sound put out.

"Letters and telegrams wouldn't have reached you." Tucker didn't bother turning from the cow he'd pulled to the side of the corral. A dry winter meant scarce forage, and the herd from Victoria proved the region hadn't seen much rain this year. Though the whole herd looked scraggly, most would fatten up for market without any trouble if they weren't rushed up the trail.

But this animal staggered straight past scraggly to skeletal. Tucker noticed the emaciated beast right away and earmarked her, along with others who showed signs of damaged hooves or lumps on their jaws, for a look over and possible treatment.

"I'm not talking about telegrams, and you know it, Tucker!" Ed huffed past him and strong-armed the cow into a headlock, helping wrestle her mouth open. "You could've answered me when I asked who she was back by the wagon, but no. My closest friend clenched his jaw shut tighter than this cow!"

"Hang on." Tucker didn't specify whether he meant for Ed to hold tight to the cow or to his patience, since it was hard to say which would give him more trouble. Tucker suspected the cow had wooden tongue. With the way she shook her head and tried to close her jaw, it wouldn't be easy to keep her steady—especially since she was a drooler.

Tucker crouched down for a better look, craning his neck left and right to get a good look at the animal's tongue and teeth. Even though the men teased him about it, every roundup he carried a pocket full of flat wooden tongue compressors he'd bought in bulk from a medical practice. If an animal needed to be cut from the herd to keep it from contaminating the food supply and spreading the sickness, Tucker saw it as pure idiocy to go poking potentially healthy specimens in the mouth with something that'd been soaking in sickness from a diseased animal.

The hardened punchers called him fussy at first, but after one season seeing their gloves caked and cracking in dried slobber flecked with blood and globs of pus, they came around to his way of thinking. It didn't matter much to Tucker that they cared more about their gloves than good sense, so long as it got the job done.

"How's it looking?" Ed grunted, tightening his grip. Like his father before him, he'd never been one to let personal matters interfere with tending the herd. "I didn't see much in the way of lumps. Wooden tongue?"

"I'd say so." The signs were there—too much drool, too little eating, and a too-big tongue—but Tucker used the compressor to verify. Sure enough, the moment the thin wood touched her tongue, the cow rolled back her eyes and shook her head as though in pain. Tucker withdrew the compressor and tossed it in the trash barrel while Ed let her loose.

"Yep. If they'd caught it back in Victoria, might've been able to treat her with iodine." He didn't bother saying the rest aloud. Ed would understand this to mean the animal was past the point of effective treatment. Together, they guided her to a small stand of woebegone cattle destined for the town butcher tomorrow. The longer they waited to be sold, the more weight they'd lose and the less money they'd fetch.

Professional interest had Ed giving the lot a once-over. "Got a lot of cases?"

Tucker nodded. "I know we didn't have a wet winter, but the forage down there must be awful rough this year. Lump jaw and wooden tongue numbers are running high for this herd, and calves are few and far between."

"I made him cut the price by another third on account of the calves." Ed scowled, obviously sharing Tucker's assumption that the owner had sold the best part of the herd elsewhere then tried to sell the remainder to the Bar None as a full brand.

"As for the sickness, usually I can spot a problem early on, but you should've seen this herd when we picked 'em up."

"Worse then?" Tucker tried not to sound too incredulous, but. . . *I told him not to take the trade.*

"They're a sorry sight today, but they were wince-worthy in Victoria. If they hadn't been slow as sludge and desperate to feed, I would've gotten back a lot sooner." Fast as a flash of lightning, Ed went back to his original complaint. "It would've been nice if you'd helped me greet Jessie properly instead of letting me flounder around, trying to figure out who she was."

Ed grumbled, but he looked almost cheerful. Certainly better than he had for weeks before going on the grueling trip to bring in this herd. And since no self-respecting rancher within sight of this sorry herd would be smiling, that meant his reunion went well.

"She would've known if I told you." Tucker forbore to mention that Jess would never have let him hear the end of it either. Ed still hadn't spent much time with his sister, and half a dozen years had a way of dimming a man's memory. He might not remember or realize the full force of his sister's stubborn streak.

"So what if she suspected you'd said something?" Ed scoffed. "Jessie wouldn't know for sure that I didn't remember her on my own. Now we both have to live with knowing I couldn't recognize her when she stood on our porch, waiting."

"You have no way of knowing she would've recognized you," Tucker pointed out. "That puts you on more even ground if she ever brings it up." As if there were any doubt she'd bring it up at some point as a conversational trump card.

"Wait a sec. Did you see me riding up and say my name?"

"No. She was the one facing the drive, trying to decide whether or not she should wait for you to get home before she tackled going to church. Looked like she was deciding not to go on account of not having any mourning dresses made up since she got back."

"Yeah!" Ed's brows bounced down then up again to land a notch higher than where they'd started, a sign of undeniable sincerity. "The yellow threw me off! If she'd been wearing black and standing on my porch, I would've figured the rest out even after coming home on the tail end of a hard drive. I can mention the yellow dress if she ever teases me about today."

"Since you're my friend and partner, I'll give you one warning. Be careful what you say about anything she wears. She gets awful touchy about her clothes." He shook his head. "The thought of the whole town talking about the color of her dress is the reason she started to rethink going to church. Otherwise we would've been gone just long enough to have missed you."

"Sorry about coming in on Sunday morning." Ed rubbed a hand over his freshly shaved jaw as though not sure he liked being so bare. "Especially since you'll be hitting the trail soon and won't be able to get to church for a couple months."

"Well, since she was deciding not to attend this morning, I wouldn't have felt right leaving her alone on the ranch." Tucker headed back toward the corral, walking around it and along the lines of the branding chute he'd just finished building. "I don't know what all those fancy lady schools were supposed to have taught her, but your sister still sets her own notions above anything else."

Tucker headed for the end of the branding chute. Long enough to easily hold twenty grown steers, only a handful up at the far end remained penned in. Since Ed and his crew trail branded the cattle and cropped their tails before hitting the road, the dehorning had gone fast. They'd brought the clippers out and had the horns cut down on every young bull or steer in record time. Now only the oldest, orneriest bulls remained.

Thanks to their advanced age and aggressive ways, the horns on these cattle couldn't be cut easily—the clippers wouldn't even fit around them. He had no choice but to chop them off, a difficult job for any man and the worst way to help a cantankerous old bull settle into his new home.

Just before Ed walked over, Tucker had sent one of the men to the barn to bring back an ax. He was thinking about how much he hated handling horns this way when Ed's laughter made him stop short. For some reason, the sound struck him as ominous.

"What's got you so tickled?"

"That you think Jessie's stubborn streak only goes back seven years!" Ed dissolved into fresh guffaws for a minute before he could speak again. "When I tried to sit on my ma's lap while Jess was getting ready to be born, that unborn baby would kick me from the other side! I'm telling you, Tucker, that girl was headstrong before birth."

"Headstrong since before birth?" Tucker grumbled. "You'd think by now she'd be ready for a change."

"She's been ready for a change since the day my father took her to England. Jessie made that change for herself by coming home. Sometimes a switch in scenery can settle your soul. It's why I had to go to Victoria." Ed shoved his hands deep in his pockets and jerked his chin to indicate the scrawny cattle. "I know you think it was a mistake on the business end, and I'd agree with you if I were calculating in time and dollars spent."

"Well, talking him down further for the missing calf count helped sweeten the deal." Tucker made a real effort to sound positive.

Now wasn't the time to tell his partner that he wouldn't have taken the trip, that the problem steers would probably cause stampedes during the main cattle drive, or that a hefty portion of the herd was already devalued from the damage done to their mouths from foraging after such a dry winter. Though they'd taken aside any cattle too far gone or who threatened to spread sickness, several of the remaining animals bore healing wounds. Even if they didn't abscess, these cattle would be slow to gain the weight they needed.

Now's not the time for that type of talk. Airing his opinion wouldn't fix the cattle or undo the decisions made. On the other hand, this was his first and last chance to remind Ed of the way they got things done and how they worked best—together, as a unit. They'd need the strength of that partnership to circumvent Jessalyn's penchant for causing problems.

"I dropped in on the Mullinses' on the way out here. Roundup will reach the Bar None land sometime tomorrow. So we barely made it in time."

"Tomorrow?" Tucker blew out a breath. "Cut it mighty close."

Ed looked over at the pen of cattle destined for the butcher and the corners of his mouth tightened. "Worse, this herd wasn't worth it, but I needed the challenge. I needed to go where everything I saw and every decision I made didn't echo with Pa's opinions. The distraction did me good. *Change* did me good."

"You make it sound like you're thinking of making other types of changes." Tucker watched one of his men swing the ax at an old bull's horns and winced. "I know your sister is."

It seemed like a God-given reminder that the traits He gave any living thing gained strength with age. Like any other hard-to-handle problem that had to be grabbed by the horns, Jessalyn was sure to put up a furious fight.

Ed's response didn't ease his concerns at all. "Jessie wants to get involved in the Bar None, like she always should have been."

"Involved like she always should have?" he repeated in disbelief. "Ed, I know you're glad to have her home and that she's gonna be a handful, but no matter how unique your sister might be, she's still a *woman*."

"Glad you noticed." Ed snorted. "Heard you had some trouble with that when she first showed up."

"That's what you talked about, the first time you see your sister in how many years?" Tucker shook his head, but he should have known. "Hair under a hat pulled low, bandanna over her face, gloves on her hands, slicker over her clothes, riding astride in a driving downpour. . .you wouldn't have figured it out either."

"Keep telling yourself that, if it makes you feel better." Ed snickered, and suddenly Tucker decided he didn't need to make such an effort to sound positive about his partner's poor decisions.

"You had trouble when she's your *sister*. Wearing a *dress*, standing on *your* front porch in *sunlight*," he shot back. "You're right. That *does* make me feel better."

"No need to get your dander up." Ed held up his hands in a hold-your-horses motion. "I didn't tease you in front of the men."

A fulminating glare was the only response needed for that asinine statement, and the only one Tucker trusted himself to provide without saying something he might regret.

Lord, I know Your timing is perfect, but I can't help thinking I could've really used a trip to church this morning. Worship has a way of working the worries out of my mind and putting the focus back where it belongs. Now that Ed's back, my focus doesn't belong on keeping Jessalyn out of trouble. He's certainly a grown man capable of looking after his own family. But I'm struggling with the idea Ed might not choose to look after her the way he needs to.

Ed looked chagrined. "C'mon. You know I wouldn't tell anyone."

"Never mind that. What else did the two of you discuss?"

"Not a whole heck of a lot yet. General stuff. Memories." He paused and looked away, voice dipping low. "Desta."

Tucker gave him a short nod, acknowledging the difficulties of that surprise scenario. Truth be told, he was grateful Ed would be escorting and introducing the "new" Culpepper women to church. Desta deserved every drop of Culpepper support.

"Even if she'd only been gone months instead of years, there'd still be too much to tackle all at once. We did touch on the terms of the will." Ed crossed his arms and quirked a brow in what Tucker knew was a challenge. "She already knew Pa made you part owner?"

Obviously Ed felt that a topic so personal and complex should have been put on hold until his return. If it had been any other woman in the world, Tucker probably would have agreed.

"We already touched on the topic of how headstrong your sister is." He chose his words with caution. "Jess disliked some of the ranch rules. Desta stepped into the conversation when Jess argued that my position as mere foreman did not grant sufficient authority for me to insist that she follow safety protocols and adhere to conventional proprieties."

Ed's jaw tensed as he took that in. "She was right."

"No, she wasn't. And neither are you if you think it's acceptable for a female who hasn't stepped foot on a ranch in seven years to buck basic common sense." Tucker fought to keep his voice a low growl, unwilling to start shouting and let the men hear him.

"She can't disappear to some far-flung corner on the ranch without a word, riding astride, skirts flying around her knees, to try her hand mending barbed wire, climbing windmills, and whatever else strikes her fancy. Jessalyn can't be allowed to go maverick. The Culpepper name doesn't entitle her to disrupt the entire outfit or risk her neck. Not on my watch."

"Lucky for you, I'm back. You don't have to watch out for her, watch over her, or send Ralph to keep watch for you." Ed's face flushed with anger, a rare sight. "She's my responsibility now."

"Good. Make sure you live up to it." Tucker decided he'd had enough of the conversation. His men had things well in hand, and Ed could supervise them for the rest of the day as they took his headstrong herd to bed ground.

I've had it, Lord. I'm not handling one more issue caused by one of Ed's stubborn creatures. Whether it stands on four legs or two, my partner can shoulder responsibility for whatever he allows to run wild on the ranch. After roundup, I won't be here to see it. Life on the trail is tough, but driving a couple thousand cattle up a trail is still a lot less complicated than trying to corral women!

CHAPTER 23

W e're just going to run over there," Jess assured her aunt, though judging by the look Desta sent her way, she didn't believe her for a minute.

If it came down to it, Jess wasn't entirely sure she believed herself. The real reason she felt reasonably honest promising her aunt it would be a quick trip was because she didn't think the men would allow it otherwise.

Especially since they weren't actually allowing it at all.

Tucker's exact words when Jess mentioned wanting to join the roundup included, "Over my dead body." And even though Ed shot his foreman a warning glare, her brother took his side. Ed kindly explained that she'd be a distraction and, since she really wasn't in possession of the skills to be of assistance, it would be best for everyone if she kept near the house.

Since she couldn't join the roundup, Jess decided to visit. And this time she didn't make the mistake of forewarning the men. Perhaps she wouldn't be much use on this final leg of the cities-wide, days-long process of rounding up every head of beef in the county, branding it appropriately, and herding the confused cattle to their home ranches after a long winter and, hopefully, calf-plentiful spring season. Jess never did like the smell or sounds of branding and never developed a taste for the bounty of "calf fries" wrought by castration. What she'd loved was feeling part of the process, riding alongside her father with a length of rope and a deep-seated resolve to help.

But a woman didn't have to recapture her skill at roping to be welcome at a roundup if she had access to the larder. It was the one consistent, unspoken rule a woman could rely on: Food magically made unwanted women welcome by most men, and tolerated by the rest. For how long depended on how good the food was and how much of it she brought.

So Jess had cajoled Desta into loading up the buckboard. She'd even packed up contingency rations, in case things went well. Jess would jump on the chance to join them around the campfire, and if that meant bringing enough dry goods and supplies to set up a fresh doughnut-making station, then by heaven she'd drag half the kitchen along to accomplish it.

She surveyed the heaping wagon with the first slight pang of doubt. There were times when a lone figure on a horse stood a much better chance of going undetected, and this was one of them. *If Ed or Tucker catch me on the way out, they'll know what I'm up to before I can say a word.*

"What about running back?" Desta surveyed the filled-to-the-gills buckboard and huffed. "Not that I think you're running anywhere with all this to slow you down."

"Maybe you're right." Jess looked from the wagon to Desta and back again. Then glanced toward the stables, where Morning Glory waited. Maybe she could still have the single rider sneakiness, coupled with the welcome-wagon advantage!

"What would you say if I rode on ahead so they'll be ready for us when you drive the wagon in?"

"I'd say you've got a mite more space you could fill before rolling out." Her aunt didn't sound enthusiastic about the idea, but at least she was trying to make the most of their plan.

"Oh?" Jess looked again at the overflowing wagon and wondered if her aunt meant she could stash something extra on the seat, since Jess would be in the saddle. "Where?"

"By the sound of that plan you just tried ropin' me into, you could pack a fair bit in the space 'twix yore ears, for starters." Desta smacked the side of the wagon. "I don' know how to drive this thing!

Even if I did, you got to know I wouldn't let you ride out there on yore own. You'd work yoreself into some kinda trouble, and we both know it even if'n I'm the only one honest enough to say it."

Sensing that her plan was in jeopardy, Jess gave her aunt a big smile. "Good thing I've got you to keep me out of trouble then. I didn't know you couldn't drive a wagon. If you'd like, I could teach you sometime."

"Better if'n I don't know. That way no one can ask me to do it." Her aunt wagged a finger at her. "And don't think I don't know when you use charm to smooth things over, 'cuz I shorely do."

"Yes'm." She tried to look appropriately penitent, knew she failed, and went back to grinning.

"'Smatter of fact, we ain't goin' that way at all until after you change. Me goin' with you helps make it more proper, but you got to be wearing a skirt like any other lady would wear."

"I'm not any other lady."

"I know. Yore still wearing proper skirts, though. It's the first time you'll meet anyone beyond the Bar None, and I won't send them out tellin' tales any more shocking than I can help." Desta shaded her eyes with her hand and made a show of looking up at the sun's progress across the sky. "Waste much more time, no use going a'tal."

At that, Jess scrambled back inside to swap her split skirts for something more suitable. Since she'd failed in her attempt to ride out, the skirts wouldn't make a difference. She climbed back in the wagon within minutes, eager to set out.

"Before we go, why don't you go on 'head and thank the Lord for this fine day and ask His blessing on our mission. Roundup's all but done. Next thing ya know, Tucker'll be taking the herd up the trail. Good time to pray for it all to go smooth."

"Again?" Jess failed to keep the astonishment from her voice, but it seemed like everyone on the ranch made praying an all-day-long priority. "Ed and Tucker prayed before they took the men out this morning. And we prayed about it before breakfast."

"And they'll have prayed once all the workers arrived, just before they sent men out along the grid." Desta nodded. "The more prayers, the more places, from the more people, the more chances for God to pour out His grace on the enterprise."

Jess rubbed the reins between her gloved fingertips, chafing at the need to pay lip service to Desta's convictions. She didn't want to hurt her aunt's feelings—or get into a conversation about the relative merits of constantly calling on a supposedly all-knowing deity who, as far as Jess knew, wasn't hard of hearing.

So she closed her eyes, opened her mouth, and...couldn't get the words out. *If I can tell when someone doesn't want to be talking to me, surely God can do the same?*

"I can tell you don't want to pray, Jess." Desta squeezed the words through a too-small windpipe as the fear she'd fought over the past few days finally found a voice and worked free.

Never seen the girl pray more than bowin' her head to someone else's words. Doesn't talk about God neither. Lord, I know Simon raised his children in the Word, and he swore those schools kept chapel. How is it my niece shies away from You now? Is it grief over her papa, or does it go deeper?

"Not so much." Jess went quiet—something Desta already knew was a bad sign. Since her niece arrived, she talked about anything and everything with a speed and passion Desta found endearing.

But she didn't talk much about Ed until he came home. And she didn't like talking about her papa—though that could come down to fresh grief. Most of all, she didn't have much to add if Desta brought up the scriptures or when anyone engaged in prayer.

Didn't take much to pin down the pattern: when it was something or someone she was supposed to put her trust in, Jess balked. Faith made her shy away quicker than a greased hog.

"And it's not just now that you don't want to pray, is it?" she ventured, voice soft so as not to set up Jess's defenses. It looked like she'd managed to slip past them in her niece's excitement over visiting roundup. Desta planned to make the most of the chance before they drove out and left the opportunity behind.

"I don't see much reason to join a chorus of voices asking the same thing." Jess hitched her shoulders as though she wanted to shrug the question away, but left the motion half undone so she sat hunched, folded in on herself. "God's not an old man with an ear trumpet sticking out the side of His head, trying to catch the meaning of what people say to Him. I'd imagine all those prayers about the same things, over and over again, are a lot like gnats circling around. Irritating. The sort of thing He'd want to slap away instead of lend a helping hand to, after a while."

The horror of that picture caught Desta and held her fast. After Jess's description, she could practically envision the entire scene, and it was enough to make anyone who didn't know better feel hopeless and unloved. But her niece knew better—or at least she once did. *And Lord willing, she'll know the truth again.*

There was a time when a hurt soul needed a healing touch. Those times called for gentle sympathy, hot tea, and hugs to warm the soul back to life—much like reviving someone who'd been caught in a blizzard.

This wasn't that time. Her niece had let lies and doubts poison her thoughts. Like a man who'd had too much liquor, Jess needed to be startled back to her senses. Since she didn't have a bucket of icy water handy, a dose of harsh truth would have to do.

"That's pure foolishness, and deep down you know it, Jessalyn Culpepper," Desta barked. "The great loving Lord doesn't want to swipe us down like bugs, though hearing you talk like that near enough makes me want to swat you. Whatever's keeping you from connecting with yore Maker, it's not on His end and you can't just brush it aside."

Jessalyn pulled her shoulders straight so fast it almost seemed as though the words had slapped her upright. "Wouldn't you get annoyed if someone kept asking you the same thing, again and again, without accepting they might not get their way?"

"You ain't been listenin' very well to the prayers around here." Desta kept her words sharp, goading her niece into defending her views. "We pray for His will, we offer thanks for His blessings, and ask for His help with what lies ahead, knowing full well we might not like His answer once He gives it. But we ask anyway."

"Why?" Jessalyn burst out. "Why bother asking Him for something you need when He already knows everything?"

"'Cuz by asking, yore acknowledgin' His power to give it." Desta sensed the time had come to soften. She'd gotten past the armor of excuses and now needed to be careful with what lay beneath it. "'Cuz you know He's in control over it already."

"Yeah, I know He's in control. He already has a plan made up and set in place. That just makes me worry *more*."

Desta sat in silence, stunned by the bitterness pouring from her niece. God's Word promised that He did not give His own a heart full of fear, but Jess was flooded with it. The living water within her niece had swollen with sorrow until what should sustain Jess's faith made it falter instead.

"Those verses yore talkin' about, like the one sayin' God knows the plans He's made for us, they's some of my very favorites." When she finally spoke, she relied on God's words. Her own would be unequal to the task ahead. "It goes on to say they're plans to prosper us and not harm us. I always found comfort in knowing I was important enough for Him to take note of. It's a powerful blessing to know I can rely on His provision. Why would that make me worry?"

"Of all people, you should know the answer to that. I worry because the die is cast. The path is laid, and I have no choice but to follow. You say you look at that and see His provision. Well, I look at it and see how helpless it leaves me. How alone." Her niece's eyes shone bright with anger and betrayal.

"He doesn't leave you helpless or alone because He is always with you, no matter if you don't feel it. He's our 'very present help in trouble,' the Bible tells us."

"No. He left me alone, far away. . .and He never gave me help." Jess shook her head. "No matter how I asked, it made no difference. All the words in the world won't change His mind. His plan. His choice. Never mine."

Heart aching for the desperation and isolation her niece had suffered, Desta suddenly understood the source of her niece's pain. The question was, did Jess? *I don't think she sees, Lord. And I don't think she'll stand much more talk about it right now. Help me reach her—without pushing her further away.*

"I see what yore saying, and how it chafes to feel you don't have a choice in yore own life. I know that better than most folks you could talk to. And I know how much it hurts to feel lonesome."

"Then how can you sit here and tell me to take comfort in God, when He's let you feel all that hurt for all that time?"

"Because God ain't never been the one to do evil in this world. He lets us make our own decisions. Every time I been knocked down, it's another human being standing there with a raised fist. Never God." Desta flexed her fingers, trying to dispel a sudden tremor. "And I bet if you think it over, you'd see the same is true in yore life."

Silence, brittle and flaking like a sugar glaze, cracked between them. Desta let it settle, giving her niece time to test the notion before she pressed any harder. Finally, she figured Jess's temper should have cooled enough to take another serving of insight.

"Now, I'm gonna ask you to think over a question—not answer it now, but really chew this question over until you taste truth in yore answer. Can you do that?" Her niece's nod was the signal for Desta to aim her only arrow.

She took a breath and let fly. "When you talk so much about not being able to change 'His' plan no matter what you said or how hard you tried. . .which Father were you really talking about? The one waiting to bring you home to heaven. . .or the one you were waiting on here, to bring you home to the Bar None?"

CHAPTER 24

B oth." Tucker watched as the new chuck-wagon cook plumped a biscuit and a crumbling square of corn bread atop the heap of pork and beans mounded in his tin, then slapped a pat of butter atop each one. Truth be told, he could've said two of each, he'd worked up such an appetite.

But a tin couldn't hold half as much as a working man's stomach, so Tucker figured he'd start with one plateful and work his way back if his stomach demanded and time allowed. Even if time didn't allow, he could always snag a couple more biscuits or hunks of corn bread. That was why it seemed like a good idea to try both now.

Usually he would've just gone for the corn bread. Biscuits were all well and good—well, not all of them were actually good, but even the worst could be choked down with a thick slather of butter or a ten-second soak in coffee. But corn bread, when it was made right, was the sort of thing that made Tucker more inclined to take Ralph's talk about food changing the world seriously.

He hadn't heard any complaints about the chuck, and not much grumbling over the new cook providing it, but Tucker believed in forming his own opinion. Particularly when the research was so rewarding. He settled himself down in a likely patch of grass, offering a short prayer of thanks before digging in.

Disappointingly, the biscuits trumped the corn bread, which didn't boast the hint of sweetness Tucker expected. Crumbly and somewhat mealy, it stirred into the beans just fine and would stick to a stomach, but it wasn't the sort of thing that made a man mosey back for more. As he finished his tin—it hadn't taken long to get through the beans, though they'd been on the chewy side—Tucker looked around with a satisfaction that had nothing to do with a full belly. Or at least, very little.

Men scattered around the campfire and chuck-wagon area, which formed the hub of the roundup. Nobody lingered too long over the midday meal—there was too much work to be done and too many men waiting their turn to fill their stomachs. And, if he were completely honest, the grub wasn't the sort of meal a man let eat up his afternoon.

Tucker spotted Ralph joining the end of the line. It was always entertaining to watch someone the first time they met Ralph Runkle, but cooks in particular put on a good show. First came astonishment, then incredulity, then inevitable mutters as they dug up an extra tin so he didn't have to eat his food while standing in line for the next helping.

Tucker headed toward the line and rounded the wagon just in time to see the new cook—Rick, if he remembered right—spot Ralph. The man's mouth fell open, and if the cowpoke in front of him hadn't been quick enough, he would've slopped a ladleful of beans straight onto the ground. Snapping his mouth shut again, he swiftly served the men until Ralph reached the front of the line. He also happened to be the end of the line, but Tucker doubted the cook could tell that. Ralph wasn't an easy man to see around.

"I don't know which outfit you come from, boy." The scrawny cook didn't stand much higher than Ralph's elbow, but waggled his ladle at him all the same. "But you best be goin' straight back there to tell yer boss I didn't find it funny to see half a mountain moving up my chuck line."

"Half a mountain, but I does a mountain worth of work," Ralph rumbled good-naturedly, extending his pan. He noticed that he'd just about clipped the cook's nose and hastily bent his elbow to lower the plate. "So Boss reckons I'm worth the extra feed."

"I didn't ask yer opinion of yer boss's opinion," Rick sneered.

"Fact is, I don't care. Anyone who'd take a payin' job and waste it on a darkie like you ain't worth listenin' to. Go back and tell him to bust out that feed bag. You ain't eatin' from my wagon."

Rage, dark and cold, crept over Tucker and kept him frozen for a beat longer than he would've wanted. But it took Tucker a moment to process the ugliness behind Rick's words, and another minute to think it through. Much as he wanted to send the idiot packing after the roundup, he didn't have the time to find a replacement for the cattle drive. It stuck in his craw worse than that mealy corn bread, but Tucker had to set the man straight without sending him down the road.

"Hey, Rick." He stepped from behind the water barrel and tried to look calm and collected. "You wanna tell me what's goin' on here?"

As if I don't know full well. Starting out by saying he'd eavesdropped weakened his position. Tucker just wanted the man to repeat it to his face so he could set him down with as little fuss as possible.

"One of the outfits here 'bouts sent this behemoth to my wagon as some kind of joke." Rick whined through his nose. "I don't take guff from no one and don't truck with those kinds of jokes, so I'm sending him back with a bug in his ear and letting him know he's plumb lucky not to be gettin' a boot to the backside in the bargain."

"What makes you think it's a joke?" Tucker gave the man another chance, reminding himself how many problems he'd reap if he sent away this cook. Aside from this snag, Rick garnered few complaints and didn't cause problems, which meant the chuck could be just this side of edible and Tucker would've kept him on.

Stark truth of the matter was, old Cookie back at the mess hall didn't have any more long drives left in him, and the contract Ed arranged meant they should've pulled out this past week. They'd probably still make it to market on time, but Tucker preferred to pad the timetable for detours and problems. More cropped up each year.

Which meant he had to take the time to iron out this wrinkle.

He didn't suffer fools gladly, but the alternative was suffering no food. . .and none of the men would go along with that.

"I don't bow and scrape for no ni—" Rick jumped back when Tucker took a huge step forward into his space.

"Don't say it," Tucker warned. "You can call him Ralph. You can call him sir. You can call him mister. But call him any other name, even when you're talking to someone else, and we'll have us a problem. Do you understand me?"

"No." The little tyrant stuck out his chin so the sparse wiry hairs atop it gleamed in the sunlight. "I don't understand why yer so het up about the fact I don't serve none but my own kind."

"Well, we're short on idiots around here, so you'll have to broaden your criteria." Tucker leaned forward until the fool almost stepped back into his own campfire. "You'll serve anyone who steps foot on Bar None property or bellies up to the Bar None campfire while we're on the trail. And you'll do it with respect, or *you'll* be sent on your way with a boot in the backside. What's more, Ralph will be the one doing the honors."

Tucker could've sworn the very whiskers on the man's chin drooped as he started bobbing his head and babbling. "Yessir. And sir." He sort of spasmed in Ralph's direction, watery eyes darting from Tucker's glare to Ralph's massive arms. "Whatever you say."

"That's all." Tucker aimed a nod Ralph's way and left the craven cook frantically stirring his pot and plunking piles of beans in Ralph's tin. As he walked away, his anger faded a bit with each step until he found the whole thing almost comical.

A few of the other ranch owners stopped Tucker for a few words, but since they saw him as hired help, directed themselves mostly to Edward. *Fine by me.*

Most of the time they wanted to compare spreads and herds and how powerful they all were—so long as none of them came right out and said it. The ring-around-the-rosie they played turned Tucker's stomach, and he happily left the jockeying for position to Ed. His partner had been raised with it and got used to playing those games.

Although, come to think of it, maybe Ed had gotten a little *too* accustomed at pulling rank. Tucker's mood soured slightly as he remembered their spat from the other day. *If he doesn't take Jessalyn in hand now, she'll start riding roughshod, too.*

Tucker grimaced at the thought, scaring away the owner of one of the smaller spreads around town who'd broken away from his friends and started over. A couple of those men—those whose spreads were in the starting-out period, usually—had tried to approach him and offer him a new position. He couldn't blame them, and truth be told it made him glad to know he'd earned respect in the larger community beyond the Bar None. But he wasn't ready to move on to anything more permanent than the trail. After that, he'd see where things with Ed stood.

Lord, maybe he doesn't realize how difficult Jess will be to look after. Once he knows firsthand how much effort it takes to rein in her enthusiasm and stand against her stubbornness, he might well be up to the task. I'd be lying if I didn't say I hope Ed experiences a change of heart while I'm gone so things settle back into a routine this fall.

Tucker kept up his stream of thought-prayer as he grabbed and saddled a fresh pony for the afternoon's work. Cow ponies were surefooted, sturdy, and steady, but worked best with four-hour shifts. Happy Jack already put in his work and deserved some quality time to feed. For now, Tucker headed to the hill near the center of camp— one of the reasons he'd chosen to center the roundup here.

Most of the Bar None boasted flat land, but this small area seemed almost as though some restless dragon below had given a mighty stretch, pushing earth and rocks upward in a haphazard, staggered pattern. It made the best place to look over the land and gauge on how the roundup progressed. It also happened to be one of his favorite places to pray.

And, while I'm being honest, no matter how much trouble she's rustled up in such a short amount of time, it's going to be hard to leave Jessalyn for the next few months. Father, You made her hardheaded as a mule, but tenderhearted underneath. It's easy to see in the way she dotes on her aunt. She's smart as a whip and means well with whatever she takes on. She's the sort of woman who—

Tucker's silent conversation with God stuttered to a halt as he saw the buckboard come bouncing into view a little ways off. As soon as he confirmed what he thought he'd seen, he set his pony in motion and turned his prayer down a different path, too.

Lord, she's the sort of woman who's going to drive me crazy long before I can hit the trail!

"We made it!" Jessalyn leaned forward and maneuvered the horses so they'd come in downwind of the chuck wagon and campfire, as etiquette demanded. She forced cheerfulness into her voice, determined not to let the day be ruined by Desta's earlier ambush.

She'd have plenty of time to mull over her aunt's question after the roundup was over and the men rode out on the cattle drive. Jess had been trying to figure out a way to convince Ed to let her go along, but even *she* knew none of her arguments would be strong enough for her to win her way.

Not this year anyway.

Next year, she'd be ready.

Until then, Jess knew she'd better drink in the day. Roundup would be finished tomorrow, and she doubted she'd be able to convince Desta to ride back up here to see the end. And when the men and the cattle all moved out, she'd be alone with her aunt. Without anything to distract her from the questions she'd promised to consider—except the memories she'd promised herself she wouldn't.

Carpe diem, she bolstered herself. It was pretty much the Latin version of "grab life by the horns and git goin'!" Jess appreciated the Texas flair, but somehow the Latin saying sounded wiser. And since she couldn't claim any actual wisdom at the moment, she'd settle for putting on a good pretense. In fact, it seemed to Jess that "a good pretense covers a multitude of ills" summed up everything those insufferable schools taught about ladylike behavior.

"Did you hear me?" Desta's voice pulled Jess from her musings and back to the roundup. "I said we should talk to the chuck-wagon cook about where he'll want us to unload everything. Don't want to step on his toes, or he'll be kickin' us off camp lickety-split."

Jess softened at her aunt's concern. No matter that Desta probed a little too far and asked questions that cut a little too deep for Jess's liking. Her aunt did so out of love and support. *I'll need to get used to the idea that having people around me who care that much means they're going to bump their noses against my business.*

It seemed the sort of thing she ought to be able to forgive— particularly since she so greatly enjoyed her own bad habit of sticking her nose where some folks might say it didn't belong. Like the roundup. Jess felt the size of her own grin as she looked around, drinking in a sight both long forgotten and achingly familiar.

The way everything worked, all the men gathered in one place and worked outward in a spreading circle, like the spokes on a wheel. The chuck wagon served as the hub of that wheel, centering the campsite. The picketed strings of cow ponies, the branding fires, and several makeshift corrals to hold the cattle of several different outfits all spread from this point. With every ranch involved, there were enough men to scour the countryside and gather all the stray cattle, then separate them out as they worked their way across the county. Everyone participated, and everyone reaped the rewards of time saved and more cows found. To Jess, it told a time-honored tale of completion, of traditions taken far away and followed right back home. Everything started out here, and everything came back to rest.

As she and her aunt hopped down from the buckboard and headed for the cook fire, Jess began to be very glad she'd listened to her aunt and changed to proper skirts. Although the sun had progressed far past the midday point, several men spread around, still eating their meal in the staggered shifts particular to cattle drovers. Almost none of them looked familiar, but almost all of them eyed her and Desta with open interest that ranged from curiosity to practically predatory.

CHAPTER 25

"Hello!" Jess called as they rounded the chuck wagon, stepping into the slightly cooler space shaded by the canvas stretched out over the back work area.

A short man with a gaunt frame and sour set to his mouth jumped to his feet at her greeting, rubbing the palms of his hands against his apron nervously. He sneered. "Kin I help ya?"

Jess decided at once that she didn't like the man. But that was where a good pretense came in handy. She summoned her most gracious manner as she addressed the scamp. "You're the cook?"

He gave a sullen nod but stood straighter, eyeing her in an obvious attempt to determine who she was and how important she might be before he spoke again. It pointed to a certain rodent-like intelligence, but again did nothing to commend the man.

"I'm Miss Culpepper." She noticed the change in his demeanor immediately, but spoke over him. The sooner she and Desta could unload their supplies and finish arrangements, the sooner she could explore further. "We've brought some additional supplies from the house to supplement your larder and reward the men after a long roundup."

"Good to meet ya, miss." The little man bent at the waist and bobbed his head in what was unmistakably—and unbelievably—a bow. "I'm Rick, and it's right nice of ya ta come out this way."

"We'll help you unload as you decide where you want things placed." Jess backed out of the shaded area to where Desta waited. The cook hadn't set things up very well, positioning his supplies in such a way as to block entrance to the work space and serving station. As things stood, men would be forced to stand in line and file through—which made for good planning on one level. Problem was, they had to file past the water barrel, so it would be unavailable when most needed.

While Jess tried to find a diplomatic way to suggest a change, Rick scurried up to the wagon, hopped in, and began rooting around. After a few minutes, he jumped back down. With empty hands, he swaggered back to Jess, thrust his sharply angled chin toward Desta, and started giving orders.

"Won't need the dry goods with one day left, and don't like loading my wagon with unnecessary weight. Yeh can take that back with yers, since the outfit will supply the wagon before we pull out later. Yeh prolly didn't know." He sounded marginally respectful so long as he spoke to Jess, but refused to acknowledge Desta directly.

"Have yer girl haul everything else on over. As she brings it, I'll tell her where to set it."

Seething, Jess found it necessary to bite her tongue and collect herself before responding. Her aunt shouldn't have to put up with anyone talking about her as though she couldn't understand plain English.

"What girl?" Jess didn't bother trying to be gracious anymore. She'd gone shrill and felt a savage satisfaction when the mean little man before her winced.

"She's laggin' behind." He jerked his wispily covered chin in Desta's direction and lowered his voice to a carrying whisper. "They do that if yer not real firm with 'em. 'Specially the lighter ones. They's lazy on account a thinkin' they's better than most their kind."

"That's enough!" She bypassed shrill and went straight to screeching, but the fool didn't realize he was the one to earn her ire.

"Now yer in fer it, girl." He cackled at Desta. "No more shirkin'. Git a move on an' grab something while yer still able."

Jess stepped to the side, blockading her aunt from the revolting attentions of this foul little man. "Rick!" she thundered, breaking through his amusement. "You will not speak to my aunt in such a dismissive manner. In fact, since you can't keep a civil tongue in your head, you aren't allowed to talk to her or about her at all. She will tell you which items to take, and you will follow her directions quickly and with utmost respect. Do I make myself clear?"

From behind her, the sound of a quickly stifled laugh gladdened her heart. Especially since it seemed like every man in the vicinity headed over to see what was going on. By now the vast majority had taken up her cause and started glaring.

"Yer aunt?" Surrounded now, the despot shrank before their eyes. His shoulders slumped as he looked at Desta afresh, craning his neck and staring as though trying to find a resemblance and failing. "Yer aunt? Yer jokin'."

Jess let loose a low growl from the back of her throat, and Rick backed up so fast he almost ran into Ralph. The cook stopped just shy of stomping on his feet then spun around with eyes slitted and mouth open, obviously ready to vent his spleen on whoever had the misfortune to get in his way.

His mouth sagged as he looked up. . .and up. . .tilting his head back to take in Ralph's expression of rigidly controlled fury. The cook spluttered for a minute, swiveled his head around on his scrawny neck, got a gander at the other glowers aimed his way, and snapped his mouth shut. Without another word, he scurried back to the chuck wagon.

"Don't pay the likes of him no mind, Miss Desta." Ralph's deep voice pulled Jess's attention back to her aunt.

"Naw." She stood tall and proud, eyes sparkling with determined good humor as she added, "Can't help but pity the man. Looks like he been weaned on a pickle. Turned him sour, so now his mind's all brine an' no brain."

Jess laughed so hard she ran out of breath, but didn't mind. The men who'd come over to watch the scene were chuckling along, and when the laughter ended, they started unloading the buckboard without being asked. It restored some faith in her fellow man, though most of that credit went to Ralph Runkle.

He looked down at Desta with such pride and admiration it made Jess's heart happy. . .and a little wistful. *Someday I hope a man looks at me that way. . .like I'm something so special he can't get the thought of me out of his mind.*

Tucker tried to tamp down his temper, but the scene unfolding before him when he descended from the point brought it surging to the fore. Men—who should be back at work once they finished eating—surrounded the buckboard, entirely blocking it from view.

I knew it, he stewed. *The second they saw her, they swarmed.*

As he neared, he saw they were unloading things from the wagon, but that did little to assuage his irritation. More helpful was the realization that Ralph's girth alone accounted for a good third of the barrier. Even so, Tucker had a hard time keeping his pace at a brisk walk. Some irrational part of him wanted to gallop at the mass of men for the simple satisfaction of seeing them scatter.

By the time he hopped from his horse, he noted the men who kept glancing toward the head of the wagon where Jessalyn stood, beaming that smile of hers. Was it any wonder some of the roundup crew looked a little stunned? Not that Tucker planned to cut them any slack.

He glowered indiscriminately as he stalked up, completing his first objective before he even reached them; the cowpunchers beat a hasty retreat back to the remuda for fresh ponies. Only the women and Ralph remained to greet him, so Tucker didn't feel the need to put on pretty manners. His scowl stayed put.

Must've been a good one, too, because Ralph took one look at him and told Desta he hadn't gotten his second serving yet. Desta slid a sideways glance at her niece, hesitating just long enough for either one of them to speak to her if they so chose. Then, without a word, she headed after Ralph, leaving the explanations to Jess.

Jess herself looked as if she wouldn't mind leaving the explanations to someone else. She stood uncharacteristically silent, one hand resting against the rough wood of the buckboard, eyes wary beneath the brim of her hat.

Maybe she's learning. Tucker crossed his arms and continued to wait. No need to demand that she justify her appearance at the roundup—she knew full well he and Ed *both* told her to stay home. Even Ed wouldn't let her off the hook for this flagrant disobedience.

Which might be a good thing. He caught himself as he started uncrossing his arms and tightened them instead. No matter if the severity of the offense convinced Ed to take Tucker's concerns more seriously—that had hardly been her intention.

Suddenly, a brouhaha broke out at the chuck wagon. Someone with a foul mouth yelped and launched into a tirade amid the clatter and clash of who-knew-what. Tucker raced for the ruckus, realized Jessalyn followed suit, and skidded to a halt, throwing out his arm to stop her advance. Had she no sense of self-preservation? A woman couldn't run into the midst of a knock-down, drag-out!

Tucker caught her before they rounded the chuck wagon. He twisted, pinning both her arms to her sides within the circle of his own. Between her momentum and the force of her sudden stop, she parted company with the ground, feet flailing until she landed none too softly against his chest.

The impact knocked the wind out of her in a huff of warm, sugar cookie–scented breath. It kept her from screeching at him and alerting the combatants to her presence, so Tucker clapped a hand over her mouth before she contributed to the commotion. Then he shifted, holding her tight against him so he could keep her still with only one arm encircling her.

Whuh. Suddenly she wasn't the only one who couldn't breathe. Tucker's thoughts screeched to a halt. Between his adrenaline and the feel of the woman now pressed far too tightly against him, all he could do was hold still and try to make her do the same. His senses flooded him with messages about just how nicely Jessalyn fit in his arms, and how good she felt pressed this close. . .and if she didn't stop wriggling around, this would become awkward in a hurry.

Tucker shifted as much as possible, trying to make space between them without letting her go. As his hold eased, she stopped struggling so much. At some point in all of this, she'd lost her hat, and he saw for the first time that she'd taken her braid and wound it around her head like a crown of summer wheat.

"Mmpf!" Jessalyn stared up at him, eyes anxious and outraged above the hand still covering her mouth. She rolled her shoulders, trying to work her arms free from his loosened hold.

"Shhh." He moved his hand, pressing a single finger against her lips in silent admonishment before taking it away altogether.

"Let me go!" She jerked her head, making the margin between them slightly wider.

"Stay put." Tucker tightened his clasp to remind her of his control, closing the space between them once more. He held her there, dimly hearing continued shouting and smashing, until she hissed her agreement. Then he intensified his hold for the merest fraction of a moment, pressing her even more firmly against him in an undeniable display of his dominance.

Tucker enjoyed her faint gasp far more than he should have, but he recognized it as the acknowledgment of his control. Mollified, he eased his hold. Not completely, but enough to let her pull free.

Jessalyn tensed, cheeks blazing, then whipped from his grip as though his touch burned. He hoped it did—hers left him singed.

Tucker stepped around the corner of the wagon, keeping his right arm held aloft as a barrier she wouldn't dare to cross. He positioned himself at an angle, keeping himself between her and the fracas.

Ralph stood slightly to the side of Tucker, having torn the folding table from the back of the wagon and upended it as a sort of shield. He'd kept Desta tucked behind him, further protected by the bulk of the water barrel. Pots and pans littered the ground. Flour and cornmeal streaked the grass, the turned-on-its-side tabletop, and even the side of the wagon. For all the mess, Ralph remained surprisingly unmarked.

Farthest away from them, seeking cover behind the pole holding up the canvas awning across the back of the wagon, the cook hopped up and down, still screaming invectives. Beans dropped from the tin mashed atop his head, splattering his clothes with graying globs.

Now that the danger had passed, Tucker caught the content of those shouts, and the banked coals of his anger burned bright once again. He strode into the open, walking around Ralph's makeshift barricade to stand in the middle of the carnage. When he came to a stop, so did the cook's raving racialism. A silence fell that was so absolute, Tucker could have sworn he heard the sporadic drips still falling from the pan on the man's head.

"You're fired." Jessalyn beat him to it, but since she said the words as she stopped by his side, Tucker decided not to quibble. Whether she meant it or not, the position declared them partners. "Get off Bar None land before we decide to press charges."

"Don't take orders from no highty-tighty hussies," the idiot sneered, brandishing a fist. "No more than I roll over to any ni—"

"I warned you about using language like that." Tucker stepped away from Jessalyn, angered anew by that waving fist. "Now I'll tell you not to threaten or insult any woman in my presence. Before you head on your way, you'll apologize to Miss Desta, Mr. Runkle, and Miss Culpepper."

He opened his mouth as though ready to keep arguing, but Tucker's gaze kicked some long-forgotten survival instinct back to life, and he shut it with an audible click. He eyed Tucker then looked up as if struck anew by Ralph's size before glancing at Jessalyn. His gaze snagged on the holster at her hip, which she deliberately reached down and unsnapped.

Gaze skittering away to meet Tucker's glare once more, he stammered a sullen "Sorry!" before turning tail with the tin of beans still perched atop his head like a hat and running from the campsite. Only after he'd become a stick figure in the distance did Tucker return his attention to the mess he'd left behind.

Dread pooled in his stomach as he surveyed the destruction surrounding them and realized the gravity of the situation. The danger had passed, but the damage done might well be catastrophic.

"Where am I going to find another cook in time for the cattle drive?"

CHAPTER 26

Right here! Jess wondered if a woman could choke from swallowing something as insubstantial—though possibly life-changing—as a single statement. The cry clogged the back of her throat, but she sensed the debacle with the roundup cook pushed Tucker to his edge, and now wasn't the time to tip him over the precipice.

After the roundup, but before the trail drive, she could tackle his temper. For now she'd sidle her way into the crew with stealth—and supper. The first step to filling the old cook's boots was to kick up the quality of the camp's grub.

"The trail drive won't leave for days," Jess soothed Tucker. "Tonight Aunt Desta and I can rustle up something to keep the roundup crew from fussing."

"No." As she'd expected, Tucker shook his head. "You women should head back to the house. After what happened already, you know it's not safe."

"I feel safer here, with you men all 'round, than I will heading home just me and Jessie." Aunt Desta spoke to Tucker's concern, but kept her gaze fixed on Ralph.

"Ralph will take you both back."

"Only if you give me leave to lay out my bedroll on the porch, Boss." Ralph looked at Tucker as he spoke, but kept his body turned toward Desta, as though still shielding her. "Can't be sure how far that Rick went, and he strikes me as stupid enough to circle back."

"Could be."

"If Ralph stays with us and you have to allocate someone to play cook, you lose the labor equivalent of three men." Jess made a sweeping motion to indicate the savaged cook site. "Four, since someone will need to help clean up while someone else is cooking. It'll draw a lot of comments."

The sound of someone riding up stopped the conversation cold, giving life to Jess's worries about unwanted attention. When the rider rounded the chuck wagon, she breathed a sigh of relief to see her brother slide from the saddle.

"What in tarnation happened here?" Ed cast an incredulous look around the area, stepping over a broken crate and edging around the cast-iron cookware littering the ground.

"We lost our cook." Tucker's mild summation amid the carnage of the fight, combined with his grim expression, hit her funny bone.

A giggle escaped before she could tamp it down, earning her a set of matching glares from him and her brother.

"That's not funny, Jess!" Edward cast another glance around the campsite as though trying to determine how much he should blame her. "You can't run off our cook right before the trail drive!"

"She didn't." Desta moved forward, shoulders back. "I'm the one who slapped a tin of hot beans atop his fool head."

"You did *what*?" Ed goggled at his aunt then repeated himself. "*You* did what?"

"Bigot spat in the dish he offered Ralph." Even amidst the aftermath of the man's hateful temper, Desta's revelation shocked everyone.

"He deserved worse!" Agitated, Jess turned to search the horizon for the weasel, but he'd long since scurried out of sight.

"So Jess and I fired him," Tucker finished. "And I was just sending Ralph to take the women home and keep watch over them."

At that last statement, Ed's confusion cleared. "Right."

"No, not right! Desta and I should stay and make supper for the roundup so you don't lose the labor. Besides, some of the men heard me call Desta my aunt when I corrected the cook. No one else said a word about it at the time, but if the men find out about this mess just after they learned about our relationship, we won't be able to avoid a scandal."

"That's right." Desta looked stricken. "They heard you call me your aunt, and not a one of them said anything bad about it except that cook. Word will spread—folks will know about the connection long before we head to town for church this week."

"Which is all to the good, as long as we clean everything up here before anyone noses around." Ed reached out to pat their aunt on the shoulder, and relief at her brother's thoughtful support swelled in Jess. "The other ranch owners swore they heard shouting, but they aren't much for moving unless something threatens their wallets. We can still make sure there's no gossip."

Jess knew better—no matter what they did about the chuck wagon or the cook, Desta's revelation would set tongues wagging. But they could at least slam the lid on this little incident.

"We'll just tell them the truth—I fired him because I didn't care for his attitude and decided we could manage without him for the last night of the roundup."

Ralph gave a slow nod. "The men saw 'nuff to believe that. So long as the grub's good and there's plenty of it, they won't ask many questions."

"Plenty might be a problem." Tucker toed the limp edge of a sack of scattered cornmeal.

"Fresh skillet steaks can go a long way to keeping a man's mouth too busy to ask questions, and no matter what's salvageable here, we have beef for miles." Ed was already reaching for his pommel. "Tucker, come with me to cut out a yearling and bring it back. Ralph, see what you can do to help the women clean things up so they can get cooking."

"Keep an eye out for Rick—just in case," Tucker murmured as he passed Ralph, but Jess still heard the worry in his voice.

His concern tugged at her heart and almost made her feel guilty about using this entire episode to strengthen her position for the trail-drive argument ahead. Almost—but not enough to make her change her plans.

Earning a place on the long drive was the perfect way to establish her role at the Bar None. *Even Papa would be impressed if he knew I managed that—and no one could say I didn't contribute every bit as much as the other owners.*

Galvanized, Jess walked right up to the end of the chuck wagon. The back of the wagon boasted a slanting tower of nooks, niches, and drawers all designed to be cleverly concealed behind the hinged door Ralph broke off and used to shield Desta. The mobile kitchen cupboard was designed like a secretary's desk, with the flat door swinging downward and resting on folding supports to form a worktable. Now broken, the table would need to be refitted and reinforced, but Jess didn't mind.

She'd have sacrificed far more for her aunt's safety—and she couldn't be anything but grateful for the situation now that the danger had passed. Besides, if the wagon needed one repair, it might be an excellent opportunity to fix a few other things. . . .

"I've fixed things now." Desta murmured the words to herself, but Ralph heard.

"Fixed 'em, how?" Funny thing about the man, now that the two of them finally got to talking, he always heard what she said.

Funny thing about her, she liked being heard.

Desta shot a glance toward the huge, handsome man who kept nearby even as he started cleaning up the carnage around them. His hands closed around the tabletop he'd torn clean from the wagon to shield her, and suddenly Desta realized her feelings for Ralph ran deeper than his easy smile or a shared fondness for conversation. *I like that he cares enough to listen. And I like knowing that Ralph Runkle won't quit caring even when he gets old and hard of hearing.*

Maybe someday she could tell him that. But right now, Desta

couldn't imagine what he must think of her.

I never lost my head so far gone and so fast. And, Lord, while the sin sits on my own shoulders and I crave Yore pardon, I can't help wishin' the whole thing hadn't happened in front of Ralph. Figures I'd make a right fool of myself in front of a man I respect. Just now I can't even look him in the eye!

Instead she ducked her head to hide her heat-pinked cheeks, sweeping dirt and coffee grounds back into a sack as she told him, "Never you mind my mutters. Yore already doin' more than yore part helping clean up the mess made by my foolishness."

Ralph tugged the sack from her hand, taking away any excuse to avoid looking at him. "You didn't make this mess, and you done nothin' to be ashamed of. Everybody knows the only fool here today's been kicked off the Bar None."

"He's right!" Jess passed the pair of them on her way to the buckboard, her grin too wide for the sad circumstances.

That girl's planning something. Desta closed her eyes for a minute. *I'm 'fraid I know what it is, and the blame lies with me.*

"Proverbs warns how 'A fool's wrath is presently known: but a prudent man covereth shame.'" Desta tugged the sack from his grasp, brushing against the reassuring strength of his fingers. "Can't sugar-dust the Word of God, and I sure showed my wrath today. That makes me a prize fool."

"Strange enough, this whole thing called Proverbs to my mind, too," Ralph rumbled. "But I'm thinking on that one 'bout how it's better to take a meal of herbs where there is love than a fattened calf with hatred."

"Especially when you think of how Rick 'seasoned' his meat." Jess wrinkled her nose. "We're all grateful he won't serve supper."

"Desta, you might've gotten het up, but even the anger yore repenting came from having such a big heart." Ralph's words had that big heart of hers melting even before he finished. "God forgives you, and you can't change what's over and done with—but don't let what you *can't* do keep yore hands from what you can."

"Ma always said God asks one thing of His children—do the best you can, where you are, with what you have now." With the weight of her guilt eased, Desta smiled and slid a glance toward the buckboard she'd helped Jess pack that morning. Then, finally, she looked Ralph in the eye again. "And it occurs to me that together, we can make something sweet come from all this strife!"

Approval warmed his gaze. "Nothin' in the world like a smiling woman offering to make something sweet to get a man moving!" With that, he picked up the broken tabletop and headed back to the chuck wagon, his jaunty whistle perking up the plains.

"No mistaking the fact that Ralph likes his dessert," Jess observed then winked. "But I'd say he's already sweet on someone."

"Maybe." For the second time that afternoon, Desta felt the tingle of a blush. Her first instinct was to shrug off her niece's comment, but her actions earlier tattled the truth—she wouldn't have lost her temper so badly if she didn't care so much about Ralph. So she took a breath and admitted her true thoughts on the subject. "I hope yore right. Ralph Runkle's an extraordinary man, and it'd be a privilege to spend my days making him happy." *Making us* both *happy.*

"Supper tonight'll be a good starting point then."

"My thoughts exactly. That no-good belly-cheat wouldn't let us unload the dried goods, so we've still got everything we need to fry up fresh doughnuts!" Desta spoke as they walked over and began to unload, a sense of purpose and hope lightening her step.

"It'll be the perfect way to end the meal! And the perfect way to butter up my brother and Tucker. . ."

"Why?" Desta already knew the answer. She didn't regret costing them that old coot of a cook, but she sure regretted the ideas it put in her niece's head.

"I'm looking to take care of the Bar None crew beyond the roundup." Jess sounded determined and downright gleeful and grabbed Desta's suddenly chilled hands. "And you could get a head start on making Ralph happy, if you want to test your resolve. What would you say if I asked you to join me as chuck-wagon cook on the trail drive?"

Suspicions didn't soften the shock of hearing her niece voice such a scandalous plan. Desta shook her head. "I'd say yore cookin' up trouble."

CHAPTER 27

"Delicious." Tucker rested a hand on his stomach and let loose a sigh of satisfaction. The best thing he could've said about the midday meal was that it sufficed to keep a man's stomach from scraping against his spine.

But for supper the women wrought a minor miracle. He'd never eaten so well at a chuck wagon, and rarely eaten so well at any other table. If he weren't so stuffed and peaceable, Tucker would've puzzled over that. He knew Ed put pan-fried steaks on the menu with far better cause than spilled supplies—he'd sampled Desta's cooking before.

Tonight he'd packed in three tins full of what the woman and her niece brought forth from a simple campfire. Butter-rubbed, pan-fried steaks cooked pink, tender, and moist. Hot onions baked in buttermilk. Skillet corn cakes hearty and sweet enough to eat plain, but served with a creamy gravy conjured from the steak drippings. Tucker licked his lips. If it wouldn't break his belly, he'd be back for another helping. Of everything.

All around him, the ranch hands lucky enough to be working a later shift groaned in satisfaction and lolled around smaller campsite fires. Worn out and well fed, none of them seemed inclined toward conversation. Even more telling, none of them seemed inclined to eavesdrop. No one paid any mind when Ed left the cluster of ranch owners—more seemed to have stayed on for the last night than usual, but Tucker chalked that up to the vittles—and sauntered over to his side of the campsite.

"We've done it." Ed voiced Tucker's own thoughts, but the grim edge to his voice gave the words a different meaning.

"Yep. No one'll run home telling tales about this afternoon and making it harder for Desta to take her place as your aunt. Thought you'd be pleased." He made it a statement instead of a question. Ed could answer if he chose or let it ride.

Ed snorted. "They'll still talk about Desta being our aunt, but that's unavoidable. No, I'm talking about Jess's introduction to half the male population of the county. That's what they'll talk about."

Tucker saw where his partner's thoughts headed and didn't care for the view. Seeking a distraction, he looked around the campsite again. What he saw offered little reassurance. The men might not be flapping their gums, but bellies full to bursting hadn't affected their eyesight. Several kept slanting looks toward the chuck wagon, and others kept heading back for another corn cake or a drink of water. At least, those were handy excuses for the treat Tucker knew the men really craved—another gander at Jess. Tucker groaned aloud.

"My sister's sudden return from England, her memorable appearance at the roundup, and the feast she prepared on site with no warning. . .she's halfway to legend." Ed sounded properly aggrieved over his sister's social triumph. "Atchkinson and Hodges have both started asking questions about whether she's spoken for. Bell danced right up to the line trying to find out about her dowry."

"Unbelievable." Trouble was, Tucker believed it. Worse, he believed there'd be more men, more questions, more hopeful hounding headed Ed's way for the foreseeable future. Or until Jess married.

Desperate for any way to stave off the inevitable, Tucker seized on the only possible saving grace. "She'll be in mourning for another year." But even as he forced the words through, Tucker knew the truth.

Men around here were too practical to be patient when faced with a woman like Jess. Ed could try to stem the tide, but he couldn't single-handedly fend off a slew of suitors forever. *Like it or not, she'll be engaged—if not married—before I'm back from the long drive.*

His stomach clenched at the realization, and Tucker almost lost his superb supper as it surged upward to choke him. Ed looked queasy, too, and for a brief moment Tucker hoped Jess had somehow poisoned them all. Violent illness might make men think twice about pursuing her.

"Won't make a difference." Ed shook his head, looking sorrowful but not sickening. "Mourning or not, unless Jess lights the wagon afire before everyone rides out tomorrow morning, we're done for."

"Done! Loaded up and ready to go." Jess beamed at Tucker and gave the side of the repacked chuck wagon an affectionate pat.

Strange as it might seem to someone else, she'd developed a soft spot for this wagon. Some carried foodstuffs and supplies, but for Jess, this one carried memories. A faded recollection of Papa hoisting her onto his shoulders years ago so she could peer into the top cubbyholes, while he explained that a trail drive revolved around its cook. The image of Desta almost breathing fire at a weedy man wearing a tin of beans as a hat. The satisfaction of successfully serving meals to the crew in between bursts of convincing Aunt Desta to join her plans for the trail. The chuck wagon carried more than foodstuffs and bedrolls—it held Jess's hope for earning back her place at the Bar None.

Home—where I belong. Not just because of my last name, but because I'm part of running the Bar None now. The knowledge energized her. It didn't matter that she and Desta scraped together only a handful of hours' worth of sleep last night, rising before dawn's first light to make another meal memorable enough to prove their chuck-wagon capabilities.

Judging from the men's reaction—and the spotless tins they returned once they'd eaten every scrap—they enjoyed Desta's Mennonite toast every bit as much as they liked last night's supper. When her aunt first suggested dipping slices of bread into a mixture of whipped eggs, milk, and salt, then frying the slices, Jess hesitated. But served alongside crispy curls of bacon and a browned hash of thinly sliced potatoes, Desta's special toast made a mouthwatering morning meal—especially when doused with syrup. It put everyone in a cheery mood.

Everyone but Tucker, who stomped up and drained an entire pot of coffee before grunting hello. After that he perked up enough to pack in a substantial breakfast, issue instructions, and get the other outfits rolling home in short order. Since he seemed determined not to let anyone lollygag around, Jess and Desta cleaned up and got ready to clear out before he said a word.

He didn't seem to appreciate the effort, surveying the wagon and the buckboard before pronouncing judgment. "If you're ready, what's keeping you from driving back?"

"I don't know how to drive a team." Desta eyed him with the same measure of disapproval he showed them. "You'll hafta get somebody to bring in the chuck wagon. We'll take the buckboard back."

"Fine." He waved them on their way without another word.

Jess gritted her teeth against her own irritation, refusing to pick an argument and undo all the hard work she'd done so far. Especially after Desta's outburst yesterday, Jess needed to prove a woman could keep calm and carry as much responsibility as any male cook.

"No. Absolutely not. I can't step in as cook!" Ed shook his head so hard and so fast Tucker marveled that it stayed attached to his shoulders. "One of us has to stay on and keep the Bar None running smoothly. If we both head out, rustlers will rob us blind in a matter of weeks."

Tucker opened his mouth to respond, but his partner rushed to add more reasons.

"Even if that weren't true, one of us needs to stay behind to keep an eye on Jess and a shotgun trained on the herd of men who're already planning to come calling." A steely glint in Ed's eyes told Tucker he wasn't joking.

Good. Thank You, Lord, for alleviating one of my worries. Between Ed's protection and Jess's own mule-headed disregard for etiquette, they'll scare off the unworthy.

Somehow that didn't make him feel any less cranky. Because without the unworthy suitors to slow everyone's progress, the viable candidates for Jess's hand would have a clear path. *And I'll be heading the opposite direction.*

It made a man reconsider his priorities, but Tucker didn't see any way he could stick around to watch over Jess. He took what comfort he could from Ed's assertion. "Can't argue about the shotgun—but if Jess didn't need you here, I would've sacrificed some cattle to the rustlers if it meant making our shipment this year."

"I know—but you'd regret it. After one day of my slop, you'd be laying into barrels of jerked beef and cracknels."

"We might have to do that anyway." Tucker scraped his boots before entering the main house behind Ed. "This late in the season, there isn't a decent cook for five hundred miles or more who hasn't already signed on with an outfit."

"Don't be so sure." Jess leaned against the study doorway, blocking her brother's passage into the room and penning the men in the hall. Everything about her, from the split skirts she'd donned once again, to the spark in her eye and her position as makeshift blockade, belied her honey-sweet tones.

Tucker sensed a snare, knew he'd set it off, but didn't know how to avoid putting a foot wrong when it came to talking with Jess. He'd find out how much trouble he triggered after he stepped in it.

"Oh? Do you have someone in mind?" Ed's delight told Tucker his friend thought Jess had found a suitable replacement cook. It also told Tucker that his friend really needed to spend some time getting reacquainted with his sister.

"You could say that." She levered herself upright and left her post in the doorway. But Jess didn't adjourn into the hall, leaving the men to conduct their business. Instead, the contrary chit led them inside the office, slid a second chair behind the desk, and gestured for them to sit! "I'll explain as soon as Desta and Ralph join us."

"Desta and Ralph?" Surprised—and insufficiently suspicious, to Tucker's way of thinking—Ed followed his sister and plopped into his seat without protest. "Join us for what?"

"A discussion about our little chuck-wagon dilemma."

Ed missed the forest for the trees, narrowing in on a simpler concern. "Why Ralph? He's not part owner of the Bar None. Does he cook?"

"'Bout three things." Ralph's bass voice preceded him into the room. He waited until Desta took a seat then folded his huge frame into the chair beside her as he added to his answer. "Just 'nuff to make a crew complain and quit within a week."

"Ralph's here on account of his role on the ranch," Desta announced before Ed could recover from his disappointment. "And because Jess and I appreciate the trust Tucker put in him to watch over us, and we both agreed we wanted him to help make this decision."

"It's important to let people know they're wanted." Jess murmured so softly, Tucker would've missed it if he'd already taken his seat.

No one else acknowledged it, but Tucker filed the comment in his memory. Jess seemed so wistful, he couldn't shake the feeling it mattered more than she would admit. That flash of vulnerability got him into his chair.

"Oh, I understand. You all want to be sure whoever we hire shows Aunt Desta and Runkle the respect they deserve, so you want to approve whoever we hire." Ed looked chagrined at the circumstance, but pleased with his reasoning.

Tucker tried not to resent his partner's cheerful ignorance. Whatever the women wanted, it went beyond approving the camp cook. "Every day we delay will cost us time and trouble on the trail. We roll out as soon as we find someone—anyone—willing to take the job."

At this point, they couldn't afford to be choosy. Not that it would be hard for the new cook to show up the old.

"*Anyone?*" The way Jess stressed the word gave him gooseflesh, but Tucker didn't have the time or patience to pussyfoot around the topic.

"Anyone."

CHAPTER 28

So long as the fellow has no problem with Ralph and produces grub that won't grumble our guts," Tucker elaborated, "I'll send prayers of thanks winging northward and have the cattle chase after them as far as Wyoming."

"In that case, you won't need to delay at all." Jess rose to her feet in a fluid, graceful motion. "You've already got two cooks who wholeheartedly approve of Ralph and made meals for your men that had them licking the tins. Aunt Desta and I will join you on the trail."

"No." Tucker gave his answer even before Jess finished speaking. "Women, facing all the danger and deprivations and drudgery of the trail? Not on my crew. I won't put the two of you through the hardship and humiliation of trying to keep up with the workload, and I won't set myself or my crew the impossible task of trying to protect two women on a journey that kills several experienced men every year."

Ed's interest turned to horror as he watched his sister round the desk, coming to a stop with her hand on her aunt's shoulder. He goggled at the Culpepper women. "You can't be serious."

"Sure we can. We're part owners of the Bar None alongside you and Tucker, and you both get yore hands dirty running things. Why shouldn't me and Jess pitch in to see our men well fed?" Desta slid a sideways glance toward Ralph. "We got a powerful investment in the outcome."

"We got a powerful investment in keeping you safe," Ralph rumbled in return. "Why else do you think Tucker set me to watch? No mistaking that you two are the most precious things on the Bar

None." One of Ralph's huge hands twitched to the right, as though wanting to reach for Desta.

"How will you keep us safe from hundreds of miles away?" Jess's demand had Tucker's stomach turning somersaults.

Lord, what do I say when I've been worried about the same thing? On the trail, she'd be safe from slobbering suitors. And with Desta and Ralph to help keep an eye on her, she couldn't go climbing windmills or riding off alone without warning. In spite of himself, Tucker found the thought tempting. But not for long—he knew better.

"The long drive endangers your very life, but the days bring drudgery." He fought to find the words to describe the trail. "You travel hundreds of grueling miles, ford swollen rivers, endure dozens upon dozens of nights with little or no sleep. You serve a morning meal before four a.m., leave not long after sunrise to drive to the next campsite, set it up, and get dinner then supper underway while the rest of the outfit works their way forward to join you. We drive slowly through the grasslands so the cattle fatten up along the way and are worth more at the end of the trail. Men work in shifts, changing mounts every four hours or so, coming in at all hours for food and coffee. There's never more than an hour or two without someone riding in hard-up, had-out, and hellfire hungry."

"When you put it like that, how can we not go?" Indignant over his attempt to dissuade her, Jess looked even more determined. She made Tucker want to wrap her up, nestle her against his chest, and keep her tied down and out of trouble. "How can you refuse your men all those things you listed, in the face of their sacrifice?"

"They sign on for the sacrifice. You won't realize how much you're giving up until it's too late! No clean clothes or baths as you face the constant threat of exposure, extreme exhaustion, and an unrelenting workload. Men find it miserable. It's no place for women—there's a reason why female cooks are unheard of."

"Not unheard of!" Jess proclaimed. "Elizabeth Cluck accompanied her husband on the long cattle drive eight years ago—with their small children in tow and another babe on the way. If an expectant mother can handle the rigors of the journey without the benefit of another woman's company, surely Aunt Desta and I can see each other through!"

"We'll be there for each other, there to see the crew fed, and there to make right what I done put wrong." Desta wondered if she ought to roll up her sleeves for the rest of the conversation.

Her niece had all the finesse of a marauding Viking swinging an ax. If the blade of logic couldn't slice through Tucker's opposition, Jess seemed willing to bludgeon him into taking her along.

"You didn't put anything wrong." A hard edge underlined Ralph's denial, catching everyone's attention. "And I want better for you than trail life. You women deserve to be looked after and taken care of."

"You men deserve to be taken care of, too, and more than anything that means good food and plenty of it. But I cost you yore cook." Desta didn't know now whether she wanted Ralph to say he wanted her alongside him for the long drive. That line about wanting better for her. . .and how he thought she deserved to be looked after. . .well, she could think of worse things than letting Ralph take care of her.

In fact, Tucker's description of the cattle trail might top that list of worse things.

"She's right—and by the law of the trail, whoever makes Cookie leave the outfit takes his place until another can be found. I fired him after Aunt Desta dumped the beans on his head, so together we ran him off, and together we'll take his place."

"We owe it to the men." Desta could've warned Ralph about the defiled food and let him handle it—she'd just gotten so mad she didn't think straight. Now she worried she still wasn't thinking straight, siding with Jess about taking on the chuck wagon.

When she knew full well she couldn't cook. Not real meals

like the men needed to fill their bellies and fuel their hard work. But what could she do but sacrifice her own comfort and do her best to lessen the damage her temper caused? Besides, she figured that if she did the baking, Jessalyn could help her with the heartier dishes.

"I would've fired him if you hadn't chimed in," Tucker growled.

"But you couldn't take his place anyway," Jess pointed out in an angelic, aren't-I-so-very-reasonable tone of voice.

"I don't see a way around this," Ed confessed. Early on, he'd stood firm with Tucker's position, point-blank refusing to even consider allowing the women to serve as cooks on the cattle drive. But her nephew boasted either more common sense or less conviction than his foreman. "I can't cook."

"Neither can Miss Desta!" Tucker burst out, shocking everyone into silence.

An absurd urge to giggle fluttered in her throat, but she swallowed it back. In all her years cooking for Simon and Ed, no one had come out and spoken the obvious truth. For it to happen now, when it mattered even less, struck her as ridiculously funny.

Jessalyn tilted her head in a motion Desta now knew indicated deep consideration. Was her niece thinking over the simple fare Desta served since she'd arrived, citing the heat and lack of men to cook for as a reason to avoid making anything difficult? Did she realize that the few times they'd worked on something hearty— mainly for Ralph's sake—she'd pitched in with the preparation work but left the actual cooking and seasoning to Jess? Her niece's eyes narrowed, but the brown depths gleamed in the firelight. Yep. Jess knew.

Ed made spluttering noises that could have been taken as protests, but Desta knew full well stemmed from an inability to argue. Her nephew and his father had filched far too many leftover dishes from the springhouse and relegated them to the compost heap or hogs over the years for him to defend her cooking now.

Only Ralph looked genuinely flummoxed, Lord love him.

"What do you mean, Miss Desta can't cook?" Confusion lightened the deep rumble she so loved listening to. "Have you eaten her shepherd's pie? I got so carried away she had to fetch another from the springhouse, and it's her cooking that's to blame."

"I know full well the power of my aunt's cooking," Ed solemnly agreed, holding his grave expression as he added, "I'll have you know I've made more than my fair share of trips to the springhouse over the years."

At that, Desta couldn't hold back her mirth. The giggles burst from her lips and grew until she panted, holding her sides and wailing with laughter. Tears gathered in the corners of her eyes before she finally regained her breath. She returned Ed's mischievous grin with a wide one of her own.

"You and yore father shoulda had more kindness than to keep taking my meals like that." She got the words out before another chuckle shook her. This time Ed joined in.

"It's not funny." Tucker, the only other person present who'd tasted her cooking, was in no mood to appreciate the irony of the situation. "Though it's a good point. Miss Desta, if I brought you along as our cook, the men wouldn't keep on through the whole trip."

Jess broke in. "I made those shepherd pies Ralph mentioned. Aunt Desta helped. Plus you all know she bakes like an angel, and I can cook circles around anyone who's run your chuck wagon before." She paused then cleared her throat and added, "But don't tell Cookie I said so."

"Baking house beauty." Ralph's murmur didn't reach anyone else's ears, but Desta stiffened.

How many years since someone called me that? She took a shaky breath and resolutely looked everywhere but at Ralph. *Not long enough.*

The phrase brought back too many painful memories. Mama shut her away in the plantation baking kitchen from an early age, as slaves learned to do with their pretty young girls. That didn't make it any less lonely. . .nor did it help prepare her for life beyond the protective prison. How much of her life was wasted as she hid from the unknown? And when would she stop hiding?

"That's 'nough." For a moment Desta didn't realize she'd spoken aloud. She'd been trying to stuff her black thoughts back into the place where she kept everything that should be forgotten, but couldn't. Now everyone was staring at her, but for once she didn't blush or back down.

"That's 'nough arguing, Tucker. You got no right to order us off the trail because we're women. We're part owners. We decided we're going. Stop squawking and settle into the circumstances."

"Two days." He sounded hoarse from too much talking. "We don't leave for two days. Ed could find someone in that time."

Ed started shaking his head before Tucker finished. "I asked around, and you know we were already having to pay Rick almost double the standard wage. There are no cooks for hire. Worse, I've already had men come up to me worried about the situation. If you can't find someone else in two days, the women earn their place on the long drive."

Lord, You know how hard I tried to find another way. Tucker hit the road the way he always did—on a horse and a prayer.

Failure lay like a bitter coating across the back of his tongue. He couldn't get the taste out of his mouth, so he turned to the Almighty for help. *I'm trying to accept that taking two women up the trail falls under one of Your designs. I know it's not one of mine. Mine are usually a whole lot more practical—and a whole lot less pretty.*

The thought snuck in before Tucker could catch it, stopping his prayer. Furious with himself, furious with her for no new reason—though the old ones were plenty strong enough—he spurred his mount to go faster. As trail boss, one of his most important functions was scouting ahead. The entire endeavor depended on his ability to locate the best campsite locations for the chuck wagon, hearty forage for the cattle to put on plenty of weight during the journey, and fresh water for everyone on the road. Along with that, he kept an eye out for trouble in the form of Indians, inhospitable settlers, cattle rustlers, and even other outfits moving on the trail.

It meant a lot of responsibility—but it also gave him good reason to leave Jessalyn and her hastily modified chuck wagon behind. For a short time at least. He'd postponed their departure so long, hoping for divine intervention, that they wouldn't move the herd off Bar None land that day. First days never did get the drive very far, but this one would be monumentally unimpressive. Yet it gave them one more day on ranch land, in case a cook came riding in for Ed to send their way.

Since he wouldn't make it far enough to use his familiar first-day site, Tucker needed to find a nice spot, ride back, then escort the women and the wagons to the campsite. The first of dozens of days he'd be looking ahead, riding alongside, and finally following behind the women and their wagons. Something about leading a woman, only to have to chase after her, seemed an eerily appropriate description of his interactions with Jessalyn.

On the trail, once he'd seen her to the campsite, he could wash his hands of her until mealtime. With a little luck, he could ditch his thoughts about her for a while, too. When a woman invaded his very prayers, the time had come to establish distance. Failing that—say, if the obstinate female wrangled herself a place on your cattle drive— Tucker could at least set up some rules and boundaries.

And top of the list came his determination to treat her like any other cook working for his crew. Tucker would hold her to the same exacting standards he'd demanded of the men before her. That included keeping the same grueling schedule as the others while producing chuck of the volume and quality his men deserved. If he couldn't keep Jessalyn off the trail, at least he could keep her so busy she wouldn't have time to get herself in trouble.

Tucker snorted at the ridiculousness of his own thoughts. The woman already landed herself in the worst trouble of her life. She just didn't know it yet.

CHAPTER 29

This is going to be the most exciting trip of my life!" Jessalyn almost wriggled with excitement.

Desta sat beside her on the driver's seat, somehow managing to stay stiff as a poker in spite of the comfortable cushions she'd run up the day before to pad the hard wooden bench. She held firm against even the sway of the wagon, only showing discomfort on the occasions when a wagon wheel hit a rock. Or a rut. Or a clump of earth. Pretty much anything that made the rig bounce up and down in addition to the creaking side-to-side sway.

Compared to that, Jess knew she wouldn't look proper no matter how many wriggles she suppressed. In fact, Desta's composure looked so eerily perfect, it went far beyond a display of decorum. Abruptly, she wondered whether someone dared play a trick and stick a stone under her aunt's cushion.

"Are you all right?" she demanded, keeping her voice low even though there was no chance any of the men would've heard her over the gentle thunder of so many hooves striking earth. "You look uncomfortable."

"I'm fine." Desta compressed her lips into a tight line that told otherwise. She kept her gaze fixed straight ahead, refusing to meet Jess's questioning gaze.

"Are you angry with me?" Her elation plummeted in the space of a single heartbeat. "Have you changed your mind? If you have, we'll have one of the men escort you back straightaway. I'll be fine." Actually, Jess wasn't so sure about that. She'd been so relieved at the prospect of having another woman along, especially her aunt, that she hadn't given much thought to the question of whether or not she'd be up to the task of chuck-wagon cook for a sizeable outfit all on her own.

The doubt galvanized her, putting enough starch in her spine for her to match her aunt's impeccable posture. *I'm up to it.* She set her jaw and slid a glance at Desta, who looked like she'd gone pale. *I have to be.*

"Whoa." She started pulling on the reins and bringing the wagon to a stop, but her aunt reached out and grabbed her wrist.

"Keep going." For the first time since they'd settled onto the seat, Desta looked her in the eyes. "I'll be fine in a bit, once I get used to it. When we was makin' all our plans, I never hopped on up here for the feel of it. Didn't see the need, since you'd be doin' the driving."

"Does the motion make you feel sick?" Jess held her breath, hoping this wasn't the case. If so, she wouldn't put her aunt through weeks' worth of torture as they covered hundreds of miles.

Desta shook her head and curled her fingers under the lip of the seat, clutching the cushion so hard it compressed almost as flat as the wood beneath. "It's just a lot higher up here than I reckoned, is all."

Jess considered this, uncertain whether or not Desta would be able to adjust. The memory of Tucker panicking at the windmill, explaining how height could make men so afraid they turned dizzy, fell from their perch, and died, made her shiver in spite of the hot summer sunshine.

I can't live with the knowledge that I helped cause the deaths of Papa and Aunt Desta.

As always, the thought of Papa wrenched her. Jess looked around to see if she could spot Tucker. One man on horseback could cover a lot of ground in a very short time, certainly far more quickly than a lumbering wagon packed pillar to post with anything and everything Jess and Desta could think of.

Well, *almost* everything. They'd talked their way into taking a second, smaller wagon so they could fit *everything*. The youngster assigned to helping the cook was driving that one.

Tucker had proved none too happy with the idea either. Since he stayed so adamantly opposed to them going at all, he made it hard to tell whether any of the extra little adjustments they made really put his nose any further out of joint. But surely his annoyance wouldn't keep him from checking in with them and making sure there weren't any major issues he needed to address? Say, for instance, if Aunt Desta suddenly discovered a fear of heights?

She craned her neck, agitated by her inability to see around the sides of the wagon. So long as she was driving, her range of vision would be very limited. She could only see ahead.

But that's all right, she told herself. *After so many years, I didn't want to look back on staying stuck right where I was. I'm used to only looking ahead.*

Ahead lies hope. Ahead lies possibility. Ahead lies anything and everything that will be better than the frustrations of today.

Except. . .today was finally exciting. She'd be having the time of her life if it weren't for her worry about Aunt Desta. For the first time, Jess had good reason to look around.

Where is he? Jess looked around again, but still couldn't spot the man. *Doesn't he know that while we're working hard to see his crew through the drive, we're relying on him?*

Wait. Only her concern about how a sudden stop might affect Aunt Desta kept her from yanking the wagon to a halt, so overwhelming was her sudden need to stop and take stock of things. *When did I start relying on Tucker?*

Fingers tightening her grip on the reins, Jess kept herself from pulling back by planting her boots against the floor of the wagon and pressing down. The physical action distracted her, a gesture to anchor her swirling thoughts.

Sometimes knowing you had the power to stop gave you the strength to keep moving. But what if you'd started to rely on someone other than yourself? How strong could you be then?

Jess drew a deep breath and shoved the disturbing questions aside. Instead of thinking about Tucker and looking for him to solve her problems, Jess did what she always did: tackled it herself. Trying to keep her voice level so she didn't startle her aunt, she probed for more information. "I didn't know you were afraid of heights."

"Me either. Never really climbed anything higher than a regular ol' buckboard before." She sounded steadier than she had a moment ago, and she looked a bit less stiff.

In fact, when Jess glanced over, she spotted her aunt loosening her grip on the bench so she could lean toward the side of the wagon and take a look over the edge. Surely a woman petrified of the view wouldn't do that?

"Feels different, don't it?" Desta stopped looking over the side and straightened back up, this time sitting more comfortably. "Bein' up this high. The way the whole thing moves seems a lot less steady."

"I know what you mean." Jess snuck another look at her aunt, glad to see she'd regained her usual, beautiful coloring. "The higher up, the more you feel the motion. It's got longer to travel so every movement seems more pronounced."

Desta snapped her fingers. "That's 'zactly so. Took me by surprise. When a body got no warning, you have a rough time telling if it's yore stomach that's doin' all the jumping, if yore gonna fall clean from yore seat, or if it's working as it should."

"The motion carries farther, like I said." Jess searched for another way to explain it. "It's like how when you walk beside Ralph, you each take one step. You start out in the same place, but he'd go a lot farther if he weren't adjusting his stride. He's taller, so the same motion carries him a longer distance. Same thing on this wagon—the higher up you are, the bigger it makes the movement."

For a moment Desta didn't say anything. "I like that. Seems to me that something built along the same lines as Ralph will be as solid and dependable as the day is long. Much more sturdy than any old buckboard."

That said, she took one of her hands away from the edge of the seat, holding on with only one as she reached up to finger her bonnet strings. She insisted on wearing one, and no amount of arguing on Jess's part convinced her to try a Stetson. She declared they were "made for men" and weren't going to help an "old woman like her" look any better.

When Jess asked whom an old woman might need to look nice for, Desta harrumphed and turned away—but not before stifling a small, secretive smile that told her niece everything she needed to know. Today confirmed it.

I made the right decision, swallowing my pride so Ralph and Desta could have a chance to get to know each other. Jess settled herself at a more comfortable angle. *If nothing else, she feels safer and more secure when he's around.*

The sudden image of a mean little man wearing a tin of beans popped into her thoughts and made her smile. *Then again, having Aunt Desta around probably makes Ralph feel more secure, too.*

A wistful thread wound around her thoughts, pulling at her earlier conviction that she could rely on Tucker. *It's the same thought I had when I knew he and Aunt Desta wouldn't let me face Ed if they believed I'd need support. I just didn't fully recognize it then. But thinking something—even more than once—doesn't make it true. Can I really rely on him?*

Then, equally important but even harder to answer, another question crept out and latched on to the first. *If I can, will he ever come to rely on me in return?*

"I'm relying on you." Tucker's vote of confidence as he helped her and Desta strike up camp for the first time made Jess wonder if he'd somehow picked up on her earlier thoughts.

Maybe we're starting to think alike? Jess couldn't decide whether or not that could be called a good thing. *Hm. . .so long as he's starting to see things my way and not the other way around.*

"We're relying on you, too." She made a wide arc with her arm to indicate the surrounding area, and particularly the river offshoot running a couple hundred yards to the side. "This looks like a great spot for our first campsite."

He grunted. "We usually camp another four miles down the trail for the first night."

Jess paused, wondering if she imagined the hint of accusation in that statement. "Desta and I had the wagons ready yesterday." Well, mostly. She and her aunt had also been waiting for the men to load up their tools and bedrolls to see if they could squeeze in any more provisions. They'd managed to tuck in quite a few little luxuries that way. . . but still they'd been ready to ride out for hours ahead of the men.

Now, having waited so late in the day, Tucker left precious little time for her and Desta to prepare the midday meal. She'd planned something special, but now she'd have to settle for something quick, simple, and ordinary. She needed to scrape every minute in order to get supper started afterward—it should've already been in the oven.

"Wagons." The way Tucker emphasized the plural left no doubt about his disapproval.

"Cooks." Desta didn't miss a beat as she returned with the younger Creevey brother, toting firewood and fresh water to make the afternoon and evening meals. Towheaded Quincy didn't seem to say much, but he followed orders with alacrity and proved to be much stronger than he looked.

"One extra person should not equate to an entire extra wagon," he muttered wearily.

"It's not for one extra person. The Studebaker Company made the chuck wagon to accommodate a crew of ten men. We have two cooks, nine men, and Ralph."

"Count him again." Quincy cleared his throat and looked down at his boots. "Twice."

"I always do." Jess chuckled and sent Quincy to water the wagon teams and pen them for the night in a makeshift rope corral. She saw Desta already mixing up a batch of dough for biscuits, and Jess hunkered down to dig a substantial fire pit.

"It doesn't need to be that deep." Tucker's criticism rankled—particularly since he stood there, cool and calm, while Jess scrabbled in the dirt trying to make up for his schedule change.

Somehow she managed not to fling a handful of dirt at him. Instead she settled for asking, "Do you know what we're serving for supper tonight, Tucker?"

"No." Interest livened his tone. "What?"

"If you don't know what we're cooking, you don't know what we'll need. But if you're inclined to sample the fare later, I'd suggest you keep your comments encouraging." The supper she planned needed a deep layer of red-hot coals from a fire burned in the pit. It held heat longer and more evenly than coals pulled from a cook fire and dropped in a pit later.

"Fair enough." Tucker sounded amused. "I'll be back in an hour or two to get that sample." With that, he rode back the way they'd come, off to keep man and cattle moving at a quick pace.

Jess picked up the pace of her own preparations to match. Finished digging, she reached for wood, swiftly constructing a fire in the pit before moving closer to the chuck wagon and setting up an above-ground cook fire for Desta's dutch-oven baking.

"Fire's started," she called to her aunt, moving back to the pit fire. "Shouldn't take too long to get a mound of embers to heat your ovens."

"Thanks." Desta laid a towel over her mixing bowl and headed toward Jess. "Good thing we went ahead and stewed beef this morning. We wouldn't have time to pull dinner together otherwise."

"Our preparations will all come in handy," Jess promised as she laid a cast-iron bar across the mouth of the pit, attached a hook, and hung a massive stewpot. "Slumgullion takes no time if the meat's already stewed."

"My kind of cooking." Desta grinned and listened, grabbing things from the wagon as Jess issued a steady stream of instructions and explanations.

"Toss it in a larded pot with onions, wait for it to warm. Then add a can each of corn, tomatoes, green beans, and peas. If we had more time I'd chop some potatoes very fine and throw them in, but an hour's not long enough to be sure they'll cook through." Once they had everything simmering, Jess straightened up and saw her aunt's smile.

"Should go good with those sourdough loaves I baked last night. For later this evening, I've got two batches of biscuits ready to bake— I can shape them now. I reckon the fire and ovens will be hot enough by the time I'm through." With that, Desta returned to the back of the chuck wagon and resumed her baking.

Jess followed, folding down the work surface she'd had the men attach to the back of the buckboard. It didn't look pretty, but it served its purpose and held a fair amount of weight. The collapsible table didn't so much as shudder when she plunked down the ten-pound roast of venison she'd soaked last night to remove most of the smokehouse salt.

"I've got the big oven larded up and tucked in yore fire pit. If you pop the meat inside, cover it, and let the fire do the work, that's just like baking," Desta mused. "I could do that, too. Roast and slumgullion—in one afternoon you near 'nuff doubled my menu!"

"We're not done yet. Why don't you cut a good length of twine— something that could wrap around this roast twice." By the time Desta handed the twine to her, Jess had covered the entire thing with slices from a side of bacon. Together the two women lifted the roast and lassoed the bacon tight. Then they sprinkled the whole thing with salt and pepper and dusted it with flour to seal in the flavor.

Once the roast was ready, they each took an end of the metal bar lying across the cooking pit and carefully carried it—and its hanging stewpot filled with dinner—and set it on its legs over the other fire.

Together they seared each side of the roast in the greased cast-iron oven nestled deep within the pit then let it settle inside. A sliced onion, some garlic, a can of tomatoes, and a can's worth of water joined the meat before Jess put down the lid and they covered the whole thing with a half foot of dry dirt, stomped flat and free of any air holes.

"And when we dig it up, it'll be cooked?" Desta looked like she harbored doubts but hoped she was wrong.

"In six or seven hours," Jess promised. "It'll be done right on time. Another hour, and we would've waited too long. This morning's delay cut things close for us."

"But here we are, dinner taken care of, supper simmering along, bread and biscuits seen to, and plenty of time to make a dessert worthy of our first night on the trail!" Now that it was Desta's turn to take charge and teach, her eyes sparkled.

"Things look better now than they did this morning," Jess agreed. "And tonight the men will be full of appreciation for our efforts. Think what we can accomplish tomorrow when we won't be so rushed!"

"Something smells good." Finished watering the cattle and corralling them, Quincy sniffed the air like a cat hoping for cream.

"Just you wait, Quincy! Today's chuck will pad your belly. Tonight's will tickle your ribs. And we'll keep on improvin'." Desta passed the boy a biscuit fresh from the oven while Jess unstrapped the jar of heavy cream she'd fastened to the side of the wagon earlier that morning.

The bouncing Desta found so unsettling served to agitate the cream, the wagon's motion working as well as any churn to turn that cream into butter. Jess spooned out a bit of fresh-formed butter and dolloped it atop Quincy's biscuit, adding a promise to sweeten the deal.

"You'll be eating so well and smiling so big your own brother will hardly recognize you in a couple of weeks!"

CHAPTER 30

T hree weeks into the trip, Tucker cracked open one gritty eyelid, only to have it fall shut. He swallowed a groan, thinking he might need to prop his lids open with small sticks to get going again. Or he could borrow a trick from one of the old vaqueros and rub tobacco juice in his eyes. It stung something terrible and made a man's eyes water for hours on end, but it definitely got him up and moving.

Tucker never kept tobacco—he couldn't abide the stuff, but if he'd had some at hand, he would have seriously considered using the vile stuff. It took that much effort to roll over, brace his forearms against the ground, and lever himself out of his bedroll. He couldn't just sit up and get his feet beneath him because he'd fallen into bed like a rooster—with his spurs still on.

Come to think of it, he should've done that. A quick moment squatting atop his spurs would've startled him awake as well as any of the other equally painful methods he'd been considering. Ah, well. He was up now, and coffee waited for him a few stumbling steps away. Tucker breathed deep, the cooler air of dawn mingled with the rich aroma of coffee strong enough to strip the hide off a lizard.

Whatever his doubts about bringing the women along, he needn't be concerned about the way they brewed that all-important beverage. If anything, Jess steeped it stronger than just about every camp cook he'd ever hired.

Something clunked into motion in Tucker's brain, making him wince at the unwelcome sensation. Were thoughts supposed to pound so hard against the inside of a man's skull? He couldn't remember at the moment, but he didn't think so.

Lord, help me not snap at the women. His morning prayer ranked among the shortest in recent memory—but then again, his recent memory wasn't as reliable as usual.

Three weeks; three stampedes. The worst drive he'd ever made there'd been five stampedes, and that was over the course of three months, from Waco all the way to Dodge City. All this trouble, and they'd barely made it from Waco to ford the Red River crossing yesterday.

Made pretty good time though. Whatever other trouble the runs caused, at least they'd been in the right direction. Now Tucker needed to get *himself* going in the right direction. After another night spent almost entirely in the saddle, Tucker knew it wasn't his own strength getting him out of bed in the morning.

Either God granted him grace, or he staggered on simply because he couldn't sleep in when Jessalyn would have been up and bustling around for hours already. Given the way this drive had gone so far, forcing the men out of bed out of sheer shame might be the best contribution the women could make. Oh. They made everyone swear less, speak nicer, and smile more, too. But that still paled beside the monumental task of getting everyone up and going. No other cook Tucker ever hauled along could've managed that. In light of that valuable service, it didn't much matter what they chose to serve for. . .

Breakfast. His clunking thoughts ground to a halt, his brain too busy sorting out the happy messages his nose sent up. *Coffee.* Thick, rich, and black as night with twice the bite, the aroma alone perked a man up. *Bacon. . .mmmmm. . .* No way to do justice to the miracle that was a pan of fresh-fried bacon. But something else jumped into the mix and made Tucker pick up his pace, sniffing his way to the chuck wagon.

"Good morning!" Jess's cheerful greeting sallied forth from behind the canvas flaps protecting the back half of the chuck wagon and extending into a makeshift shelter where the women slept at night.

Or rather, where they *would* have slept if the cattle didn't keep spooking. Even under the best of circumstances, camp cooks had to be up three hours before sunrise to get the grub ready for the men coming back from late shift and the group riding out to spell them.

"You have no right to sound so cheerful." As soon as the words left his mouth, Tucker wished he'd bitten his tongue. "Sorry. You have every right to be cheerful. It's a wonderful thing that you can run on so little rest and still sound happy to greet the morning."

"Yes, it is. I'm glad you can see that I have a right to be happy." Jess poured a stream of dark, luscious liquid into a mug.

Something uncurled inside him with a hopeful sniff. When he didn't follow up that smell with an immediate gulp of blessed, bitter brew, the thing snapped and snarled.

"Yeah," Tucker snapped right along with the nameless impulse. "The right you don't have is rubbing your liveliness in everyone else's faces when the sun isn't even shining. It's downright indecent."

She drew in a deep breath, as though breathing took all her concentration. Then she held the mug out toward him and asked, "Coffee?"

That bright smile of hers didn't falter this time like it had the first eleven times he'd gone in grumpy. Either she'd done something awful to his coffee, or she'd stopped taking his bad moods personally.

Thing of it was, women were like barbed wire. They all had their good points, but they got awful prickly. Jess proved no exception to that rule.

Tucker frowned. The pounding against the inside of his skull made it hard to be sure, but he sorta had the notion he'd decided she still took things personal. Which meant—

"Just drink it." She nudged a blessedly warm mug into his hands. "You barely count as human until you do. I've got it figured out. With coffee, you're Tucker again. Without coffee. . ."

"Don't you go givin' him no options." Desta woke up more like a normal person, showing no signs of Jess's revoltingly chipper attitude. "There ain't no Tucker without coffee. It's somethin' he'll need to turn an eye toward fixin' someday, but not till after this drive gets done."

"Dunno what you two are yammering about." He glared at each of them, then glared down at the mug he'd wrapped both hands around. Tucker let the steam wash over his face and stopped trying to figure out whether or not this was some sort of perfectly plotted female vengeance.

So what if it is? He downed the whole mug in two swallows, letting the liquid scald him awake. Smacking his lips, he thrust the cup back toward Jess in wordless demand. So it went. She filled, he emptied, and when they'd done this dance four times, the pounding in his head packed up its bags and left him in some semblance of peace.

Guilt struck him almost immediately—or maybe it had already been knocking, but hadn't made it past the pounding to be heard. Tucker hung his head, the whiskers on his chin scratching against his rumpled collar. "Sorry. Usually I make a point of not talking to anyone until after I've put away half a carafe or so."

"You mentioned that afore." Desta arched a brow at him. "In fact, every morning after you've turned back into Tucker, you run remorseful like this. We promise we won't take it personal if you rest yore voice a few extra minutes every morning."

"We'll probably like you better for it," Jess called from the side of the wagon, where she fetched more water to put on another batch of coffee. No doubt about it, the woman was a marvel.

How could I have ever argued against her coming along? Without her, we'd probably be three days behind. Tucker leaned against the side of the wagon and accepted another serving of the black fuel that kept him running when he'd been run ragged.

Maybe if he put away enough of the stuff, he'd feel half as friendly and full of energy as the woman who continued to surprise him.

If the man had any idea what ran through her head when he staggered in here every morning, he'd run as though fleeing the hounds of hell.

No, Jess silently amended. *He'd grab the coffee* then *run as though fleeing the hounds of hell.*

Then again, if he thought to turn around and treat those poor creatures to the same snapping and snarling he aimed at her, they'd probably slink back to perdition with their tails tucked between their legs and their hearts full of gratitude that *they* weren't the ones stuck working with him day in and day out with no end in sight!

But instead of giving Tucker the telling-off he so richly earned every day, she smiled and served him more quickly. Sure, he earned another notch on the stick she kept hidden in her barely used bedroll, but he didn't need to know about his growing tally. He'd settle that score with her when the drive was done. Until then, she figured she owed him both her service as black-coffee supplier and her silence about his even-darker morning moods. If she'd listened to the man, she would have been spared all of it.

Every time she caught him looking or acting as miserable as she felt, it broke her heart a little more. *Tucker tried so hard and fought all of us for so long, trying to spare us.* And when they hadn't listened on the night of the roundup, he'd still ridden the length and breadth of the county, wired telegrams, and done everything in his power to inflict this terrible journey on anyone else. But the worst part, to Jess, had been how hard he took his own failure. She'd thought him annoyed and aggrieved at having gotten saddled with a pair of women. Now she knew better. Tucker understood the hardship ahead, and he grieved *for* them.

If I'd only known, I would've grieved for us, too. Jess sighed and started slicing yet another slab of bacon. Once, she'd loved the sweet-savory flavor of the smoky meat. Now she could scarcely stand the smell. It was added to the list of disappointments plaguing her.

The grand adventure she'd envisioned, filled with miles of changing scenery, tall tales swapped with the men, and deepening conversation with the only female relative she could claim, had proven false. In place of these happy dreams, they got a brutal serving of drive life. The men worked in rotating shifts, which meant someone always needed to be fed—and food always needed to be ready. This meant that at least one of the cooks always had to be ready.

No matter how and when they tried to snatch sleep, Jessalyn never caught more than a couple of hours at a time. In spite of the cushion, long miles took their toll. Combined with sleepless nights, neither of them had much energy left for conversation. It was all Jess could do to keep driving the team while her aunt dozed next to her.

Throw in enough stampedes to make the men miserable and cranky, and every day dragged into the next with unceasing, unrelenting monotony. *Drive, cook, dishes. Drive, cook, dishes. . .* The cycle spun on endlessly, punctuated by these delightful morning visits with a pre-coffee Tucker. To be fair, post-coffee Tucker was a vast improvement.

It might take a mountain-range worth of bitter beans to sweeten the man's outlook, but no one could deny he took care of his own. Jess's irritation eased as she thought of the many small kindnesses Tucker showed along the trail. From the sites he chose to the shifts he assigned and the gear he inspected, Tucker kept busy making sure they had everything they needed to get through the long days.

They were fortunate to have such a capable trail boss. Whenever and wherever possible, he tried to ease their way.

But nothing could make the journey easy.

Increasingly, Jess found herself turning to her father's Bible in search of a way to stay awake. And, as time went on, in search of answers and inspiration.

Papa always cited psalms of praise when he rode the ranch. Aunt Desta held a fondness for practical proverbs. But Jess treasured the

Old Testament tales told to her as a child—stories filled with larger-than-life heroes handling hardship through faith. Now she sought out those stories with fresh eyes, finding comfort from traits she shared with the greatest of God's chosen people.

Abraham believed in a future beyond what he could see. Born with no birthright, Jacob fought for his father's blessing. Esther remained true to her heritage, and her heart, in the face of death. Joseph, discarded by his family and sent to a foreign land, proved his worth beyond any doubt.

And so will I. Jess slipped a ribbon between the whisper-thin pages of Papa's Bible, marking Joseph's story so she could read it again later. *Papa already sent me away, I survived the foreign land. . . and after this cattle drive, no one on the Bar None can say I haven't earned my place and proven my worth!*

If she lost sight of that, she lost everything.

CHAPTER 31

Wen did you lose it?" Tucker eyed the boy's burned cheeks and the sunburned stripe of scalp dividing his white-blond hair, and winced in sympathy. *How did I not notice one of my men riding around without a hat?*

"Charge before last, sir." Porter Creevey, the young man in charge of the outfit's horse remuda, bowed his head. The vantage point displayed his sunburn even more brilliantly.

"We'll get you a hat as we go past town today." Luckily, there were enough outposts scattered on this side of the trail after Monument Hill for them to get this taken care of. A cowboy without a hat wouldn't make it far.

It wasn't a question of if he'd die. It was a question of *how long* until he succumbed to sunstroke or dehydration.

"It's Sunday." Creevey sounded apologetic as he broke the bad news, but Tucker understood. Finding a shopkeeper who'd do business on the Lord's Day could get tricky.

Giving the order to keep the herd grazing and let them drift north at a leisurely pace, Tucker took the kid to town. He knocked on the back door of the mercantile, figuring the shopkeeper might be more willing to work out a deal privately. The man carried a good bit of extra weight around his middle, but sadly seemed to have missed out on such bounty between his ears.

"Can't sell anything on the Lord's Day," he steadfastly maintained, jaw jutting forward. "'Sides, I'm about to leave for church!"

"You'd rather sacrifice this young soul to death by exposure?" Tucker clapped a hand on the youth's shoulder and nudged his neck so his head fell forward, exposing the bright line of burned skin already beginning to blister.

"Ain't my sacrifice," the self-righteous shopkeeper maintained. "In any case, a mortal life is little cost compared to the loss of an immortal soul. Around here, we follow the Lord's laws!" With that, he yanked the door from Tucker's hand and slammed it in their faces.

Tucker fought the urge to break the man's windows, walk inside, and steal a hat. He stood there for a long time, banging on the door and bellowing for all the world to hear. But it did no good. The shopkeeper had escaped through the front of the store to seek peace in the House of the Lord.

The man needed to be taught the difference between peace and quiet and the peace that passed all understanding. But Tucker didn't see how he'd be the one to manage it. The best they could hope for was to wait until church got out to see if God worked in the man's heart and his conscience kicked up a fuss.

Failing that, Tucker would rig some sort of head covering for the boy. A bit of bedroll or some of his slicker would do in a pinch. Both were thick enough and treated to withstand rain to some degree. It wouldn't be pretty, it wouldn't hold water, it wouldn't sit high enough to allow the luxury of an air pocket to lessen the heat. . .and it'd slide off in a stiff breeze. Useless.

They only had one choice. Tucker's jaw clenched as he slapped the hat back on his head and addressed his hapless puncher. "We aren't leaving this town today without getting you taken care of."

"I'll take care of it." Jess patted Quincy Creevey's shoulder, trying to soothe the sixteen-year-old who'd been such a big help to her and Desta throughout the trip.

The boy suffered from a lisp severe enough to keep him from saying much, but he worked hard. The smallest and youngest member of the crew, he gathered firewood or buffalo chips, stocking the leather swing stretched across the underbelly of the chuck wagon. He drove the spare buckboard the women insisted on bringing along, sparing Desta from the strain of learning to drive a team.

He scrubbed and carted pots and pans, peeled potatoes, took on some of the latest night watches, and above all remained unfailingly polite. She and Desta would've crumpled into heaps long ago if it weren't for Quincy's unassuming assistance and quiet camaraderie.

So when he struggled his way through a speech about his brother losing his hat, Jess was horror-struck. From what she gathered, Tucker already took the older Creevey brother to the township a couple miles up the trail. But the shopkeeper there had an unflinching reputation for refusing to do business on the Lord's Day, no matter how important the person or how great the need. From the fear on Quincy's face and the few facts Jess knew about the dangers of exposure, the need was great indeed.

"Can you stay here and pass out coffee and splatterdabs to the men as they come in?" His nod was eager and apprehensive all at once. It tugged at her heart.

"Then I'll take the buckboard into town and make sure this gets handled, quick as can be." She glanced over to where her aunt stood, eyes narrowed in speculation. "Miss Desta might come with me, if you're sure you can handle things on your own?"

"She can't go ridin' into town on her lonesome, son." Desta shook her head. "No stickler of a storekeeper who balks at sellin' needful things to honest folks on account of the day of the week will take kindly to requests made by an unescorted woman."

"Isth fine," Quincy assured them. "Go holp m' brosther."

"It's a big job we're trusting to you, but it's a big job you've trusted to me. So I figure that makes things even," Jess called over her shoulder, hoping to build the boy's confidence as she and Desta took off.

"Smart boy," her aunt approved when they reached the buckboard and found the team already hitched and waiting. They wasted no time hopping aboard and setting off.

For some moments in life, timing turned out to mean everything. Jess knew that full well even before she'd raced into the shipping office, desperate to book passage to America, and discovered that if she'd arrived even three minutes later, she would've missed meeting the captain of the vessel. At the time, she'd called it luck and gone on her way.

Now, after weeks spent with Aunt Desta, Tucker, and even some time spent with Ed, she knew they would call it something else. Divine providence sounded awfully presumptuous to Jess, but at the same time there was something comforting in the idea that God went ahead and arranged little appointments in a person's life. It seemed intensely personal, and at the same time, it fit in with the way He didn't seem to step right up and show Himself to people anymore.

From what she'd been reading in Papa's Bible, and what she increasingly remembered learning as a child, in olden days gone by He used to show up more often and in spectacular ways. That seemed to have ended with the New Testament. Jesus came to earth, went home to His heavenly Father, and they both stopped making house calls.

This was the part she had trouble with. Jess never had much patience with waiting, and even now she didn't understand how she was supposed to believe if someone really wanted to be close with her and bring her home, they kept her an ocean or an entire world away. With nothing but some aging letters bound in leather or tied in a ribbon to keep her company when she felt alone.

Maybe that's why she'd latched on to the idea of divine providence. It fit better with Desta's ideas about how God's plans could be comforting instead of constricting. Maybe it wasn't about making your own way in life. Maybe it was more about the way your life could be used to help someone else. This morning she aimed to test that idea.

"Almost feels like I'm headin' for church." Desta gave a little laugh. "Does my heart good to think I'm on my way to a meeting with the Almighty this morning, even if we don't see a single pew."

"Maybe we're on our way to a meeting He arranged," Jess ventured.

"Might could be." No longer laughing, her aunt looked at her with an approval Jess rarely enjoyed from just about anyone. "We'll find out soon as you stop this here wagon."

"Here we are." She pulled to the side of the street and jumped down, hitching the horses and looking along the main drag. At the northern end stood a small, whitewashed building with a spire stretching from the roof. "Look, Aunt Desta. Just like you hoped for. Sort of surprising they have one in such a small place."

"Don't question the building." Desta looped her arm through Jess's and headed toward that spire. "Question the people you find inside until you find someone who can help!"

"Wait a minute, Aunt Desta." Jess had to dig her heels into the ground to effect a stop. "Aren't you supposed to find help within a church even when there's no one you can see?"

"No doubt 'bout it. But you can find that same source of help anyplace, Jess." Her hand tightened its clasp, as though trying to press her words as deep as she could. "It's one of the beautiful things about God. No matter where you are in life, He's willing to meet you if'n you do yore part by comin' to Him in prayer."

"All right." Jess squeezed her aunt's hand in return.

As they walked down the street, Jess heard someone shout her name. She peered in the space between two buildings and spotted Tucker heading her way in a hurry, with a blond boy in tow who could only be the other Creevey. Neither one of them looked very happy.

"Jess! Desta! What are you doing here?" Tucker turned the question into more of a demand for an explanation than anything else.

"Quincy asked us to come help. He's handing out splatterdabs this morning while we rustle up another hat for his brother, here."

Jess smiled at the silent young man, whom she suspected suffered from the same lisp as his brother. "Desta and I think the best chance we have is to head to the church, ask for help, and hope for guidance."

"Fair enough." The men fell into step alongside them. "We already paid a visit on the shopkeeper. He roared a refusal, shut the door in our faces, and snuck out of the building to get away from us. Your way, at least you get to go to church!"

The sound of voices raised in a hymn greeted them through the open door, and they followed the song inside. A handful of half-filled pews faced a plain wooden podium, where a man with more enthusiasm than talent led worship.

Jess smiled as she moved forward, looking for a pew with room enough to fit all four of them. Only the empty front row offered enough space. She pushed aside her discomfort at walking past the entire town, obviously late for service, and forged ahead.

When the song ended, it seemed everyone finished at a different time—on a different note. When the final, quavering voice died away, the man up front raised a hand as though bidding people to halt. Jess couldn't say whether or not he was a preacher—he wore no cleric's collar—but he obviously exerted the authority here.

"Before everyone gets to their feet and finds their way back out the door, why don't we take this chance to thank our visitors for joining us this morning?" He gestured toward them, making Jess blush. "They might have missed the message, but they don't need to miss the feeling of finding fellowship so far afield. Am I right?"

From the sounds of the response rising behind them, Jess thought he'd wrangled an agreement. He must've thought so, too, because his cheerful grin grew even wider before he spoke again.

"Let's take this opportunity to pray over these folks, asking God's provision for their journey and safe travels until they reach their destination!"

CHAPTER 32

Tucker pushed past his disappointment that they'd missed the message—it would've been a much-needed bright spot in a dismal day. A dismal drive, in truth.

He snuck a sideways glance at Jessalyn, smiling to see her place her Stetson so carefully on her lap. She was chock full of funny little quirks like that. Men removed their hats, but women usually kept their heads covered in church. But to Jess, respect for her hardworking Stetson—and the people who'd have to see around it—outweighed feminine pride.

Tucker found good cause to be grateful for lack of vanity. Jess had plenty of pride and more feminine charms than she knew what to do with. If she ever figured out a way to harness the power of that smile of hers, well. . .

For a girl so rough-riding and rule-breaking as to pass for a cowman—if only in a driving downpour—Jessalyn Culpepper sure turned out to be a looker. Even now, as she sat in a shadowy church pew sporting split skirts and a Stetson instead of frilly skirts and a fancy hat, she shined. What little sunlight squeezed through the single window above the door sought her out, gleaming golden along her mussed-up braid.

The preacher's voice pulled his attention back where it belonged. It sounded like he was wrapping things up. "Let's take this opportunity to pray over these folks, asking God's provision for their journey and safe travels until they reach their destination!"

From your lips to God's ears. Tucker bowed his head, then realized he wasn't praying along with the church because Jess grabbed everyone's attention.

"I'm sorry to interrupt." Jess jumped to her feet so everyone could hear, shaping the words with those high-fallutin', parsed-and-proper syllables they'd taught her in England.

Until now Tucker hadn't realized how much he liked it when she did that—and how much *more* he liked knowing that she did it less the longer she spent back home.

"But an introduction like that was too tailor-made to resist trying it on for size!" Her joke met with appreciative laughter from the audience, but Tucker understood the earnestness behind it—and her purpose as she parlayed the preacher's words into a plea for Porter.

"I'm being honest. When your. . .leader, here, spoke of fellowship, provision, and safe travels, I couldn't quite believe it! Those three things brought us here, searching, to see if God would provide the means for this young man to continue safely on our travels."

Jess reached down and tapped Porter's elbow, so he stood up with her and faced the audience. The light filtering through that one window went from golden glow to silvery halo at her command, bathing Porter's white-blond hair with angelic light. Even with his hair sticking up in a hundred different duck-fluff directions, it gleamed bright enough to make some of the women gasp with admiration.

"Bow your head," she whispered from the corner of her mouth, so slick and sly no one but he and Tucker heard.

Porter obeyed, bowing his head to reveal the stripe of angry red slicing through the gleaming crown. Holding his hands clasped in front of him, his head bowed low at the front of a church, the posture turned him into a portrait of wordless suffering—and, better yet, silent supplication.

She's brilliant. Tucker marveled at how easily Jess snagged the spotlight and turned it on Porter's problem. Alone, Tucker hadn't swayed the shopkeeper. Jessalyn herself might have managed it, but she'd taken no chances. Instead, she marshaled the entire township to her side.

"Through no fault of his own, this fine, hardworking young man stands here, suffering. A stampede cost him his hat." She held up her own. "I know it doesn't seem like much, but a simple Stetson provides vital protection from the elements. Exposure for even a day does damage, as you can see. Even one more day and he could fall victim to far worse."

"So soon?" Tucker recognized the quavering voice of the music lover who'd drawn out the last warble of worship.

"Absolutely." He decided it was time to stand alongside his crew and offer up his authority on the subject. "Exposure to the elements doesn't mean one risk. Extreme heat. Dehydration. Sunstroke. Any one of these kills. Combined, they can cost a man his life in a matter of hours. I've seen it firsthand."

By now folks were shifting in their seats, darting glances toward the dour shopkeeper before turning to the man who'd led them in praise. But for all the shuffling and glancing, no one spoke up.

"We aren't looking for a handout." Tucker raised his volume, and the stakes. "The worth of a life can't be measured, but I am fully prepared to be more than generous in return for the gear this young man needs."

"It ain't about the money!" The shopkeeper lumbered to his feet, shaking his head like a crotchety old mule. "This is the Lord's Day, and around here, we make it a point to remember the Sabbath and keep it holy, like the Good Book tells us."

"The Good Book also asks us to be kind, love one another, and treat others as we wish to be treated." Jess stepped in to soften the altercation. "You wouldn't want you or yours left to the mercy of a blazing summer sun."

Far from looking convinced, the man puffed out his chest even farther. "You don't have the first idea what a man like me wants, and it ain't seemly for an upstart of a girl to try and guess."

The women in the room burst into distressed exclamations and angry murmurs. If he hadn't been pinned in behind the pews, Tucker would've stepped forward. For now, he held his ground while Jess stiffened her spine and stared the man down.

That's my girl. Tucker didn't catch the thought—it caught him. *To help Ed look after. . .like I promised Simon. She's not* mine. He tried to correct it, but now that he'd claimed her in his mind, the idea spread. Trying to dislodge the feeling made his chest tight.

Lord, is it possible You brought Jess back before Ed and I would have for this purpose? Not so she could mourn her father and rebuild her life as part of the Bar None family, but so she could become such an important part of mine?

Tucker tried not to look too dumbstruck, glad she'd drawn attention to herself so his stare wouldn't seem so strange. He poked back at the idea that just about knocked him down. Instead of agreeing or denying, he decided to open himself to the idea. *Mine?*

As he pondered, he watched her. Plainspoken and plainly dressed, Jess possessed the sort of beauty most women went out of their way to fake. But once a man got to know her, he could look past all that to the true appeal of Jessalyn Culpepper: that everything about her, from the way she looked to the way she acted, was absolutely genuine.

MINE. This time the desire didn't surprise him. Tucker wasn't stupid enough to pretend he hadn't been intrigued from the moment he spotted her through that curtain window. The tightness in his chest eased. Thinking of the two of them together felt right.

He'd been trying to regain his balance since Simon pulled the rug out from under him with that surprise inheritance. Jess struggled to find her footing in the home she hadn't wanted to leave. *Maybe God threw us both off balance so we'd have even more reason to lean on each other.*

Tucker wondered if Jess saw it that way. *It makes good sense.*

Then again, sense wasn't her strong suit.

He watched as she broke out in a dazzling smile and made his decision. *If she doesn't see it yet, I'll bring her around. Persuading her that we should be a team has to be easier than trying to rein her in.*

Besides. . .he planned to be *very* convincing.

꧁⚬꧂

I have to convince him to change his mind! Jess searched for a way to turn the conversation back around, grasped on the shopkeeper's insult, and beamed as inspiration struck.

"You're right, sir. I can't presume to know the mind of a grown man. But I can certainly enlighten you as to the tender heart of a woman." She turned things around so quick the shopkeeper couldn't hope to keep up. "We can't stand to see needless suffering. We want to help. What's more, we want to see that the people we rely on for what we need—especially every day—feel the same way."

A great swell of agreement filled the room, women waving their hands in the air and nodding to each other.

"It's not that I don't want to help." He tried another track, bellowing over a chorus of demands that he go ahead and help already. "But I can't engage in commerce on the Lord's Day!"

"Christ Himself went out of His way to heal others." The preacher Jess had half forgotten stepped in. "Even on the Sabbath."

"And by His example I'm more than willing to lay hands on the boy and pray for his health," the shopkeeper declared. "Healing is only a business if you're a doctor. But I don't heal by trade. I sell things. And seeing as how Christ also turned over the tables of the money changers at the Temple, I can't sell anything today."

I can't believe he's still arguing! Jess would have been impressed by the man's mule-headedness, if it wasn't about to cost Porter so dearly. The whole thing was downright ridiculous. What kind of callous idiot would risk a boy's life—and withstand the anger of his entire town—over something so trifling as a *hat*?

She didn't believe his protests about biblical principles for a second. A man who truly lived the Christian creed would've given Porter a hat and been done with it before coming to service. If he weren't selfish right down to the soles of his boots, by now he would've made the concession simply to save face.

"You aren't obligated to accept payment just because it's offered." Apparently Tucker's thoughts ran along the same rails as hers. "I said I wasn't asking for a handout, and I stand by the notion that charity should be reserved for those in need. But today, this boy is in need." Tucker clapped a hand on Porter's shoulder, but stared so intensely at the slug-like shopkeeper he missed the boy's look of admiration. He missed Jess's, too.

Standing at the front of the church with his shoulders thrown back, his baritone voice deepening with the force of his conviction, Tucker Carmichael blazed with righteous anger. The force of his character exuded an almost magnetic appeal. Not a woman in the place could look away, and Jess found herself thinking it was a shame there weren't more of them present to enjoy the display.

After all, how many modern men could evoke the ancient strength of mythical heroes while denouncing hypocrisy and protecting those in need of aid? Hours ago, Jess would've laughed at the thought. But that was before Tucker took up the cudgels on Porter's behalf.

"What?" Selfishness begat a certain shrewdness as the shopkeeper played dumb. "I don't understand what you're trying to say."

"I'm saying. . ." Tucker lowered his voice even more, as though confiding a promise and offering a warning all at once. It gave Jess chill bumps, and she hoped it did the same to their opponent. "That if you're offering to be charitable so you won't break the sanctity of the Sabbath, then I won't let my pride stand in the way of you honoring your principles."

"Oh, well, I, er. . . ," he stammered, eyes a bit wild around the edges as he searched for some way to escape the corner he'd backed himself into. When he straightened up, Jess feared he thought he'd found one. "That is to say, I—"

"Wanted to offer all along, but didn't want to embarrass us?" Jess finished the question on a high note of glee then produced a girlish gasp. "I've misjudged you, sir!"

"What?"

"This whole time I was thinking such terrible things about your selfishness, when all along you were willing to let everyone think the very worst about your character, just to spare strangers from embarrassment."

"I wouldn't put it that way."

"We would!" Tucker stepped back and pushed Porter forward so the boy headed down the aisle toward the grudging generosity of the shopkeeper, extending his hand in gratitude.

"Oh yes." Jess grinned at Tucker, relishing the success of their shared conspiracy. "Now's the time to take credit where credit is due!"

CHAPTER 33

For a moment there, when the tide turned and everyone knew the boy would get his hat, Desta fought the urge to follow Porter up the aisle and ask for an extra. The man deserved to lose the money from as many sales as possible after he acted so shamefully, then had the nerve to try and pass off his pettiness as piety.

Jess turned from watching the tiny troupe of townspeople rush to the store. "Are you sure you don't want to join everyone and watch Porter get his new hat?"

Desta shook her head. "Sometimes it's nice just to pause." They left the church and reached a patch of shade where Desta halted, leaning gratefully against the rough clapboards of the building.

Jess edged into the cool patch along with her, and Desta wondered whether her niece was really holding up to the rigors of the trail drive as well as she pretended.

Jessalyn refused to fail, admit defeat, or even show signs of weakness. In some ways, Desta admired that about her niece. In others, it made things downright difficult. How could she confide how much the heat bothered her, and that she wished she'd listened to Jess and brought along a sensible Stetson instead of her bonnet, while her niece rushed around faster than a tumbleweed with a tailwind?

It seemed too hard to catch her to hold a conversation in the first place, and that made it a shame to waste that time with whining. Looking after the men kept them hopping from—well, Desta would have said from morning till night, but these days morning began at three and night nudged right up against it.

Everyone's sense of time was fluid, flowing in a different direction depending on what the day brought and how the terrain stretched out. The night hours, in particular, streamed by. Desta wished she could say the same when the sun rose, but daytime minutes moved like mules—the hotter it got, the slower the seconds crawled by.

Unless she was stealing a moment with Ralph, of course. Then the sun fair flew across the sky. During some of her less-charitable moments, Desta considered asking Jess to arrange more of the "breaks"—not so she and Ralph could see more of each other, but so the entire trip would speed up! Not that she needed to ask her niece for assistance, when Jess already tried to help her sneak those increasingly precious snatches of time. Every time he walked up to the wagon, Jess started clucking at her to go sit a spell.

Desta tried doing the same thing whenever she spotted Tucker making his way over. But her efforts yielded such poor results, with Jessalyn speeding up instead of slowing down, that Desta finally stopped giving any warning. She feared those two would never drop their defenses.

But today things changed, and I got a front-row seat to see it. Tucker couldn't keep his eyes off Jess, sneaking peeks every time he thought no one would notice. Jess didn't display the same sort of interest until later, when Tucker brought the force of his strength against his opponent and revealed the warrior within.

"'Sides, just watching you and Tucker join forces and wage war against that shopkeeper leaves me with plenty to think over." Since she and Jess were alone, Desta confided her most important observation. "Brought out a side of Tucker I've never seen before, like a warrior come to life. I swear, if'n he'd been swinging a sword at that man instead of shaking his Stetson, Tucker would've looked right at home riding with King David."

"I know what you mean." Jess looked off into the distance as though calling the memory to mind. The longer she enjoyed the memory, the more her smile blossomed. "He tried so hard to come alongside me and be civil, but when that wasn't working, Tucker transformed."

Her niece had a habit of tiptoeing right up to what she most wanted to say, then stopping if she thought she'd sound silly. Desta raised a brow, but didn't respond, hoping the void would keep Jess talking to fill it.

"One minute, he was the man we know. The next, well. . .he called to mind heroic deeds and ancient titles. Provider. Protector. Defender." Jess rubbed her arms as though afflicted with a sudden chill. "It made me grateful he fought for our cause this morning. I wouldn't want to be the one going up against him."

"As though that's not exactly what you've been doing almost since you first laid eyes on each other." Desta hooted. The look on her niece's face as understanding dawned struck her as funnier still, so she had a good chuckle. Especially after Jess joined in. There was something about sharing laughter that made it restorative.

"You might have a point," Jess admitted sheepishly. "But if he'd ever turned all that intensity loose on me, I wouldn't have wanted to stand against him."

"What 'bout standing alongside him?" Desta pressed. "Seems to me the two of you make a real good team."

"We did, didn't we?" Pride and surprise mingled in her expression, finding release in a sigh. "But that was for Porter's sake. Truth of the matter is, once you fall into the habit of disagreeing with someone, it carries on. It takes both people wanting more than an argument to make it stop."

"Well, what if he wanted you on his side more of the time?" Desta pressed. "Maybe what you need isn't a stop—do that, it's mighty hard to start over, and yore not looking for an end to anything. You want a change."

"A change. . ." Jess got that faraway look again that told Desta her niece was thinking of Tucker from church. "Might be a wonderful idea."

"I've got a great idea!" Tucker tried to make it sound as if something just popped into his head. A man just couldn't admit he'd been antsy over every extra minute it took for them to grab the goods and get going.

Those minutes added up when the entire town populace insisted on squeezing into the store behind them, cutting off the exit and refusing to let them leave until every woman present personally told Porter how fine he looked in his new hat. Neither of the Creevey kids talked much, so Tucker got the feeling Porter didn't get too many compliments. He didn't mind letting the townsfolk shore up the boy's confidence.

He minded not knowing whether or not Jess and Miss Desta would wait for the two of them before heading back to the campsite. They hadn't had a chance to make plans before the triumphant town pushed Porter and him out of the church and into the shop. Would the women wait, or would they hasten back to make up lost time making lunch?

They stayed. Tucker spotted them soaking up a square of shade and picked up his pace.

"Yeah?" The kid loped along beside him, trying to keep up.

"Miss Jess loves riding more than most, but she's been busy driving the chuck wagon ever since we pulled out." As soon as he said that last part, Tucker could've kicked himself for not noticing sooner. It wouldn't have been hard to assign someone to drive the wagon for her every once in a while.

"Yep. Got m' brother thinking beesth don't keep busthier than her." Panting slightly, Porter couldn't hide his lisp. *S* was a hard letter to avoid saying. "Good cookin', too."

Taking note of the kid's hard breathing, Tucker suddenly remembered he'd been out without a hat all day yesterday, becoming burned and worn out. No wonder he winded easily. Tucker slowed his pace.

The kid could use a chance to catch his breath, and, truth be told, he wasn't the only one. The whole outfit was run off its feet after so many stampedes. Envisioning the route ahead, Tucker decided to take it slow that afternoon and arrange for an extra day's rest. The cattle could put on weight, and he could put some hours of sleep between his morning moods and Jess. *Jess. . .*

Tucker got back to the plan. "What say you take the reins of the buckboard and escort Miss Desta back to camp, and we'll treat Miss Jess to a little ride?"

"Whatever you sthay," Porter agreed right as they reached the women.

The boy blushed beneath a barrage of fresh compliments, while Tucker suddenly realized he probably didn't present such an appealing sight. He rubbed his jaw, wishing he could've shaved sometime in the past week. Or better, taken a bath. The closest he'd come was an icy dip in a cold creek two days ago, so he didn't smell his freshest.

Suddenly this didn't seem like the best idea. What if he'd gone past less-than-fresh to offensive? Tucker gave a surreptitious sniff and winced. His clothes ranked—and "rank" was clearly the right word—as offensive. His only hope was to keep the conversation on horseback. From a mount away, he wouldn't risk offending her.

At least, not with my clothes. Tucker shrugged. Any area of the conversation he could control ahead of time should make other things easy to manage. And he needed all the easy-to-manage factors possible, since Jessalyn herself wouldn't be one of them.

Not that I want her to be easy to manage, Lord. Just. . .easier.

He noticed when the women ran out of compliments and started to stir, signaling their readiness to hit the road. Tucker drew a breath, prayed for the words to start things off right, and made his move.

"You're wearing some of your split skirts again," he blurted out. Not the most romantic start, but at least he had a lead-in to invite her riding.

Jessalyn's cheeks flushed pink, and Tucker could hardly believe she'd started blushing already. Her jaw thrust forward, and suddenly he realized she wasn't flattered or embarrassed at all. Like some sort of thermometer, the color in her cheeks rose to an outraged red while she hissed at him like an angry cat.

"Don't you dare give me grief about wearing split skirts to church, Tucker Carmichael!"

CHAPTER 34

Is that what's got you so riled?" Relief and disbelief coursed through him in equal measure, restoring his hope. Tucker let out some of his tension with a small chuckle.

"Don't laugh at me either! What else am I supposed to think?" The flush began to recede, but leaving her pretty and pink and utterly appealing. "You constantly criticize my clothing."

Realizing he might not make it to the stirrups before sticking a boot in his mouth, Tucker hastened to explain. "No, I've been thinking it's too long since you went riding. You're wearing the perfect thing."

"Really?"

"Yep." Now that she'd gotten past her preoccupation with defending her clothes, Tucker figured they'd put the worst behind them. "Porter and I had a little talk, and he's more than willing to drive Miss Desta back to camp in the buckboard if you wanted to take his pony."

She looked completely nonplussed, stretching her neck to the side as though working out a crick before accepting his offer. "Well, in that case, I'd love to spend some time in the saddle."

If she said she'd love to spend some time with me, it would've been too easy, Tucker told himself. *The challenge makes the chase.*

Porter clicked his tongue and got the wagon in motion while Tucker waited. He figured they'd let the other two get a decent distance ahead, then follow. Dodging the dust and debris kicked up by those wheels wouldn't suit his romantic intent.

Someday Jess will appreciate how thoughtful I was about this. He braced one hand on his pommel and another against the leather rest curving to form the back of his saddle. Tucker applied pressure first on the right, then the left to loosen his back and leave him as relaxed as possible for what lay ahead. A man only proposed once, so he might as well enjoy it.

Tucker settled back into his seat and turned his head to tell Jess they could probably get going. Except. . .Jess wasn't there. While he'd gotten comfy, she'd gone and kept pace with the wagon!

He spurred his mount and caught up in a blink, determined to lure her away from an audience.

"I don't know about you or that pony you're ploddin' along on, but I'm in the mood to feel the wind in my hair and the sky in my smile." Tucker figured that, as a bonus, a stiff breeze could carry away some of the smell from his jacket. "How 'bout it, Jess?"

She glanced at Desta then, without a word, goaded her pony to pick up the pace. By the time she broke into a gallop, Jess's smile matched his. Side by side, they raced the wind for a finish line neither of them could see.

Tucker made sure to angle his mount so they raced off course instead of straight toward camp. When he spotted a small stream snaking through the grass, he called to her that they should give the animals a drink. *And slow down long enough to hear me out!*

She let the horse carry her straight into the shallow water. Droplets splashed her boots, but she didn't seem to mind. Jessalyn's smile looked carefree and joyous for the first time he could remember in weeks as he rode in right alongside her, grateful she hadn't dismounted. Seemed strange, but until he held a meeting with a bar of soap, he'd stand a better chance of getting close to her if he kept his distance.

"Thank you," she told him. "For arranging this with Porter. It's almost like I forgot how freedom feels until the ride reminded me."

"Freedom," Tucker repeated. That wasn't the way he wanted to start off. It brought to mind independence and going it alone, not pairing up with someone as a team. He tried to make the best of it. "Freedom isn't how you ride or even where. It's living as open as you can and sharing that joy."

"You're right." Jess kept smiling as she surveyed the land around them. "Breathe deep, take it all in, and give back your best. . .that's how Papa taught us to tackle each day. I wish more people lived that way."

"It helps if you're not going it alone, I think." *I hope.*

"Sometimes." Jess looked at him, brown eyes warm and searching. "I guess it depends on who you're with and how they treat you."

"You should always be treated well," he assured her. Tucker paused to make sure she'd heard him. When she gave him a questioning little head tilt, he forged ahead. "You were amazing this morning, Jess. I think we made a great team."

"We did." Her swift agreement had him sitting a little straighter in the saddle. "And I'm glad you brought it up because it got me thinking. Up until we left the ranch, we squared off about almost everything. Now, I'm not saying I'm willing to follow all of your orders, but I'm tired of standing against you when we accomplish so much more if we come alongside."

Thank You, Lord!

He kneed his horse to carry him closer to hers. "I'm glad to hear we're thinking the same way. Fact of the matter is, I like having you close by no matter what stance you take, but I liked it best this morning, when we stood together."

"I think we could take on a lot if we don't waste time squabbling." Her brows drew together in thought, making her look so serious and sweet it was all he could do not to sweep her off her horse and onto his.

"I think we could take on the rest of our lives." Tucker figured he wouldn't get a better chance than this, so he grabbed it with both hands. "What if we decided to breathe deep, take it all in, and give our best to each other, every day? There's a lot we could share, if you choose to."

She'd already agreed they made a good pair and could accomplish a lot. Wasn't that the biggest part of marriage? Staying together and working hard to reach their dreams?

Tucker thought the decision would be simple, but as time dragged on and she didn't so much as blink, he began to think differently. An icy numbness settled in his veins and started to spread. *Is it me she doesn't want, or is it the life I pictured us sharing?*

The numbness offered no relief from the weight pressing against his chest, giving the sensation that he'd never be able to "breathe deep" again. Soon the sinking feeling grew so powerful he couldn't believe he and his horse weren't flailing in the water below.

Lord, did I make a mistake? He didn't want to believe it. *And if I did, how can I possibly fix it? When a woman tells you she doesn't want to share her life with you, where do you go from there?*

I can't move. Jess knew Tucker expected a response, but his proposal came as such a shock she couldn't stop staring at the man. Even when her eyes started to water, she couldn't seem to blink. *Aunt Desta was right. Starting over again is so much harder once you've been stopped. . . .*

The longer she sat and stared and struggled to say something, the more Tucker withdrew. He didn't move any more than Jess did, but she could tell the difference anyway. The spark left his eye. Those lines around his eyes and mouth that usually crinkled with sun and smiles deepened into grooves. His smile slipped away like something she'd only imagined.

Frustrated, Jess shook her head, hoping to shake loose something that made sense or at least dislodge the source of her confusion.

"You don't have to say anything, so don't worry about shaking your head. The silence worked just fine." His deep voice flattened into something cold and hard and impossible to sink into the way she normally did.

I didn't even realize I did that! Her heart howled at the revelation. *How did I not notice how much I loved listening to his voice, even when I didn't like what he said?*

The answer came back quick; honest and ornery. *Probably because you were too busy arguing with him.*

Well, the man did manage to say an awful lot that rubbed her the wrong way. It occurred to Jess that, instead of trying to marshal her fluttering thoughts, maybe she should focus and consider what Tucker had actually said. Then maybe she could dredge up a more acceptable reaction than stunned silence.

He'd gone from agreeing with her about them making a good team and wanting to stand together. . .to taking on the rest of their lives. Then he'd quoted what she'd shared earlier from Papa's favorite advice, changing the end to make it personal. *"What if we decided to give our best. . .to each other?"*

That was nice. Jess appreciated the way he'd listened closely to the things she thought were important and offered them back to her with the promise of forever.

If it weren't for the shock, Jess would've found it incredibly touching. *It's not every day a man wants to marry you.*

Jess gasped. Her thoughts, which had taken wing like a flock of disgruntled birds, grudgingly lighted on their perches once again. Only one stayed in motion, flying in the face of her romantic ideas. *He didn't actually propose!*

For all the talk of partnership, sharing, and giving one's best, Tucker hadn't mentioned marriage. He hadn't asked for her hand. He didn't say he wanted her for a wife. Each omission was like being thrown by a bronco—and Jess remembered the sensation all too vividly.

He didn't say he loves me. The most heartrending realization of all trailed behind the others, dead last as though the extra time could soften the blow.

It couldn't.

Eyes stinging, heart aching, Jess no longer felt remorse at seeing Tucker so dejected. *The man has no right to be dejected when he didn't even give me a proper proposal!*

"Stop slumping," Jess snapped. "Don't say my silence gave you any sort of answer. You sprang that on me with no warning, got my head spinning, and now you can't imagine why I'm having a hard time coming up with something to say?"

"I don't know much of anything that goes through that head of yours." Tucker sat straight and pinned her with a pointed look. "Up until a few minutes ago, I would've sworn we were thinking the same thing."

"And that would be?" In spite of her annoyance, Jess softened her tone. She couldn't help it, when his voice had lost that cold edge she'd hated hearing.

"That we're good for each other. More than that." His brows eased apart, the frown fading. "We're good together. And if you wanted, we could build a future for ourselves and the ranch that would make both us and your pa proud."

Part of her heart sang at the words, hearing notes of commitment and companionship, admiration and appreciation. . .but logically, Jess knew he hadn't mentioned any of those things. For the second time, he'd skirted around the important issues.

"Well, that didn't clear anything up. For the second time, I've heard you mention things like"—Jess held up a fist, thrusting up a digit for each point she made—"taking on our lives as a team, giving our best to build a future, making my papa proud. . ." She paused. Making Papa proud was a good way to get her to agree to just about anything, but this time it wasn't enough.

Jess cleared her throat, clenching the points of his proposal as though she could crush them. Then she started anew.

"You didn't mention anything about love, wives, or marriage." Jess paused to look from her upraised fingers to her would-be husband, noting with satisfaction the chagrin on his face.

"So tell me, Tucker. Are you proposing an improved partnership?" Jess crossed her arms, creating a barrier between her and whatever answer he came up with. "Or are you proposing marriage?"

CHAPTER 35

Now came Tucker's turn to stare without offering any answers. A whole herd of responses stampeded in his skull, but he couldn't get a grip on anything to pull him out of the hole. Every single idea he caught hold of would dig him deeper.

Arguing with Jess wouldn't get him anything but a headache. Besides, the woman made a solid case. Some fellows could polish a proposal slick enough that women slid into their arms. *But me?*

"I'm not good with lovey-dovey language and decked-out declarations." For some reason, this manful admission didn't smooth things over.

"You certainly don't strain yourself with trying." She spoke with those starched syllables—the ones that meant trouble.

"Yeah?" Tucker didn't like where this was headed. "Well, I haven't practiced this."

"You should have practiced before you asked!" Her words weren't so crisp around the edges anymore. They tilted together with the passion he found so appealing. No mealymouthed mouse, his Jessalyn.

"Do you want a man who soft-soaps his speech to win women over?" he challenged, refusing to retreat. "I may not talk sweet, but I stand by what I say."

She gave a quick, sharp nod to acknowledge his honesty before prodding her horse to the riverbank and leaving him standing midstream—alone. *All washed up?*

Tucker shrugged off the dismal notion and chased her right up to the scant shade of a scraggly oak. He might've lost control of the conversation, but he'd get things headed the right direction again.

Women always had something more to say, and Jess in particular loved getting the last word. *We're not done yet.*

"I do trust you to stand by what you say. So, to be fair, I'll give you the chance to say it better." Jess raised a hand and made a circular "carry on" sort of motion.

"Whatever I say next is bound to be as bad as before." If honesty was the only good point he could claim in this conversation, he'd make the most of it. Much as he wanted things settled between them, a little time might make her anticipate his next try—which would be a darn sight better than today.

"Since I'm not improved enough yet, we can take this whole thing off the table, ride back to camp, and avoid each other for the rest of the trip. I can get one of the men to bring me my food and coffee."

"No you can't." Her jaw angled forward in defiance. "You won't find a single soul on the whole crew who'll take on the responsibility for your coffee. I've seen bears trapped in cages that snarled and swiped at folks less than you do every morning."

By now she should know it's just the way I wake up. Suddenly Tucker remembered his short-lived concern about her unnatural cheerfulness. He considered for a minute, then dismissed the notion that he'd proposed to a woman who'd spit in his coffee. *Nah. She wouldn't.*

Tucker's relief drained away immediately. *Except she thinks I didn't actually propose.*

He offered the ultimate sacrifice, hoping the depth of his devotion made an impression. "I could make my own coffee."

His spirits sank to the soles of his boots when she didn't immediately refuse, but looked like she was considering leaving him coffeeless and without consolation. Even worse, after everything that came before, Tucker knew he'd have to stand by what he said.

"Maybe." Jess looked far too thoughtful for it to bode well. "It might do you good to go without the one thing you seem to depend on."

"Is that what you think? That coffee is the only thing I depend on?" No wonder she had reservations about his desire to get hitched.

"Maybe not the only thing—but certainly the first thing."

"Wrong."

Her eyes narrowed. "We both know you like to be in control of everything, but depending on yourself doesn't count."

"I don't count myself." Irritated at this glimpse of how she saw him, Tucker realized they had a lot of ground to cover before he'd propose again. "For the record, even if I did, I wouldn't count myself before coffee, since I'm near 'nough useless in the morning without it."

She chewed on the inside of her lip as she tried to solve his puzzle. The longer it took, the more it aggravated him until he cast his gaze heavenward with a silent prayer for patience.

"Oh!" She noticed his glance upward. "Faith! You rely on God before coffee and before yourself."

"I try to. Sometimes when something rubs me the wrong way, I react on my own terms and take charge before turning to prayer. I'm working on it."

She drew a sharp breath, staying silent for a beat too long before replying shortly. "Something we have in common then. I've never been much for prayer, but I'm working on it."

"Not one for prayer?" It surprised him, but now that she mentioned it, Tucker realized she didn't volunteer for or request prayer. *How did I not notice this, Lord?*

"No." Jess withdrew, wrapping one arm around her middle. "Never seemed to do any good when I asked for Mama to get better or Papa to bring me home, so I stopped asking God for things and started questioning Him instead."

"What changed that?" Some of the tension in her shoulders eased at his gentle response, and Tucker realized his botched proposal might still provide an opportunity to reach her heart.

The intensity of her gaze belied Jess's shrug. "Papa's death, the memories once I got home, the way Aunt Desta and Ralph and you and Ed drag God into everything."

"I've seen you reading by the light of the campfire."

"Papa's Bible." She lowered her lids, thick lashes hiding her eyes. "I wanted to bring a part of him with me on the trail and try to find a few answers along the way."

"Anything you want to talk over, I'm here. I won't have all the answers, but by now you know I've got strong opinions." He hoped to make her laugh, but had to settle for a small, swiftly lost smile.

"Another thing we share."

"Many marriages have been built on smaller patches of common ground." he pointed out.

"Many marriages are miserable," she shot back. "Are you willing to settle for that?"

"No. That's not what I want for or from my wife."

"What do you want?"

You. Tucker didn't say it aloud, afraid to sound flippant when he felt anything but. "I want a marriage centered around shared faith, caring, and trust as we build a life together."

"Shared faith. . ." She caught the clincher right away, but seemed more thoughtful than afraid. "Biblically, marriage usually means the man takes control."

"Marriage isn't about control," he countered.

"But you *are* controlling, Tucker. Even your proposal was all about how you wanted to handle the ranch and our lives." Her words were getting clipped again. "You'd be the type of husband to want a biblical wife, and we both know I'm not the submissive sort."

Tucker heard the fear behind the accusation, and it softened his response. She wasn't trying to insult him—she was being honest. And if he were to be honest, he'd given her cause for concern.

"The man is set as the spiritual head of the household, but if you look closely, that's because he's supposed to show his wife the same depth of self-sacrifice Christ showed the church." He paused to see if she understood, but she didn't speak, just circled her hand in a motion bidding him to continue.

"Christ died for the church. If a husband is willing to live out that commitment every day, it means he puts his wife's needs above his own." He struggled to reassure without pressuring her.

"Is 'putting her needs first' another way of saying 'decide what's best for her'—like you've been trying since I first rode up to the Bar None?"

Tucker saw her jaw clenching again and hurried to finish. "I proposed a partnership, not a dictatorship. When you arrived, I didn't know how independent or capable you were then. All I knew was I couldn't stand to see you hurt. Just like with the barbed wire."

She didn't reply, but he saw her rubbing a finger over the palm of her glove, as though retracing his touch from memory. A small gesture, but just enough to give him hope.

"Something on your mind?" he encouraged. Anything that gave her pause and possibly put him in a positive light was worth nudging her to share.

"Just wondering. . ." The dreamy expression slowly sharpened as she looked from her hands to focus on his. Her glance flicked upward, brushed his, and skittered back to his hands. Then she spoke softly, words just above a whisper. "Did that count as us holding hands?"

"Counts," Tucker confirmed without hesitation. She needed it to count, and that meant he needed it, too. Besides, he'd carried the memory of her sweet, sun-warmed skin since that morning. He hadn't forgotten, and that meant it shouldn't be discounted.

"Otherwise, you proposed—almost—when we haven't even held hands." Jess didn't look so sure. "I don't know. . . ."

"I do." He cut in, not letting her think her way around it. That "almost" stung.

"You would say that, though, wouldn't you? Without even taking time to think it over!" Jess pulled her hands apart, clenching them into fists. Fighting his attempts to reach her.

"I don't need to take time when I've been thinking about that morning almost every day since." Tucker saw her startle, fists easing and eyes widening. He pressed his advantage. "The memory marked me as much as your hands mark you."

"What do you mean?" Curiosity warred with a sudden vulnerability in her gaze, making him want his words to reach out and reassure her, since he couldn't.

"The man in me noticed your soft skin, warmed from the sun. How delicate your hands seemed in mine, how finely God made you." Tucker saw her glance back at her hands, as though searching for what he described. "But I also noticed your scars, signs of skill earned with hard work. Your hands show the same supple strength I've seen in you from the start."

Silence, brittle as glass and every bit as transparent, separated them. But Tucker saw the way Jess stared at her gloves, toying with the edges as though impatient to yank them off. As though she wanted to see what he'd seen when he touched her.

"Is that why you held on, even when I tried to pull away?"

"Yes. Notice that I didn't let go of you then." He leaned as close as he could, given the circumstances. "And know that I don't plan to let you go now."

"No?" She sounded so hopeful and hesitant it wound his heart-strings a little tighter.

"No," he promised. "I'm never going to change my mind about wanting you for my own."

"Oh." Something between a gasp and a sigh, the breathy sound made him smile. "That's better."

"Good." Tucker sent up a sincere prayer of thanks that he'd somehow turned the tide.

Suddenly she shot him a saucy look. "Until now, your attempts at romance fell so short they couldn't see over a sway-backed burro."

She wants romance! He could've thrown up his hat and hollered. Of all the things she could've been thinking about, he couldn't imagine a better beginning. Unless he'd courted her properly to start with, but from where he sat, things looked good. *Good, but a bit too far away.*

"I can work on that." He tried not to sound too eager as he nudged his mount forward, closing some of the distance between them. "Why don't you slip off those gloves for starters?"

It would've been awful romantic if she whipped off her gloves, tucked her hand in his, and let him stroke the back with his thumb while they talked.

Instead she edged her horse—and herself—farther away. "It's more than holding hands!"

"I'd be happy to hold more!" Not hiding his enthusiasm for the best idea he'd ever heard, Tucker followed hard on her heels and leaned forward. Holding her close, maybe stealing a kiss. . .

"That's not what I meant!" Exasperated and enticingly breathless, Jess stayed beyond his reach. "There's more to courting than holding hands, holding close, or holding tight!"

"I thought the whole point was finding someone you wanted to hold on to for the rest of your life." For the first time in the conversation, Tucker got the impression he'd said the right thing without even trying.

Jess visibly softened, her lips curving in a small smile and parting to let loose a chuckle. "Someone to hold on to. . .or at least someone I'm happy to see every morning when he heads for my coffeepot."

Tucker let his laughter join hers, relieved he wouldn't have to make his own coffee and rejoicing in the return of her good humor. "I'd do a lot more to start courting you, Jess."

"I worked that out when you offered to take responsibility for your own brew." She shot him one of those special smiles.

Inspired, Tucker made a vow: "Tomorrow morning, I'll start proving myself."

CHAPTER 36

What on earth's gotten into that man?" Desta rounded on Jess the minute Tucker walked away the next morning. "Nary a grumble or a mutter this morning, even before he made it to his mug."

"Tucker's trying to be a better man." Jess smiled.

"Well that's sayin' something, since Tucker Carmichael stands head and shoulders above most men." Desta figured the time for subtlety had passed. If the man could transform for a woman so greatly after a single afternoon ride, he deserved to be taken seriously.

"*Most* men." Jess's raised brow said her niece caught on, and planned to give as good as she got. Jess shaded her eyes, peering toward an advancing rider before adding, "Though Ralph might have an edge."

"Point taken!" In spite of Jess's teasing, Desta straightened and smoothed her hair, squinting against the sun to spot the one man worth all the trouble of the trail.

Desta had some time before Ralph would head over to the chuck wagon. He'd see to his horse's needs first then wash up downstream before presenting himself for a long-overdue meal.

Most of the other men came in to swap shifts earlier that morning, and they'd decided to let Quincy help his brother with the horses so Porter could rest up after suffering too much sun. This presented her with a rare moment of privacy with her niece without the pair of them gritting their teeth against the bone-jarring bounce of the wagon. Desta planned to make the most of it before Ralph stole her attention.

"What happened on yore ride yesterday to make Tucker change his ways?"

Jess sprinkled flour atop the folded-down work surface at the back of the chuck wagon, rolling out pie dough and taking her sweet time before answering blithely, "I might've mentioned how impossible he is in the mornings and that he has a persistent need to control everything. It looks like he decided to make a virtue out of two vices and control his morning grumpiness."

"Now if that ain't a prime example of taking what you're stuck with and making the best of it, I don't know what is!"

"*I* know." Jess waved her rolling pin from the chuck wagon to the campfire and back again. "Every blessed meal we cook on this trail is a prime example of making the best of things!"

"And we're mighty grateful yore so creative with yore cookery." Ralph's deep voice rolled across the campsite, warming Desta's cheeks.

I thought I'd have more time! She tossed a smile over her shoulder and hustled to the back of the wagon, ducking beneath Jess's table and retrieving another pan of scrapple from the compartment below. Shielded from the sun by the wagon itself and the folded-down table, the nook kept the dish cool and its contents firm enough to fry.

By the time she turned back to the fire, Ralph already made himself comfortable beside it. Of all the men, only he and Tucker were permitted to take their ease by the cook fire. The others gathered around the campfire several yards away, knowing not to come between the wagon and the cook fire where the women worked.

"I see the hashed taters—but I'm smelling something I can't pin down. Like corn mush, but more. . ." Ralph breathed deep, eyeing the dish she carried with enough anticipation to make her glad to be holding it.

"Scrapple, which Aunt Desta stayed up late last night getting ready for this morning. About time she rested for a minute. Make sure she sits down and eats some herself!" Jess interjected. After so many weeks on the trail, Desta deeply appreciated Jess's consistent, cheerful ploys to let her spend time with Ralph.

"Sure thing, Miss Jess." The glint of humor in Ralph's dark gaze warmed her heart. "I'll see to it she gets a good-sized portion of. . . whatever you called the thing that smells so good!"

"Scrapple," Desta repeated. "Last night I browned and boiled sausage, then stirred in cornmeal sweetened with a touch o' molasses for flavor. Spooned into pans and left to chill overnight, it firms up so I can slice and fry it quick as can be come morning."

"Sounds like good eatin'. I'll fetch us some water and a pair of tins and forks while you finish yore fryin'." Eager as the man was to eat, he never stopped thinking of ways to lend a helping hand.

The air soon smelled of sausage, syrup, sweet corn, and strong coffee. By the time the scrapple browned and went crisp around the edges, Ralph toted over tins, forks, a dipper of water, two mugs of coffee, a crock of butter, and some syrup he'd snuck from the chuck drawer.

Desta raised a brow as she took in his bounty. "Good thing God gave you arms long enough and strong enough to fit yore appetite."

"There's always room for something special." He quirked a brow and chuckled at the blush she felt darkening her cheeks. Settling beside her, his voice lowered to a rumble that ran straight through her. "Give me the word if you ever want to test these arms of mine, and I'll drop everything else."

"Ralph!" She batted his forearm, far too pleased by his forwardness to really scold him for it. No one could hear him, so no harm done.

"I've also got a broad set of shoulders to lean against." He slanted his torso closer and nudged her back with one of those shoulders. His rumble of approval when she let herself lean against his strength had her swallowing a giggle. Ralph bent his head so only she could catch his words.

"And if you don't need arms to catch you or shoulders to lean on, I've got ears to listen, lips for praying, and a heart happy to know yore near."

Desta's heart fluttered in response. After so long avoiding men, she'd finally found one who spoke to her soul. Desta tilted her head back so her whisper warmed his ear.

"It's a mighty good thing you want me nearby, since it's where I plan to stay. Yore heart finds its match in mine, but my arms can't stretch half so far as yours!" She managed not to squeal with delight when he gave her a squeeze and rumbled right back.

"All the more reason to keep you close."

"Follow me." Tucker's smile made it an invitation instead of an order, so Jess fell in step alongside him.

A two-word summons might not seem overly romantic, but anything that broke up the tedium of trail life seemed an adventure. And Jess found the idea of adventures with Tucker more appealing than ever before. After all, the man promised to prove himself, and he'd already made a good start this morning, almost managing to be pleasant before his coffee. Jess couldn't help but wonder what he had in mind next.

"Where are we going?"

"Nowhere. We're staying an extra day so Porter can recover in the shade and the cattle can bulk up on roughage. We'll take every advantage now since we're sure to run into some tough stretches up ahead with homesteaders."

"Seems to be a recurring problem." Jess felt her own frown mirror Tucker's. "Soon there'll be less trail to travel than detours and delays!"

"We've earned a rest." He shot her a playful glance. "Yesterday wasn't enough to let everyone enjoy some free time with the plentiful water supply hereabouts."

"Water? Is that where you're taking me?" She didn't even try to conceal her eagerness. A handful of times during the past several weeks, he'd hunted out a small offshoot of a stream. Someplace with a few trees or big rocks, where he and Ralph rigged the canvas wagon coverings to give her and Desta some privacy. Cool, clear water. Strong soap. Heaven on earth.

Tucker chuckled. "One hint of a water hole, and you're jumping like a June bug."

"Bugs. Dust. The very reasons why every bath is a blessing!"

Tucker looked mighty pleased with himself, and Jess decided he had good reason when Desta bustled up, her smile as full as her apron.

Jess spied a hairbrush, soap, and their precious stash of clean garments. Even with the "extra" articles, Jess never felt so grubby in all her born days as she did on the trail. Nor had she ever felt so grateful to get clean. Ages ago, the academy instructors informed girls that women did not perspire—they glowed. *If that ladylike malarkey were true, by now the pair of us could light the way on a moonless night!*

After days of tending cook fires beneath a blazing sun, she and Aunt Desta felt anything but glowing as they eased into the cool, clear water. With Tucker and Ralph standing watch on the other side of the canvas coverings, Jess and Desta silently washed more than a week's worth of weariness away. They helped each other thoroughly soap up their hair, work out the suds underwater, and comb through the tangles of trail life. Jess poked her head between two canvas flaps and craned her neck until she caught sight of Tucker.

"Looked like the stream is rockier to the west, a good spot for laundering." Cleaning their clothing came a close second to cleaning themselves. They hadn't brought many changes of clothes, but their provisions certainly beat out any the men could claim.

"There are other nice spots hereabouts for swimming or laundry." Tucker held up a few makeshift fishing poles. "What would you say to fishing for supper?"

"Wonderful! That way we can hang the laundry here instead of slapping it up on the wagons." For everyone to see. Modesty didn't take precedence over getting clothes washed and dried, but it still didn't sit well with her to air undergarments in view of the entire outfit.

"Sounds good to me." Ralph's voice joined their conversation before the man stepped into view.

"We'd be happy to add your washing to ours," Jess offered. "And since we have the area all rigged up and Desta and I will be upstream, seems only fair you and Ralph take a turn."

Tucker looked surprised, but Ralph wasted no time agreeing to the arrangement. They made quicker work of collecting their things and washing up than the women, already finished by the time the girls rinsed and wrung everything out.

As Jess smoothed damp fabric over the makeshift laundry lines, she took advantage of the partial cover to sneak glances at Tucker. For the first time in weeks, he'd shaved properly, revealing the strong lines of his jaw and the creases at the corners of his mouth. She'd secretly wondered if his beard would scratch or tickle beneath her hand, but somehow forgot just how handsome Tucker was without his whiskers.

Flustered by her forgetfulness—and the strength of her response to Tucker's transformation—Jess slapped a wet shirt across the line and received a face full of wet material as thanks for her efforts.

If Tucker looked like this yesterday, she assured herself as she batted away the damp fabric, *I still wouldn't have accepted his proposal.*

She snuck another sideways glance and admitted, *But I might not have been as quick to turn him down!*

Things were looking up.

Tucker didn't want to get ahead of himself, but he'd come a long way with Jess in less than a day. His heroic effort to be pleasant this morning earned him several smiles—even some from other members of the outfit. Then the bath he'd arranged washed away more of her defenses.

Even better, the bath washed away yesterday's need to keep his distance. Now that he'd cleaned up, he could get as close as she allowed once he got her alone. Jess's bare hands tempted Tucker to make up for lost time and give her the sort of hand-holding session that could only be taken seriously.

From here on out, she won't need to ask, he determined. *Every moment counts.*

"How about here?" She prodded a thick growth of brush with the end of her pole to reveal a shady pool.

"Perfect." Tucker forged ahead, using his own legs and fishing pole to clear a path for her. After she'd passed, he followed, narrowly avoiding a lashing from those low-lying branches. He didn't mind, since that brush kept the spot clear of cattle. He swiftly spread a blanket beneath the tree closest to the bank, where the ground remained firm enough for sitting.

She cast a look at the muddy bank before granting him a smile. "Good thinking on bringing along a horse blanket. I'd hate to dirty my fresh dress for a few fish!"

"It pays to be prepared, especially since my fee is so reasonable." He remained standing, splaying his legs to keep Jess from sitting down. In response to her raised brow, he waggled his own and held out a hand.

Her eyes and mouth rounded in surprise as Jess looked at his outstretched hand. A small smile played about the corners of her lips almost immediately, and Tucker knew she'd figured out what he wanted.

"You want me to dig up the worms?" she offered sweetly.

Tucker couldn't help but chuckle right along with her, but he stood his ground. "Think again."

"You want me to shake your hand?"

Tucker let some of the heat of his attraction show through his gaze. "Try me."

CHAPTER 37

Tucker kept his hand out and his smile hidden, certain Jess wouldn't be able to resist an invitation wrapped in a challenge.

Her chin lifted, telling him his ploy worked. She took a step. . . away. Only then did Jess extend her arm, straight out, keeping as much space as possible between them.

Too much space. His instincts screamed to pull her close and hold tight, *right now,* but Tucker stepped back to widen the gulf between them even more. He looked pointedly from his boots to hers as though gauging the distance.

"First catch of the day!" he teased, gently tugging her toward him. "Reel her in, and she's all mine."

"Catch and release!" Jess ordered, laughing while she dug in her heels. But the muddy riverbank offered no traction to stop her swift slide. Slipping closer than he'd planned, Jess steadied herself by placing a palm against his chest.

Close enough to kiss. Her fingers curled into the fabric, and Tucker's self-control started to fray. Her gaze reflected the same spark he felt, but where his burned steady, hers flickered with doubt. Doubt he needed to dispel.

"I won't cross the line, Jess. I'll always try to pull you close, but I'm not going to do something that pushes you away." Tucker drew a deep breath before removing her palm from his chest. He kept both her hands cradled in his and gave a reassuring squeeze before loosening his grip. "So for now, catch and release."

She squeezed back to show he hadn't scared her off, then skirted around him to settle atop the blanket. "You're the one who wanted to fish."

"Still do. But tell me. . ." Tucker grinned and settled beside her. He reached out and snagged one of her damp curls, looping it around his forefinger. "What do *you* want, Jess?"

To belong. Jess shook her head against the thought, sending the lock springing free from his finger to bounce against her temple. It seemed too intimate a thing to say aloud, so she turned Tucker's question back on him.

"What do *you* think I want?"

"This is probably where I oughta say a man can never know a woman's mind." His grin received an answering one from her. "Truth of the matter is, I think men and women both want the same things. Maybe not the little things, but deep down, at the very heart, I think all of us share the same simple need."

He reached over to bait her hook, brushing the back of her fingers with his. Despite the tingle from his touch, Jess couldn't help but see the parallel between the fishing and the conversation. If the fish took his bait half as well as she did, they'd eat well tonight!

"All of us?"

"Do you want to hear about that, or do you want to know what I reckon it is you'd say if you'd answered the question yourself?"

Jess didn't know whether to wince or smile. Tucker paid close attention to what she did—and didn't—say. Even when it put her on the spot, she couldn't help but appreciate being the focus of attention.

"The first one."

"Some will say it sounds silly spoken aloud, but I think no one wants to be alone unless something's gone very wrong. Every one of us wants to be chosen. It's the fundamental human need, to be needed by someone else." Tucker slanted a glance toward her.

"How'm I doing so far?"

"Why do you think we all need the same thing?" Every word spoke to a longing Jess never put words to.

"God Himself wants to be chosen and loved." Tucker drew in a deep breath. "He made us in His image, for the purpose of companionship. . . . It only stands to reason we'd crave that same thing."

"I suppose you might be on to something there." Jess turned the idea over, fitting it against some of her own questions about the Almighty. "You know, I wondered why God allowed distance between our hearts and His. I struggle to understand a Father who leaves His children hurting, letting us choose wrong when He could make everything right and bring every soul to Him so easily. Now I'm starting to see the reason."

Tucker's gaze seemed to burn straight through her. "With Him, just like with us, love has to be a choice."

"Sounds obvious when you put it that way. Simple, even." Jess rubbed her fingers along the nubby weave of the horse blanket. "But love between people isn't so easy. It has to be earned with trust and understanding."

"Do you understand that I choose you, Jess?"

"I do now." Tears stung her eyes and nose as she confessed, "But I don't know why."

"Because you don't hide behind a mask, telling people what they want to hear. You're smart and strong and stubborn, but you always take the time to be kind. Even when we argue from opposite sides, I understand what you're fighting for, and I want to work with you to achieve those dreams."

"Some things a person has to do alone."

"Some things don't have to be done at all." He raised his voice then softened it again. "You don't have to prove that you belong at the Bar None, Jess."

Jess sucked in a sharp breath at how closely he'd guessed her heart's desire—and how swiftly he'd rejected it. "Everyone needs to prove themselves!"

This time he reacted to the swift hiss of her breath, rubbing her elbow in reassurance. "You don't have to prove yourself, and you never did. Everyone knows and accepts that you belong."

"Papa didn't." If Jess could snatch the words from the air before they reached his ears, she would've. But she couldn't take the words back, and she couldn't change the truth behind them. Tucker's pity at her pronouncement would be her undoing, so she swiftly tacked on, "You didn't either. You didn't want me in the stables, in the corrals, on the windmills, on the roundups, or on the drive. Of all the people in the world, how can you be the one to sit here and tell me I don't have to prove myself?"

"Everyone has to prove their ability before they're trusted with the responsibilities of the ranch." Tucker had the gall to agree with her right when she most wanted some splendid, impassioned statement that made her feel special and wanted again. "I meant you don't have to prove that you deserve a place. You belong on the Bar None simply because of who you are."

"I don't want people to tolerate me because of who my father is." *Not when he sent me away in the first place.* "I want them to respect me as a working partner who contributes to the outfit!"

"I didn't say you belong there because of your last name." A muscle worked in his jaw, though he kept his tone even. "Trust that folks are smart enough to respect you because you care about the ranch, the land, and the people who work it. That's who you are, and that's why you belong."

"You're probably the only man who can tell me off and make me feel better at the same time, Tucker Carmichael." Jess sniffed and turned her attention to her fishing pole, but smiled anyway. "There were *years* when the only thing I wanted was to come home."

"But that changed." She could hear his smile through the words, even as she kept her focus on the fishing hole. "Because you were barely home for a week before you started pushing to come on the long drive."

"Pushing, was I?" She stiffened at the description. Knowing it was true didn't make it any more flattering after she'd already been put through the wringer. "Here I thought you were glad for more chances to pull me close."

He scooted closer, pressing his leg against hers and sliding one strong arm around her waist and bracing his hand against the blanket. "I am. Never doubt that."

"You can pull me close or you can keep me far away, but you can't want both."

"Have you never wanted to shove someone away and yank 'em nearer all at once?"

"That's ridiculous. Of course not."

"Oh?" Tucker shifted his weight to lean closer, teasing her with his nearness. The spicy scent of his aftershave snared her as he taunted. "How 'bout now?"

Jess realized she'd leaned toward him, savoring the closeness until his challenge brought her to her senses. She held perfectly still, barely breathing as she wondered whether he'd keep his promise not to cross the line. If he tried kissing her, he'd find himself swimming in the fishing hole.

But he didn't try any funny business. He cocooned her in his half embrace, simply sitting alongside her as though their nearness were enough. It made her believe what he'd said before and appreciate how much effort he'd put into holding her hand.

Which made her want to push him in the swimming hole for *not* trying to steal a kiss.

"It always comes down to the same struggle for a woman," Jess muttered. "Being respectable means you can't do some of the things you want most."

"Are you trying to say I'm right? You do want to pull me close and push me away?" He didn't look overly pleased at the prospect of victory, which made things a little easier.

"It means I'm not ready to move fast, and it doesn't feel right for me to pull you close." Jess slid her hand across his, twining their fingers together and relishing the way his breath hitched. "Even though I don't want to push you away anymore."

In the space of a heartbeat, he swung his other arm around her and closed the distance between them, holding her as though he'd found the missing piece to happiness. He rested his cheek against hers, so she felt his words as much as heard them. "I'll always want you as close as possible."

"Go back." Barefoot, riding bareback, and brandishing a motley assortment of shotguns and pistols, the homesteaders issued their ultimatum.

"Trail's been here for years." Tucker tried reasoning with the men, more in desperation than hope. Every year more homesteaders claimed land in southern Kansas, directly northward along the trail. And for the past three years, he'd had trouble with farmers running the outfit away from the best watering spots. But he'd not been turned away from the trail itself. *Lord, You know how dire this situation is. Please help us get through Kansas one last year.*

The only detour available offered no drinkable water. Even pushing the livestock as fast and far as possible, it would take five days to pass through the Saline Reservation, where the waters were so impregnated with alkali salts that they'd poison man and beast. He had to gain passage, so he plastered on a smile and kept talking.

"Whole area was mapped by cattle drives. Without us, there'd be no paths, no stores, no outposts. Surely we can pass through without causing you any trouble. We'll keep to the trail and steer clear of farmland. I give my word on that."

"Yer word ain't gonna keep our livestock from catching Texas fever germs!" One of the men shifted his shotgun to aim at Tucker's chest.

Once again, Tucker rued the day he'd agreed to let Ed's scraggly bunch join the trail herd. The livestock showed no signs of fever, but those scrawny additions didn't look like health on the hoof either. "My cattle aren't ill."

"Texas cows don't come up feverin'. They carry the disease and leave it behind to poison the livelihood of God-fearing farmers!" The loudmouth who'd aimed at him ended on a yell, rallying the others to shout alongside him.

"We'll press on at top speed." Tucker kept trying to strike a bargain. "Keep our herd closely contained, out of any fenced fields and away from any other cattle we spot. You'd barely know we passed through."

This time the leather-faced leader didn't let the surly troublemaker get a word in. "Cain't let in one outfit but block the rest."

"Why not? Your land, your decision." Tucker wasn't above groveling when it came to the safety of his crew. Especially this season.

"And it's already been made, so don't waste time clackin' yer jaws!"

The trigger-happy lout waved his weapon as further warning. "Step foot on our land, we'll see to it you and yours never leave it."

CHAPTER 38

Whata do you mean, we're not leaving?" Jess dusted floury hands on her apron and wondered what made Tucker so tense after such a pleasant afternoon yesterday.

"Homesteaders have laid claim to the trail. When I went scouting for the next campsite, they rode up and denied us passage. They'll shoot before allowing the risk of Texas fever." As he spoke, a muscle ticked in his jaw.

Jess reached out to pat his forearm, wanting to soothe both of them but refusing to show any distress over the prospect of a detour—or the added days they'd have to spend on the trail. "It's not the first time that's happened. We went through the same thing two weeks back, and it only added an extra day or two to go around."

"Not this time." Tucker shrugged away to point northward, and Jess realized she hadn't dusted enough flour off her hands. A powdery print stood out in sharp relief against the dust-darkened cambric of his once-white work shirt. "The trail goes north for good reason—it follows the water. The detour will take us through the Saline Reservation, where the only water is so laden with alkali salts it will poison man and beast. Even going full-bore, we won't find drinkable water for at least five days."

Jess heard Desta's sharp gasp and narrowly managed to gulp back her own. Doubts and questions roiled, but she whittled it down to the most crucial concern.

"Five days? Can the cattle make it that long?" If the cattle couldn't survive, they wouldn't make the attempt. Better to turn back and sell for far less than lose everything.

"If we keep night watch, keep them away from the water, and stampede them over the Cimarron crossing without letting them drink or turn back, most will survive." He slapped his hat against his thigh in agitation. "We can't afford another stampede, or we'll lose them all. Ralph?"

"Time to blind the three?" Ralph's forbidding expression rivaled Tucker's.

"No choice now."

"What?" Jess knew the situation was dire, but the idea of "blinding" anything sounded beyond belief.

"The three young bulls what caused most of the stampeding earlier on. Sometimes a group of 'em will get a taste for trouble. We been keepin' 'em apart to cut back on problems, but with a hard push ahead and no water, ain't no leeway to spare them no more."

Desta looked every bit as appalled as Jess felt. "Be kinder to kill 'em and take the loss than to put out their eyes."

"We don't put out their eyes, Desta." Thankfully, Tucker looked disturbed at the thought. "We sew the lids shut. The stitches wear down in about two weeks, but by then they've learned to follow the herd peacefully instead of leading them into trouble."

"Most of the herd will go blind from lack of water anyway. They'll regain their vision once hydrated again, but at that point the real danger will be losing the herd to overdrinking."

"I still don't like it," Jess stated. "But the safety of our men has to be the priority. We can't waste even an hour controlling renegades if we'll be pushing so hard to reach water."

The detour loomed as a death sentence. Even with the extra water barrel they'd had rigged to the spare wagon, it wasn't possible to carry enough water for the entire outfit. Not to mention water for cooking and washing the skillets and dishware.

Tucker's grim expression told her he knew that all too well, so she bit her tongue to keep from listing the concerns surging through her thoughts. For the first time, she regretted their showdown with

the shopkeeper. They'd won Porter's hat, but now there'd be no dealing with the only merchant in town. Whatever containers they had
on hand would have to be enough.

～✦～

Tucker watched as Jess sprang into action, making plans and issuing
orders.

"Tell the men we aren't rationing the pickles or the watermelon
rinds anymore. I want it all gone by the end of the day. We'll use
the pickled eggs to make salad as part of the midday meal, too. Any
water we put in those vessels will taste a bit briny, but it'll be fine for
boiling up later." As she spoke, she hauled out the gallon and two-
gallon jars. "Aunt Desta? Let's combine all the remaining preserves
as best we can to clear out those jars, too."

"I'll get to soaking enough beans and salt pork to last us the
next five days." Desta dove into the thick of things. "And I'll bake
up breadstuffs to see us through at least three days and make up an
extra batch of corn mush for frying. Small things add together to
make a difference."

"Coming together's the only way to make it through," Tucker
approved. "I'll admit I was wrong about the extra buckboard. The
added water barrel is nothing less than a blessing. You ladies do
everything you can, and tomorrow morning you'll leave the outfit in
better shape than we had any right to expect."

He half hoped she wouldn't catch that last part, what with bustling around getting things ready, but Jess froze at the words. Slowly
she turned, her brows slammed together as though already blocking
out his reasoning.

"Leave?"

"Once everything's ready, I'll ride you into town and put you
up there. You can catch the next mail coach and head home. You'll
have each other, and it's safer than trying to push through the Saline
Reservation with the rest of the outfit."

"So much for pulling close, keeping near, and coming together." Anger and indignation blazed in her gaze, burning hot enough to hide the hurt from anyone but him.

Tucker heard the betrayal beneath the words and mourned the renewal of a distance he'd thought they'd crossed. But seeing her safe took precedence over seeing her smile, and he'd settle for the chance to make it up to her.

"You need us." Her whisper echoed with undertones of yesterday's conversation, a plea for him to confirm that he needed her.

"I need you safe. That's my priority, and that's my decision."

"We're women, not troublesome bulls to be led about blindly. How can you think to make this decision for us?"

He moved toward her, his hands enveloping hers and holding tight when she tried to jerk free. "It's not just a decision, Jess. It's a sacrifice. I will always sacrifice to do what's best for you."

"No." She twisted away from his grasp. "Desta and I started this journey, and we'll see it through. You'll need every man—even Quincy and Porter, whenever possible—to help move the cattle, stop stampedes, and keep up the pace. There's no one extra to do our job, and we won't leave things unfinished." With that, she turned on her heel and started to leave.

"What about this?" *What about us?* He knew she understood what he was really asking. "Will you leave this unfinished, Jess?"

"This conversation might take a while, and I don't have a second to spare." Jess turned back to her chuck wagon. "Talk to me after we've made it through, Tucker."

"We made it." Too tired to savor her triumph, Jess wearily sank down beside her aunt and ran the tip of her finger across her cracked lips. "We can leave out the chili and let the men fend for themselves while we catch up on some sleep."

"My bones fair ache, and my eyes are heavy, but I'm wound tighter than a church key still." Desta sighed and sipped some of the blessedly pure water they'd finally reached that day. "Cool evening breeze feels too good to leave it behind and lay down in the tent just yet."

"After some sleep, I'll be hunting down another spot for a bath." Jess sipped from her own mug. Earlier, she'd belted back an entire canteen's worth without taking a breath. Everyone in the outfit did the same, and had been nursing canteens and mugs ever since. Maybe the men half-felt the way she did—as though if she left the water out of reach for more than a minute, it'd disappear again. Five days didn't seem like a long time until you had to ration every swallow, stop washing up, and still put in round-the-clock hours on a grueling trail ride.

"Mercy, the thought alone of sliding into cool water makes me light-headed. I covet that bath same as you."

"Tucker'll see to it as soon as he can," Jess soothed.

"That's the first positive thing I've heard you say about Tucker since we took off across the Saline Reservation. You two were getting along so much better, then he tries to spare us this awful trek and you stop wasting words on him." For an exhausted woman, Desta could work a glower like nobody's business. "What happened 'twixt the two of you?"

"The usual." Jess drained her mug and eyed the water barrel. "On the ride back from getting Porter's hat, Tucker tried to propose and botched it badly. Not one word about love in the bunch."

"Don't know how to tell you this, but that ain't usual." Desta snorted with laughter. "Then again, maybe it is. Even the smartest of men sometimes can't speak his heart."

"He got better at it. The day we went fishing, we'd just about reached an understanding. Tucker kept talking about working as a team, coming alongside, wanting to keep me close. . . ." Jess would've sworn she had no moisture left for tears, but found herself blinking a few back at the recollection.

"Then he tried to send you home, and you took it wrong."

Jess stiffened. "What other way is there to take it when a man says he wants you close but tries to send you off at the first opportunity?"

"He was willing to sacrifice having you with him to know you were safe." Between Desta's plain speaking and the experience of the past five days, Jess felt a bit more ready to consider the point.

"That's what Tucker says, that a husband is supposed to sacrifice for his wife, and that's the reason she submits in love and trust. But how can I trust that he'll make the right choices when we don't see things the same?"

"Nobody makes the right choices all the time. But if you think about it, you already trust Tucker with all sorts of things. Even if his judgment may be flawed at times, do you trust him to seek out the Lord's will?"

"Yes. But even so, he gets things turned around sometimes."

"But not most times. Who do you trust to run the Bar None?"

"Tucker."

"Who do you trust to manage the trail drive?"

"Tucker—mostly. He's made a few mistakes there, too."

"Who would you run for if something went wrong?"

"Tucker."

"Who is it yore lookin' for first thing every morning?"

"I think we both know the answer to that."

"What I hear you sayin' is that you trust Tucker with yore home, yore cattle, yore loved ones, and you even trust him not to leave you alone. All the most important things in a person's life." Desta pushed to the heart of it. "So there must be somethin' in particular yore worryin' on. What is it you don't trust Tucker to do?"

"It's more what I don't trust him *not* to do." Jess picked at a loose thread as though it could unravel her concerns. "He's already tried to send me away, same as Papa."

"No, honey." Desta folded her hand over Jess's. "Tucker tried to keep you home, then tried to send you home. He's never tried to send you off. Every step of the way, he's done his best to keep you safe and sound in the center of things."

Neither of them spoke for a long while. Desta didn't have any-thing to add to what she'd said, and Jess closed her eyes, thinking and praying things through before making any decisions. When she opened her eyes again, they shone with unshed tears.

"What happens when I mess up? Perfect love isn't possible for imperfect people, and we both have plenty of flaws."

"That's what love is for in the first place, Jess. To fill in the flaws and keep the heart full." Desta stood up. "Don't let fear of being hurt keep you from being whole."

CHAPTER 39

Aunt Desta?" Jess passed off the last of the breakfast dishes and sent Quincy to the stream. Then she looked around for her aunt. When she didn't spot her right away, Jess bit her lip.

They'd brought along a jumped-up wooden frame and canvas to set atop the buckboard and angle to the ground. They set it up every day as part of base camp, and Desta liked to go there to rest out of the heat of the sun. If her aunt were resting in the slapdash tent, Jess didn't know if she'd have the heart to wake her up.

Desta seemed to tire so easily these days that Jess suspected she wasn't sleeping well. Before making a decision either way, she slipped over to the tent and peeked inside. Sure enough, her aunt lay inside. But to Jess's horror, this was no restful nap.

Desta stretched out directly on the ground, without so much as a bedroll for a cushion. And though she clearly slept, she muttered and moved her arms and legs in agitation, as though trying to fight something off.

Is it a nightmare? Worry clutched at her. It didn't seem possible that Jess wouldn't have noticed her aunt suffered from nightmares, when they'd spent so many days sleeping in separate shifts. If her aunt had been groaning and thrashing around, she would have noticed long ago. *If not a nightmare. . .then what?*

Her aunt kicked her legs, tossing the hem of her skirt upward and revealing her ankles and feet. Jess gasped. Desta's ankles were so swollen, Jess didn't see how her aunt could have gotten her shoes on that morning, much less walked around helping with breakfast.

She crawled inside the tent, reaching to feel her aunt's forehead and drawing her hand away covered in sweat. *Fever.*

That was all it took to have her stumbling away from the canvas and racing for the horses. When she reached the remuda, Jess didn't bother asking Porter for a saddle, even though two of the men were bound to be off duty and their gear would be free.

I don't know how long she's been feverish or what to do about it. Panic thrummed through her as she spied a horse near a convenient rock and vaulted onto its back. Winding her fingers through its mane and leaning forward, she pressed her knees together. The pony understood, as the best horses always did, and headed for the rope serving as a gate for the makeshift enclosure.

Porter opened it and Jess spurred her mount forward, racing in the direction she'd seen Tucker take with Ralph. Not knowing exactly where to go, Jess was surprised to find herself praying. Nothing fancy or formal or probably even coherent. Just a string of thoughts and frantic pleas, sent to the Father who might not answer in time to save Aunt Desta.

It didn't matter. Jess had to ask for the help anyway. For the first time she understood what her aunt had meant, about prayer being one of the ways she could do her part. Jess wasn't in control, but at least she had a direct line of contact to the One who was.

As the horse flew over the landscape, she searched in vain for some sort of tracks to guide her way. But traveling with a herd of cattle made short work of any imprints, so she started scanning the horizon instead. It seemed to take hours, but finally she spotted two figures on horseback.

Twining her hands in the mane even more tightly, Jess urged the horse faster, ignoring the unstable sway of the creature beneath her. She hadn't ridden bareback in almost a decade, but it didn't matter. For all she knew, minutes might make the difference. And if not, they made a difference to her because she knew she'd given all she had to find help.

By now the men caught sight of her and were weaving their way around cattle, coming to meet her. Jess barely managed to keep her seat and not go flying over her horse's head when they came to a stop. "Desta's sick!"

Until she tried to talk, she hadn't realized how hard she'd been crying, or how hard it was to take a breath. "Fever-swollen feet," she catalogued. "Must be alkaline p–p–" She couldn't get out the last word. It was too terrible to be true. Desta couldn't really be poisoned. . . . She would be all right. . . .

"Deep breaths." Tucker's voice broke through her anxiousness enough that she was able to obey. When she started breathing more regularly, he rode up right alongside her, slipped an arm around her waist, and tugged her off her horse and onto his.

"Oh!" she gasped, still crying, but surprised and already somewhat calmed by the warm strength of his arms around her as he settled her across his lap.

"You'll take care of her, won't you, Tucker?" she pled, desperate to hear that her aunt would be all right. That she hadn't given Desta a death sentence by convincing her to come on the cattle drive.

My stubbornness got Papa kicked by the bronco, and now it's got Aunt Desta, too. Lord, I didn't mean any harm. How can I be responsible for the deaths of two of my closest family members? She can't die.

"Ralph's already on his way to check on her." Tucker didn't tell her everything would be fine, and Jess couldn't hold back a ragged sob.

"Take me back to her?" she half asked, half demanded.

"Ralph's gone to her. But I know a homestead hereabouts who might be able to give us more help. We're going there." The simple fact that he had a plan went a little way toward easing her mind.

"Help is good," she agreed. "Let's go get help."

"We will. But first I need you to hang on so we can put on some speed. Wrap your arms around my waist or my neck, whichever's most comfortable, and lean your head against my chest." He sounded so wonderfully sure of himself, authoritative and in control, that Jess didn't think twice.

She wrapped her arms around his waist, pressing her cheek against his chest and finally finding comfort in the strong, steady beat of his heart.

"Poisoning from alkali salts," Ralph confirmed, stepping down from the buckboard after arriving at the homestead. He stood by the wagon, reaching down toward Desta. He hesitated, glanced at Tucker, then went ahead anyway. Gently, he used the back of his finger to brush a lock of hair from where it had fallen against her forehead and stayed, stuck against her fever-flushed skin.

Tucker wasn't surprised by the tender gesture—he'd seen Ralph sneaking pockets of time to sit with Miss Desta, and at some point, even *he'd* realized what an idiot he'd been when his friend worked on the garden. It hadn't been the desserts that put a spring in Ralph's step—though they certainly hadn't hurt any.

The gleam in Ralph's eyes hadn't been the Light of Pies Past. No. The something sweet he'd go the extra mile for had always been Miss Desta. Tucker had been so busy keeping an eye on his own preference for savory spice, he hadn't noticed. Jess had a way of occupying his imagination the same way Miss Desta distracted Ralph.

If they could get her through this—and get Jess through helping Desta get through this—what a pair of pairs they'd make.

Ralph's bass rumbled with remorse. "I shoulda guessed. She bin tired, but kept sayin' as how she'd sleep after our talk. Asked if she drank enough water, and she'd tell me yes." His Adam's apple bobbed before he finished. "I shoulda done more. Shoulda made sure."

"We'll make sure she's taken care of now." Tucker reached up and clapped Ralph on the shoulder, wanting to bolster him without mollycoddling in a way that might embarrass them both after this ended. "You already started—looks like you lined the buckboard with every bedroll from the outfit."

"Yes. I didn't want her bumpin' and jouncin' around and hurting herself any worse."

"Good idea. The Burles are giving up their bed for her, so it's all ready and waiting inside. Just as soon as we figure out the best way to move her—" Tucker broke off as Ralph leaned over the side of the wagon, carefully slid his massive hands beneath the unconscious woman, and lifted her as though she weighed no more than one of those bedrolls.

Ralph crooked his arms slowly, tucking Desta tight against his chest before heading for the door with a slow, measured tread. Without another word, he opened the door and disappeared inside.

Jess waited in the tiny homestead house, her nervous pacing making Mrs. Burle bustle about in a great hurry without actually accomplishing much. All the extra movement in such a crowded space was just the sort of thing to drive Tucker crazy in a real hurry. So he'd left the women stoking the fire, folding blankets, tightening bed ropes, plumping pillows, boiling broth, and heaven only knew what else they'd gotten up to.

It was a real shame Miss Desta wasn't awake to appreciate the warm welcome. Tucker figured there were queens who hadn't been received with such care. But it was Ralph's stricken expression and stoic determination that really brought home the severity of her condition.

Until he'd seen her lying in the bed of the wagon, insensible, Tucker held out hope that Jess went a little wild in her reaction. It would've been understandable. After all that time away, to come home and discover her aunt made for a wonderful surprise. Losing that aunt mere weeks later over something as senseless as alkali poisoning—particularly so hard on the heels of her father's death... Jess might never recover.

Lord, protect the ones I love. Especially Desta now. She's come so far, Lord, and been so brave in opening her heart. Please grant her healing, and share Your peace with Jess and Ralph as we wait to see Your plans revealed. Amen.

Tucker shoved his hands in his pockets and slowly started toward the small house. Desta wasn't the first person he'd seen fall victim to alkali water along the trail, but it still surprised him. Cooks usually stuck close to the water barrels and zealously guarded their contents to keep them cool and pure.

Because of that, cowpunchers out riding the cattle with nothing more than a canteen were the ones who succumbed to the lure of any water that looked reasonably clean. Not the cooks. It made him wonder how Desta came to be the one afflicted.

Because if it happened to Desta, it could just as easily have affected Jess. Tucker stopped midstep then broke into a run. Icy fear prickled across the back of his neck. *I didn't check. What if Jess is affected, too, but not showing the symptoms as quickly?*

In no time, he burst through the door, knocking it into Ralph. The big man looked like he was trying hard to shrink down and stay out of the way, but in spite of his best efforts he swallowed up half the space. Tucker stepped around his friend, knowing nothing could convince him to leave the room so long as Desta lay there.

"Jess!" He reached out and snagged her wrist, tugging her around a table and swinging her a bit so she sat on a chair. "Stay put."

Having given his order, Tucker knelt down before her, reached beneath her skirts, and pulled her foot toward him. He propped her boot atop his raised knee, one hand wrapping around the heel, the other sliding beneath the fabric of her skirts to cup the top of the boot, where it lay against the soft skin of her calf.

Ignoring her splutters and Mrs. Burle's squawking, Tucker curled his fingers and pulled. He paused then repeated the motion until he'd worked the boot completely free of her foot. Thin black stockings, warmed from close contact with her flesh, covered an ankle every bit as trim and dainty as he remembered seeing it in the kitchen that first night.

Just to be sure, Tucker smoothed one hand along the light fabric, down the front of her leg, stopping to gently massage her ankle before sweeping forward over her foot. Once he was satisfied that she hadn't started swelling, he reached back for her boot and helped her step into it again.

"No other signs?" He didn't whisper with everyone crammed in so close, but kept his voice low. "No stomachache? Sore throat? Dizziness?" At each symptom he listed, she shook her head. And with each shake of her head, Tucker felt a little better.

He rose to his feet, careful not to touch her now that the diagnosis was done. No matter how much he ached to keep touching her, he owed her more respect than to take advantage of her distress.

"I have to see to the herd and make arrangements to pass them off at Caldwell. It's not far, so don't worry."

"When will you come back?" The bleakness darkening her gaze tore at him, especially when he saw her hand lift as though to touch him, then twitch and fall back to her side.

Neither of them were ready to let go, but they both knew they had work to do before they could hold tight. The memory of how sweetly Jess clung to him on their ride for help spurred him. For a brief time, she'd turned to him and found comfort in his arms. Tucker wanted to provide that comfort whenever she needed it. Just so long as she needed *him*.

"Soon," he promised, and he meant more than just when he'd return. Yesterday he'd told her to take her time. Now, in light of Desta's condition, Tucker knew he wasn't willing to wait much longer. He coveted every moment they could spend together.

He nodded to Ralph on his way out the door. "Take care of them for me." Tucker saw Ralph nod his acceptance of the charge as he walked through the door, moving fast.

The quicker he could settle the cattle, the sooner Tucker could return. *Because once I'm back at Jessalyn's side, no power on earth is going to make me leave.*

CHAPTER 40

Go on, now." Desta waved her hand at Ralph, trying to hide her weakness. "Get yore hide outside and soak up some sunshine for a change, Ralph Runkle. Yore fading like leaves in wintertime, and I don't aim to be responsible for you turning white as a ghost."

"Don't think to be sassing me with such nonsense." He shook his head, but the smile she so loved to see gleamed once more.

"Sassing?" Of course she was. If that was what it took to help him break past his lingering expectation she would up and die on him, Desta would sass the man clear back to the Bar None.

But first, she wanted a few minutes with her niece.

"Now, is that any way to be talking to a woman who darted past death without so much as an inch to spare?"

"'Zactly so. You say you sidled past Death himself 'cuz he gave you an inch and you took a mile. Well, I'll learn from his mistake and keep you even closer." He hunkered down, sitting on his heels so he could meet her gaze. "I don't plan to ever let you get past me, Desta."

"I wasn't gonna try," she whispered, then shook her head and reached for a handkerchief. "But you can't go making me all teary. After you and Jess poured half a lake down my throat to help me get well, I can't be wasting water on womanly foolishness."

His hand wrapped around hers, warm and strong. "Don't go getting foolish on me, but keep the rest. I like yore womanly ways."

"And I like having you around to make me buck up and get better." She wriggled a little until she worked her fingers through his, then gave a squeeze. "Seeing what I've got waiting for me helps hurry the healing."

"But here you were, trying to send me away." Ralph tapped her on the tip of her nose, making her eyes cross so he could laugh at her. "Don't be in such a hurry that it turns you contrary."

"I'm not contrary; I just want a moment or two with my niece while the Burles is getting supplies. Go on and get her, then go out and soak up some sun!" She slid her hand away and shooed him again.

This time he followed her directions. Desta suspected he hung around close by, but she didn't mind. She'd grown used to having Ralph Runkle close by and wasn't going to give him any reason to give up the habit.

"You're looking much better." Jess carried in a basket of eggs and set it on the table before moving closer to the bed.

"I feel better, though for a time I thought you all planned to boil me. Atween the heat of the fire against my feet and all the water you got down my gullet, it wouldn't have taken much."

Jess grinned, but just as she'd been noticing for the past two days, the smile didn't quite reach her niece's eyes. "You're welcome."

"Come on over here and siddown a spell." Desta patted a corner of the bed. "Now that you done such a good job nursing me back to health, it's time you tell yore aunt what's troubling you."

"Ralph took on more than me," Jess demurred. "And looking after you wasn't any trouble. The trouble would've come if we'd lost you."

Tears clumped up the last two words so they barely sounded English, but Desta understood. She patted the bed again. This time Jess skirted around the frame and sank onto a free corner.

"Now tell me what's weighin' on yore mind." *And heart.*

"Nothing at all, and everything all at once."

Desta snorted. "And to hear Ralph tell it, I'm contrary!" This brought out the hint of a smile.

"Sometimes two things that seem like opposites can both be true." From the way Jess said it, a world of meaning lurked behind the words.

"Gimme an example. I ain't so sure what yore sayin'."

"Well. . ." After brief consideration, Jess decided to get the conversation started. "Our talk about God letting love be a decision stuck in my thoughts, and it makes sense that the deepest desire of our hearts would be the reason He made us in His image. We all want to be chosen and valued."

"I like the way you put that. 'Smatter of fact, I like it so much I don't see the problem." But she saw one looming in the darkening expression on Jess's face as she gathered her thoughts.

"It's the next part. Once we choose Him, why doesn't He want us with Him?" Jess twisted her handkerchief as though the mangled scrap of fabric could help unknot her thoughts. "Why leave us here, hurting and far away, instead of bringing us home?"

"Maybe you and God got differing ideas 'bout what makes a home," Desta pointed out. "For me, it's not a place so much as the people you share it with. Since He lives within those who accept Him, He's already as close as can be."

"I never thought of it that way. Since Christ says He's preparing a place for us in heaven, I always thought that was supposed to be our home together."

"Yes. But for now, He's working in our hearts to prepare us for that heavenly home. Most of us aren't ready yet—we have a lot of growing to do before we've become our best selves."

"Do you think that's the reason Papa didn't bring me home either?" Jess rocked forward, then back again before bursting out, "He didn't think I'd grown enough? I wasn't good enough yet? Because now it's too late. . . ." Her breath hitched. "He's gone!"

"Honey, I'm going to tell you something." Desta reached for her niece's hand and clenched it tight. "Yore papa wasn't God. Not even close. He was a regular man, who made regular mistakes. Some of those bigger than others."

"Me." Jess sighed the word with resignation. "I'm the big mistake. My foolishness helped kill him. No wonder he didn't want me back."

"You weren't the mistake." Desta shook the hand she held. "Listen to me. His mistake was thinking that other women could give you what you needed, and that he couldn't. He hated having you gone, but he made the sacrifice because he thought it was best for you."

"No." Horror filled the denial. "Don't tell me that's how Papa sacrificed for me."

"Sacrifice means giving up something for someone else. But that doesn't mean every sacrifice is the right choice." Desta went whole-hog and wrapped her arms around Jess, rocking them both back and forth until Jess calmed down enough to work out one last worry.

"So how do I trust Tucker not to make a mistake like Papa did?"

"We're all imperfect people, but we're all different. Tucker won't make yore papa's mistake—he'll find brand-new ones instead. But love holds us together through the hurts."

"You make it sound so simple!" Jess sighed, but looked wistful instead of woebegone.

"It's one of those contrary true things you meant. Sacrificing for the ones you love is the easiest thing in the world—and the hardest. But I'll tell you a secret my mama told me: the more you give up, the more you find you've got left inside you to keep on giving."

"Tucker!" Jess let out such a shriek she could only be glad he was still too far away to hear. Just as she'd known Ed from an impossible distance when her brother came home to her, Jess knew Tucker had come back for her.

Thank You, Lord. Her prayers still might not amount to much when it came to counting the words, but Jess figured God felt the gratitude behind them. What's more, she figured He understood that as she learned to be stronger in prayer, she'd be growing more into the woman He was waiting for in heaven.

Waiting's not so bad when it's something you're willing to work toward. Even though it took every ounce of self-control to hold back, Jess didn't go flying across the field to meet Tucker. *He worked to come back for me, and I can wait an extra minute so he can see it through.*

It looked like she wasn't the only one eager to cross that final distance. Tucker galloped toward the house and slid from his saddle long before his horse halted. Then Jess gave in and went to meet him. Three steps, and he caught her in his arms and spun her around, stealing a squeeze before he set her back on the ground.

"I'm so glad you're back!" It was a silly, obvious sort of thing to say, but Jess didn't care. It would do him good to hear her say it, and it did her good to tell him. She planned to be telling him the same sort of thing for the rest of their lives, just as soon as she could coax a halfway-decent proposal out of him.

And maybe tease him into tending a few steps he's neglected along the way. Jess beamed. She'd been planning how to have this conversation ever since Aunt Desta got better.

"I'm glad to have you to come back for." He stood so close she could feel his warmth. His hands lingered at her waist long after he'd put her back down.

"You don't have me just yet." Jess placed her hands atop his and slid from his hold. "We have some questions to ask each other first. And some answers to give. I hope you've been thinking and praying about this while you were away?"

"Yep." He reached out and snagged one of her hands. "Other than making arrangements for the cattle and passing them along to Ed's man in Caldwell, and praying for Desta's recovery, thinking and praying about our future was about the only thing I managed to do."

A month ago it wouldn't have mattered to her whether or not he'd sought God's will. Now Jess took pride in the knowledge that she'd joined him from afar. The way she saw it, God might be up in His heaven, but when two souls sought His guidance for the same thing, He connected their hearts no matter what distance lay between. His love completed the story and helped make them whole.

"So, would you like to go inside and check on Aunt Desta and say hi to Ralph?" She swung the hand he held, and he swung right along with her for all the world as though they were children playing in a schoolyard.

"Not just yet. I'm hoping to go in there with good news to share." Tucker took a step closer. "Why don't you start asking those questions you've been keeping?"

"All right." Jess took another step away, tugged her hand back, and started walking across the field. "Come on. Private conversations won't last long if you're standing in front of a house full of people wanting to see you!" *I should know. If someone else saw you first, it would've been impossible not to come running.*

He went with her, but stopped behind the first shrub tall enough to give them some cover. "This is far enough."

Jess figured she'd waited long enough to start teasing him. "First question: Do you promise to stop criticizing my clothing?"

"Done." Tucker reached forward and smoothed a strand of hair against her temple. "Better get to the next one, Jess. My patience is wearing thin."

"After just one question?" She shot him a disgruntled look and tugged her hair away from his questing fingertips. "Well, that doesn't bode well for the next question."

"Which is?"

"The most important one!"

"I'm sorry, sweetheart. This *is* important." He gave a sheepish shrug. "It's just hard to hold off on holding you tight when I've waited for so long, but I'll try to be more patient."

"That means a lot because what I need to know is that you'll listen to me." She prayed he gave the right answer. "When you say you'll sacrifice to meet my needs, do you promise to listen when I tell you what it is I really need?"

Tucker stopped teasing her at once, instead looking deep into her eyes so she could read the promise in his. "I'll listen, but I won't always agree."

"All right. As long as you value my judgment, I'm willing to trust yours."

"Thank you." He bridged the gap between them, sliding one arm around her waist to hold her close, but raising the other hand to cup her cheek. "Do you have any more burning questions, Jess? Or are you ready to hear my proposal?"

"No more questions." She held her breath, refusing to miss a word of what was to come just because her chest felt tight and her breath might sound loud.

"Jessalyn Culpepper"—Tucker cinched his arm a little tighter around her waist—"you're the first and only woman I ever considered sharing my life with—the only woman I think has enough life in her to make the sharing worthwhile.

"We argue, and you drive me up the wall. We work together, and you drive me to be a better man. You make me smile without even trying, and when I see you, my hands itch and my arms feel empty. God's been working on my heart since the moment I saw you, and I pray He's been working on yours the same way."

He loosened his hold on her, bending down on one knee and asking her the question she'd been longing to hear. "Jessalyn Culpepper, I'm telling you now that I love you, and I want you for my wife. And if you'll have me, I'd be honored to keep you forever."

"Yes!" Joy lifted her high, and she realized Tucker had gotten to his feet and picked her up again. As he lowered her back down, she slipped her arms around his neck and kissed him back with everything she had to give until they were both breathless.

"For the longest time, I thought I'd find my home at the Bar None. But I was wrong. I'll marry you, Tucker Carmichael," she whispered, tracing the line of his lower lip with her fingertips. "Because with you, I'm finally home."

Kelly Eileen Hake received her first writing contract at the tender age of seventeen and arranged to wait three months until she was able to legally sign it. Since that first contract a decade ago, she's fulfilled twenty contracts ranging from short stories to novels. In her spare time, she's attained her BA in English Literature and Composition, earned her credential to teach English in secondary schools, and went on to complete her MA in Writing Popular Fiction.

Writing for Barbour combines two of Kelly's great loves—history and reading. A CBA-bestselling author and member of American Christian Fiction Writers, she's been privileged to earn numerous Heartsong Presents Reader's Choice Awards and is known for her witty, heartwarming historical romances.

A newlywed, she and her gourmet-chef husband live in Southern California with their golden lab mix, Midas.

Other books by Kelly Eileen Hake...

PRAIRIE PROMISES

The Bride Bargain
The Bride Backfire
The Bride Blunder

HUSBANDS FOR HIRE

Rugged and Relentless
Tall, Dark, and Determined
Strong and Stubborn

Coming soon from Kelly Eileen Hake

Trails & Targets
The Dangerous Darlyns – Book 1

After their father's death, the four Darlyn sisters discover the family farm is mortgaged to the hilt. With an unscrupulous creditor proposing indecent solutions to their uncertain future, the girls leave their childhood home—and childhood itself—behind. Soon an unexpected hero finds himself saddled with the slew of sisters and their surprising skills. But only one thing's for sure: the sharpshooter named Beatrix hits the mark of his lonely heart. Plagued by past failures and forced to make their own way, find out what happens as the Dangerous Darlyns take to the road in *Trails & Targets*!

Available wherever Shiloh Run Press titles are sold!